Acclaim for Jo
Pulitzer Prize

D0468785

The Late George Apley

"Wicked and delightful.... A picture of a Bostonian that is perfect to its last detail. The character-work is glorious: Boston
male and female, Brahmin and toady, Puritans and Irish, young
and old, Mr. Marquand has them all down to the life. In the dis-
guise and labored style of a minor man of letters undertaking
to write the life of a friend whom he admired to idolatry, Mr.
Marquand manages to be most hilariously funny."
— D. B. Collins, *American Review*

"A beautifully precise dissection of a man, a class, and a way of
American life.... The work of a man who writes of his own
themes in his own way and writes of them with a skill, a style,
and a sense of acid comedy that may, perhaps, outlast a great
deal of admired laboriousness and earnest breast-beating. In
other words, here is a novelist — and a real one — with all that
that word implies."
— Stephen Vincent Benét, *Saturday Review*

"The little world that George Apley and his kind have made is
reproduced here in such accurate detail that its bitterness can
be more easily endured between covers than in real life."
— Quincy Howe, *New Republic*

"The distinction of *The Late George Apley* lies in its economy
and terseness, its very accomplished satirical form and style."
— Mina Curtiss, *Nation*

"*The Late George Apley* and now *Wickford Point* are examinations of a society — the fag end of the New England aristocracy — that Thackeray would have understood and smiled at, just as Mr. Marquand understands and smiles at it. Their attitude (Somerset Maugham shares it also) is that of the extremely intelligent clubman who knows that his select club is populous with fools, bores, and triflers, tells to perfection iced and acid anecdotes about them, and yet rejects with well-bred horror the very notion of resigning. Such an attitude, when implemented by a sound craftsmanship, produces social satire not sufficiently devastating to change readers' ideas, yet not so light as to be merely 'amusing.' This middle-ground attack is rare in our country, and at the moment Mr. Marquand is its most effective practitioner."

— Clifton Fadiman, *The New Yorker*

"*The Late George Apley* is satire, but it is satirical by indirection only; it is cast in a delicate irony, one that smiles, sympathizes, and almost forgives; it relies for effect entirely on tone, risking the indifference of the hard of hearing."

— Bernard DeVoto, *Saturday Review*

"Mr. Marquand has done a whacking good job."

— C. P. Curtis Jr., *Atlantic*

"In *The Late George Apley* Mr. Marquand selects what he considers a characteristic Beacon Hill family whose blood is running thin and whose qualities of conservatism and self-sufficiency are therefore constantly heightening, and chronicles two of its generations through the agency of a family biographer who inadvertently tells all. . . . There is hardly an aspect of Boston life of recent history which in some way is not linked with the saga of the Apley family, usually in a vein of sarcasm. . . . It often makes for downright hysterical reading. . . . Everyone should have a good time with it."

— Lucius Beebe, *New York Herald Tribune*

THE LATE
GEORGE APLEY

THE LATE
GEORGE APLEY

A Novel in the Form
of a Memoir

by
JOHN P. MARQUAND

BACK BAY BOOKS
LITTLE, BROWN AND COMPANY
NEW YORK · BOSTON · LONDON

Back Bay Books / Little, Brown and Company
Hachette Book Group
1290 Avenue of the Americas, New York, NY 10104
littlebrown.com

Originally published in hardcover by Little, Brown and Company, January 1937
First Back Bay paperback edition, March 2004

Back Bay Books is an imprint of Little, Brown and Company.
The Back Bay Books name and logo are trademarks of
Hachette Book Group, Inc.

The publisher is not responsible for websites (or their content)
that are not owned by the publisher.

ISBN 978-0-316-73567-4
LCCN 2003115659

CONTENTS

THE LATE
GEORGE APLEY

———•———

CHAPTER I

A FOREWORD AND APOLOGY

A Necessary Exposition of
Circumstances Permitting a Certain Incorrect
Liberty in the Penning of
This Memoir

GEORGE WILLIAM APLEY was born in the house of his maternal grandfather, William Leeds Hancock, on the steeper part of Mount Vernon Street, on Beacon Hill, on January 25, 1866. He died in his own house, which overlooks the Charles River Basin and the Esplanade, on the water side of Beacon Street, on December 13, 1933. This was the frame in which his life moved, and the frame which will surround his portrait as a man. He once said of himself: "I am the sort of man I am, because environment prevented my being anything else."

It is now my task, to which I have agreed under somewhat unusual circumstances, to depict the life of this valued friend of mine through his own writings. I can think of no more suitable way of beginning than by resorting to an explanation which is, in a measure, personal. It has been my privilege many times in the past to edit the notes and letters of other prominent Bostonians under the advice of the family. In this case, as is usual in such matters, the advice of the family stands first. In this case, however, the advice is not usual.

Shortly after I read the obituary notice of George William Apley at the annual meeting of the Berkley Club, when our departed members for the year are customarily remembered, — a work which was welcome to me because of our friendship, — I was surprised by the following comment from his son, John Apley: —

Dear Mr. Willing:—

I did not have time to thank you the other night for the appreciation which you read of my father at the Berkley Club. As I might have expected, you did yourself and the old man proud. I only had this one criticism to offer: As I sat back in the dim part of the room watching you stand on the stage beside the secretary with your papers, I could not avoid thinking of all the other lives which I had heard read out from that platform in sonorous, periodic sentences. Perhaps I had had a touch too much of champagne at the dinner downstairs, but if so I think it only sharpened my perceptions, or did it make me see more than double? At any rate, I seemed to see, through the passage of the years, a string of members with their medals and their colored seniority waistcoats rising from the darkness on the floor and possibly stumbling over somebody's glass, as they walked one by one up to the platform with their papers in their hands. I seemed to hear the lives of all our fellow members read out with the usual comments, and those comments were always similar. You made Father seem like all the others, Mr. Willing. You shaded over the affair of Attorney O'Reilly and some other things we know. You talked about the Historical Society and about the fight against the electric signs around the Common, but you did not mention his feud with Moore and Fields; you told what he had done for the Art Museum, but you did not tell how the New York dealer gypped him on the pre-Han bronzes. You mentioned his graciousness as a host at those Sunday luncheons at Milton and when the Monday Club had its meetings at our place on Beacon Street. Do you remember the gold chairs in the two upper rooms and the creamed oysters and coffee waiting in the dining-room downstairs when the speaker for the evening was finished? You mentioned all these things, but not a word of how Eleanor and I disappointed him and Mother.

Perhaps you were right, given the time and place, but I wonder if Father would have liked it? You can answer that better than I can, because you knew him better. Personally, I think he would like the truth for once. I hope so because I was rather fond of him. He was kind to me when I was a kid; he was swell when we used to go camping and I shall never forget the picnics on the beach, and the days of the Harvard-Yale game.

Naturally Father always kept up his façade. Naturally we never quarrelled actively even inside the family, but I remember one thing he said to me once. It sticks, when so much of his advice eddied into one ear and out the other. He was angry at the time and bitterly disappointed with me, because I would not go into the firm of Apley and Reid, thus changing it to Apley, Reid, and Apley. This is what he said: "I'm the only father you'll ever have, and you're the only son I'll ever have. Let us try not to forget it."

With this in mind — and I know this letter must seem rambling to anyone with your eye and your sense of style — I come to my purpose in writing you. You may have guessed already that it involves your capacity as a compiler of distinguished pasts. You are now Boston's Dean of Letters, Mr.

Willing, and now that the mantle has descended upon you, the earnest request of another dutiful son follows that mantle, if the simile is not too involved. I, and the rest of the family, would be very proud and grateful if you could find the time and inclination to take in hand my father's notes and letters. You know he was getting them together himself shortly before his death.

My Aunt Amelia has probably spoken to you already of this project, as Aunt Amelia has somehow taken upon herself the conviction that she is the head of the family, and the custodian of its heirlooms and documents. Nevertheless, my request will be different from hers in its essentials; or perhaps it is not a request, but rather a humble suggestion. Do you not think it would be possible to edit and comment upon my father's letters and papers so that the result would be more distinctive than your exposition before the Berkley Club? How would it be if these letters should tell the truth about him? Not that I insinuate that you do not always tell the truth — I mean that on this occasion you leave matters in the record which your conscience and loyalty might otherwise blot out. Do you think it would do any real harm, provided we put a limit on the copies of this book, say fifteen, for circulation among only the immediate members of the family? This might, of course, be hard for you in that you would be denied the customary public acclaim which your skill so well deserves. But I should insist on paying you, of course, as though the work were to have a wide circulation, and also you might have the artist's satisfaction, rare, as I have heard you say, for one who must earn a living by letters, to deal with your subject veraciously. This seems to me your chance and mine to do a last piece of justice to Father, and I have an idea that Father would appreciate it. Will you think it over, Mr. Willing? I'll be glad to consult with you at length, if you should care to have me.

My main preoccupation is that this thing should be real. You know, and I know, that Father had guts.

As ever yours,—

JOHN.

I may say frankly that I was challenged by John Apley's letter, although its style has made me wonder what there is which is wrong with a Harvard and Groton education. Any graduate of any English Public School, any British journalist, is so much more familiar with the structure of his language. It is disconcerting to find John Apley, the product of the two best educational institutions which I believe America can offer, standing against a background which has prized culture for many generations, resorting finally to the monosyllable "guts" in order to define his meaning. It may be a small matter, but it is one which I think is important. The answer lies somewhere in the perpetual revolt of youth from tradition. Considering the matter broad-mindedly, I believe that George Apley had something more than this in his character. He had the essential, undeviating discipline of background, which the letter of his son has given me the incentive to display.

Certain aspects, which I might ordinarily have eliminated in dealing with a portrait to be painted by the subject's own words and interpreted by mine, I shall now allow to stand in deference to his son's request.

And now arises a final question and one which has perplexed many another biographer. What *is* truth in a life? In order to delineate character there must be an artistic stressing of certain qualities — but are these the vital qualities? Who has the right to say?

Like many other families imbued with the Puritan tradition, the Apleys have not been in the habit of destroying letters or papers. As a fortunate consequence of this, John Apley has been able to deliver to me a surprisingly complete dossier of his father's life, beginning with the letters which were scrawled out in his boyhood to his father, Thomas, and to his mother, Elizabeth Apley. The letters continue through his life stream, notes to relatives and friends, notes to business associates, and conventionally composed pieces of correspondence, such as those relating to the widening of the Esplanade and to the display of electric signs across the Common. Besides these, George Apley has preserved portions of his own works such as his address to his class on its fortieth anniversary, his paper at the Centenary celebration of his Harvard undergraduate Club, and the papers which he read at intervals before the Monday Club and the Historical Society.

To a casual observer, from another section than our own, these works may not seem worth preserving. Taken individually this may be so, but collectively they reveal the spirit of the man and his influence on the life around him. They reveal too, I think, the true spirit of our city and of our time, since Apley was so essentially a part of both.

———•———

CHAPTER II

THE FAMILY BACKGROUND

Apley's Own Account of Antecedents,
Which Must Definitely Motivate the Life of
Any Man with a Family

BIOGRAPHY, like every other branch of art, must have its form and its conventions. Conventionally one starts with ancestral roots in order to answer the question: What made the man? In this instance we are so fortunate as to be able to supply the answer, given by the man himself in one of his random papers. One cannot do better than to let him speak in his own words of the Apley family, as set forth in a memorandum written to his son John and his daughter Eleanor from his Beacon Street library in the year 1912. I have spent many an evening with him there in that snug room situated at the head of his stairs on the second floor of the Beacon Street house, walled in by the leather backs of good books, with the prints of sailing ships above the shelves and his collection of shaving mugs just below them. His interests may have been varied but his discrimination, undeviating.

Dear John and Eleanor: —
The other evening when I was seated here in the library I had the door half open for the sake of ventilation. You

know how the wind whips up across the Basin on a winter night, making it impossible to open the window even a crack. That was why my door was open, not from any desire to pry into the affairs of another generation.

It may not occur to you how distinctly voices carry up our stairs, particularly the voices with the Apley enunciation, and you two, I am pleased to observe, have the Apley voice. I heard you talking to the Burrage boys about your Uncle William. Don't think that I mind that. You were speaking about his plumbing and his stair carpet in Fairfield Street. You were suggesting that, with his income, your Uncle William might make certain renovations. It may seem strange to you that the idea surprised me in that it was new to me.

Your Great-Uncle William's house has always seemed to me a part of him and, therefore, not subject to change. The plainness of its furnishings, the draughtiness of its halls, the worn tines of the forks on his dining table, and the darns in his table linen have been to me an expression of his character and an intimation of inherent worth. Your Great-Uncle William, if he wished, could live with the ostentation of the *nouveau riche;* but he does not wish it. He has a dislike for external show, which is shared by others accustomed to money. He still goes to his place of business in the trolley cars. He buys perhaps one suit a year, as I heard you both observing. In commenting on this you must not forget his generosity to others. You have seen the row of Rembrandts he has given to the Art Museum, but you do not know that he contributed anonymously three million dollars to the South Boston playgrounds, and that he has supported our family charity, the Apley Sailors' Home, for the last twenty years.

I do not object to your laughing at Uncle William, for I have done so myself in my time. The only thing that surprises me is your belief that he should change, when his care in living is a part of his philanthropy. From the time of the Roman Empire down, indulgence in the externals of wealth has never benefited a community. Your uncle realizes that there are more important things than modern plumbing; I pray that you two will come to that realization in time. I wonder if you will. Besides, William Apley is a lover of music, and owns one of the largest and best Chinese porcelain galleries in America. You have heard of the Rockefeller Hawthornes? Ask Uncle William to show you his.

From your comment on your relative the drift of your conversation trended naturally to families, particularly to Boston families. I heard you laughing at the pride which certain of our connections take in the family tree, and I could almost have laughed with you, although this is a Boston joke that was *vieux jeu* even in my day. I heard you say that we all came from yeoman stock, small English shopkeepers and farmers. You were quite right in this. I was only surprised that you had not discovered the fact before. The simplicity of our beginnings makes for your Uncle William's simplicity, but do not forget that these ancestors of yours had their beliefs and convictions.

I have heard certain things about the Apley family passed down by word of mouth which I shall pass to you now in writing, for there'll be a day, perhaps, when you may wish to be identified with a family.

The Apleys have lived in the town of Totswold-Fearing in Sussex as far back as there are any parish records. There are Apleys there still, as I found out for myself during the last trip which your Mother and I took through rural England. The first American Apley, Thomas, known in the town records as "Goodman Apley," settled in Roxbury in the year 1636.

If you recall your early American history, this date coincides with the great period of emigration from the Mother Country, not of persons struggling to find a new home because of poverty, like the starving Irish who overwhelmed us in the middle of the last century, but of solid citizens, many with substantial properties, who desired to take up a new abode because of conscience. It is true that few gentlemen entitled to a coat of arms were engaged in this adventure; but there was good society in Salem, Roxbury, and Watertown, as Sewall's diary bears witness — a far more cultivated society, I believe, than any which existed in the early Plymouth Colony. I, personally, do not think that persons who boast of ancestors coming over on the Mayflower have very much of which to be proud, but this is beside the point.

Thomas Apley at his death in 1672 left two dwelling houses, fifteen acres of land, and rights in the Common pasture for forty cattle; two feather beds, two silver tankards, and an Indian slave named Tomfrey, who had probably been captured in some of the troubles with the Narragansetts that led to King Philip's War. During his career in this country he had three wives and twenty children, half of whom died in infancy. None of those surviving appears to have made a name for himself except your ancestor John Apley, second son by the second marriage, who was selected by his father for the clergy. John Apley attended Harvard, graduating with the class of 1662, and I may add there has been an Apley at Harvard since in each succeeding generation.

This John Apley, whose life has been touched upon by Cotton Mather in his "Magnalia Christi Americana," became, after his ordination, one of the ministers in the township of Barnstable on Cape Cod. He was influential there in converting the Indians, and is known to have delivered a sermon to them in their own language on an occasion when these people met in great numbers on the beach to play a game which has been called "football." I have never been able to determine what sort of a game this "football" was except that several hundred Indians took part in it, but I am often pleased to think that John Apley interested himself in football, as the game has always fascinated me. You must remember that the position of an ordained minister in the days of Massachusetts Bay was a very high one, socially, in the community. Thus it is not strange that John Apley should have allied himself with Martha Dudley, not a direct connection of the able Thomas or of his arrogant son, Joseph, but from a collateral branch which many believe is better.

In consequence their eldest son, Nathaniel Apley, took his place in Boston as a young man of some cultivation and fashion. You may have seen his portrait by Dummer, the Essex County silversmith, which was presented by your great-grandfather to the Boston Athenæum. The picture, which hangs to-day in the oval Trustees' Room opposite the case of volumes from George Washington's library, shows a thin young man in a blue coat and a brown wig. In the Harvard Catalogue of 1687 Nathaniel Apley is listed as "Mr." — an accurate indication of his social position in those days of gentlemen and commoners. Presumably because of his relationship to Governor Dudley he seems to have left for England during the troubled period two years later, but returned shortly to marry Maria Gookin, a daughter of that family which can honestly claim as great distinction and gentility as any in the early Commonwealth.

Nathaniel engaged in trading ventures with the West Indies, bartering fish and lumber for sugar, and I suspect investing in shipments of blacks to the Carolinas. In those days the slave trade was strictly honourable. He prospered in this business and bought himself a dwelling house on the north end of Boston Peninsula. You may see his house marked on Bonner's famous map of Boston. His stone is in the King's Chapel burying ground.

His son, Joseph, from whom we are descended, was in the Harvard class of 1733, but was expelled for using profane language in Massachusetts Hall. On a business visit to the town of Portsmouth he wooed and won the local belle, Elizabeth Pringle, in the old Pringle homestead now fortunately preserved by the Colonial Dames of America. Her picture in the dining-room downstairs probably does not do her justice, since it was painted by one of those journeyman artists who travelled up and down the Eastern seacoast.

Their son John graduated from Harvard with the class of 1757 and I have two of his pamphlets in my possession, dealing with arguments in favour of the Writs of Assistance. His portrait, painted by Copley when John Apley was eighty-seven, fell to your Aunt Amelia when your grandfather's estate was divided. Before that time it used to hang directly above the sideboard in the dining-room at Hillcrest in Milton — where I personally believe it should have been left, if only out of sentiment to your grandfather's memory. Your Aunt Amelia thought differently, however, and the portrait now has its place among her Burne-Jones pictures in her front parlour in Louisburg Square. Even in these Pre-Raphaelite surroundings the features of our famous ancestor reveal the deadly reality of Copley and his pitiless and seldom complimentary probing of character. For Copley, as you know, probably because of his plain beginnings, did not have the politeness or the graceful tradition of either Stuart or Blackburn. The features of our ancestor in this Copley — and I have heard Charlie Jones and Briggs Danforth and other leading instructors from the Museum Art School say that this is Copley at his finest — have the wintry grey whiteness of old age, with just a touch of pink at the cheekbones that verges into purple. The left hand, beautifully executed, is clutching at a faded, purplish brocaded dressing gown.

Although in the pre-Revolution days John Apley's sentiments appear to have been distinctly Royalist even down to the time of the Boston Massacre, his name is mentioned among those who contributed secretly a sum for powder and arms at the eve of the Bunker Hill battle. Yet when the Revolutionary War was over, we find him deploring the anarchy of the times, and some of his letters suggest the advisability of a monarchical form of government. I can remember when I was ten years old hearing my Great-Aunt Jane, then in her ninety-second year, speak of him with affection.

"You will never know," my Aunt Jane said to me, "how very close we come to being nobility. In a sense, indeed, we are nobility."

My great-aunt was not the only one whom I have heard speak in this vein. It amuses me to think of her in these days when pandering politicians in Bulfinch's State House are discussing such socialistic nonsense as an income tax and old age insurance.

I have never discovered why John Apley quarrelled with his son George and cut him off in his will with a shilling, except that George married out of his social sphere. At the age of sixteen he became enamoured of a Maria Cabot from Beverly. Her family at that time were people of good plain stock, engaged in coastal shipping, but only in a small way. When young George persisted he was turned incontinently out of doors and communications between him and his father came to an abrupt and permanent termination. I imagine that certain distant branches of the Apley family are sorry for this to-day; for the Apley ability went with George and his young wife, Maria, to the farming community of Sudbury where the young couple occupied a farm of some eighty acres near the marshes of the Sudbury River, lived in great want, and were blessed with a family of five sons.

The early days of the Reconstruction Era — so aptly termed by my dear late friend, John Fiske, "The Critical Period of American History" — found these five boys and their parents wresting a meagre living from the soil. I have told you that the Apleys were plain people, but this short account of mine is evidence enough that good stock will not entirely disappear.

At this point George Apley's narrative breaks off abruptly, and the memorandum certainly never went farther than his desk. The life and customs of Colonial days were a source of deep interest and of not a little amusement to him in his late middle age. He gradually acquired from collateral branches of the Apley family various heirlooms of his early ancestors, including a magnificent pair of silver tankards by Hurd, which are now on loan in the American Wing of the Art Museum. It must be added in all fairness that George Apley's attitude in ancestral matters was not always the same as that reflected in the foregoing paper. In this connection it may be as well to insert a portion of a letter which he wrote in 1902 to his classmate, Henry Schuyler Wilkie, after a visit to New York.

Dear Schuy: —

Seeing you in the modern Sodom and Gomorrah did your poor friend Ap a good deal of good. Of course, no one from my cautious part of the world is entirely at home in New York. The lights of the theatres and the noise of the traffic around Twenty-third Street upset us, but I hope I did my

best once I caught the spirit of it. I shan't forget for quite
a while the race we had in hansom cabs through the Park.

Now I am back in the land where the gold grasshopper
swings above Faneuil Hall to the bidding of a damp east
wind. I have had family dinned in my ears ever since I have
been able to think. My life has been governed by the rigours
of blue-nosed bigots who have been in their graves for a
century. . . .

Such erratic changes in his mood as these, although they became less frequent in George Apley's later life, were a part of
his character which endeared him to many friends. Several
years after he composed this first memorandum he evidently
discovered it in going through his desk, for we have a con-
tinuation, penned in 1916, from exactly where he had left off.

Dear John and Eleanor: —

I may as well finish this, though I shall probably destroy
it before you read it. It is a bad habit to break things off
halfway.

Moses Apley left the farm at the age of fourteen (your
great-grandfather) to enter the Derby countinghouse in
Salem. This position, as far as we know, was obtained for
the boy through the intercession of the Cabot connection.
Moses Apley's own autobiography, which I must say reveals
very little, is now in the library as I write. His other letter-
books and business papers have been loaned, quite properly,
to the Essex Institute in Salem. Moses Apley appeared at
one of those rare times in the history of the world when wars
were besetting civilization. At the age of fifteen he sailed
as a clerk on the Derby brig *Stella* for the Baltic. At the age
of eighteen he was master of the Derby brig *Good Hope*
bound for Madagascar and China with a cargo valued at

fifteen thousand dollars. This, as you see, was the beginning of our commerce with the Orient. At Madagascar, on hearing of the outbreak of war between France and England, this boy — somehow boys in this part of the world matured more quickly then, in spite of there not being a Harvard Business School — contrived to sell his cargo for three times its value and place the proceeds in currency, which itself doubled its value, before the *Good Hope* left port three months later. Finally at Canton, he contrived to put aboard a cargo of tea purchased at panic prices. This was due to the fortunate suicide of the agent of the British firm of French and Daniels at the Canton Factories. Returning by way of the Cape of Good Hope your Great-Grandfather Moses touched at the vicinity of Fernando Po on the African coast and was able to trade a consignment of rum, which he had purchased in Canton from a New England shipmaster who was dying of flux, for ivory tusks. These had been accumulating for some time at a Portuguese factory on the Fernando Po coast; and owing to unsettled world conditions, and an ocean thick with privateers, there seemed little chance that this ivory could reach a market. These details are treated with meticulous accuracy in your great-grandfather's autobiography, and I only mention the superficial aspects here to show why Moses Apley, through his determination and judgment, ended his life as one of the richest shipping men in Boston, the beloved and respected friend of the houses of Peabody and Perkins. When the brig *Good Hope*, after eluding a French privateer and a British sloop of war, finally returned to the Derby wharf in Salem at the end of a two years' voyage, Moses Apley, not yet in his legal majority, was able to present the Derby countinghouse with a cargo valued at well over one hundred and fifty thousand dollars. His own share of this, as Master, was sufficient for him to purchase a vessel of his own, the brig *Pretty Pearl,* then building at the yards in Essex. The name, as you may suspect, was sentimental. She was named for Pearl Frear, of the Frear family in Salem, who was later to become your great-grandmother. Though it has been said that your great-grandfather was somewhat relentless in his later dealings, no one has questioned his uprightness or his probity. His two-hundred-thousand-dollar endowment of the Apley Sailors' Home, an immense sum in those days, is proof enough of his charitable instincts.

There is one story about him which you may not have heard, but one which seems to me worth repeating. Moses Apley was summoned to his father's bedside when George Apley was dying in the Sudbury farmhouse; the old man was in his bed, well toward the end of his last illness, and he was troubled in his mind. He had willed his farm and his personal possessions to the remaining four brothers, leaving Moses out of the estate. He wished Moses to understand that his only motive in making this testament was because he had heard that Moses had done well in business.

"Father," your great-grandfather said to him, "don't worry. A vessel of mine has just come alongside the wharf with a cargo which can buy the whole town of Sudbury."

The old man groaned and turned his face to the wall.

"To think," he said, "that I must die and know my son a liar."

We will leave your great-grandfather now. I have only known him from his portrait in the parlour, for he died before I was born, leaving a family of seven children, but we have Moses Apley to thank that we are financially comfortable to-day. What little we have is due to Moses Apley, and I think that we may be proud of him with reason. His house, in what is now our business district, was torn down even before the Boston fire; but there is a drawing of it in your great-uncle's hall, just by the hatrack near the stairs. The next time you go to see Uncle William ask Bridget to turn up the gas a little; explain to her that you want to see the picture. She will understand you, if you shout at her loudly enough. It is well worth looking at.

———•——•———

CHAPTER III

THE PARENTS

*Continuing Our Subject's Own Account of
the Early Struggles of Thomas and Elizabeth Apley*

YOUR great-grandfather's estate, though large, suffered
somewhat during the decline of Boston shipping and
from a fire on the waterfront. Yet even when it was divided
my father, Thomas Apley, was comfortably off. His own
business acumen was responsible for conserving and enlarg-
ing his estate so that it amounts to the little we have to-day.
During his entire life your grandfather, who might have lived
upon his income, rose at five-thirty every morning; at nine
o'clock each evening he took his candle and went upstairs.
He had been educated for the law at Harvard, as I have been,
but his proclivities were always those of a businessman. He
and your Uncle William, when they formed a partnership to
administer their and their brother's and sister's share of the
Moses Apley estate, turned instinctively from the sea. In
those grim days of depression before the Civil War they
understood that New England's future was essentially industrial.

The mills in the town of Apley Falls on the upper Merrimack River are the direct results of their vision. The success
of our family venture, the Apley Mills, has been due in its

broader aspects to the more mature mind of your grandfather. It was he who arranged the financing and for the useful employment and the suitable accommodation of labourers from the great horde of Irish then pouring into the port of Boston. The aspersions cast upon the living conditions of the mill hands at Apley Falls by certain propagandists of the South was always a source of pain to your grandfather, as well as one of just indignation. The Southern apologists for their "peculiar institution" of slavery published reports in Richmond and Norfolk papers to the effect that a slave on the average Southern plantation had better food, better care, and greater prospects for happiness than the workers in the Apley Mills. My father contended to the last days of his life that no more untrue or unjust comparison was ever made.

These Irish peasants, coming from a land of starvation where they had existed beneath absentee landlords in a situation little better than serfdom, were given good brick houses at Apley Falls, steady labour to keep them out of mischief, and a wage equal to that which they might have obtained elsewhere. Their children received the benefits of common schooling, and they themselves, though nearly all illiterate, had the blessings of free thought and action.

More than this, these people were grateful for it, as I know myself. When I was a boy of seven, on a visit to your Uncle William at Apley Falls I remember walking (between him and your grandfather) up a street made up of these long brick rows of millworkers' cottages. The evening's work was done; the men and their womenfolk were seated placidly on their porches with nothing before them but the prospect of a comfortable supper and a working wage the next day. Their looks of pleasure and affection were certainly not purposely assumed when Uncle William and my father walked by. I can see them still, the women bobbing and curtsying, the men pulling their forelocks. They regarded my uncle and my father each as their friend and protector who gave them shelter and livelihood, and advice and assistance in family difficulties. There was no such thing as labour trouble in those days at Apley Falls, because there were no such things as unsound ideas, and no desire for shoddy luxuries. There was no desire for luxuries because there were none, and I wish it were the same to-day.

My father was responsible for the broader policies of this venture. Your Great-Uncle William, still a boy in his teens, had the direct charge of the enterprise and lived at Apley Falls and worked as hard as, if not harder than, any labourer in the Mills, and carried the burden of his responsibility home with him at night. This responsibility must have been enormous, for nearly the entire capital of the family estate was involved in the infant textile industry and it is only due to the unfaltering assiduity for work, the abstemiousness, the watchfulness, and the acumen of these two men that we are as comfortable as we are to-day.

Considering their responsibilities, both for family and employees, I think it is natural that they were not greatly in sympathy with the agitators of the time. The Abolitionist Movement was anathema to my father, who saw, as so many other solid businessmen also saw, the blind folly of a political war between the North and South. It must have been hard on my father to take this position, for in many ways he was a liberal and stood firmly for the freedom of human initiative; also in his leisure he was interested in the arts. I have often heard him speak with affection and pride of that fine flowering of New England genius, the Transcendentalist Colony at Concord. He always spoke with deep respect of the works of Mr. Emerson and of many of Channing's sermons. He was particularly amused and delighted with the vagaries of

Thoreau. He had the deepest respect for the views of our essayists, and even of our novelists, although he felt, I think rightly, that fiction was the most trivial and ephemeral of all the arts. While maintaining this interest, he had no great patience for the unsound, radical inclinations which always seem to be tied up with a literary society. He stated his views to me once in terms which are as sound to-day as the rest of his philosophy.

"Your poet," he said, "your minister, your essayist, is not a man of affairs. He is completely unsuccessful almost invariably in the realms of banking and business. Being unsuccessful, it is beyond me why his views on economics and politics should be given the slightest attention."

At the time of the outbreak of the Civil War your grandfather had been married for a year to Elizabeth Hancock, a good match for both of them, based primarily on love but also on a community of friends and interests. As a young husband who was about to become a father, and as the head of an important business enterprise, upon which hundreds depended for their daily bread, my father, although as staunch a Unionist as anyone in Boston, when the fatal die was cast could not fight in the Civil War. At the time of the Draft Act he was obliged, much to his own regret, to hire a substitute. Clarence Corcoran, the head gardener of his country place at Hillcrest, took your grandfather's place in the ranks, receiving the usual bounty and with it the promise that his little family should be cared for comfortably in case of any accident. I once saw some letters that my father wrote to Clarence at the time of the Wilderness Campaign; letters of affection and good cheer, each with a financial enclosure.

It is gratifying to add that Clarence came back safely and that a friendship existed between him and my father which endured even after Clarence was obliged to leave Hillcrest, on account of drunkenness and an unfortunate infatuation for your grandmother's maid. Clarence and the Corcorans have been pensioners of the family ever since, even down to his grandson, John Apley Corcoran, whose tuition I paid myself in Boston University and later in the Suffolk Law School.

Your grandfather bought and improved the place at Hillcrest when its former owners were faced with hard times. In his later days he felt a deep affection, which I have inherited, for every stick and stone of it. I have often stood with him, as a child, on a spring evening, watching the purple and white festoons of the wistaria against the columns of the veranda. When one of the elm trees sickened on the driveway circle, his concern was as great as if one of us had been dying. Your grandfather, also, bought this house on Beacon Street when the Back Bay was filled in, and this leads me to a single amusing instance of his unfailing business foresight.

Shortly before he purchased in Beacon Street he had been drawn, like so many others, to build one of those fine bow-front houses around one of these shady squares in the South End. When he did so nearly everyone was under the impression that this district would be one of the most solid residential sections of Boston instead of becoming, as it is to-day, a region of rooming houses and worse. You may have seen those houses in the South End, fine mansions with dark walnut doors and beautiful woodwork. One morning, as Tim, the coachman, came up with the carriage, to carry your aunt Amelia and me to Miss Hendrick's Primary School, my father, who had not gone down to his office at the usual early hour because he had a bad head cold, came out with us to the front steps. I could not have been more than seven at the time, but I remember the exclamation that he gave when he observed the brownstone steps of the house across the street.

"Thunderation," Father said, "there is a man in his shirt

sleeves on those steps." The next day he sold his house for what he had paid for it and we moved to Beacon Street. Your grandfather had sensed the approach of change; a man in his shirt sleeves had told him that the days of the South End were numbered.

I shall not speak at length of my mother, not because I could not but because of the tenderness of my memories and my admiration for her. These make me shy and self-conscious even with my children. Beneath the discipline of my father the routine of our family life was very strict, but I do not think too strict. Through it all my mother was a cheerful, loving wife and a kind friend to everyone who knew her, firm in her convictions, but charitable to weakness. Her love of literature and music and of painting was very great, but she did not over-indulge herself in any of these directions. I think that she feared that such an interest would overbalance her responsibility to her home. Even when her mind failed in the latter years of her life, she still felt that responsibility very keenly. You remember her in her wheel chair at Hill-crest, knitting mufflers on the porch. Your Great-Aunt Jane, of course, you may remember better, but your grandmother, though quieter, had all your Aunt Jane's determination.

I have gone on with this longer than I had intended but it has given me a pleasant evening, so pleasant that I am afraid I have not achieved the purpose I undertook when I began. It was my intention to give you something of our family background, that you both might understand the character of the people from whom you spring. You were right in believing that they are simple but there is an importance in their simplicity which you must not forget. I think there is no reason why you should not be proud of the Apleys, as proud as any Virginian is of his own ancestry. The other day I heard your Aunt Amelia say: "When I am depressed I remember I am an Apley." At the time I was amused by the remark. Her self-importance often exasperates and amuses me. Yet, granted that her remark was poorly phrased, so that it was silly, the fact remains that it is worth while for anyone to have behind him a few generations of honest, hard-working ancestry.

This memorandum is necessarily short. Its author has left out many important facts, but in its essentials it conveys some impression of George Apley's point of view. Pride in family, place, and tradition were inherent with the man; his realization of their importance grew with the years, until many of his activities became centered about genealogical research.

Nevertheless, it must be remembered that this is a later development of his character. Time changes all things.

———•———

CHAPTER IV

THE BOYHOOD SCENE

*A Hasty Evaluation of the
Background and Philosophy of a Golden Era,
Much of Which Fortunately Still Survives*

HAVING dealt briefly with the family background, our
next task is inevitably a reconstruction of the scene upon
which George Apley's eyes first opened. It will be the pano-
rama of the Boston known to George Apley, the child, the boy,
and the youth. I shall try to give this background clearly in
the earnest hope that such a reconstruction is possible, for in
it must lie my interpretation of George Apley's character. At
the age of thirty-two, George Apley once wrote to a friend: —

I move along a narrow groove. With the exception of two
months in Europe when I was twenty, ten trips to New York
and one to Washington, I do not believe that I have been
farther away from Boston than Portsmouth, New Hampshire,
to the North, Lenox to the West, or Providence to the South.

It is painfully trite to say that the Boston of the early seventies is vastly different from the Metropolitan Boston of the
present; yet if one lists some of the changes which have occurred since then, the difference is so immense that this trite-

ness is overpowered by significance. At no time in the history
of the world have such material changes occurred as those in
John Apley's life span. The impact of these changes upon the
mind of an individual must necessarily be portentous and immense. Let us sum it up in a single homely detail that may
convey an impression better than reverberating facts. Let us
start, without any wish to appear humorous, with the mud-
scrapers on the houses of Beacon Hill.

In the constantly shifting American scene the appurtenances
essential to another generation are only too apt to be swept
away by the ruthless hand of what is so incorrectly called
"progress." It is to the credit of Boston that these changes have
occurred slowly, and only after a struggle with the sounder
element. There is still a decorous pause between innovations,
although this pause is admittedly briefer than it was. In the
midst of this haste for tearing down much of what is fine, it is
not unpleasant for one of the writer's age to be able to walk
peacefully through a part of his city, there to observe a few
vistas which have not changed greatly since the days of his
boyhood. One can turn the clock back without great difficulty
as one ascends Mt. Vernon Street toward the State House, or
turns left, through Louisburg Square, up the even steeper
paths of Pinckney.

Here the brick sidewalks are still at such an angle that several pedestrians each winter suffer from broken hips after an
easterly sleet storm. With but few exceptions the hitching
posts have been removed from the curbs of these sidewalks,
but here and there an iron ring set in the curbing is a silent
reminder of the days of the horse, when a child might coast
down Mt. Vernon Street. The covered alleyways and the
lanes which lead from Mt. Vernon toward Beacon Street are

still extant, and the property deeds still include their clauses for the right to lead through these lanes one or more cows for pasturage on the Common. Such matters as these, of course, were curiosities — like the purple windowpanes in some of the Beacon Street houses — even in the early seventies. But this was not so with the iron scrapers on the Cape Ann granite steps. They stand alone on Beacon Hill as memorials to a muddier Boston, a Boston of blacksmiths and cobblestones. The details of these bits of ironwork vary in design, and, if one observes them closely, one may detect something of the spare grace of line which is so manifest in the doorways and façades above them. Given the time for research, a highly informative paper might be written about this ironwork.

At the time of Apley's birth, although his parents were better than comfortably off, the Apley establishment was sensibly rigorously simple. The summers were spent at the country estate of Hillcrest in Milton, then a considerable distance from town, a large estate with driveways under arching elms, with a rambling house dating from the forties. The Apley children, when at Hillcrest, were under their mother's serene and careful guidance. It was she who gave them their taste for literature and directed their attention to the saner beauties of country life. It was there that they began to form friendships and associations which remained with them as an unaltering legacy. The Calders with their five children dwelt upon the right, and the Bromfield children on the left, so that, altogether, these three families made a noisy group of boys and girls who wandered over their common acres in a rare childhood kingdom.

All who knew her have united in the opinion that Elizabeth Apley, the young mistress of Hillcrest, was a person of outstanding character. Not alone a competent and practical housekeeper, whose calm hand controlled every branch of the establishment, from the stables and kitchen to the nursery, she was careful as well to cultivate the leisure, to continue the development of a painstaking education. Her sensibility to literature was very marked. Several of her poems, among them "Blue Hill at Eventide" found their way into print in the pages of the *Atlantic Monthly*, and show the accuracy of her keen reaction to the New England landscape. "Blue Hill at Eventide" is the description of Blue Hill in that hour just before the twilight of cool October. It speaks of that clarity of air and of the local perfection of silence through which the faintest noises of the southern-going bird come so distinctly to the ear. The simplicity and finality of her last line is peculiarly effective: "And may our voices, too, rise up so true to God."

The accomplishments of the young mother were not solely confined to verse. Hunt himself has spoken highly of her skill at water-color sketching, and several of these works of hers, in the hall at Hillcrest, prove that he did not wholly exaggerate. Also, she never gave up her music. George Apley has often spoken of the hour before his bedtime, as a child, when the notes of the piano directed by his mother's fingers winged through the house. Religion, pure Unitarianism, was also a part of the Hillcrest life, for both the Apleys and the Hancocks had been converted to its New England intellectualism. It was to be expected, with such a mother, that conversation should have been on a high plane, but her interests did not end there. She was careful also that each of her children should engage in a practical avocation. Each child at Hillcrest had a small square of garden, devoted not only to flowers, but to vegetables, and each child was held strictly accountable for the care of his or her garden plot. This was probably the reason for George Apley's interest in flowers, which brought him finally to the vice-presidency of the Boston Horticultural Society.

The clear tranquil beauty of Elizabeth Hancock Apley, combined with her unvarying graciousness as a hostess, with her never-failing interest in the affairs of others, and with the charm which she could give to a world seen through her own intelligence, made her parlor throughout her life a meeting ground for exceptional men and women. A Sunday afternoon would customarily find the best conversation of Boston around her tea table. Dr. Horsford would frequently be there, embroidering on his interesting theory regarding the settlement made by Leif Ericson at Norumbega on the Charles River. The fine face of Charles Eliot Norton was often seen, and Child and Shaler of Harvard, and Celia Thaxter, the poetess, and Mrs. Julia Ward Howe whose "Battle Hymn of the Republic" trumpets down the corridors of time. By her magic Mrs. Apley could cause the peculiar talent of each to be given forth for the benefit of all with no other stimulation than the cup that cheers but does not inebriate. Her capacity for friendship, which drew so many around her, drew among others Nathan Pettingill, the brilliant young minister of the local Unitarian Church. From the association of these two eager intelligences a friendship finally blossomed and was terminated only by death, one of those friendships of the spirit, rare in other parts of the world, but with many parallels in this congenial atmosphere. The character and understanding of the husband, Thomas Apley, concealed from so many beneath a cool and somewhat austere exterior, manifested itself in the complete trust and comprehension, akin to a deep pride, with which he observed the activities of his wife. Modest always of his own attainments, in spite of the weight which his word was given in State Street, Thomas Apley would sit, during such afternoons, an intent and generally a silent listener.

The Apley children, two little girls in their new white pinafores, and young George in a tight brown jacket — the style of their dress is apparent from an early photograph — were encouraged to share such occasions with their parents. In the democracy of this family there was no barrier of age, and so the children were led into the drawing-room of a Sunday afternoon, where, after shaking hands and exchanging remarks with whoever might be present, they were placed in a silent row upon the sofa, obeying the maxim that "children should be seen and not heard." It was Elizabeth Apley's oft-expressed belief that their offspring should assume with the parents a part of the responsibility for the teatime entertainment. Thus, at some propitious moment during the afternoon, the mother might call upon one of the little daughters for a snatch of song, which she herself accompanied sympathetically at the piano. On other occasions, little George would be called to render some dramatic recitation, perhaps a few humorous lines of Lowell, or again, Burke's famous speech on the American Revolution, ending on the ringing words "You cannot conquer America!" This declamation was taught him by his father, painstakingly, with the appropriate gestures. George Apley has contributed a brief account of one of these scenes, which gives something of their flavor.

It is no small ordeal for a boy of seven to stand up before his elders and to deliver a declamation. How my voice would shake at the beginning! And I can remember the attentive silence which greeted me. Father would sit watching me, stroking his black side-whiskers. Mother would watch me, too, now and then exchanging a glance with Mr. Pettingill, whom we called "Uncle Nathaniel." There is one occasion which sticks in my mind as though it were yesterday. I had eaten very heavily of roast beef and Yorkshire pudding, and was not feeling well, when Father said: "George, stand up and give Burke's Speech." I started out mechanically, but when I got to the part about the savages I stopped and my stomach seemed to turn about. Father rose quietly and took my hand. "George," he said, "come with me." As I went upstairs I told him I felt sick. Father's reply was the right one. "You must learn to do a great many things that you don't want," he said. "Now let us go over this so that you may get the end correctly."

Other more informal hours were spent at Hillcrest in the company of Tim, the coachman. His learning consisted almost entirely of Irish folktales, concerned with black ghosts and white ghosts and banshees. Sometimes in the kitchen Bridget, the cook, would sing snatches of ballads. One in particular dealt with a fiery-tempered young man who went walking with the girl of his choice down an Irish lane. For some reason which George Apley could not understand, this young man suddenly hit his sweetheart over the head with a club, and threw her body behind the thorn hedge. Later, on his return home, the girl's sister had him tried for murder, and the ballad ended "And well she might, for she knew the night, when I took her sister out." Since this ballad-narrative puzzled young George he went to the one source he knew, where the puzzle might be resolved: his mother. After listening carefully, Elizabeth Apley brought him to the library, where his father was arranging books, and there George repeated the story. Thomas

Apley also listened carefully and made no comment, but Bridget thereafter lost her gift of song.

These details of the life at Hillcrest may seem of small importance, but out of such trivial incidents are woven the fabric of a life. This is proved by George Apley's own letters to his friend Rhodora Calder, which he wrote her some forty years later. Despite the lapse of time, they give a vivid picture, sometimes grave and sometimes gay, of the fine free life which a child could lead. We cannot leave the Hillcrest days without including a few excerpts.

Dear Rhodora: —

Hester tells me that you are not feeling well, and so your old friend Georgie Porgie writes you. I remember a girl he kissed who did not cry, behind the hedge, near the hotbeds and the brook, after we had been playing "Deerfield Massacre." You had been frightened when Joe Bromfield scalped you, do you remember? I think of those days a good deal now, and I wish I might get as far as Mattapoisett so that you and Charles and I might laugh at them together. How closely our little crowd has always stuck to each other! I think that is one of the fine things about Milton — the way childhood friendships last. Dear me, it doesn't seem so long ago. Do you remember the suppers in the nursery when you used to come to play dolls with Amelia and Jane? Do you remember the games of hide-and-seek we used to play in the upper hall, and the time Grandmama hid me behind her dress when she sat in her rocker, knitting? Poor old lady, I had been forbidden to go in there, because she was not well, you know. She called me "Little Tom," she thought I was my father. And do you remember your good old Newfoundland, Tony? The way his tongue lolled out of his black muzzle, like a piece of red flannel; and Wash, your colored coachman —

do you remember how he used to sing "Swing Low, Sweet Chariot" when he sat in the harness-room?

Are children always like our crowd, do you suppose? It seems a little ironical how much of our culture seemed to come from the stable and the kitchen when we had such opportunities to meet the greatest figures of our time. But grown-ups were something else, weren't they? The dark gods who ruled the world, but our world was not theirs. . . .

Dear Rhodora: —

Your answer to my scrawl of the other day bearing with it your own impressions of that distant time has blazed a path far backward in my memory. To plagiarize from Emerson: the daughters of time, the hypocritic Days, have taken my hand and led me backward down that path to the old Milton, of which you and I are really the most pleasant exponents. No wonder that Milton absorbs so much of the thoughts of everyone who was brought up there. The shadow of Blue Hill lies deeper than the charm of Brookline. The Thayers may have their Lancaster and the Storrows their Lincoln, and all the rest their other favourite bits of domain, but we Apleys and Bromfields and Calders know they are not Milton.

Yes, I remember very well the day I ran away from my nurse, Norah. I stood on my own two legs that day until Corcoran, the gardener, finally found me, catching polliwogs in the swamp. Yes, Rhodora, I remember how we got kerosene over ourselves in the lamp room; and I remember Sundays too — they were not as pleasant at our house as they were at yours. We were all more afraid of Father on Sunday than on any other day of the week. He was larger and more silent then. Father could laugh loudly enough, he could even play, on weekdays, but not on Sunday and neither could we children. After breakfast Father would summon me to the library. He would want to know everything which I had done and learned during the week, and then would talk to me on some interesting subject on which I suspect he had prepared himself the night before. Perhaps it would be Mr. Darwin's Theory of Evolution, or again a snatch of Roman History. When all this was over, Mother and the girls and Father and I would mount in the carryall for the ride to the Church at Milton Corners. The hour and a half at Church was a period of complete quiescence and, must I say it frankly, an interval of such boredom as I have never known since.

You must have felt it too, Rhodora, because I remember you across the aisle, and I remember that Church smell. What made it, do you suppose? I think it had something to do with the building which had been closed during the week. There was that aura rising from pew cushions and hymn books mingling with the scent of flowers about the pulpit and lavender and camphor from the clothing of the congregation. Do you remember how the silk dresses rustled when everyone stood up with a sound something like the leaves in autumn? — without the wildness of the leaves. Do you remember the hats and bustles? I used to wish that Mr. Pettingill would not keep making us jump up to sing the hymns and make responses. Every time we were comfortably settled it would be his pleasure to make us move. Then there was a period of standing close to Mother's skirts, but not so close as to step on them, while all the dark people of the grown-up world stood talking. Then there was the drive home again, and Sunday dinner with Sunday guests. Oh well, so much for Sunday, and now I come to the strangest thing about it — I would give half of what I possess to be back at Hillcrest on one of those Sundays if I could have the assurance of living into a Monday morning. How I have run on! Your letter is

to blame for it, Rhodora. It has given me the will of speech.
You must get well soon and join us at Hillcrest. Catherine
has just come in this minute from her dressing room, and has
asked me to whom I am writing. She joins her love with
mine and her hope with me that all is well with you. . . .

The feelings expressed in this letter are such as have no lasting significance. For the last twenty years of his life, George
Apley was a pewholder in King's Chapel, where he attended
services regularly each winter.

"There is nothing," he once wrote to his son, "like the discipline of Church. It is a fine thing for the spirit. I cannot see
why you do not understand this."

The scenes and the hours of Hillcrest, which were to play
such a continued part in George Apley's life, were occasionally
interrupted in his boyhood by visits to other members of the
family, particularly to his Aunt Jane Brent, who lived of course
in that charming community of the Brents, on Pachogue Neck
on Buzzards Bay. The theater of his life was already broadening, and with it the field of his human contacts. One gains a
sense of this and an impression of a boy's naïve enthusiasm in
a letter which he wrote to his mother from his Aunt and Uncle
Brent's in the summer of 1874. This is among the earliest of
George Apley's letters. It is done in the careful, copybook
hand that speaks well for the discipline of Hobson's School in
Boston.

Dear Mamma: —
    I am very well. I hope you are well. I have brushed my
teeth every night and said my prayers. I play all day with
all my cousins. I like the sea. Uncle Horatio has a sailboat.
He has a dog, too, and a goat that pulls a cart. We press

THE BOYHOOD SCENE 39

flowers in the dictionary. Can Father send me ten cents? With love . . .

This letter was evidently referred to Thomas Apley, for his reply has been kept with it.

My dear little man: —

Here is your ten-cent piece and do not forget that this is a good deal of money. Think of it this way: it can buy ten lead pencils or two tops and a string, or enough candy to make you very ill. Please try to think carefully exactly what you want, before you spend it, because there is no satisfaction as great as spending wisely, and few annoyances as great as feeling that money has been wasted. I am glad you like the sea. . . .

On other occasions he was sent to visit the family of his maternal uncle, Henry Hancock, at Nahant, and again we have a letter, written in the summer of 1876.

Dear Mamma: —

I hope you are well. I hope everybody is well. I am well. I like Uncle Henry. He makes me laugh. I like Aunt Mabel, too. She is fat. My Cousin Tom and I go fishing off the rocks. Uncle Henry plays cards. When is Father coming to get me? With love . . .

This letter was answered by Elizabeth Hancock Apley.

My dearest little son: —

You are getting to be a big boy now. You must grow used to seeing some things of which your parents do not entirely approve. If your Uncle Henry plays cards you know he has a perfect right. I have not the slightest objection except I think that card playing is a waste of time. That is why your Father and I do not play cards. I am glad your Uncle Henry makes you laugh. There is nothing like a good joke. There is only one thing in your letter I am sorry for. It is not right to make remarks on the appearance of other people, particularly of your dear relations. Your Aunt Mabel would be very sorry if she were to think that you had written of her stoutness. Your dear father will come to take you home in the steam cars on Monday. . . .

———•———

CHAPTER V

BEACON STREET AND SCHOOL DAYS

Further Glimpses
Toward the Broadening Horizon of
Custom and Environment

THUS ONE sees that the world of George Apley is already growing broader. This correspondence opens vicariously, to the reader, a quiet world of mind and order. Already this world was reaching for George Apley, as it has reached for all its children, tying him by invisible bonds to this person and to that, directing him in his tastes and his associations, and offering him a particular position which was his by right of birth.

To those of us who know it and are a part of it there is nothing unnatural in the preoccupation of a Bostonian with his environment; for order — so lamentably lacking in other cities — tends to make him so completely at home and so contented with his social group that he is unhappy in any other. Starting with the nucleus of the family and its immediate friends, and next to it the school attended by these same contemporaries, he finally reaches the dancing class, and then the Thursday afternoons, and next the Friday evenings. A young girl will be introduced into society and will join the Sewing Circle of her year; a boy will be taken into his father's Club at Harvard. There is a simplicity in this procedure which emanates, I think, from the laudable similarity of ideas which makes up Boston life. These ideas have their foundation on the firm substratum of common sense which runs back to the beginnings of our colonial founders. This common sense, combined with an appreciation of what is truly fine, has given us a stability and a genuine society in a chaotic, nervous nation. If this society has moulded an individual in conformation to its principles, I, for one, cannot see why this is a deplorable situation, as every human being must conform to the social demands of his group, whatever that group may be. If George Apley failed to meet certain challenges, let us admit that we all have failed in some respects, and let us remember that we stand together peculiarly as one large family. Collectively, in habits and ideals, our group is a family group where kinship, however distant, stretches into the oddest corners.

In the winter home of Thomas Apley the boy George found himself exposed, however indirectly, to the events surrounding the active life of his father, which differed from the cultivated leisure of Hillcrest. By regular habits of life he was made to feel his own responsibility and he was aware, though vaguely, of the unsettled events of that period so aptly named by the recent writer, Claude Bowers, "The Tragic Era." The unpleasant affair of the *Crédit Mobilier* and the "Black Friday" on the New York Stock Exchange could not help being reflected, to an observant boy, in his father's face and manner. Thomas Apley, like every other New England industrialist, was piloting his craft through difficult financial waters, where politics not infrequently were lashed to banking. Thus it was George Apley's privilege to meet, during his boyhood at his father's house in Beacon Street, figures from the world of practical affairs and politics — who differed in some essentials from the leaders of scholarship and letters who sought the companionship of his mother.

"I wish," he once wrote, "that I could better have appreciated the value of these side-whiskered gentlemen in their tall silk hats. I can only recall most of them as tall, heavy-set strangers, whose faces shared the stern resolution of my father's own expression. Yet vague though they seem to me to-day, they had a vitality which I cannot forget. They are a type which is not seen in Boston at present. I often wonder where their kind has gone."

As is true with nearly every man of property, the political convictions of Thomas Apley were essentially conservative, and of a sort which confined themselves principally to the needs of the textile industry and to the industrial growth and prosperity of New England. He was, from the course of events, an ardent Protectionist, particularly for leather and textile products. Although he never coveted any political office, his influence — which was greater than many knew — was always thrown on the side which he considered would best further New England development; and thus he was a liberal contributor to the Republican Campaign Fund. His eminent good sense in these matters is illustrated by an extract from a letter to his brother William.

You appear worried for the aptitude shown here by "Paddy" in politics. I cannot share this alarm; instead I am quite willing that he should interest himself in municipal affairs as long as there is a firm hand at the top, which is I am sure the case at present. What concerns me more is your account of an element in Apley Falls that is giving wrong ideas to our mill labour. I hope you will soon get the names of the moving spirits and send them packing.

Referring to this further issue of stock, I think matters are going very nicely, but I beg you to leave the arrangement entirely to me. If these Wall Street men press any further demands, I think they will be sorry. I have, by the way, purchased a few thousand shares in young Agassiz's copper mine. This was partly out of friendship to the family of the great naturalist — for, as you know, I do not think much of mining speculation. However, it has elements which might interest you.

I am seeing H. to-morrow and G. and I am confident that everything will go well in that direction. That block of holdings is absolutely sound, an insurance for the future, and I think we would be wrong in entertaining any offer, however attractive. . . .

This is a glimpse, perhaps too intimate, into the lifework of one of the most active and respected men of his generation. It displays excellently the serene, practical capability of the father and throws an amusing sidelight on the early history of the Calumet and Hecla mines, which were to do so much for the prosperity of Boston. The astuteness of Agassiz was eminently congenial to Apley, and reminds me of a story which Thomas Apley once told his son George and myself when we called at his house one Sunday.

On an occasion some Harvard students went to great pains to construct an insect for a naturalist which had never been seen on earth, air, or water. They used the thorax of one species, the wings of another, the legs of a third, and the antennæ of a fourth. When the professor was confronted with the final result, and was asked what it might be, he smiled.

"I think," he said, "that it is called the humbug."

This story is an example of Thomas Apley in one of his lighter moods, which have perhaps been too much neglected. One must not forget that life in those days had its own modicum of robust gayety. One may obtain a glimpse of it, if one is interested, from the pages of the little book entitled "Rollo in Cambridge," published at that time, a satire which is full of laughter. Nor must we forget Lucretia Hale's inimitable satire of the time, the "Peterkin Papers," which deal with the mirth-making vagaries of the Peterkin family — which were surely parodies of her own flesh and blood — and the practical Lady from Philadelphia, who rescued them from so many difficult situations. Yes, the generation of the seventies had its moments of rollicking amusement. Their own long friendships with each other, dating also from childhood, enabled them to unbend at times and to be almost children again. Parties of charades, dealing with abstruse words amazingly acted, and games of quotations did more than test their intellectual skill of an evening. On such occasions there was an undertone of carefree merriment and friendliness that we youngsters now growing old have never been able to recapture. Then there were the outdoor days, the afternoons of skating on Jamaica Pond and the afternoons of coasting on some friendly hill. I have seen with my own eyes Elizabeth Apley, dressed in her grandmother's made-over woolens, coasting down the slope at Hillcrest boy-fashion, and enjoying it as much as the rest of us. George Apley himself has spoken of long peals of mirth coming through the closed doors of the dining-room when his father and his guests sat alone after dinner. Thomas Apley was in his office frequently at seven in the morning, and did not return home until the children's bedtime; thus his real impression on the family must have been shadowy, as George Apley has suggested — but it was an all-embracing shadow.

His ninth year saw George Apley established at Hobson's School on Marlborough Street, that institution which so many of us have to thank for our early education. In it he met the scions of his own social class, in it he cemented many of the friendships which were to endure through life. It was there that the present writer himself met George Apley.

It may be well to give a brief description of Hobson's School, for it is an institution which I regret to say is passing. I regret, because it had so many of the essentials of high thought and plain living. It had few playgrounds and not much fresh air, but these were replaced by wholesome, undeviating discipline. The school was housed in the two lower floors in Mr. Hobson's own dwelling, in rooms bare except for desks and blackboards. The presiding genius was Mr. Hobson himself, — "Old Hobby," we called him, — a stiff, melancholy man, with black sideburns and stern gray eyes. His dress was unvaried, a black Prince Albert coat, black cravat, and a pair of noiseless Congress boots. He had two assistants who had recently graduated from Harvard; one, a Mr. Weems, had the first two classes under his particular charge. This Weems was somewhat of a dandy; to our simple and censorious eyes his cravats and his waistcoats had a dash of immorality, and of a Saturday afternoon he would ride a high-wheeled bicycle. The second master seemed to us a tall, fine giant because he had rowed on the Harvard crew. Later, he had attended Oxford for a year, and this had given him an accent and a manner which excited our secret amusement — especially as we considered, so incorrectly, that the British were our hereditary enemies. In the savage

humor of childhood we nicknamed this master "John Bull
Godfrey" and secretly used to imitate his voice and walk.

George Apley shared with the rest of us the perpetual mis-
chievousness of boyhood, though not an unwholesome mis-
chievousness. A sprightly, likeable force in George Apley,
perhaps suppressed at home, had a freer rein in Mr. Hobson's
school and gained for him among the rest of the pupils a distinct degree of respect. In his dealing with constituted authority he was a past master of sophistry, and possessed a very accurate sense of that difficult limit where transgressions cannot
be overlooked but must be punished. This writer, his schoolboy
friend, is able to recall a single amusing instance.

Mr. Hobson, during the hours of school, had laid down the
law that there must be no whistling or disturbance on the stairs
or halls as the boys walked from one classroom to another. On
one occasion when George and I were walking up the stairs,
George began to whistle. The ubiquitous Mr. Hobson, as was
his custom on such occasions, descended upon us out of nowhere.

"Apley," he said, "I heard you whistling."

"No, Mr. Hobson," George answered, "I was not whistling,
I was *sissling*. I know that it is wrong to whistle in the hall,
but no one had told me that it was wrong to sissle."

As one views Mr. Hobson from the perspective of age, it
is interesting to reflect what his real reaction must have been
to this remark.

It is such encounters as these, I verily believe, absurd as they
may be to the ears of an adult, that play an important part
in the triumphs of a boy. Such adventures add to his self-
confidence and to his knowledge of human nature. There is
another, of which George Apley himself speaks, in a paper

which he once read before the Monday Club, not very originally entitled "Memories of a Boston Boyhood."

There is one adventure in Mr. Hobson's school in which I can take no pride, and to which I have not alluded for a great many years, although it sometimes returns still to my thoughts in the watches of the night.

Once a week at Mr. Hobson's school there would come before us a being who had never obtruded into our ken until that time. He was a wanderer upon our shores, a Frenchman whose name had been anglicized to "Mr. Treete," who gave us lessons in his language. I do not know what there is about a Frenchman which seems invariably to amuse young Anglo-Saxon savages. I only know that Mr. Treete's tight waist and dainty leather shoes, his difficulties with our idiom, his unvarying politeness and his volatile temperament, made most of us giggle and laugh and play, as did the children who saw the lamb that followed Mary to school. Poor Mr. Treete possessed no powers of discipline, and we soon had an instinctive sense of this defect, so that every scholar in Mr. Hobson's school set out to make the life of this poor polite scion of a cultivated nation as miserable as possible. To my greatest shame I must confess that I was a leader in this movement. With the skill of a Chinese torturer I would think of ways to goad the poor man to the limit of his endurance, and finally I drove him beyond the limit. I did so by the composition of a little poem, the doggerel of which still is with me —

> Mr. Treete, he has big feet,
> And all he eats is boiled wheat.

This for some reason reacted so strongly on Mr. Treete that he drew me out of my chair, dragged me before the class, and boxed my ears. This humiliation was richly deserved, but it

occurred at an unpropitious moment. Just as Mr. Treete's
hand descended on my ear the door of the classroom opened,
disclosing Mr. Hobson and my father, who had come to
honour the school with a visit. The frown on my father's face
was like that on the brow of Jove before he cast a thunder-
bolt.

"What is this man doing with George, Mr. Hobson?" he
inquired.

I shall draw the veil over the final explanations. When they
were over, Father sent me home in the carriage with orders to
go to bed, and when I returned to school, it was to discover
that Mr. Treete was no longer with us.

The same afternoon Father sent for me to visit him at his
office on State Street, the first time that I had ever laid eyes
on this establishment. I remember the clerks standing at their
ledgers and the huge safe and the great iron letterpresses and
Father's private offices, distinguished by a fine soft coal fire
in the grate and, save the mark! a large brass cuspidor — for
visitors I am sure, because my father never chewed.

"George," my father said, "your mischief has caused a great
deal of trouble and misfortune. Mr. Treete, of course, has
been obliged to leave Mr. Hobson's school; you have cost him
his position. I hope you are very sorry." Truthfully, I had
never been so sorry in my life for anything. I did not see why
Mr. Treete had been obliged to leave, and I told Father so.
His answer was characteristic of the older generation to the
younger. "You are too young to understand," he said, and that
was all. I can still only conjecture; I still do not understand.

Thus it is that a childhood life is filled full of imponderables.
There are many things which a child does not understand, and
I am not sure that the attitude of our fathers, of refusing to
discuss certain matters with their young, was not fully as whole-

some as the frank and detailed explanations which are retailed
to the child of the present. It must be an open question, which
is the more confusing to a young mind, the explanation or the
silence. Personally I prefer the latter; George Apley, like the
rest of us, was obliged to cope with the silence and to put his
trust into the maturer knowledge of another generation. At any
rate boys were no different in our days than they are at present.

The accusation of snobbery has been leveled at a certain section of our society so frequently that one is reminded of the
proverb that where there is smoke there must be fire. It is true
that a stranger coming to Boston, without the proper introduc-
tions or family connections, unless he is an Englishman or a
Frenchman is apt to receive a somewhat perfunctory reception.
Nevertheless, this noticeable trait, of which one hears so many
strangers complain loudly, is due neither to pride in family nor
to pride in intellectual attainments. We have alluded before
to that final factor which, one must admit, does tend to close
the door of careless social facility. It is the intense congeniality
of our own society which has its inception in a unique community of ideas resulting in a common attitude toward life.
When the individuals of one group find a complete peace and
happiness and fulfillment in the association with one another,
why should they look farther? This, I think, explains an evident but completely wholesome element of our self-satisfaction.
It explains also our many marriages between our childhood
friends and cousins. It explains why so many residents of
Boston flock together when abroad, instinctively seeking the
relaxation gained from each other when confronted with an
alien environment — why Boston has her own hotel in New
York City and in London and on the right bank of the Seine.

Yet, let us repeat, this congeniality bears in it no element of superiority toward or of dislike for the world around it.

Once admittance is gained inside this circle, one encounters the democracy of trust and friendship in its finest flower. It is manifested by a serene assurance that discounts the externals of dress and, indeed, of income. This explanation — tedious though it may be, and one already consciously felt, if not consciously analyzed, by all who read these pages — is an explanation for the unusual emphasis one places on George Apley's boyhood acquaintances, for these must inevitably become the friends of youth, the pillars of manhood, and the props of declining years. It furnishes also an explanation for the intimacy of nomenclature, and why the nickname of the school day has followed so many of us down the sunset path.

Unlike Gaul, the pupils attending Mr. Hobson's school may be divided into two groups: those who shared our background, and those who did not. We will concern ourselves with this first group primarily; and chief among them I shall mention George Apley's friend and contemporary, Winthrop Vassal. The name in itself describes his family — the Loyalist branch of the Tory Vassals, so many of whom left Boston for Halifax at the time of the Revolutionary War. Let us hasten to add that distinguished ancestors did not turn Winthrop's head, then or on any other occasion. He was a snub-nosed, reddish-haired, freckle-faced schoolboy who never lost the divine merriment of his youth. "Winty" Vassal, the life of our class and our Club at Harvard, the toastmaster and inimitable story teller at our class reunions, has ever maintained that fresh interest in youth. His imitation of the Irish conductor in the Brookline car, slightly mellowed by potations, is as side-splitting to the youngsters to-day as it is to us oldsters.

"Chick" Chickering was another of our group, musical even then, who has since distinguished himself for his studies in the art of English bell-ringing. Indeed, as one looks back at Mr. Hobson's school, one may take a pardonable pride in the later accomplishments of so many of our friends. "Tweaker" Sewall, who could catapult a spitball more surreptitiously and accurately than any boy at school, is Sewall, the surgeon, who developed a new and successful technique for the removal of the gall bladder. The voice of "Tom" Partridge, whom we knew for no good reason as "Daisy," has been heard for many years in pleadings before the Supreme Court at Washington. Geoffrey Broughton, whom George Apley once referred to as "Bookworm" Broughton, a name which was later contracted to "Wormy," is now known for his exhaustive study "The Massachusetts Fishing Fleet Before the Civil War." We may mention also George Apley's cousin, Horatio Brent, whose advice and loyalty have done so much to ensure the success of the Boston Symphony Orchestra, and his second cousin Nathaniel Apley, the collector of the "North of Boston Colonial Letters," which this writer had the pleasure of publishing and editing.

These were our particular intimates at Mr. Hobson's school, and we have stayed together ever since as a little band. There were others — not many — who, I regret to say, have been less fortunate. Kindness compels one to skip briefly over the subsequent career of Jonas Walker, whom we knew in our school days as "Mike," and who later was fullback on our Harvard football team. His lurid affair with one of the dancing girls in "Floradora" is still a matter of talk as is his disappearance to Chicago and his return thence to New York. Yet through all these vicissitudes George Apley remained his steadfast friend, ready always to defend old "Mickey" from what he considered, wrongly, unjust censure. One must include in this same category the most brilliant, though erratic of our companions, Henry Joyce, the head boy at Hobson's, who was the first of his class to enter the Phi Beta Kappa at Harvard. What might have been a brilliant and successful career has been clouded by an unbalanced preoccupation over social injustices. Garrison-like, he has dissipated his notable abilities in an unbalanced espousal of various lost causes, which led to his arrest while picketing the State House in the unfortunate Sacco-Vanzetti dispute, and again while assisting the agitator Mencken in his struggle against the Watch and Ward Society. These brief sketches, treated more frankly and informally than they would be in another type of work, and with the complete confidence that they will be read only by friendly eyes, may serve to show that the personnel of Mr. Hobson's school was an adequate cross-section of our world. If one could adjust oneself to this environment, it was surely safe to assert that after-life would not present the problem which it might have had one's life been more sheltered. In this instance George Apley's efforts at adjustment appear to have been easy and natural, as excerpts from his diary illustrate. This was one of the sporadic diaries which he kept at the instance of his mother, who offered him a tangible reward for making regular entries. She realized, as she said herself, that the discipline and perspective gained by even the brief jotting-down of the day's events were valuable to character.

"I know," she once wrote to her son, while pleading with him to continue his diary during his Freshman year at Harvard, "that a diary may have its disadvantages. It may be an unpleasant breeder of egotism, my dear, though I like to think that egotism is not strong in your father's family or in mine. Yet if one recognizes this difficulty, it will surely conquer itself. A diary will make you able to "know thyself." Furthermore, when your mother reads it she will not be so far away from the interests of her own dear son."

Boston, Monday, 1879. Damp, chilly, rainy. I went to school. I missed in Latin. I wish I had a football. Amelia got mad this afternoon. Father put a blot of ink on her nose when she came home, he says it is the way to punish girls. I wish he would punish me that way.

Tuesday. Sunny and cold. Going home from school there were some toughs. Mike fought one of them. Then Jane and I played "lotto." There are too many girls, I wish I had a brother.

Saturday. No school. Horatio and I played in his back yard. We started walking back-yard fences. You can go a long way on fences. Old Mrs. Burridge opened a window and told us to get off. In the afternoon "Tweaker" came over to see me. We made such a noise that Father came out of the library and told us to stop.

Sunday. Father talked to me about Romulus and Remus, then we went to church, then Dr. Holmes and a professor from Harvard, I don't know his name, and some other people came to dinner. Amelia and I got giggling and she had to leave the room. Then Great-Aunt Jane came to tea, and she gave me ten cents. And that is all, except the Bible Game.

Wednesday. Snowing. We go to Hillcrest to-morrow for Thanksgiving.

In keeping with the Puritan tradition, one is not surprised to find that the Apley family, like so many others of the Calvinist extraction, observed Thanksgiving with a greater punctiliousness than Christmas, that former "Popish holiday" once so inveighed against in Boston. One finds, indeed, that only community pressure finally weaned Thomas Apley away from the good old custom of his fathers — the giving of gifts on the New Year instead of on the Yuletide; but always through his lifetime that essentially New England day, Thanksgiving, was the high festival of the year, combining as it did pious thanks for plenty which the year had bestowed and a refurbishing of family ties. The group around the Hillcrest board was some-times forty strong, composed of many branches of the Apley line whose members would not appear at Hillcrest for another year. Near the head of the board, in George Apley's childhood, would be seated his father's surviving brothers and sisters — with the exception of Edward Apley, whom an unfortunate nervous complaint, bordering on hallucination, prevented from attending the family function. Until her death in 1875, George Apley's grandmother, for whom the brig *Pretty Pearl* had been named so long ago, occupied the seat of honor at her son's right hand, and a toast of cider for the youngsters and Madeira for the grown-ups was always drunk to her, standing. Though the old lady's mind was failing in these latter years, she in-variably enjoyed these family meetings; and one has the pic-ture of her, in her neat lace cap, beaming down the length of the dining-room table, and out to the smaller tables in the parlor beyond. It has been said that the plenty of the feast sometimes disturbed her to the extent of her asking her son, Thomas, if he was quite sure that he could afford this extrav-agant outlay, and often she cautioned those near her to be spar-ing in the use of sugar. There is a story told of her on one of these festive occasions that displays the vagaries of a dear old lady's mind as it groped through the dark avenues of the past.

Once, it is said, when the Reverend Nathaniel Pettingill, who always attended these dinners to ask the blessing, was assisting her upstairs, she turned to him with this remark: —

"Young man, should you ever go blackbirding, be sure to select Negroes that are brought down from the mountains, they are stronger and healthier than the Blacks from the coast."

Where she may have picked up this stray bit of information was sometimes an interesting source of speculation in the more intimate family circle. But Thomas Apley assured his son George, and once assured the writer, that the remark was germane to certain incidents in old Salem shipping days but had little or nothing to do with the Apleys' former mercantile interests.

Close beside this "last leaf on the tree" there sat her sister, Jane, a brown-eyed, determined old lady, whose wit was pungent and quick and who was credited with a predilection for certain bits of scandalous gossip which had better have gone with their subjects to the grave. Once, in later years, she shocked the table with an incredible tale of illegitimacy and a forced marriage in a distant branch of the family, which caused a pall of surprise and embarrassment to hover over the entire table. In all justice, one must add that such indiscretions were of the rarest. The younger generation, quite surprising in its numbers, occupied small tables in the parlor, where merriment sometimes rose to a pitch that obliged Thomas Apley to take a hand.

Such is a glimpse of another childhood scene, which must be dear to all that boast a New England heritage. The gastronomic demands of this single day were at times immense, for family obligations frequently obliged guests to look in on other dinners of collateral branches, so that the sight of that noble bird the turkey, and his attendant collection of pies, was frequently anathema for weeks thereafter.

These childhood diaries of George Apley, of which we have given a brief sample only to show their quality, are obviously not worthy of quotation in themselves, except in so far as they give a light of reminiscence.

December 15. Went to dancing school and had to sit with the girls.

Here is truly a segment of boyhood, which cannot fail but hold memories, fond or otherwise, for all of George Apley's contemporaries, for Papanti's Dancing School was as much a part of the life of the time as the lectures and the evening class. It was to Signor Papanti's that George Apley and the rest of us repaired, whether we would or no, to be taught the graceful intricacies of the waltz, so different from and so superior to the negroid steps and the drum-beat rhythm of the present. Mr. Papanti, whom we all must remember as a graceful Italian gentleman, had a power of discipline over his young charges, perhaps as a result of early military training, far superior to that of the unfortunate Mr. Treete. A stern look from Signor Papanti's dark eyes, and several sharp raps of his bow upon his fiddle, were sufficient to quell the exuberancies of the wildest rebel; yet now and then revolt would break out in some small way.

George Apley, in his "Memories of a Boston Boyhood," already quoted, alludes to certain reluctant youths who would persist in hiding behind the greatcoats in the boys' dressing room, rather than mount the stairs of the Tremont Street hall to join the fairer sex. These malingerers, when they were discovered, were ushered upstairs by the agile dancing master himself and were obliged to walk across the floor from the boys' row to the girls' row amidst subdued tittering.

There was one girl [George Apley writes, to quote from his very quotable paper] by the name of Elizabeth Freer, the sister of Jimmy Freer, whose family dwelt on Chestnut Street, the same Jimmy who was the Harvard halfback. Elizabeth was prone to burst into unreasonable fits of giggles at Papanti's, which at times she was unable to suppress. When I discovered this weakness, I regret to say that I abetted it by every means in my power, and found that a few simple changes of facial expression would frequently throw the unfortunate child into convulsions. . . . "Poor girl," as Whittier so aptly says, "the grasses on her grave have forty years been growing."

It was here at Papanti's, as George Apley once confided to me, that he first set eyes on Catharine Bosworth, one of the Bosworths who dwelt near the corner of Mt. Vernon and Walnut Streets, another instance of how attachments ripen early in our environment. It is not difficult to perceive that these early days at Papanti's leave behind their trains of friendly memories. Many a romance had its inception in this atmosphere, particularly at the more grown-up series of evening dances which we attended later. The auspices were always suitable for the meeting of young people, as the list of those attendant was under careful scrutiny and represented the best of our group.

CHAPTER VI

REVEALING MEMORIES

*A Few Instances
In Which Apley Meets Life in Its
More Challenging Aspects*

A LETTER to his elder sister, Amelia, written in the middle of his fourteenth year, evidently when Miss Apley was on a visit to New York, sets another mark to the broadening of George Apley's horizon.

Dear Am: —

I hope you are having a good time and going to lots of parties. What do you think — Father took me to the theatre — the first time I've ever been to a real theatre. We went to the Museum to see a play called "So Lies the Dew, or A Confession of Conscience." I wish you would dress like Miss Janeway. They tried to pretend that she was only a poor governess when she was really the heiress to Lord Roxbridge. . . .

The rest of the letter, which we will refrain from quoting here, indicates a boy's enthusiasm for the dramatic arts, as well as a dawning understanding of life, which has caused the writer to repair to the dramatic shelves of the Boston Athenæum in order to refresh his memory on the details of this production.

"So Lies the Dew," one recalls, was a highly successful and popular piece in its day, written by the actor-author George Willoughby, who played the part of the villain, Hugo Sayre. Admitting that the plot has not aged well, there is none the less a sparkle to Mr. Willoughby's dialogue which explains the great popularity of the piece. The theme was one of a genuine moral significance, which probably explains why young George was allowed to see a production which furnished much discussion around Boston teatables. Briefly stated, this drama was designed to show that deceit and covetousness meet their own retribution when facing the impregnable front of integrity. The three virtues of Tennyson — faith, hope, and chastity — are quite accurately unveiled in the action of five acts, centering around the dramatic question of whether a forgotten heiress will lose both her virtue and her inheritance. It may be added that the dialogue concerning this former attribute was couched in terms probably vague enough to be above the head of a boy of fourteen years, and at best was a minor element. Though the oversophisticated youth of the present may well laugh at the artificiality of the plot and the ridiculous contrivances of concealment in "So Lies the Dew," one shrewdly suspects that this drama in its reticences will prove in the course of time no more outmoded than the bald, inaccurate, and unintelligent realism of the present theater.

This drama is only mentioned here as an illustration of a new side of life which was confronting George Apley and which a boy of his generation was obliged to meet single-handed, with little or no explanation from his elders. The practice of ignoring many basic facts of relationship between the sexes, which was prevalent in George Apley's boyhood, one must repeat again was probably no more dangerous or absurd than the franker expositions which are now presented to confused and uninterested youth. If a boy in those days was permitted to find out about such matters for himself, he generally did so quite accurately and with no great harm. As a schoolboy grew older there were certain parts of Boston which he was generally forbidden to visit, and needless to say he visited them.

It was in such localities in our late 'teens that we boys heard bits of conversation quite different from the talk in our parents' parlors; and yet, on the whole, perhaps this was not detrimental. Youth has its own capacity to absorb surprises, and the natural conservatism of a proper home environment put these surprises for a healthy boy in a suitable perspective.

George Apley and his boyhood group were now reaching that interesting, if difficult, period of adolescence when a curtain rises which has obscured the stage of life partially from the accurate but unsophisticated eyes of childhood, and when life, seemingly overnight, assumes a new significance that reveals the characters of those about us. For some this revelation, close to religion in its sudden illumination, brings in its train an awkward tongue-tied silence and an introspection, particularly on religious matters; and with George Apley this was partially the case, though we find him also developing that capacity for tolerant observation which will prove one of his outstanding and lifelong characteristics, and which stood him in such good stead over trying intervals.

In the summer of George Apley's fifteenth year he encountered an adventure which could not but have a profound effect upon his viewpoint in that it brought to him very vividly the presence of impending death. He had been sent from Hillcrest on one of those customary visits to the country estate of his uncle, Horatio Brent, which as we have already mentioned is situated at Pachogue Neck on Buzzards Bay. Horatio Brent, who was the founder of Brent and Company, the banking house on Congress Street, was from boyhood an ardent sportsman whose collection of early shotguns still betrays his avidity. His windswept acres on Buzzards Bay were a haven for duck and quail shooters, and already he had interested George Apley in the sport by presenting the boy with a fine, light Parker on his birthday. It was here, also, on Pachogue Neck, as well as on the John Apley estate at Hamilton, that young George had his first experience in riding. But, more than these interests, sailing held him spellbound.

"When I am aboard a boat," George Apley once wrote, "tending the sheet myself, I am away from everything. I have always felt this to be true."

George Apley, already growing large and endowed with the wiry Apley physique, was allowed that summer to share one of those broad-beamed twenty-foot Cape catboats with his cousin, Horatio Brent, Junior. At five o'clock one summer afternoon, while they were off the South Rip Shoals some five miles off Pachogue Neck, they encountered a sudden thunder squall. Boylike, neither of them visualized the force of the gale behind its curtain of steamy water until it struck them suddenly with its full weight. They jibed, and the boat turned over. Fortunately, as it was discovered later, her ballast broke loose, and thus she floated, bottom up, affording the two boys a precarious hold. They remained clinging to the bottom, and encountering a high but warm sea, for some two hours, feeling their strength gradually ebbing away and their desire for life ebbing with it.

It was fortunate for the boys that Horatio Brent, disturbed by the suddenness of the storm, was on the lookout on the veranda on Pachogue Neck. When the squall lifted he saw the bottom of the capsized boat and put out at once, with a local lobster fisherman to the rescue. Arriving, he found that George Apley had managed to get a piece of rope under the arms of Brent's half-unconscious son Horatio, and was thus preventing his cousin from being washed away. This is a matter of which George Apley has never spoken, and it may not be known to many of his family.

Letter from George Apley to his sister Amelia.

Dear Am: —

I had a chill when they took me off and Uncle Horatio made me take a glass of whisky. I felt better when I had the whisky. I seem to know a lot more. I am going to take that boat out again just as soon as I get up. I do not want anyone to think that I am afraid. . . .

Whether rightly or wrongly, this last wish was not gratified, at least in its entirety, as is shown by a letter from Thomas Apley which the writer found among George Apley's papers.

Dear George: —

Under no circumstances will you sail again this summer unless you are accompanied by a competent boatman, preferably the elder Nickerson from Beach Road. You were careless in handling that boat. You should have let down the peak and allowed her to ride it out. Instead, you allowed the full force of the squall to hit square on your sail. You have caused your mother a very great deal of worry and anguish. She was unable to attend the meeting of her Sewing Circle yesterday afternoon and has been in bed this morning with a severe headache. You are growing old enough now to remember that your actions have a direct effect upon all those who are interested in you. I am enclosing my check for five dollars which I wish you to present personally to the lobsterman who was instrumental in getting you off that capsized boat. . . .

There is a further sequel to this incident which may not be known to the family but which reveals itself in a letter from Elizabeth Apley to her son. Normally it would not be quoted, and it is done so here at the risk of delicacy, to fulfill the writer's promise of holding nothing back in the life of the boy whose character as a man the writer has always revered: —

It is very dear of your cousin Henrietta to be taking such good care of you and naturally, George, you are very grateful to her. Being two years older than you, she must be a delightful and sympathetic companion and it must be at some sacrifice to her that she gives you so much of her time, though of course she is a sweet girl who has much of her mother's outgiving nature. Now, George dear, I am going to add a word of caution, because your happiness and your development are my greatest interest. It is hard for me to realize that my little boy is growing up to an age when he can take a different view of girls. You are close to the age when you may grow attached to someone a few years your senior. Mind you, nothing is more wholesome than cousinly friendship, but for your own peace of mind remember that anything else may result in unhappiness.

And, George, I do not need to tell you to revere womanhood, for that reverence is a part of the code of any gentleman. Reverence of womanhood, or at least a deep respect, is the cornerstone of life's structure. Give my dear love to Cousin Henrietta and all your other cousins.

Tragically enough, the experience of elders can seldom be translated to youth. That eminently sane advice of Elizabeth

Apley, one has reason to believe, went unheeded. The evidence of this is contained in several poems in one of the boy's stray notebooks which were probably never placed before the eyes for which they were intended. A few lines from one of them, entitled "To Henrietta," will be quoted here, if only because they reveal an attitude of chivalry which George Apley never lost. To the boy and to the man, the good woman was a creature of another world, to be protected at all costs.

There are things I dare not do, Henrietta
I would like to say, I love you, Henrietta,
I would like to touch your hand, but would you understand,
My love for you is true, Henrietta?

Though one may suspect that these lines came partially from the songs which George Apley heard rendered by his sisters and their swains around the piano in the Beacon Street parlor, they have, in spite of their triteness, a sad sort of beauty. To one who sees them scrawled on the yellowing pages of a notebook, they speak a little sadly of a boy's first love. They tell of the glamour and the beauty of an early comprehension of the world. They foreshadow the inevitable tragedy, and with it the half-ludicrous disillusion, of a boy's first love; but in spite of disillusion George Apley remained throughout his life steadfast in his attitude, which was one of chivalry and restraint. This thought may be best expressed — before leaving the subject — in a letter which George Apley once wrote to his son John, and which is now in the hands of the writer.

You must not be shocked to discover, as I was in my early 'teens, that there are two kinds of women in this world, good women and bad women. The latter class you must learn to treat somewhat differently than the former, as they concern your life only indirectly. But always remember this: Treat them all respectfully. You may be amazed to learn how much good there is in the very worst. At any rate, it will please you in later years to know that you have always been a gentleman, and, believe me, that is something.

Until now we have been describing the background of George Apley, important because it furnished the mainsprings of his character. But now the stage is set. Before George Apley's eyes, his own sisters and parents, his school friends, his masters, the Brents, the Hancocks of Nahant and the John Apleys at Hamilton, and many others in the family circle, were beginning to assume a new and more rounded relationship. They will now step forth on these pages as people seen through a young man's eyes.

George Apley and the present writer and other members of his school group were graduated from Mr. Hobson's school in the spring of 1883. Having passed his preliminary examinations that same spring and his final examinations that autumn, George Apley became a member of the Harvard class of 1887, for the first time actually launched into a larger world. A letter of his father's at the time contained some common-sense admonitions. The letter was dated from New York.

Your examination marks, which are before me, while not of the highest, are on the whole satisfactory as far as I can judge by comparing them with the results achieved by the sons of my other friends. The radical views of Charles Eliot are changing Harvard into a place which I no longer wholly understand. Nevertheless, I feel that some views of mine, those of an old "fogey" if you wish to call me so, still have a certain pertinence. You have always seen wine upon our table. You have seen it used, not abused. If you wish to drink moderately at meals, it is now your right. As for smoking, although I have enjoyed a cigar after dinner for many years I had rather that you avoided the habit. As for women, I mean to talk to you sometime, George, about this matter. You may now and then fall in with a "fast" crowd; you may be subjected to temptations. My great hope is that your bringing-up will cause you to see them in a sensible light. I have no objection to your taking part in the various college sports now becoming so fashionable, nor has your mother any objection. I only wish you to remember that you are primarily at Harvard to broaden and to improve your mind and I want you to remember that how you behave reflects both on your parents and your family. I do not think I need say any more, because you are my son. While I am anxious you should live comfortably in keeping with your position, I do not wish you to live on the scale of the "swells." There is nothing more ill-bred than the over-lavish spending of money. Your allowance, above your living expenses and a reasonable amount for books, will be fifty dollars a month, I think a generous sum. Out of this you must dress and amuse yourself.

Business will keep me here for another two weeks. Your mother will settle you in your rooms and I shall hope to hear a good report from you at our first Sunday lunch together at Hillcrest.

CHAPTER VII

HARVARD DAYS

"About these halls there has always been an
aroma of high feeling not to be found or lost
in science or Greek — not to be fixed,
yet all-pervading"

THERE are certain persons of whom it has been said, partly in jest though partly in earnest, that their clock struck twelve while they were undergraduates at Harvard and that in the interval remaining to them between youth and the grave their personalities underwent no further change. This is an indictment, though the writer does not believe it wholly a fair one, which may be leveled against a number of his contemporaries. It might be more suitable to consider it not an indictment but rather a tribute to Boston and Cambridge that so many of her sons succeed in staying perennially young in spirit, that by some magic the scenes of their youth and the triumphs of their youth remain indelibly before them. Considering that George Apley's preparation for his college years had a peculiar adequacy, it is not strange that he should have been one of that happy band who derived much inspiration from college life. By tradition and position George Apley's group, of which the writer was one, was truly fitted for a college career.

The friendship with the leading spirits of our class was open to us by right, as were the doors in the best houses during many events of the social season.

It is not strange, therefore, as one attempts to reveal the thoughts and actions of his most intimate friends through the "shortest, gladdest" years of his life — a line unfortunately written by a Yale man, but none the less true — that one feels a certain thrill of anticipation. Even the stupidest, least observant of us were confronted with a certain something at Harvard, indescribable but unmistakable, which could not fail to add to our stature and our manner. It is an attribute which has best been described by the late Oliver Wendell Holmes, Junior, the soldier and the jurist, in his answer to a toast at the Commencement of 1884.

"It has been one merit of Harvard College that it has never quite sunk to believing that its only function was to carry a body of specialists through the first stage of their preparation. About these halls there has always been an aroma of high feeling not to be found or lost in science or Greek — not to be fixed, yet all-pervading."

Our task will now be to show how George Apley, like so many another son of New England, took to himself a portion of this feeling and how his Harvard associations formed him, in spite of a single interlude which was to test his character, into a high-minded gentleman.

The present writer, in an article "Harvard in the Eighties," which received much favorable comment at the time of its publication in *Harper's* magazine, has described something of the life of the period with its swift change of taste and fashion, and perhaps a portion of it may be quoted here as the setting of the new scene of George Apley's activities.

The Harvard of our day was undergoing a great transition which reflected the material growth of the country. This change largely expressed itself in the form of bricks and mortar, and its cycle may be marked by many fine contributions to the older building groups. The architectural triumph of the towering Memorial Hall, the informal yet important façade of the Hemenway gymnasium, the Gothic of Gore, the pleasantly sculptured cornices of Gray's and Matthew's Halls, are some of the more interesting examples which this Harvard has passed on to posterity. Although the present may criticize the architecture of Richardson it bears witness to an undeniable intellectual vigor which has its prototype in many of the figures who adorned the Harvard scene, the scholars whose personality formed the taste of succeeding Harvard generations, the Childs, the Shalers, the Hills, and the Nortons. Harvard was more truly the repository of the *best* of New England culture than it has perhaps ever been since. Cambridge was emerging with this Harvard from the status of a small university town into something that was larger.

These impressions may be supplemented by some of George Apley's own, given in a letter which he sent the writer on the occasion of the fifteenth anniversary of their class.

Cambridge is indeed growing a dizzy place since we were there, Will, but I'll warrant some of the old landmarks are left. There is the livery stable at Inn Street, for instance, where I kept my horse and trap. Cousin Jane lent me the money for it, you remember? There is Bow Street where we had our Club Table; that old house is still there, frowning upon the sybaritic magnificence of Beck Hall, and there are a number of tobacco shops and billiard parlors about the Square, suspiciously like those we once frequented, and the old *Lampoon* rooms on Holyoke Street, and the house where the Club had its quarters.

The new building to which we have all contributed is certainly more in keeping with its dignity, but I like the old one better. What a gay place Cambridge was! Full of light and laughter — "Sweet college years with pleasure rife" — we may not have learned much, Will; we may have had our heart-burnings and our jealousies, but we had a high old time. I'll tell you something confidentially. Although I don't understand it myself, I seemed to be standing a good deal more on my own two feet out there than I am to-day in spite of everything. I wonder why — what's happened to us, Will?

Even to the writer that question is sometimes haunting and disturbing, for there are certain enigmas in the past. The truth was that we were much the favored few, moving in an exclusive circle that was the envy of many less fortunately situated.

The pictures of George Apley at this period might well be those of the typical Harvard man. There is one before me as I write, taken with the rest of the Club Table. It shows him a muscular, rangy, sharp-nosed youth, with thick yellow hair and a hint of laughter at the corners of his mouth, wearing a striped blazer and boasting a wisp of mustache on the upper lip. Besides this picture, there is also a word portrait of him by his friend, Dr. Sewall, in a letter of reminiscence now in the author's possession.

I think the one in our crowd who had the best time of all was George Apley. George was quite a figure in those days in our little world. Once he was away from home he blossomed out, though perhaps all of us blossomed out in that congenial atmosphere. George was never a wild rake, like Mike Walker, but he was full of honest fun. We all know how he won the middleweight sparring his Freshman year, in the Hemenway gymnasium. But more than that, he applied himself to his work — not that George burned the midnight oil. You and George were the literary ones in our crowd, Will, though of course you have gone much farther. Your magic gift of words, to bear such fine fruit in the later world of letters, was getting you on the *Lampoon* already, but George honestly applied himself to writing; he was sensible, too, most of the time, a good influence on the rest of us. Except for one lapse we all know of, George was a steady boy, but there must have always been that erratic strain. He had a bit of the rebel in him; the Apleys are too high-strung.

This picture may serve, although it is not accurate in all of its essentials. Though lacking perhaps in brilliance, George Apley was endowed with a peculiar gift for friendship and with a certain generosity which even caused him to espouse the interests of others who were not in his own circle. He had a way of making many acquaintances among eccentrics who could do him no great good; and this tendency, we shall see, grew more pronounced during his undergraduate career, causing him to go against the sound sense and expostulations of his father and of many of his friends. This leads one to mention a single instance, brought out by the following correspondence.

Extract from a letter to his father, December 1883.

I am studying very hard and I have been taken on the tug-of-war team. I am also going out for the debating society and I have written a few "bits" which the editors of the *Lampoon* think are quite good. I have only been to Boston one night all week and that was to the Barrows' dance. Several of us rode home in a cab. In case you have heard some talk about it, I want to assure you that it was not our fault that the horse ran away. Yes, I am making a number of friends. There is one here whom I like very much, his name is Henry Alger, who sits beside me in English. His family come from Springfield and I should like very much to bring him home some Sunday for lunch.

Letter from Thomas Apley.

Dear George: —

Your mother and I were both somewhat worried by your letter. We neither of us can understand why you did not stop to see us if you came to Boston to the Barrows' dance. Surely you might have given us a moment of your time. I hope that excessive drinking did not cause the horse to run away, and your mother hopes so too. Your account of your many activities indicates to us both that you are spreading yourself very thinly over too large a surface.

What worries me more is a fear that you are not meeting the right people. The Westcotts, who were kind enough to agree to keep an eye on you, have told me you have declined two of their invitations to tea. No doubt you have more important business, but nothing is more important than social consideration. You must bear in mind that the friendships and associations which you are now making at Harvard will be with you for the rest of your life. In my experience there is no truer axiom than that "a man is known by the company he keeps." Besides this, the connections you are now forming are of definite importance to your subsequent career, both in college and in business.

It is the fondest hope of your mother and me that you will be taken into the Club which has had an Apley for a member for many generations. But, your worthiness to be one of its members depends to a certain extent upon yourself. You must be sure to see the right people, which should not be difficult for you, as you have been born among them. Your mother and

I have been greatly worried by your mention of this fellow-student named Alger. It is all very well to be democratic and pleasant to an acquaintance who sits beside you in the classroom, by an alphabetical accident. I have no wish to limit your circle of acquaintance, as acquaintances are valuable and instructive, but you must learn as soon as possible that friendship is another matter. Friends must be drawn from your own sort of people, or difficulty and embarrassment are very apt to be the result. Who is this man, Alger? Though I have not heard of any Algers in Springfield, my acquaintance there is not large. I simply want to feel that he will be a useful and congenial friend. . . .

Letter to Thomas Apley.

Don't worry, Harry Alger is first rate. We box every afternoon in the gymnasium. He says his father knows you. His father owns the West Springfield Yarn Company. . . .

Letter from Thomas Apley.

Dear George: —
    That is capital. I remember Mr. Alger now, and I am very glad that you know young Harry. Have him around to lunch by all means. Your mother and the girls will be glad to see him. The West Springfield Yarn Company is a very sound organization. . . .

Between the lines of this correspondence one who has been a parent may readily read and sympathize with the anxious solicitude for the welfare of a son who is leaving the family roof and entering the world. This desire to control the destinies of one's offspring is a difficult one to check, for it contains all that is best in instinctive parenthood. If the anxiety of Thomas and Elizabeth Apley for their son's welfare may have been too great, they may have had their own reasons for anxiety which they never communicated to the world at large.

Letter from Elizabeth Apley, December 3, 1883.

My dearest George: —

Your life in Cambridge sounds like a very happy one, though it is far removed from mine. Sometime we must have a good long talk about it. I was sorry we could not have done this last Sunday at teatime, but my guests made it impossible and then you, yourself, had to hurry back to do your lessons. I don't want you to overdo your studying, George. So many have ruined their eyes from overwork and I was worried at your appearance at Sunday luncheon. Both Amelia and Jane were worried too. Your eyes looked badly and you did not have a hearty appetite. Don't sit up too late studying another Saturday night but arrange it so that your Saturdays can be the beginning of a healthful relaxation before a day of rest.

Yesterday I saw dear Mrs. Westcott, who told me that you had been in to tea and that my George spoke well and intelligently about his courses of study. I am so pleased that you have seen the Westcotts and that you may now and then have a bit of home life during the week. I have heard from the Bosworths, too, that you attended their party of evening games. I am so pleased that you like them. I suppose you think me an old lady now, but I still love charades and I do think that Catharine is turning into such a sweet girl. You may not realize it as I do, because you two have played together for so many summers in Milton, but you will realize it some day. Some day you will know that there is a beauty of the soul that is more important than worldly beauty. Remember this when you see worldly beauty. . . .

Though this sort of admonition and encouragement could not but have a definite result, George Apley had patently reached a stage where youth must make its own adjustment, and must do so by the painful system of trial and error. With the world at one's feet, adventurous youth must explore its lights and shadows. In the following college theme, which evidently formed a part of his exercises in Freshman English, one suspects that there is more than a little firsthand experience. If so, it will serve to add to the veracity of George Apley's portrait. If not, it will do no harm. Although this early attempt at composition deals with a social problem not frequently mentioned, it must not be forgotten that every man has faced this problem in some one of its forms. The theme is entitled "A Night of Regret."

The two young men had been drinking more than was good for them. They did so because they wished to prove proper companions for the older members of the party and they learned their lesson. When it was suggested that everyone should go to Mrs. Bryant's, Hugo said he did not know the lady and was afraid that he might not be in a fit condition to go anywhere. He was surprised that the others laughed heartily at his remark, assuring him, at the same time, that Mrs. Bryant would not mind. Next, this thoughtless party was in a cab, headed for a part of Boston out of the fashionable district. They stopped before a large house whose hall was lighted dimly. The hour was late, but Mrs. Bryant seemed glad to see them. Hugo had never seen anyone like Mrs. Bryant; she was richly dressed and spoke with an Irish brogue, but she was most hospitable. She said the girls were in the parlour. Hugo's ignorance was such, or perhaps his condition, that the painted cheeks and carmined lips of the creatures in that close, heavily scented, brilliantly lighted room gave him no message of warning. It was not until one of these singled him out and signified her profession in a way he could not doubt that Hugo knew he was in a house of ill fame. The knowledge shocked him to sobriety. He saw then where a thoughtless man might be led by heedless companions and he left the place at once, filled with fear and loathing and tortured by remorse. Such are the pitfalls that lie around us in a great city.

This exercise, the rest of which is not worth quoting, was given the deservedly low mark of C-minus, but it shows something of George Apley's sensibility.

It is only fair to add that the extra-curricular activities of our set led only a few of its members on such expeditions more than once. There was little incentive, with the opportunity so freely offered to meet girls of one's own class at the social assemblies of the Boston season. Though the laws of chaperonage were strict in our day, it was possible for young people to meet, skating on Jamaica Pond or walking in the suburbs. These casual meetings which occurred now and again afforded enough of wholesome romance and were protected usually by an honorable reticence. There was also the wholesome outlet of vigorous competitive sport; the important connection between a sane mind and a healthy body was fully realized in the Harvard of that day. Somewhat light for the hard scrimmage of the football field, George Apley's attention was directed to sparring, then a very popular pastime. At the winter meeting in the Hemenway gymnasium, much to his surprise, he found that he was proficient in the manly art and actually outclassed the University titleholder of his weight — Higgins, a senior. This triumph could not help but have a profound effect in George

Apley's college world. It not only gave him a new confidence in relation to his fellows but a new respect for himself. He suddenly became deservedly popular with the athletic set. In a letter which he wrote much later to his classmate, Chickering, he speaks amusingly of his own reactions at that time — probably, as he said, one of the most important periods in his life.

I suppose I must have been quite insufferable for a while, but I don't believe that the rest of you fellows at the Club table ever knew what that triumph in the Hemenway gymnasium meant to me. I felt that I was somebody in my own right. I think I stood up straighter after that and did not back down so readily in an argument, but I must have been insufferable. . . .

If he was, it was a phase which the writer does not remember. As a matter of fact, George Apley's prowess was causing him to be considered favorably in other directions. The editors of the *Harvard Lampoon,* the little group which is brought together by its own merry humor as much as by its literary capacity, began to find in George Apley a congenial companion. Toward the end of the year, he was made a member of the Board; and also, greatly to his own pleasure but somewhat to his father's alarm, he was made a member of an organization, now defunct, known as the Racquet Club, whose membership was composed of an element known to some of us as "fast."

The chief function of the Racquet Club was to spend a day each spring in a Tally-Ho coach on a country party. George Apley, who was able to handle the ribbons himself, acquitted himself well on such occasions, but perhaps what he enjoyed most were evening meetings in the rooms of his friends, where certain musical spirits raised their voices in choruses that perhaps may still be heard beneath the College elms: "A Health to King Charles," "Seeing Nellie Home," "After the Ball Is Over." The approval of his class was finally accorded George Apley by his selection as one of the first ten of the D.K.E. Society, and Thomas Apley, himself, was keenly aware of the importance of this honor.

Letter from Thomas Apley.

Dear George: —

This last bit of news is capital. I am very, very proud. So are your mother and your sisters, and many of the doubts which I have felt about the wisdom of your course in college are now favorably resolved. I do not believe that you know, yourself, the importance of what has befallen you. The approval of your classmates so expressed will, in a sense, be yours for life, and we need no longer have any fear about your election to the Club early in your Sophomore year. Again, I say that this is capital and I am sending you my check for fifty dollars, with only a single word of caution. Remember, though you have justly earned it, this honour comes to you in a sense because of your family's position. Thus, we feel honoured with you. . . .

Although the mantel in George Apley's study at Gray's was now beginning to bear its burden of athletic trophies, and its walls the medals of the clubs, the study lamp upon the rosewood desk which his mother had given him was not entirely dimmed. He was already laying the foundations of his later tastes, but for these he was also under obligation to the sensitive discrimination of Elizabeth Apley. It was she who guided him away from much that was trivial and valueless, and so we find him years later saying, in a letter to his son: "My mother taught me one important thing about reading, which I shall now hand on to you. It is simply this: Distrust the book which reads too easily because such writing appeals more to the senses than to the intellect. Hard reading exercises the mind."

This bit of Puritan tradition did not, however, blind George Apley to the lighter side of letters, for one often found him at Gray's laughing over his Dickens and his Thackeray; and his marks in the final examinations of his Freshman year, though they set him only in the middle of his class, were not at all discreditable.

Early in his Sophomore year, as his father predicted, George Apley was taken into the Club and joined that band which links each member in its peculiar brotherhood, no matter how far from kindred this meeting may take place. Once in this Club, much of George Apley's period of experimentation was over and his interests necessarily became centered in the Club itself. Though his acquaintance with outside members of the student body continued, he could not help but feel the weight of his added responsibilities which he gracefully expressed in a toast at one of our annual dinners: —

"All things which are worth while demand vigilance and sacrifice. To be a good Clubmate requires these attributes, for one's first effort must be for the Club. Critics have said that this is a narrowing of interest, but the reward is proportionately great."

It must not be supposed, however, that the Club limited George Apley's student activities, as this was far from being its purpose or its spirit. He had put on weight in the summer of his Freshman year, so that in the next season he offered himself for the varsity crew and rowed at Number Six for the next two successive seasons.

He appeared also in his Junior and Senior years in two musical extravaganzas of the Hasty Pudding Club, the lyrics of which were written by the present author and the music by Chickering. The writer well remembers the nights of vigil and the weeks of nervous suspense while the first of these efforts was in rehearsal, for upon its success depended in a great measure his own personal vindication. The knowledge that there would be present many graduates well known in the literary world, and that most of Boston society would occupy the stalls when the curtain rose, did nothing to assuage his doubts and fears. A glance at the old score now reminds him that the action took place in a Balkan palace, where, by a really ingenious twist of circumstances, the princess changed places with the lady's maid, little realizing that a handsome duke from another kingdom, madly in love with this heiress to the throne, had already insinuated himself into the palace as "boots boy."

Amazed by his sudden infatuation for the little lady's maid, this duke is about to resign all to follow the path of his love, when the old king, who has fortunately been hiding under the bed, emerges, deeply moved by the entire scene, in time to explain that the pretty little menial is, after all, the princess. At several of the rehearsals the more serious-minded members of the cast questioned the advisability of laying the scene in the King's bedroom, feeling that its implications might be misunderstood; but one and all agreed to risk it on account of its mirth-provoking qualities. The author's word is not necessary for assuring the reader that the whole production was an immense success. The critic from the *Boston Advertiser* was kind enough to write the next morning: "We have a true dramatist in our midst. His name is Willing. . . . George Apley as the prince interpreted his rôle magnificently, and Edgar Sleed as the princess, though somewhat muscular, was on the whole a dainty sprite in lace and muslin." When George Apley, in an apron smeared with shoe blacking, sang the song "My Heart Is in My Boots," the author knew for the first time how really good his words were. Many still rank them with that classic "Odd Fellows' Hall," and they have been revived at least ten times in entertainments before the Berkley Club.

Such triumphs as these, though not sedate, have a way of exercising a peculiar importance through the years. Whenever those of us who have joined in that boyish merrymaking get together, memory binds us and lends an unconscious mellowness to our conversation that is as sound as a good rare wine. Back to our minds come a hundred pictures, made dear because we shared them together, and we know that the bravery of youth is recaptured and indeed that it has never left us. It is before me now, in a paper which George Apley read at the dinner celebrating his forty-second birthday.

Do you remember the fishing trip we took to Lynn in a four-in-hand one spring? I think that every one of us here around the table was in that party, which outdid the escapades of the boys in Wister's "Philosophy 4," to my mind one of the most perfect stories ever written of college life. It was Mike Walker's idea to hire the trap and drive to Lynn, there to produce poles and to start fishing in Lynn Square. I wish that we were setting out for Lynn again to-night, instead of sitting around this Beacon Street table.

Such examples of the serious and the gay college life give an indication, one hopes, of George Apley's development, without there being need to cite many others. They show a normal progression from boyhood to manhood, and an enthusiasm and a loyal spirit. From his contact with Harvard democracy and with the cross-section of the world which was presented to him there, George Apley was emerging, as a type perhaps, but a type of which Harvard may be definitely proud. He adhered to the strict conventions of youth loyally, on the whole; but now and then something in his spirit was irked at these conventions. If this occasional impatience lent him a certain instability, those who loved George Apley will all admit that the instability made him human. With this in mind, the writer must now turn reluctantly to a difficult incident in George Apley's private life, which he still feels should be eliminated, in spite of the insistence of George's son, John Apley, that it be aired.

———— • ————

CHAPTER VIII

INTERLUDE

*Dealing with a Subject
Which Would Not Ordinarily Be Discussed in a
Work of This Nature*

IT SHOULD be stated at the outset that nothing which will be published regarding a youthful lapse discussed in this chapter reflects to the discredit of our subject. It serves rather to illustrate that anyone at a certain stage of life may be beset by vagaries which must not be considered seriously. It must be remembered that through it all George Apley remained an outstanding success, not only in his Harvard class, but in society. That he did so, speaks well for his tradition and for his self-control.

As one approaches the age for marriage there are many of both sexes who find it difficult to settle their lives finally in the direction where their real emotions and convictions should lead them. If it is so with George Apley, others of us have faced the same problem. The solicitude of his parents at this time is manifest by the correspondence which was kept intact — as may be illustrated by these extracts from a few letters.

Extract from a Letter from Elizabeth Apley.

You are probably too modest, George darling, and too pre-occupied with your Club and your College activities to know what a swathe you are cutting here in Boston. This makes me very proud, within limits, but you must not use that attractive-ness, George, as a means of playing fast and loose. I do not need to say any more, because I know that you will be the gallant knight.

I think it is time for you to realize, though, now that you are in the middle of your Senior year, that there is a certain young thing, and a very sweet one, who is taking you quite seriously. Your father and I are very glad and very much approve, because the Bosworths are quite our type of person. Catharine Bosworth has what my dear Jane Austen would call both "sense and sensibility." She has been brought up as you have been, to know that true happiness in life, such as your dear father and I have shared, is not based on external show. I think it would be very nice if you were to pay Catharine some little particular attention the next time you come into town. You and she have so much in common.

Letter from George Apley to Catharine Bosworth.

Dear Catharine: —

Mother is coming up to my room for tea on Thursday after-noon, after the meeting at the Hemenway gymnasium. She and I would both like it very much if you and your mother would drop in afterwards at Gray's. . . .

Letter from Elizabeth Apley.

Dear George: —

I enjoyed the little tea party. I thought that dear Catharine looked very beautiful. Mrs. Bosworth could not help but say how well you two dear children looked walking across the Yard together. . . .

Letter from Thomas Apley.

Dear George: —

The portion of your grandmother's estate which came to you under her will makes a small but comfortable sum that under certain circumstances is enough to start life on, modestly. I am holding it in trust for you, as the will directs, using the income for your further education. I am also conserving a part for another contingency, in case you wish to speak to me about it. . . .

These beginnings, so intimately connected with George Apley's future happiness, had an unforeseen and erratic interruption. This takes the form to-day of a bundle of letters, taped and sealed, with a superscription in Thomas Apley's handwriting, which reads as follows: "To be given to my son, George, at my death, with my request that he burn them." It is the writer's opinion that they should have been burned, either by George Apley or by his son, and this suggestion was made when this work reached the present stage. The reply of John Apley to the writer's request, which is appended here, is his authority for delving into a painful and needless detail.

Dear Mr. Willing: —

I have been over these letters very carefully myself and cannot see the harm in them. That you do only makes me feel how different your and Father's world must have been from mine. My one desire is to see Father depicted as a human being. Having read what you have written up to date, and it is phrased as only you yourself could phrase it, I think this business is a good deal to his credit. It must have required a good deal of initiative on his part to go as far as he did. . . .

We will, therefore, continue in the light of this advice. The letters begin on May 1, 1887.

Letter to Miss Mary Monahan.

Dear Mary: —

It is eleven o'clock at night. My roommate has gone to bed, so naturally I am sitting writing to you, because my mind keeps going back over every minute we have been together. I believe in fate now, I believe in destiny. Why should I have been in Cambridge Port, and why should you have been there? When I picked up your handkerchief and we looked at each other, I remember every shade of violet in your eyes and every light in the black of your hair. You called me a "Back Bay dude!" Do you remember? You said we shouldn't be seen together but you met me that Sunday on Columbus Avenue. You make me see things as I have never seen them. I am not what you think me, Mary, and now I am going to show you. I am going down to Worcester Square to call on you next Sunday. If your brother Mike doesn't like it, it's time he knew better. I'd be glad to see Mike any time. . . .

For reasons too obvious to be specified, any letters which George Apley may have received from the young woman, Mary Monahan, are not at present in existence, but information gathered from conversation and correspondence with members of the family and friends gives one a glimpse of this young woman who appears so abruptly in Apley's life. This glimpse, it must be admitted, reflects favorably on George Apley's taste, granting the impossible elements of this escapade. It appears that the Monahans, in their class, were respectable. The girl's grandfather, a small farmer who held title to his own land in County Galway, left hurriedly for America for political reasons during one of those abortive revolutionary efforts near the middle of the last century. The girl's father, a contractor, who had inherited the family's political proclivities, was in a position regarded as comfortable by many of his nationality in South Boston. There was, it appears, a sufficient amount of attractiveness in this family circle to appeal to some weakness in George Apley's makeup, for there is no doubt that on many occasions he found actual relaxation at this girl's home. It may have been that George Apley's athletic prowess furnished him an additional entrée, in that further correspondence reveals that the Monahans were personal friends of the notorious pugilist John L. Sullivan.

As for the girl herself, she appears to have been superior to her class, even to the extent of being sought after by a young attorney and by a son of a member of the City Council. Apley's classmate, Chickering, who once accidentally encountered the pair in a canoe, on the upper Charles River, gave the writer a description upon which he will draw, not having himself seen the young woman. According to Chickering, who at that time was something of a lady's man, Miss Monahan had many of the externals of a young person of a higher position. She was well and quietly dressed, and of a striking beauty that was more romantic than vulgar. Her figure was slender, as were her hands and ankles, her features delicate and interesting, her hair dark, her eyes deep violet. Her manners were quiet and polite; she was even mistaken once, when George Apley was seen walking with her on Commonwealth Avenue, for a visiting Baltimore belle. It need scarcely be pointed out that all these favorable attributes only served to lend to the affair most serious complications.

Letter to Mary Monahan.

My sweet wild rose: —

I hope your people liked me as much as I liked them. Dearest, I had a very good time. Darling, I love you more than anything in the world. You give me something that makes me feel free for the first time in my life. Nothing, dear, has made me so happy as this sense of freedom. Will you let me read you Browning again sometime? Poetry itself is real when I read to you. . . .

Letter to Mary Monahan.

Sweetheart: —

I am glad that Tim thinks I am all right, because I think that Tim is the same. I suppose Tim thinks so because when I went out with him I did more than shake the hand that shook the hand of Sullivan. Of course it wasn't anything, my darling. It was very kind of big John to let me stand up to him for two minutes with the gloves on and something I won't forget in a hurry. When can I see you again? Nothing here amounts to anything. Everything is a travesty until I see you. . . .

Letter to Mary Monahan.

Darling: —

Once and for all I want you to know that I mean every word I tell you. I never knew how dull existence was until I saw you. If your father is worried by my attitude towards you, I think I had better speak to him myself. I shall gladly tell him what I have told you, that I love you and want to marry you, that I shall try all my life to make you happy. If my own family were to see how sweet you are, how unutterably beautiful, they would want it, too. Believe me, believe me, everything I say I mean. . . .

Letter to Mary Monahan.

I should not care what they say, there are other places besides Boston and we can go to them. There is the West, for instance.

Letter to Mary Monahan.

For the life of me I can't stop thinking of the sailboat we hired, and of the clearness of the day, so like your soul. Though I remember every minute of it, it all goes together into something delicately sweet like music, so that I cannot take one moment from another. You took me away, just as I hope you will take me away forever from everything which binds and ties me.

The language in which these letters are couched betrays only too clearly the seriousness of George Apley's infatuation. Many passages must be left out for delicacy, as they might probe too intimately into the secrets of a high-minded idealist. It is certain that his intentions in this direction were always of the most honorable, and if latitude was offered him by the young Monahan woman, that he took no advantage of it. This is the one pleasing aspect of an affair which obviously could not be of long duration. It was only natural that in the course of time George Apley's aspirations should come to Thomas Apley's attention. Much of the ensuing detail can now be supplied only by the imagination, but the following letter suggests how the truth may have found its way to Thomas Apley.

Letters to Mary Monahan.

Mary, darling: —

Why do you always have in the back of your mind the feeling that this is not permanent? Nothing, I tell you, nothing can stop my love for you. All the things you speak about mean nothing to me. If you could see you would know that I am right. I am tired of being brought up in this atmosphere of self-assurance. I am tired of everything but you.

That is why I do not worry about rumours. What if old Clarence Corcoran has seen me in your company and has expressed surprise? It is true that Clarence was my father's gardener just as you say, and still calls me "Master George," but I don't see why this is alarming. I am proud to tell anyone that I love you. I am prouder still that you love me, because I do not deserve it. . . .

Poor, sweet darling: —

You must leave this to me. It is very dear of you to be afraid, but I am not in the least. If my father and mother were once to see you they would understand everything. Once they do, you'll find that all the Apleys stick together, and that you will be one of us. . . .

Darling: —

You must not be afraid. You are the only person I shall ever love. It has been very dreadful, but they cannot stop me, my sweet, and you cannot, because I love you, I love you. . . .

Since these letters are not dated, one is obliged to guess at their chronological sequence. It will be left for the reader to fill between the lines himself, and to draw his own conclusions regarding such events as these lines foreshadow. Since this correspondence comes to an abrupt end, it may be assumed that rumors finally reached the ears of Thomas Apley, but the natural reticence of a man of affairs and of a family confronted with such a problem leaves his exact reactions to it, and his methods of dealing with what must have been, to him, a shocking affair, considerably in the dark.

The reactions of the Monahan girl, whom one suspects betrayed better sense than many another in her position and of her connections, lie also behind a blank wall of silence.

CHAPTER IX

EUROPE

The Important Initial Impact
of Continental Sights and Scenes

ON THE twenty-seventh of June of this same year, George Apley's nervous reserves were greatly depleted by his anxiety over his final examinations and by the duties which devolved on him as an officer of his class. Very sensibly his family recommended a sea voyage and a change of scene, and thus unexpectedly he entered on an adventure which must always be a bright one in the days of any youth. On June twenty-seventh George Apley, in the company of his aunt and uncle, Mr. and Mrs. Horatio Brent, and his elder cousin, Henrietta Brent, embarked from New York to England and for a summer tour on the Continent. The following letters, written him by his mother for his perusal on the day of sailing, show Elizabeth Apley at her best. They combine the tenderness of a mother's care with the cheerful courage of a brave woman who faces a crisis courageously and hopefully.

My dearest George: —
    I hope by now you are feeling such a great deal better, less tired and much less worried and better able to see things

as they really are. Your aunt and your uncle, my dear George, are such understanding people, who both love and admire you so deeply that you could not be in better company. I think it was very generous and sweet of them both so gladly to leave everything they love best in life, which is, of course, Pachogue Neck, to go with my poor tired boy who will be better very soon. You must not worry them, George dear, but be very thoughtful of them and particularly of your poor cousin Henrietta. You know as well as the rest of us that the man she met at that unfortunate Ball in Philadelphia, which I did my best to prevent her attending, is only a little short of a mere adventurer. The wealth his family has gained from the steel mills at Pittsburgh only puts a very thin veneer over his vulgarity. His crudeness of speech and his utter obliviousness to the finer things of life, you know as well as I, render him most unsuitable. You, my dear boy, when your strength is back, have such a fund of common sense and good humor that you can be of the greatest help to Henrietta as well as to your aunt and uncle, in this unfortunate phase. We older people understand these phases and know that they are soon over. . . .

My darling boy: —

I reproach myself so much for my selfishness and for a preoccupation with my own affairs which so entirely prevented my perceiving that my dear boy was getting overtired. I can only say now that I shall know better at another time. You shall not want a mother's love, a father's love, or sister's love, when you come back to Hillcrest in the autumn. Your dear father, who is so thoughtful, when harm falls to his own brood, is already planning to have a study arranged for you in Beacon Street, so that we may all be together when you embark next winter on your readings in the Law School. The walk or the ride in the cars from Boston to Cambridge will be sure to do

you good. But now no more of this. Your one thought must be
to get well and to be happy.

How selfishly I wish I were to be with you so that I could
see my dear boy's face light up with pleasure at the wonderful
new sights which are in store for him. It has been many years
since I was abroad, not indeed since before I was married, and
I still treasure the impressions I have gained there and these
do so much to help my reading. Westminster, the Thames, and
the Embankment, how beautiful they are! How solemn and
how majestic is Whitehall! And France! If these people have
a certain frivolousness in their conversation and their art which
is a little hard for us quite to understand we can honestly love
the sunny beauties of Paris and the countryside immortalized
by our dear Rosa Bonheur. The Seine, Notre Dame, sad Ver-
sailles, forest-girded Fontainebleau, Chartres — and oh, perhaps the châteaux on the Loire! What a box of history's jewels
are opened to you! If many of the characters who trod the
paths of this history possessed a different code of morals and
honour from our own, you must remember that they are different people who lived in a darker age. With this letter comes
a packet of books which I have marked for your reading. They
will be your guide in this new adventure. The poems of Mr.
Longfellow are particularly beautiful. . . .

Letter from Thomas Apley.

Dear George: —

I hope this finds you much better than when I saw you last.
A sum of money in the form of a letter of credit has been
placed in your uncle's hands for you to draw upon at his discretion. I think it better that we both refrain from discussing
various matters until you return. I want particularly for you
to consider your mother. She has been so unwell that I have
been deeply worried about her and I will not have her upset

further. You will view matters in quite a different light after a change of scene and will understand your obligations as a member of our family. . . .

Letter from Amelia Apley.

Dear George: —

There is one thing which I think you will be glad to know. No one is talking about you. I have told everyone that you were overtired by your examinations and everyone is most understanding. If you see any sort of brooch in Paris or any pin with pearls, I wish you would buy it for me.

Your loving sister,—
AMELIA.

Letter from Jane Apley.

My darling brother: —

There is one person who knows how you must be feeling. George dear, brothers and sisters always seem to be so reticent. I wish we had not been. It would have been so much easier if you and I could have talked. You have always been so sweet to me. You have always made your friends dance with me at parties, you have always known when I was lonely and unhappy. I don't see that anyone is really very happy.

Always your loving,—
JANE.

There are no copies extant of George Apley's answers to these letters, if indeed he did answer them. For a mind as deeply disturbed as his he may quite probably have gone on the New England principle that the least said the soonest mended. He was meeting the severe shock which comes to all of us who must reconcile inclination with obligation. There is no doubt that he struggled with the difficult horns of this dilemma, for his friends on his return from Europe were aware that he had undergone a spiritual change. Much of the irresponsibility which may have endeared him, but had also made him difficult, to many of his associates seems to have left him at this phase of his career. He had departed from New York as a youth; he returned as a man who could thank his own reasonableness, and the watchfulness of his parents, for this change. It is now a pleasant task to publish excerpts from a series of letters to his mother, — bound in a packet entitled "George's Wanderjahr," — which show the chemistry of new scenes at work on the resilience of youth. The healthful contact with new faces and new environment was serving to heal what must have been, to a man of his sensitive feelings, a deep and painful wound.

Letter from George Apley to Elizabeth Apley.

We had a safe and pleasant crossing and here we are at Southampton. Aunt Martha and Henrietta were ill most of the time but Uncle Horatio and I managed quite well, playing cribbage in the smoking-room. I know you do not like cards; my excuse is that time had to be passed and that I was not well enough to read. It is very true, I think, what so many of our friends have said: that an arrival in England is like coming home. It seems to me that it is everything nice about Boston, with none of Boston's problems. There is a beautiful orderliness and a cheerful acceptance of fact which has meant a very great deal to me. We are staying at a little inn before leaving for London, the sort that Dickens and Washington Irving have written about. Please tell Father that I delivered his letter to Mr. Murchison, who received me very kindly. I am all agog to see London.

Letter to Elizabeth Apley.

Why did no one tell me how much old England is like New England? The country out of the train window reminded me of our own Ipswich and Rowley, and London after all is only a greater Boston, except that I think our air is better. Hyde Park may be larger but I do not think it is in any better taste than the Public Garden of the Common. It is only that there is more of everything. There are more Louisburg Squares, more Beacon Streets, and more Clubs. We are putting up at the Chiswick Hotel and we were very glad to get there, for we immediately encountered friendly faces. Whom should I meet but Professor and Mrs. Brokin from Cambridge, and Winthrop Vassal and his mother and sister, also out to see the world, and the Sellers from Chestnut Street, and Miss Marie Coffin from Nahant? It was quite like a family party. Under Aunt Brent's guidance half a dozen of us have arranged to do the galleries, Westminster Abbey, and the Tower to-morrow. Uncle Horatio has some business at a gunsmith's and later wishes to see some Springer trials. I am planning to-morrow to leave Uncle John's letter on Sir William Fewkes.

The determined gayety of these letters, one is led to believe, was largely assumed for the benefit of Elizabeth Apley, of whom he was always thoughtful. A letter to his sister Jane, of the same date, reveals an undercurrent of deep unhappiness: —

I wish I were more in the mood to enjoy the sights around me, but they seem to pass by me like shadows of a dream. My mind is so engrossed with other subjects that I seem to be walking by myself. Uncle Horatio has been very kind to me; he took me to the play last night.

Letter to Thomas Apley.

Dear Father: —

I gave Cousin John's letter to Sir Thomas, in which you were so interested, and received a reply the next day asking me to his country place in Hants. Uncle Horatio went with me because I suppose he feels I am better when I am not alone. The place at Hants was beautiful, with a fine maze of box. It reminded me very much of Hillcrest, except that it was larger.

I respect your judgment but I have not changed my mind. . . .

Letter to Elizabeth Apley.

Dear Mother: —

Miss Marie Coffin took us boating on the Thames and we compared many of the sights to scenes along the Charles River. We are going to Paris to-morrow. . . .

Letter to Elizabeth Apley.

Dear Mother: —

No sooner did we arrive at the hotel after a very rough channel crossing than I found again what a very small place the world is. There in the dining-room were Dr. and Mrs. Jessup from Mt. Vernon Street, and Jane Silby and her aunt from Commonwealth Avenue, and the Morrows from Brookline. Aunt Brent says that the Hotel Metropole is one of the few hotels in Paris where one can be sure of meeting congenial people. We all made a party for a drive this afternoon up the Champs Elysées. It is surprising how very much it is like Commonwealth Avenue. You will be glad to know that many of the waiters and cab drivers understand my French.

Uncle Horatio and our driver had great difficulty over the fare, as Uncle Horatio does not believe in giving more than the usual ten per cent fee extra. We are going with Dr. and Mrs. Jessup through the Louvre to-morrow, where I am looking forward to seeing the Mona Lisa. . . .

Letter to his classmate Walker.

Dear Mike: —

Well, here I am in Paris and I wish you were here too. I saw Wintie over in London and we split a bottle together in a Public House and talked about the Club. I have always heard how pretty the French girls were and I am disappointed. If you and I were to walk up Tremont Street we could see a dozen prettier ones. Uncle Horatio and Dr. Jessup and I have been out several evenings to "see the town." We have been to several shows. There is no doubt that the French are a very immoral lot, even when one does not understand everything that is said. They certainly seem to enjoy and thrive on immorality. Uncle Horatio is really quite a "sport" and once he has got Henrietta and Aunt Brent safely out of the way you would be surprised at some of his goings-on. Several evenings we have both of us been quite tight. He is very glad to have a vacation, he says, from Boston and so is Dr. Jessup. I am learning a great deal about the older generation. Again, I wish that you were here. . . .

Letters to Elizabeth Apley.

Dear Mother: —

We have now done Paris pretty thoroughly. I particularly love the enormous painting by Rubens in the Louvre and the marvelous Titians. As for the Winged Victory, I cannot keep my eyes off her. I love Notre Dame and the crooked streets along the Left Bank. I am ashamed to say that I have been playing a game with myself. It consists of reading "The Three Musketeers" very carefully and then trying to follow the footsteps of Athos, Porthos, and Aramis along the streets which Dumas has mentioned. Though the book is slight, it is a rather interesting way of seeing the city. Uncle Horatio and Dr. Jessup have also taken up my idea and are amused by it. We now call ourselves "the Three Musketeers." To-morrow we go to Fontainebleau. . . .

The beech forest at Fontainebleau reminded me very much of Uncle Horatio's virgin stand of beeches at Pachogue Neck. The courtyard where Napoleon took farewell of the Old Guard was very solemn. It reminded me a little bit of the space in back of the State House.

On the whole I like France. The people are all amusing, but they are very anxious to please. This has been a very profitable trip for me and I only hope that I am really getting the most out of it.

Here we are in the city of Tours, staying at the Hotel Univers on a large open square. We were very glad to find the Bromfields and the Winstons from Milton and we all went together to see Loches. We all agreed that the country around Milton is more beautiful than the Touraine country. The wildness of Milton I like very much better than the intensive cultivation of the land here. I shall be glad to be coming home.

Letter to his classmate Chickering.

Here I am reaching the end of my trip through Europe. I have seen much of England and not a little of France, but I have been impressed by a similarity existing between almost every scene, the reason for which I think I chanced upon to-day. It seems to me that all this time a part of Boston has been with me. I am a raisin in a slice of pie which has been conveyed from one plate to another. I have moved; I have seen plate after plate; but all the other raisins have been around me in the same relation to me as they were when we were all baked.

It is strange that instead of gaining much impression of different cultures, we have succeeded in transferring our own culture momentarily upon every place we visited. We had no wish to lose our identity and we did not lose it. We have succeeded in interposing a barrier of polite conversation, dealing principally with relatives and personalities, against the façades of the cathedrals, the collected works of the masters, and the walls of Chinon. When we were not doing this we were quoting from observations made by our own poets and scholars and thus we have seen the world through a local haze. This has had a strange effect on me. This effect is composed of a desire to escape plus an admiration for our tradition.

I taxed my Uncle Horatio with the idea the other night over a bottle of Vouvray. The bubbles of this wine must have quite gone to my head to have made me do such a thing, but Uncle Horatio did not seem surprised. This is what he said: "I see nothing astonishing in all this. People of the same tastes and inclinations naturally flock together. As a matter of fact I am quite convinced, and you will be convinced in time, that our own culture and our own morals are a good deal better and finer than those of the people around here. Find a Bostonian and you will find a citizen of the world."

Well, he may be right but I have seen more of Boston than of Europe. By and large, I have seen a great deal of Boston since I was born.

These letters have been quoted thus fully because they display random thoughts coincidental with full development.

In spite of his criticism of the Boston barrier, George Apley was succeeding in storing up a number of valuable impressions. He brought home with him two notebooks filled full of careful observations of the places which he had visited — so like those of nearly any youth of George Apley's years that they are hardly worth quoting. We will content ourselves with one excerpt which may seem both unusual and disturbing: —

As I stood on the edge of this village and looked up the white road winding between its hedges through that rolling farm country, I wished that I might be walking up that road entirely alone, away from everything I knew. I wished that I might be walking up it to see something by myself and for myself without guidance and without advice. I wonder, will I ever walk up any road alone?

It is safe to assume, however, that such thoughts did not arise often to haunt him and that the following letter to his sister, Amelia, is more in keeping with his usual outlook, so we shall allow it to strike the last note of his European tour: —

Here we are, back in London. Henrietta is having some clothes made for her here, according to some ideas of Aunt Martha's which are different from the theories of the French *modistes*. Aunt Martha says that no one over here understands the rigours of a New England climate. When she came over to England her mother had some very nice tweed suits made for her which lasted very well. Some of the same are now being made for Henrietta.

Father has done something for me which has both surprised and touched me. He has opened an account at Wilson and Maxwell's on Albermarle Street, so that I may buy a new wardrobe. I am afraid mine is going to look a good deal better than Henrietta's. Aunt Martha has bought six canvases by a Frenchman named Monet, of landscapes which are made in blotches. They seem to me quite mad, but Aunt Martha says they will be a good investment. Uncle Horatio has purchased six Springer puppies. I have a box of books and some presents and Uncle Horatio has given me a twelve-gauge Greener out of several he has bought for the gunroom.

Thus concludes our glimpse of a trip through Europe much the same as the travels of other liberal families in comfortable circumstances, and interesting only in so far as it sheds light upon our subject's character. He had expressed a desire, not unnatural to youth, to journey up the road alone. How little one can estimate one's own future! Only too soon, probably without his realizing the pleasant imminence of the fact, George Apley was about to proceed up the road of life hand in hand with a helpmate whose choice he was never to regret. We find that his next year in Boston quite artistically foreshadows such an event.

CHAPTER X

———————

LAW SCHOOL

*Aspects in the Settling Down to the
Actual Tasks of Life*

GEORGE APLEY returned to Boston in late September
with his reservoir of health refilled, to take his position
as a student not only in the Harvard Law School, but also in
the more carefree ranks of unattached young bachelors. Although both Thomas and Elizabeth Apley were keenly de-
sirous that their son's struggle with Blackstone should be successful, they evinced a growing preoccupation that he should
take the position intended for him in society. Thus the Apley
papers of this period deal not only with the abstractions of the
law — George Apley was immediately taken into one of the
Law Clubs which occupied much of his time — but also with
the gayer side of social entertainment. On Friday evenings the
Apley house on Beacon Street became the scene of frequent
"semi-formal" dinners given for the son, and in addition the
hand of Thomas Apley is seen at work, as is shown by the
following letter.

Letter to George Apley, Esq., from Thomas Boylston, Esq.

My dear George: —

The conversation with your father at the Club this afternoon leads me to hope that you will be willing to have your name come up for election as one of the Board of Trustees for the Boston Waifs' Society. We are anxious to get young blood on our Board and you are doubtless aware of the Apley contributions to this cause.

The Boston Waifs' Society, perhaps I do not have to tell you, was founded by Nicholas Brattle in 1802 for the care of unprotected children in this city. Our work now comprises the oversight of many waifs, rendered such by no fault of their own, until to-day this charity has assumed the importance of being a definite obligation to that section of Boston more fortunately situated than the rest. . . .

George Apley was made a member of this Board at the annual meeting in the first week of January, 1888; and at nearly the same time he became the recipient of another letter, which is self-explanatory.

Letter from Minot Pickens to George Apley.

Dear George: —

Some of your friends, including myself, want to know if you would not like to have your name put up for the Berkley Club. You know what this Club is, a congenial place of friendship, made up of interesting people like yourself, where informality is the watchword and where anything may happen of an evening. . . .

The Berkley Club, which needs no introduction, was already something of an institution. Started by an artistic set who desired to while away their leisure, it was fast growing to include in its list many young lawyers and men of affairs and the informality of its earlier days was giving place to a light-hearted ritual. The Club's patroness being Aurora, the goddess of dawn, there follows the natural implication that many of the members sat up all night, as was indeed the case; and these evenings gave forth many interesting bits of song and story which are now embalmed in the Club records to be perused by those who are privileged to open the pages. From the very beginning of his membership George Apley became an ardent devotee to the goddess of dawn, and much of his life may be traced to the plays and pageants in the Berkley Club House. George Apley also was on the list of the Saturday Evening Assemblies.

Letter to his classmate Walker.

Dear Mike: —

It seems strange to think of you in a banking house down in New York and not back here with all the rest of us. Well, we are all very sober now. We have to be, to keep in the Law School. Some of us meet in the Club for lunch on Tuesdays. As you know, I am living in Beacon Street this winter, so that I do not have the chance to get out as I once did. The only break I have in my routine is occasioned by the Berkley Club. I am glad to say that my mother approves of my being a member there because there are some very good writers and scholars on the list, not to mention musicians. I do not believe she realizes that the conversation is not exclusively scholarly and I do hope that no one will disabuse her. One has got to let off steam somewhere and I can think of no safer place. It is good, free, unconfined merriment. When half the evening is gone we do not seem to care very much who we are or where we came from. We are able to laugh and talk, quite confident that the walls have no ears to speak of. . . .

Letter from Thomas Apley, New York, January 1888.

My dear George: —

It seems one must leave home to learn the news of home. At a dinner of some business associates the other evening I heard your name mentioned in connection with certain activities at the Berkley Club which had been relayed to my host by some young relative. It seems that you dressed up as Robin Hood in some sort of a pageant and later in the evening actually appeared upon Tremont Street with certain other Club members who were clad in similar costumes.

This letter is not intended as a reproof. I flatter myself that I am broad-minded in such matters and that I was once young myself. I could tell you about certain sleigh rides and races which I indulged in, but I will not. A certain amount of this merriment is all very well, but one must be careful of the company which one chooses for such occasions. They must be from your own class.

The Berkley Club is amusing enough and may sometime in the future have a definite social value, judging from its more recent members, but at present it is a very informal place with an atmosphere of fiddling and writing about it which cannot command serious attention from the rest of the community. As I say, this is all well enough and I am glad that you are enjoying yourself but you must not forget that you are reaching a time in life when your name will carry certain implications. I have been meaning often to talk to you about this responsibility; and will, when I return from this trip. You must realize how much appearances count in a world of business and credit. You must realize, too, the economic system of this country is not in a perfect sense of balance and I can foresee many grave difficulties in the very near future. You must also remember that your name is up, as my son, for the Province Club and that you are being watched.

In quite a definite sense, I think, you must be setting the pace of your own set. I do not want you to display any lavishness or eccentricity, but I want you to enjoy yourself. You may feel free to use either of my two trotting horses, any of the carriages or sleighs. . . .

Letter from William Apley, February, 1888.

My dear Nephew: —

Your father, who was at Apley Falls last week, tells me that he wishes you to be employed about the Mills here for the coming summer. I think this is an excellent idea. But for the sake of appearance, you must take this position seriously. Just because you have been born with a gold spoon in your mouth gives you no privileges up here. I shall want you to call on me at the Boston offices the next time I visit town. . . .

Letter from Martha Brent.

Dearest Georgie: —

Your Uncle Horatio and I were so very proud of our young handsome nephew last night at Catherine Bosworth's party. When you led the cotillion your aunt could not keep her eyes off you and I suppose you know that a great many younger eyes were on you too. I have told your mother, for I think she should know about it, what Henrietta has told me, that you are quite the centre of the younger set. This makes us all very pleased. . . .

Memorandum from Elizabeth Apley.

Dearest George: —

I am putting this in writing in case it may be of value to

you. I am so very pleased that you have set pen to paper seriously and it was sweet of you to show this effort to your mother. I wish in turn to show it to Dr. Holmes and Mr. Howells, for I feel, and so does Mr. Pettingill, that it has promise and a real merit of its own. Your little sketch "Beacon Street" betrays a real insight into our human comedy and a delight in nature which you must inherit from me. There is nothing more interesting and more useful all through life than a knowledge of letters. George, darling, I am so glad that you have turned to this recourse, but you must not let your sense of humour get away from you. You must be careful not to offend. Some of your accounts while travelling abroad, while amusing, are neither just nor true. Neither your Uncle Horatio nor your Aunt Martha — nor Henrietta — would be greatly flattered by their portraits although they make me laugh and laugh. You must try again, dear, and do something more serious. . . .

These letters all indicate a broadening of activity. George Apley, in his first year at the Harvard Law School, was giving a full indication of those varied interests which were to be his through life. His mind, while it was being drilled in the precisions of the law, was moving in these other directions. In a light social way he appeared at many parties of young people. He began to be a useful committee member upon an important charity, a clubman of the very best sort, a sportsman, a student of business and finance, in short a man who was rapidly preparing to undertake family responsibilities.

The summer of 1888 found George Apley in a new rôle — with his Uncle William Apley at the mill town of Apley Falls.

This experience [he once wrote to his own son] was a most valuable one to me. There I was, obliged to make my way with common labourers. They were most of them good fellows and taught me something of the mind of the people. I do not believe that anyone knew my status in the mills except the foremen and the superintendent. I must say, after my daytime experience, a comfortable bed and the hearty dinner at Uncle William's was very welcome, and there is one thing I am sure of: work in a cotton mill is neither hard nor difficult. It does no harm to rough it for a summer and I very much want you to do it yourself.

At the end of six weeks of this labor at Apley Falls, Thomas and Elizabeth Apley evidently felt that there must be a period of relaxation, for we next find George Apley upon a series of visits up and down the New England coast.

During this formative period at the Apley Mills, young Apley engaged in what was probably his first business transaction, and from it he gleaned an insight into the burdens which were being borne by the elders of his family. Several letters from his Uncle William Apley show that the young nephew was evidently sent to Boston, probably as a part of his education, to attempt the purchase of a few lots of cotton for the Apley Mills.

Letter to George Apley.

My dear George: —

I find the order for the Number 4117 tickings, of which I spoke to you, before you went to the city, will require two hundred bales additional "Strict Middling" good body and staple. I am therefore asking you to inquire around the Boston market with a view to picking up these two hundred bales at a reasonable price. I ask you to remember that *every cent or fraction thereof* which is added to raw materials and labour costs detracts from the *eventual profit*. The last price we paid for this variety of cotton was $6\frac{7}{16}$ cents. From my estimate of present market conditions, I am of the distinct impression that this figure may be shaded $6\frac{13}{32}$ cents, as there seems to be a little more pressure to sell. Besides, I happen to know that the Quanset Mills up-river here have lightened their demands on the market a trifle this week.

I should suggest your trying Forbes and Son, first, and if they seem difficult to deal with, try Cabot and Steele. *Do not commit yourself in any way* but make an estimate of the situation. I may warn you to be very watchful in dealing with Mr. Steele.

I give you this lengthy advice as this is your first chance to show what you are made of. I hope very much that you can prove that you have inherited some of the family instincts, exemplified by your father and grandfather, which may eventually render you a fit member of the Boston business community.

Yours truly, —
WILLIAM APLEY.

P.S. If Mr. Jessup, of the firm of Forbes and Son, should deal with you, I am much afraid that he may take advantage of your youth. The man has a cordial exterior. It is his custom to invite you to some hotel where he will probably attempt to ply you with liquor. If this should be the case, you could probably afford to take one glass with him, or even two, as I understand that drinking is the fashion at Harvard, but after this refuse politely to do any business with him until the next morning. *Commit yourself to no agreement which is not made over clear, cold water.*

The problem laid down by this letter was truly not simple of solution. In the late eighties trade in Boston was conducted with the conservatism and the shrewdness which characterizes State Street to-day; although, alas, certain great figures that might have conserved fortunes in our last financial *débâcle* are now gone forever. Behind the granite façades of State Street the business offices were still conducted along the lines of old tradition. Many a head of an organization who controlled vast interests still wrote his own correspondence, kept his own books, and saw all customers. The tempo was quiet. There was a scrupulous care in small matters which to-day is unfortunately lacking. One can picture George Apley, imbued with the careless qualities of youth, learning his lesson at this hard school. The next letter from his uncle proves that his first attempt was not wholly successful.

Dear George: —
The two hundred bales arrived to-day from Forbes and Son and considering the high price paid, 7¾ cents, this is the poorest lot of cotton that has been received at the Apley mills since the Civil War. I have spent some time to-day in the classing room, pulling the staple of every bale, with the help of Mr. O'Shaughnessy, and I am mortified that O'Shaughnessy, who has our interests deeply at heart, should know that an Apley made such a purchase.

It is even my impression that you did not examine this cotton before purchasing, for surely in your summer here you must have become conversant with the length of staple and with its importance in the finished product. I am further convinced that Mr. Jessup was the one who approached you and that you were in no condition to pull the staple properly or to grade its length. I want you to remember that whatever small profit our family has been able to extract from Apley Mills (which is now growing measurably less due to cut-throat competition and the vicious disposition of labour) has been made by unfaltering attention to such small details.

Should you see Mr. Salter in the office of the Boston Waifs' Society, you may tell him to count on me for my usual contribution of fifteen thousand dollars. . . .

There can be little doubt that this experience made upon George Apley a profound and permanent impression, for many years later we find him alluding to it in a letter to his own son, John: —

It is the small things in life which count the most. There is nothing which pains me more than your jesting about small sums of money. I learned their importance very early, from your Great-Uncle William. You must learn that there is a zest and a genuine satisfaction to spending money properly as your Uncle William spent his. There is not much place in this world for personal gratification, nor is this particularly becoming to people of our position.

During this summer also George Apley visited his father's cousin and his own namesake, George Apley, who dwelt in the old Apley house on the great Square in Salem. This was an experience which also left a wholesome influence and we find him writing of it long afterwards in a random paper.

The romance of our family and its inherent importance in this section of the country was never greatly conveyed to me until I visited my cousin George in Salem. There, lingering in a ghostly way, were the shades of the Orient and Africa. The genius of an Apley had built the fine McIntyre house, and had filled it with curious things — lacquer boxes, rare embroidery, Chinese ware and Malay swords. Exotic as these things were, I could somehow see their connection with the

Apley Mills and our house on Beacon Street, with my father and with my Uncle William, with many things they thought and felt, and, indeed, with all of Boston, and the connection was very fine.

In short, when he entered his first year at Law School George Apley was maturing rapidly and as always his father watched him across the gulf of years and pathos which always must divide a father from his son. There is extant a letter of about this time, written from New York by Thomas Apley to his wife, Elizabeth.

I am glad to hear from you that George seems to be pursuing his studies and seems to be tranquil. Let us both hope that this one escapade of his will be the only one to mar his life and that it is now a thing of the past. I cannot understand why youth to-day seems so much more extravagant and unsettled than was the case in our own generation. I hope Jane seems happier than she has lately. Amelia is really the member of the family who should have been the boy. I am glad to hear that George has been calling on Catharine Bosworth.

Business matters here are very difficult. These Wall Street bankers are unstable and have a wholly exaggerated idea as to the future growth of this nation. I shall be here for at least three weeks longer. If the cook wishes another dollar a week, I think you would do better to let her go. These insistent demands which come from every section of labour are growing very trying. Why these women should want heat on the upper floor of Beacon Street is more than I can see. I never had any heat in my bedroom when I was young and I doubt if you did either.

Thomas Apley's hope that his son George might be settling down was reaching to some extent a species of fulfillment. In his second and third year at the Law School one observes an increasing interest in his studies. The second summer found him again at Apley Falls, striving once more to win the commendation of his Uncle William Apley, which was accorded to him only grudgingly. The keen eyes of William Apley and his precise and logical mind estimated the young man's capabilities. In the following letter to his brother Thomas, the firm strokes of an expert penman which are as steady as the legend beneath a copperplate engraving betray this insight: —

The greater part of my life up here has been spent in weighing the possibilities of men. The foremen and minor officials whom I have selected are almost invariably a success. I have seen George and I do not think that he is a businessman. If he succeeds me here at Apley Falls I am convinced the Mills' earnings will show a corresponding drop. He is popular with the men but he is too easy-going. As a cotton buyer he has not the shrewdness of soul, and when he sells he lacks the pliability, so necessary. He lacks also the capability of understanding the other party's intentions. I regret to say besides that there is an erratic streak in George. It is my experience that when someone "goes off the handle" once he may very well repeat the process. I am much afraid that in him the Apley stock is running wild. It is my belief that he should be set up in a law office without too much responsibility, where he can eventually become a trustee with the advice of effective junior clerks. I am very sure that George would be a successful guardian of other people's money, but not of his own. What little he may inherit I strongly advise should be put in trust, rather than under his own management.

How closely this advice was followed by Thomas Apley will be seen a short time later, and in following it he added

ammunition for a certain writer of Boston, who shall be name-
less, but whose article in a recent magazine bears a certain
distorted element of truth. It seems quite probable, as this
writer suggests, that the men of Thomas Apley's generation,
bred in the hard amphitheater of uncertain commercialism,
were only too prone to distrust the ability of their sons. The
writer's further hypothesis, however, that large sums which
had been left in trust have atrophied the abilities of those to
whom they have been left, is most untrue. Relieved of the
burden of caring for a large financial estate our leading citizens
have never shirked their duty to the community. Their mode
of living has remained plain, their bequests to charities have
been liberal. Their libraries, their pictures, and their clubs of
chamber music are not excelled by any in the world.

Moreover, though one must admit it reluctantly, it is only
too probable that the judgment of Thomas Apley and his
contemporaries may have been correct. They may have seen
more clearly than others the growing complexities of finance.
It is, at any rate, regrettably true that certain of our larger
financial institutions which have met in recent years with serious
reverses, in the present writer's opinion, have not owed their
misfortunes to lack of integrity on the part of the heads of
these houses as much as to the fineness of their tradition.

There is one other piece of firsthand evidence which forms
a picture of George Apley at this time, given by his tablemate,
William Prentice of New York, who dined with Apley for
two years at a Law School luncheon table in Hilliard Street.

I remember Apley well, as someone who was solid and fine.
I think of him to-day as a true son of New England. I see him,
lean and a little pale, seated at the table listening to the good-

natured chaff and chatter. Sometimes a look of bewilderment would cloud his features, but when he understood the joke he was always quick to join in the merriment.

I well recollect when some of us thought it would be highly amusing to have Thomas Rolfe, a somewhat silent and bookish member of our group, seat himself inadvertently upon a sheet of flypaper, Apley's eyes flashed when this occurred, and I don't think that any of us present have forgotten his reproof. "Fellows," he said, "that isn't funny." At that time and indeed ever afterwards, George Apley was a man's man. His genius for friendship was unassuming but he made many friends.

————•————

CHAPTER XI

MARRIAGE

*Circumstances Surrounding an Important Step
in a Well-Rounded Life*

THOUGH APLEY was a "man's man," he was soon to become very satisfactorily a woman's man as well. The emotions and upsets of courtship, so characteristic of certain undisciplined elements in other sections of the country, are, fortunately, no part of our best tradition. Here, marriage has always been taken in the stride of life, as a sacrament to be entered into soberly, cheerfully and irrevocably. In February, 1890, Mr. and Mrs. James Bosworth announced the engagement of George Apley to their daughter, Catharine — in every way an eminently suitable match, not only from the point of view of property but, more important still, from a community of healthy tastes and tradition. These two had played together in childhood and had trod the same paths of youth with a similarity of upbringing which could not but make them congenial. The Bosworths, who could boast among their ancestors James Bosworth of the Assistants' Court in Massachusetts and Ephraim Bosworth, a ringleader in the Boston Tea Party, joined the Apleys in expressing their pleasure in the approaching union.

Letter from Mrs. James Bosworth to George Apley

My dear George:—

Catharine to-day told me her great news in the sweetest way, that we were to lose a daughter but were to gain a son. Of course, when she spoke of losing a daughter this was a most complete jest. Neither her father nor I would possibly tolerate losing what we hold more dear than life itself. It simply means that you will now become a member of our family and join our happy circle. James is already arranging to have the old barn at Mulberry Beach made into a very sweet little cottage, so that you and Catharine can start your life this summer only a stone's throw from us.

We must both insist on this. I know you will understand, because you are your own dear mother's son and must have her own sensibility, that Catharine, though she seems robust, is actually very sensitive and is wholly dependent upon her parents. I know that you will not think of separating any of us, and that is why James and I are both so pleased. . . .

Letter to George Apley from James Bosworth.

Dear George: —

I am still somewhat shaken by our last interview, as my love for Catharine transcends my love for anything else. My worst fears are allayed by your assurance that we would never be separated by any greater distance than the suburban limits. Our business talk, coupled with a letter from your father, has been eminently satisfactory. It is our joint wish to have you two start life comfortably, but simply, and I feel that we can make the necessary arrangement. . . .

Among the other letters received by George Apley from his family and his many warm friends, all of them expressing the pleasure so natural for such a felicitous and suitable occasion, it is fortunate that we have the wishes of his father. It appears that Thomas Apley was in New York at the time, where he was detained, as seems to have been so frequently the case in those years, by business negotiations.

Dear George: —

Your letter reached me at the Park Avenue Hotel this morning as I started down to Wall Street. I only wish I were out of the confusion of this place to tell you at first hand the happiness and relief which I must now set down on paper. I have always had a feeling that the Apley stock is solid at bottom. We may sow our wild oats, — I was young myself once, — but now, thank God, we are out of the woods.

Catharine, whom I am looking forward to greeting as my daughter, has always seemed to me a very noble girl and her position and yours in the scheme of things are such that there will be none of the frictions due to divergent backgrounds, which might occur for instance in a New York and Boston union. You have shown the good sense, too, to realize that beauty is only skin deep and that there are more important elements in the holy bond of matrimony.

The income from the little which your grandmother has left you, which is now invested in sound railroad bonds, except for a few thousand dollars which I used some years ago for taking a "flier" in telephone stock and which I will make up to you in case this invention eventually becomes only a fad, should be enough for you to start a modest establishment. In addition to this, I shall continue at least a portion of my allowance to you.

This, unless my belief is wrong in Catharine's sagacity as a housekeeper, will be enough to keep the wolf from the door. Mr. Bosworth has told me that he plans to do the barn over for you at his summer place. It happens that I was obliged only the other day to foreclose a mortgage on a small dwelling house in Gloucester Street. This was one of a parcel of three. As I have already turned the other two over at a profit, I have nearly cleared this one house on the transaction, and I shall turn it over to you as a wedding gift. In order that things may not come too easily, however, I am putting a small mortgage on it, which your Uncle William has kindly consented to hold, and you must be responsible for the interest.

The time is coming also when you must be launched in business, and I shall talk to you soon about a suitable law office for you to enter. I am very glad to hear from several older men that you are generally well thought of, and that shortly your name will come up for the Province Club. There will, of course, be no difficulty here, particularly if you separate yourself a little more from the amiable nonsense of the Berkley Club.

There have been some very disturbing rumours lately that a small group of hare-brained meddlers is agitating to have the Charles River dammed, so that the flats of the rear of our house on Beacon Street, which I have always enjoyed watching at low tide, will be covered at all times. This is only another example of the constant inroads being made upon the rights of individuals who have had the good sense to amass a small amount of property. Something must be done to stop this at once, but I shall talk to you about this on my return. . . .

The last paragraph of this letter, referring to the project of the Charles River Basin, now a veritable jewel of water resting on the bosom of our city, may seem curious in the light of the present. It was to play a significant and somewhat sad part in the life of George Apley, as we shall see in a later chapter.

Now, however, we continue on a more happy strain and quote a letter from Elizabeth Apley to the bride-to-be: —

My darling, darling Catharine: —

My own dear George himself told his first love, his mother, his tender news this very morning. He told it in such a manly way, so simply and so sweetly, that I wish you could have been there to have heard him. He came up to me at the front window, as I was holding a bit of burning tobacco leaf in a dustpan to kill the aphids that have attacked my dear geraniums, and he said: "Mother, I think you will be glad to know that Catharine Bosworth has consented to be my wife." Of course, the first thing I did, dear Catharine (and would not any woman do the same?), was to give way to a few tears, as I thought of this impending change in my dear boy's life — but they were most of them tears of gladness. The rest, let me hasten to add, were foolish tears betraying the weakness of a fond parent who feels that her nest is being broken up and that her brood of dear ones is flying from her. But then, as my dear Georgie brought me a glass of water, I remembered, as I hope you will, that Georgie hates tears and I knew how foolish I was. I had only to say to myself that I was not losing a son but was gaining a dear, sweet daughter — how sweet I think I know. Indeed, I know very well that you will never take my Georgie from me, for nothing can sever the love of a mother for her son. I know that you will let Georgie and me have as many friendly, playful chats as we ever had before. I know that you will realize as well as I do that George is a dear, sensitive boy who needs a mother's understanding. I know that you must love the same things in George that I love and we two will share that love together. Darling, darling Catharine, will you come to me this afternoon so that we may have a quiet and intimate little talk?

There are so many things that I can tell you about dear George. . . .

This interest in and this solicitude for the welfare of George Apley forms the theme of letters from many other relatives, since the position of both the Apley and the Bosworth families was such as to render the approaching union one of extraordinary significance. That friendly concern for the affairs of others which so characterizes our society gave rise to inevitable speculation as to the future happiness of the fortunate young couple. The devotion of Catharine Bosworth's father on the one hand and of George Apley's mother on the other received a particular and deserved meed of praise from all who knew them. Thus the correspondence nearly all deals at length with efforts to make George Apley understand the sacrifices of these two parents. The letter of his Uncle Horatio Brent is almost the only one which sounds a slightly different note.

Dear George: —
I must congratulate you on marrying Catharine Bosworth but I wonder whether you know exactly what marriage means. It is, my boy, a damnably serious business, particularly around Boston. Remember, George, that you not only marry a wife but also your wife's entire family. Much as you may love your wife, it is hard even with all the good will in the world suddenly to love the whole new group of extraneous people who fall your way, simply because they are relatives of your wife. You're fortunate in that you know most of these people already but you are going to know them differently now. I'm afraid you're going to find it a little hard to love old Bosworth. I know I never did, but don't let me discourage you.

What bothers me most is that I am afraid you don't know

much about women. I didn't when I married your aunt, but I know a great deal now and I have been around a bit in my time. I think it might be a very useful thing if you were to have lunch with me at the Club and let me give you a few bits of advice which are not printed ordinarily in books. I feel sure you'll need it later. Personally, I never became so seriously interested in sport as I did after I was married. By this autumn you may want to go with me down to Carolina for the quail shooting and next spring we must go up to Muskeg River where I have salmon rights. The great thing about marriage is not to think too much about it. Your affectionate uncle, . . .

It is the writer's belief that nearly any man must look back to this important period in his life with somewhat mingled emotions, in that the new social contacts and this new and beautiful relationship cannot but cause a certain amount of mental confusion. The excitement resultant from the preparations for the event probably explains why the bridegroom is so frequently an abject and harassed object by the time he finally approaches the altar. It explains, too, the reason for many unfortunate crises. Thus the writer can recall, without mentioning names, as indeed many others also must recall who read these pages, several persons with the very best background who have disappeared from Boston on the eve of matrimony. Most of these have re-established their position at some time later, but two, to the writer's certain knowledge, have never been heard of since; and it may be added that their names are now never mentioned by their relatives. Though George Apley was of a different stamp, he revealed something of the turbulent uncertainty which has beset so many in a letter to his intimate friend Winthrop Vassal.

Dear Winty: —

Thanks for your note about Catharine. I know that I am very, very fortunate because I don't know what she sees in me. She is so vastly finer in every way than I am, more generous, more intelligent and a great deal more sensitive. There is one thing about her I did not know until after we were engaged. For several years Catharine has been collecting butter knives, and she now has one of the best collections in the country. That is quite remarkable, isn't it? What with preparations for our house in the country, and what with wedding presents coming in, and what with everyone being so kind and anxious to help — there cannot be kinder people in the world than those in Boston — I don't know exactly where I am or what I am doing. Everyone wants to give us tea parties and dinners. My Uncle William has already sent his wedding present, a fourteenth-century tapestry; it must be put somewhere where he will see it, but I don't know where. Uncle Horatio has sent me a pair of Irish setters and I don't know where I am going to keep them either, particularly as it appears that Catharine doesn't like dogs. Aunt Hancock has sent me a dining-room table, and so it goes. Marriage is a very serious business, Winty. Catharine has set the seventeenth of June for the wedding. What frightens me more than anything else is that I may never see my old friends again. We must all stay together, Winty, things must be the same between us. You and Mike and Chick and I and the old crowd at the Club mustn't drift apart. . . .

This preoccupation of George Apley, not indeed unusual to one who is embarking on a new and untried stage of existence, that the friends of his own incarnation might be leaving him, should have been very quickly dissipated by the loyalty of these same friends at numerous small dinners which they gave

him in the interval between his engagement and his marriage
in early June. Nevertheless, though Apley was fully aware,
as he often said himself, that he was the happiest man in the
world, he often gave way on such occasions to a strain of sentimental sadness. This was particularly true at his own bachelor's
dinner, attended of course by the ushers, among whom the
present writer, his old friends, Chickering, Walker, and Vassal,
and several of his contemporary cousins were numbered. The
writer remembers this occasion very well indeed. Though not
unlike many others which he has attended, the group around
the table was of the best. With such people around the board,
all from very much the same section of life and each known
so well to the other, there was no need for anyone to display
the care or reticence which his caution and sense of fitness
might have demanded of him at another time and place. The
atmosphere in the private dining-room of the Parker House
was one of a complete and unalloyed friendship as course followed course. Thomas Apley, sensing the importance of this
dinner, had sent over a half-dozen Madeira which had been
to Charleston and back in ballast fifty years before, and had
instructed the management to serve unlimited champagne.
Vassal told several of his inimitable stories and Walker sang
songs in his fine baritone until everyone in the room, including the waiters, joined the chorus. Then there followed
a round of toasts, one given by the writer himself. It was
noticed at the time that Apley seemed distrait, but no more
so than might be expected, until the company, each placing a
foot upon the table, sang "Should auld acquaintance be forgot . . . ?" — at which point Apley actually gave way to
tears. This sign of emotion was received with hearty applause,
marred only by a display of carelessness on the part of one of

the guests, who stepped out of a window. The dining-room, fortunately, was on the second story, so that a broken arm and two shattered front teeth were the only results of an accident that might have cast a gloom on the whole company.

The wedding, which was solemnized behind the brownstone façade of the Arlington Street Church, was, as has already been said, an occasion of importance. The agitation of George Apley, as he waited in the small cloakroom, could readily be explained if one took a glimpse at the pews of that great edifice. Like many another happy bridegroom, he was pale and perspired freely, and several of his remarks may be quoted as completely characteristic of one in his position.

"Good God," he said, "is everyone in the world here?" Shortly afterwards he said in a spirit of pure facetiousness: "Perhaps Catharine has backed out — but she wouldn't, would she?" Later he said: "Has it ever occurred to you that marriage is an accident?" And finally he added, "Well, this is the end."

This perturbation and bewilderment left him when he stepped before the altar to meet his bride; he was calm though pale, and he made his responses in a clear, firm voice. Catharine Bosworth, in the lace veil and the wedding gown which had been worn by her mother and her great-grandmother and had been altered only to fit a different figure, was a truly beautiful bride. When she cast back her veil and the united couple walked side by side down the aisle on the straight path of their married life they both seemed happy and relieved. The ensuing reception at the dwelling of Mrs. Penn Scott, the aunt of Catharine Bosworth, on Louisburg Square, was solemn, staid, and beautiful. The line of carriages driving to the house stretched well into Charles Street, and the fresh green leaves of June upon the streets around the Square were symbolically significant. The young couple stood by the rear windows of the great parlor, behind an embankment of ferns, mosses, and wild flowers gathered by Elizabeth Apley's directions from Hillcrest in Milton; and thus George Apley and Catharine Bosworth were embarked on their new responsibility of marriage.

It may be added that marriage in those days was a more serious matter than it is at present, where the possibility of the breaking of ties may from the first be treated plausibly. At the time of George Apley's marriage such an eventuality was beyond even faint consideration, and this is the reason, as the author earnestly believes, that so much of the life of his period moved tranquilly without friction. Those concessions so necessary in the bond of matrimony were more readily arranged because, in a sense, they were inevitable.

It was Catharine Bosworth's wish to spend their two weeks' honeymoon at some point distant from Boston where both she and her husband might be intrigued by a change of scene. She had therefore selected the Narragansett House at Rye Beach, New Hampshire, and thither the young couple repaired. She could not have made a happier selection or one more temperamentally suited to them both.

The following is a letter written to the author by George Apley at this time.

Dear old Will: —

Thank you very much for everything. I am feeling like an old married man already. Though the Narragansett House is rather "swell" it is at the same time comfortable. I am a little glad and I think Catharine is, too, to be such a long way from friends. Hardly anyone here knows us and though Portsmouth is near by, Portsmouth is not as closely knit as Boston. I have a sense of great freedom looking at the sea. Catharine says we never really knew each other until we came here, and I am inclined to agree with her. In the morning we generally go for a long walk whether it is raining or not. In the afternoon we drive, although the local livery is very expensive considering what they give us. At teatime we read Whittier and his descriptions of this part of the country chime in very well with our mood. In the evening when Catharine is not busy writing "thank-you" notes for our presents I read to her out of Emerson, while she starts crocheting a bedspread. This consists of a number of squares which she will eventually sew together. She needs a hundred and sixty of these squares and has finished eight. When I told her it would take a long time to finish she said that there would be a long time to finish it in, and I daresay she is right.

We are moving to Mulberry Beach next week. Catharine's mother has been through a number of old trunks in the attic, looking for curtains. She found there some of her grandmother's brocade curtains, which Mrs. Bosworth had entirely forgotten. They were better than the ones she had intended to give us but as she had forgotten them entirely, she decided to give them to us at any rate. You see, Mr. and Mrs. Bosworth came yesterday and are now staying with us at the Narragansett House. Catharine is pleased, because two weeks alone is rather a long time. . . .

CHAPTER XII

———•———

ACHIEVEMENT

The Writing and the Results of Apley's Paper,
"Jonas Good of Cow Corner"

MULBERRY BEACH on the North Shore must be as
dear to-day to the children of George Apley as it is
to the author himself, for they have shared in common its
wildness and its beauty. They have seen the rocky islands and
the headlands of Cape Ann in sunshine and in storm. They
have taken the same walks and have known something of the
society which existed there before the turn of the last century
and shortly after it. In those days of the horse-drawn vehicle,
the trolley car and the bicycle, Mulberry Beach was at its best.
Its summer residents who built their rambling shingled cottages along its cliffs came almost exclusively from near-by
Boston. The gatherings at the Mulberry Club, which boasted
one of the first turf tennis courts and later one of the early
nine-hole golf courses, were intimate and friendly. With the
coming of the automobile and with the advantages of our
North Shore being finally recognized by New York, Baltimore,
and the Middle West, Mulberry Beach has changed for the
worse, although in sections much of the old tradition still
prevails. At the time when the young Apleys took up their

residence in the barn of the Bosworth estate, "The Oaks," the Mulberry Club was unpretentious and the Yacht Club only a small building for the storage of oars and other gear. The simplicity may indeed be gauged by the existence of a cove in the rocks where men and boys of the colony customarily bathed in the nude of a Sunday afternoon. The beach to-day has been changed by the chauffeurs and extraneous personalities from other parts of the United States. Professor Chiswick of the Harvard Observatory no longer talks of a summer Saturday night to an audience at the Mulberry Club about the mysteries of the stars, nor does Godfrey Hallowell Rogers, author of "A Century of American Criticism," sail in his twenty-foot catboat or discourse on literature, nor does Mrs. Salter Trask have her Thursday Mornings of essays and conversations, nor does Dr. Stanhope, who did so much toward importing unusual shrubbery for the extensive plantings in the Fenway, any longer tend his garden. The Wanderers' Bicycle Club is gone, and so are the singing parties by evening bonfires. In short, the tide of time has swept away many of the personalities and the ideas which made life intellectually and socially agreeable. In their place is the Mulberry Beach of to-day with its swimming pools, its bridge parties, and that abomination of social intercourse the cocktail party, its golf tournaments, its tennis tournaments, its S-boats and its Q-boats. This change, the writer is sure, is in no sense for the better.

There is a consolation that something of the old life still remains. Not all these newcomers, seeking to gain social prestige by the weight of new-found wealth, have always been immediately received. There are many out-of-town families whom no one knows, although they have purchased neighboring estates and have lived on them each summer for over twenty years. In this connection there is an amusing, though significant story, connected with a Cleveland family which came to Mulberry Beach with the idea, presumably, of gaining some indirect social distinction by being members of this community. At the end of the summer, the head of the house was heard to remark that he had met everyone. Although he had heard much of Boston manners and cultivation, he asserted that he might as well have spent the summer in Cleveland, or some place worse. On being questioned further, it appeared that he and his family had made their acquaintances on the beach every afternoon! Coming from an inland city, they had not realized that beaches in the afternoon are customarily left open to the servants.

Such, in brief, is the community where George Apley spent his summers for several years; and it is not strange that Catharine Bosworth was reluctant to go elsewhere, for "The Oaks" in those days was wholly delightful.

A place had been found for Apley in the firm of Ripley and Smith, which was already noted for its management of real estate and for its searchings of titles. George Apley's inquiring turn of mind during the hours he spent in the Registry of Deeds soon bore fruit in a significant way which added not a little to his reputation. It had been intimated to him in August that there was a vacancy in the Browsers' Club, one of the many dinner clubs in Boston, founded in the Golden Age of New England literature, and he received an invitation to become a member. As it would consequently be his task sometime in the early winter to read a paper, the idea occurred to him to trace in some detail the history of a certain Boston business corner in which his firm was interested. The search for the title had taken him back to the holdings of one Jonas Good, who owned this same corner, then situated on a way known as "Cow Lane" in 1636. On that first summer of his marriage he proposed to trace in a discursive paper the vicissitudes of this property and its owners from Jonas Good to the present. One Saturday afternoon, after a game of tennis, at which George Apley was becoming something of an adept (indeed two years later he was champion of Mulberry Beach), he broached this idea of a paper to the present writer. At the time he was fully aware of the seriousness of his undertaking and of what it involved in the way of accuracy and research. It was largely due to the interest of Catharine Bosworth that he persisted in what he then started.

Letter to Elizabeth Apley.

Dear Mother: —

I will give you three guesses what I am doing and not one of your guesses will be right. I am working on a paper which I am thinking of calling "Jonas Good and Cow Corner." I know how interested you will be, as you have always urged me to do something of the kind. Catharine takes the matter so seriously that I sometimes think it is more her paper than my own. Each evening before supper, after the drive from North Beverly, she has pen and ink ready in the parlour and sets me to work while she does her sewing. She asked me to thank you particularly for the little blanket which you knitted. She says it is the prettiest of all. . . .

One of the most lovable characteristics of George Apley was his desire to give pleasure to others and on this occasion the results surely equaled his expectations. The answering letter from Elizabeth Apley is not only full of tenderness but rings with a triumphant sense of maternal vindication.

I have always known [she writes] how wonderful my own dear boy is, and now I am sure that the world is going to know. Many of your ancestors on my side have been literary, George. That you should have inherited this gift is to me like the passing on of a torch, and may the flame be bright!

I do not believe I have ever told you this but it is a memory which I have always treasured. Louisa May Alcott saw you once when she attended one of our tea parties at Hillcrest. I shall never forget how her kind face lighted up when she reached out and touched you, while everyone in the Hillcrest parlour leaned forward to hear what she would say. "Perhaps he will be a writer like you, dear Elizabeth," she said. It was at a time when I had published a bit of poetry in the *Atlantic* which dear Dr. Holmes was kind enough to feel had merit. That night I prayed that her prediction might be true and now my prayer is answered.

My only fear is that Catharine does not understand the significance of your undertaking and what it will mean to her and you in after-life, since dear Catharine must be now somewhat preoccupied with her own sweet secret which now is mine since you told me. I am sending your own dear little porringer and mug, because I know it will be a boy.

Thomas Apley's reaction, although perhaps not as enthusiastic, clearly betrays his latent pride.

Dear George: —

I have to-day established a trust fund for the new Apley whom I trust will be with us before long, the income of which when compounded and suitably re-invested should much more than equal the principal at the end of twenty years. I am very glad that you are writing a paper, particularly as it has pleased your mother, who has been in a rather serious nervous condition since the inexplicable actions of your sister Jane. I must talk to you about this in private sometime this week. In the meanwhile I am considering placing Jane under the care of Dr. Colton at his place in Brookline where she may do some simple handwork.

I am much pleased that you have started to write papers, as this sort of work creates a very favourable impression and opens many doors which might otherwise be closed to you. If you can do a sufficiently good article I do not see, everything else considered, why you cannot be on the Harvard Board of Overseers by the time you are thirty-five. There is nothing more useful than combining scholarship with business. If you are too busy to attend to all the small details of this paper yourself, I know a young instructor in History who would be very willing to help you for a small sum. He did very well for me, looking up facts, brushing up details, and fixing the language in a paper I prepared on banking, which I read before the Saturday Consideration Club, although the actual work on the paper was entirely mine and purely my own idea. . . .

This last suggestion displays a doubt in his son's capacity common to many a father. But the present writer can say from firsthand knowledge that George Apley availed himself of no such assistance. His paper, "'Jonas Good and Cow Corner,'" was entirely original with him in conception and execution and manifested a diligence and a conciseness of thought which were peculiarly his own. Those who were privileged to read it before it reached its final draft could foretell accurately the impression which it would make when it should finally be read before the Browsers' Club. As it happened, these predictions fell short of the actual result. We are fortunate in having the scene described by the Club's secretary in a volume of the minutes of the meeting.

After the coffee and cigars were served, the evening's host, Mr. Theodore Caldwell, called for the Treasurer's Report, which showed a deficit of seventeen dollars and thirty-three cents, the Club's contribution to a fund for protest to the City Council against improvements about the Frog Pond on the Common. After the report was accepted our new member, Mr. George Apley, read for an hour and ten minutes an absorbing paper entitled "Jonas Good and Cow Corner." In it Mr. Apley traced, with painstaking thoroughness, the fascinating vicissitudes of this well-known parcel in the North End of Boston, and showed how it had been deeded to one hundred and fifteen owners from the time of Jonas Good to its present owner, Luigi Martinelli, who now maintains a restaurant and a laundry on the site. Trenchantly and briefly, yet with an undeviating devotion to historical fact, Mr. Apley gave a sketch of the various personalities connected with "Cow Corner," even going so far as to locate the sites where fifty-six of them are now buried. This work of Mr. Apley's held the attention of every member about the table, not only because of its scholarship and veracity, but because of the indirect method he used to display the ironies and the pathos of the growth of Boston from the time it was a village of cowpaths to our present metropolis. At the close of the paper our senior member, Professor Judson Hall, made the unqualified statement that this was one of the five best studies which he had heard during his fifty years' attendance at the Browsers' Club, a statement which was heartily seconded by other members.

Nor did the matter end here, since those who had heard "Jonas Good and Cow Corner" went forth to spread its praises. To one who understands the significance of the Browsers' Club, it will be clear that the importance of its commendation cannot be overemphasized. The congenial membership of this organization, made up from Harvard University, the Bar, State Street, Beacon Hill and Beacon Street, was maintained after a strict tradition laid down by its founders. On the night in late November when George Apley sat down at table, he was known only because of his family connection. When he rose from that table he was known for his own intrinsic worth, and thus almost overnight he took his place with the intellectual element of the city. It may be added that President Charles Eliot himself read this work, which was privately printed a week later, and commented upon it favorably; and it is now too well known to those who read this book to make any recapitulation necessary. It formed, incidentally, the basis of many of his future efforts and gave a new and permanent direction to his life. Other groups, eagerly alert for merit, were quick to recognize the potentialities of George Apley; so that somewhat to his surprise and embarrassment, — for quiet modesty as to his own attainments was a trait which Apley never lost, — he found himself the recipient of a number of flattering invitations to take his place in other organizations of a social and cultural nature, including the Historical Society, the Colonial Society, the Board of Selections for the House-to-House Library, the Centennial Club, and many of the other evening Clubs, generally named for a day in the week, which reflect so accurately the cultural aspirations of our city. Thus it may be safe to say that "Jonas Good and Cow Corner" not only gave George Apley a knowledge of his own capacity, but made him face the full impact of our actual cultural life.

To gauge the effect which this life cannot help but have upon an individual, it may not be amiss to pause for a moment to indulge in a brief description.

It is the writer's belief that few of us, though we have spent a lifetime in our city, fully realize the time and attention which is given to intellectual and artistic pursuits. In the early nineties, the impetus toward scholarship and cultivation which had been given Boston by her Motleys, her Prescotts, her Lowells, her Emersons, her Clarks, her Everetts, her Hales, and her Hunts was now reaching its finest flower. Although the actual period of growth may have been over, the complications had not ended. It is the writer's belief that no city in the world possessed such intriguing facilities for intellectual, artistic, and philanthropic stimulation. In proportion as Boston furnished the fundamentals for an ideally cultivated life, it is not surprising that Boston should have received her share of gibes and jests from many larger but less fortunate neighbors.

That Boston is the center of music is demonstrated by the Symphony Orchestra. The Boston art collections and Museum Art School are known to everyone, as are, of course, the free lectures of the Lowell Institute, not to mention lectures at Harvard University, but not all are privileged to step behind the scenes to perceive the mass of discussion clubs, chamber music clubs, and afternoon lecture clubs which furnish daily and nightly serious entertainment for those who are privileged to join them, not to mention the various more formal scholarly societies which have made the name of Boston famous. In addition to these there are the private philanthropies, such as the Apley Sailors' Home, whose advertisements often fill an entire page of the *Boston Evening Transcript*. In view of these manifold and congenial activities, it is not strange to find many who have devoted the better part of their lives to the pursuit and furtherance of them, and this in a measure was to be George Apley's future lot. There was little time in those days for laziness in Boston. Indeed, the frequent attendance at Board meetings, the activities of intelligent discussion and the necessity for taking a part in them, have led many of the author's acquaintance, toward the end of a Boston winter, into periods of great nervous weariness, sometimes ending in actual nervous breakdown. The demands made upon the individual were, and still are, in proportion to his willingness to meet them, and called for a certain amount of judgment. It was George Apley's task throughout his life to face this problem; and the tax which it made upon him, in the belief of many, materially shortened his span.

He shows his own amazement, when confronted by this new vista, in a letter to his friend, Walker, who was then residing permanently in New York.

For some weeks I have been too busy to send you a line, because I seem to have "arrived" in Boston. Quite suddenly I find myself nearly every evening sitting down to a heavy dinner with learned people, and listening afterwards to a paper; not infrequently many of us go to a later evening party where there is music and another evening paper and a supper of creamed oysters. Catharine enjoys all these very much, but sometimes I don't know that I am entirely up to them. My afternoons are now given over to attending the board meetings of certain charities. I have been on the Boston Waifs' for some time but now I am on half a dozen others. It is all very interesting but I am somewhat confused and tired. I really don't know when I can ever get to see you in New York but I must, Mike. I can't and I won't lose touch with my old friends. Surely you'll be at the Club dinner in February. I shall be there, I don't care what happens.

---•---

CHAPTER XIII

PROBLEMS

Dealing with
Inevitable Difficulties of a Domestic Nature,
In No Sense out of the Ordinary

THE FIRST and only son of George and Catharine Apley was born at their house on Gloucester Street, March 21, 1891, an event which was hailed with an equal enthusiasm by both the Bosworth and Apley families, until it appeared that the young couple for some reason best known to themselves had reached no mutual agreement as to the name of their offspring. They should perhaps have been advised by certain well-known disputes regarding the choice of a name, and should have taken some precaution. Instead of foreseeing the discord and the clash of wills which would inevitably arise, they found themselves without any preparation cast into the storm. Though George Apley preserved a calm and considerate exterior through what must have been an interminable family debate, amusing to an outsider but certainly not to him, it may be safely said that he felt the strained relations very keenly. As he has said himself in another letter to his friend Walker: —

Well, Mike, I am the father of a son, and a very strange sensation it is, when one comes to think of it. I can understand a great deal about my own father now that I am one myself. I find myself looking toward the future, wondering what the world will be like for him and wondering what I can do for him, and even what pieces of silver he will get when I am dead. I have a strange idea that I should be an example for him, though he doesn't need an example yet! Between me and my son, who looks like a wizened old man in miniature, there is already the same formality, the same constraint, and the same unnaturalness which I believe has always existed between my father and myself. I know the reason now — I have the same desire that my father has to see my son get on in the world. I wish him to do better than I have done, I wish him to be happier, although I have every reason to be happy enough and more than I deserve to be grateful for.

I have learned one thing since I have become a parent. I thought that he would be *my* son, but I have been disabused of that. It now appears that Catharine and I have simply been the means of bringing another member of the family into the world, a baby which belongs to everybody. I can see nothing in his features which resembles anything, but everyone else can. Mother says he has my nose, my father sees a striking resemblance to the portrait of Moses Apley in the dining-room. Mr. Bosworth and Catharine say he is the spitting image of a Bosworth, and so say all the Bosworth great-aunts and uncles. I do not know exactly what they mean by "spitting image" of a Bosworth, but the point is that the Bosworths wish to name him one thing and the Apleys wish to name him another. Catharine is siding with the Bosworths and I have suddenly found that I am violently an Apley. God knows how this is going to end!

Many who remember the occasion will recollect that the matter became a piece of public property, the justice of which was discussed with some acrimony. To one who knows our world this is not peculiar, since Boston always has been hospitable to problems involving a moral issue. The situation eventually became regrettably acute between Mr. Bosworth and the senior Apley, and each adhered to a definite point of view. They even deemed it necessary to place their views in writing.

Letter from Thomas Apley.

My dear George: —

I am sending you this note as Mr. Bosworth and I, through no fault of mine, are no longer on speaking terms. When he approaches you, as he no doubt will in his somewhat hysterical manner, I should like to have you place these views of mine squarely before him. You may show him this letter if you wish.

It has been the custom in our family and, I believe, in every other well-conducted family, to give the first son of a new generation one of the Apley names, and these names in my opinion have considerably more importance than anything which the Bosworths may conceivably contribute. I should feel that I had been very lax in my moral duty if a grandson of mine should be anything less than an Apley. Beyond this question of custom and social justice, the child from his appearance and manner is indubitably an Apley, as is attested by everyone who has seen him and who knows the family. He has every one of your grandfather's features and his manner of holding himself in his bassinet needs no comment from an unprejudiced observer. The world is indeed becoming a strange place, and different from the world I used to know, when such a matter even admits of argument. In my opinion the trouble is entirely due to Mr. Bosworth's stubbornness and egotism, which is no doubt augmented by that of his wife.

For reasons which anyone would understand, it is obvious that the child should be named William Apley, after your Uncle William, who is not married, and is not likely to be at his time of life. Your uncle, as you know, has already manifested an interest in the child, and has opened a five dollar account for him in the Water Carriers' Savings Bank. I need not tell you that this interest is important. I must only add that the matter is entirely up to you. You have justice on your own side.

Letter from Mr. Bosworth.

My dear George: —

I feel that I must write to you as the father of my dear only child, your wife. You know, better than most, how close and how very precious Catharine has always been to me. I wish you to understand my point of view, and to lay it before your father, because, on account of his well known high temper and a baseless arrogance, we are no longer on speaking terms.

Dear Catharine's wish is always the same as mine, and at such a time as this, when she has made the greatest sacrifice to you that woman can make in this world, the least you can do is to heed her wish. Not unnaturally she wishes and I wish too that her little son should be named Theophilus Bosworth Apley. Catharine's mother feels, as do the rest of the family, that this concession is only right and should be conceded gracefully. No one can deny that the child has every resemblance to the Bosworths, and that already he is a Bosworth through and through. I am sure that you will see the justice of everything I say, and will do what you can to make it right.

The difficulty finally resolved itself, and the child was given the name John Apley, the given name being common to both the Bosworth and the Apley families. When their second child was born — a girl — she was named Eleanor, distinctly a Bosworth name.

It is difficult in a life as active as that of George Apley to do justice individually to his many interests and actually this task cannot be wholly accomplished, nor need it be, for it is the author's single purpose to give the portrait of the man. At this time his life was that of many of his contemporaries, divided between his work in the law office, where he became a partner in the year 1897, his duties as trustee and director of various enterprises which we shall list later, as business was already paying him its tribute, and finally his clubs and his charities. These were making his life a very full one and were drawing him somewhat away from home.

"The Apley I knew in the nineties," one of his friends has written, "seemed to be always shy in the company of women. He did not try actually to avoid them; he treated them with invariable respect, but he seemed often puzzled and subdued by their attitude of mind. In their society he was far from being the Apley whom we knew and loved at the Club. At the Club, on Tuesday afternoons when many graduates made it their duty to go to Cambridge to lunch with the undergraduate members, George Apley lost most of his shyness and reserve. He was the Apley that we knew in the old days, carefree and full of merriment. He seemed to welcome these interludes with distinct relief, particularly as time went on, just as he welcomed his long vacations on cruises and in the woods. I remember a remark he made to me once which seems to me peculiar in view of the fullness of his life: 'I seem to be busy all the time but I don't seem to be doing anything. I seem to be getting nowhere.' "

The author has heard other friends of his — too many — make this same remark. He believes that it reflects merely the restiveness of a man who sees the course of his life lie clear ahead. This restiveness of Apley's is characteristic of the man, but on the whole he overcame this handicap. He was wrong, as he probably knew himself, in the feeling that he was getting nowhere.

A conscientious sense of public spirit, which is one of the finest attributes of his environment, was bringing him into city affairs. It was here that he encountered, both to his amusement and to his amazement, certain professional politicians who represented an element hitherto unknown to him; and here also he took a side in one of those controversies resulting from the growth of the city — which had for him painful consequences, in that he was forced from a sense of duty to take issue with his father, Thomas Apley. This decision of his was the more difficult as the senior Apley had been in poor health for some time. It was clear to those who knew him that the strain of business in the depression of the period was taking a severe toll on the older man, and that he was losing something of his old skill in negotiation, but none of his determination.

We have quoted in one of Thomas Apley's letters his hostility to the project of what is now the Charles River Basin, a hostility that was shared by many owners of real estate on the water side of Beacon Street. When a more progressive group, made up mostly of younger men, proposed building a dam so that the mud flats of Beacon Street would be permanently covered, Thomas Apley was one of the first organizers of a defense organization which employed the best legal talent to stop what was considered an encroachment on the landholders' rights. He also set forth his opinion clearly in a letter to the *Boston Evening Transcript*.

It is beyond my ability to see [Thomas Apley wrote] what good can come of this extravagant expenditure of public sums, or why Boston should want another pool of stagnant water at her gates. There is enough water around Boston; there are enough stagnant pools in the Fens already. The Charles River, which now bears daily on its rising tide the invigorating salt water of Boston harbor, will become a pestilential mud-hole, a breeder of disease. This proposed step is also an infringement upon owners' rights. The clams on the mud flats will be killed. Many owners whose drains flow into the river will be forced to take other measures. Much of the river beauty to which we have been used for a lifetime will be irreparably ruined — and why? It will be done to gratify the unbalanced whim of a small group who believe there are not sufficient places for the citizens of Boston to walk and play. It is not the purpose of those who built upon the Charles River to have playgrounds in their back yards. The Boston Common was intended for recreation, and also the Public Gardens; and these generous contributions to the city's welfare are enough.

Issues have always been evenly drawn in Boston, where high-minded men and women have been quick to take sides on a question of right and wrong. In this instance the issue was of supreme importance, for it involved a radical change in the very appearance of the city, a physical change greater than any which has since eventuated. Knowing the force of his father's desire, the stand of George Apley is a tribute to his courage and his sense of public spirit. Deliberately, clear-mindedly, knowing full well that he would strain many ties of family and friendship, we find George Apley lending his name to the cause of the would-be builders of this dam. Nor was it his way to be content with a passive interest. He was actually present at several State House hearings, although he did not speak.

The shock incurred by the elder Apley as a result of this defection can only be gauged by those familiar with what is now, alas, almost a dead generation — the firsthand builders of New England. That their works and much of their fortunes still continue so many years after their death is evidence enough of their vitality in life. George Apley himself has left an account of this scene in a memorial sketch which he wrote of his father. It was read before the Centennial Club, and afterward before the Board of the Apley Sailors' Home, and later still, was privately printed for circulation in the family. The quotation we give has a vivid significance and indicates something of the latent power behind George Apley's pen.

This scene — and I believe it was the only time I ever crossed my father — occurred toward the end of his life, in his private office at Apley Brothers. The simplicity of that office, with its sea-coal fire, its heavy roll-top desk, and its two oil paintings of former Apley ships, was a part of my father's own simplicity. I remember his silk hat beside the letter-press, for he never gave up his custom of going to business in a silk hat and a Prince Albert coat. At that time he was in his seventieth year, but he was remarkably well preserved. Except for one other occasion I had never seen him as greatly agitated. He was striding up and down the carpet before the fire, alternately clasping his hands behind him and pulling at his iron-gray side whiskers. As I look back upon them, some of the things he said have an almost prophetic significance.

"Thunderation, George," he said, an expression he used

only when deeply stirred, "I do not care as much for the water, as I do for the principle of the thing. It is a bitter blow, at my time of life, to know that my son has turned traitor to his class."

I tried to explain to him that my position in the matter was actuated entirely by a sense of common good, that I could only conscientiously do what I was doing because of the public welfare. I tried to explain the benefits which would accrue to a vast number of people, but he raised his hand in a signal for me to stop.

"It isn't that," he said, "it is the principle of the thing. There is ruin in this sentimentality. You do not understand, and I fear you never will understand, that affairs will always be controlled by a small group. I, and my group, have controlled them, but you young men are all weak. It is not a pleasant thing for me to feel that the Irish are going to run the affairs of this city, and I do not see anyone in your generation who has the force and skill to guide them. This talk about the common good is arrant Socialism and nonsense. You and I do not stand for the common good. We stand for a small class; but you don't see it. Thunderation! Nobody sees it but me and my contemporaries. It is our fault, I suppose, that our sons will never handle business and affairs as we have handled them. You represent to me the definite end of an era. When control is gone, and it is slipping fast, Boston will become moribund, atrophied; and I for one shall be very glad to leave it."

I tried to explain to him that this was not so, and I quoted certain persons whose opinion I knew he respected, but with that prescience and insight of his he stuck unerringly to his point.

"That is all academic bosh," he said. "For decoration, it is well enough; but actually it is stuff and nonsense. This is the end, and I am very, very sorry. Think of it this way, if you like.

I am an old man now; when I was young there were great men
in Boston and they were here because they were men like me.
Where are they now? Mark my words, this place is becoming
decadent."

My father was deeply moved as he spoke and definitely convinced of what he said. I do not think that he ever understood
that the individual must conform to a new era. Yet, I sometimes wonder if in certain respects he was not right. There
are surely no men like Thomas Apley left in Boston. With
all respect for their integrity it sometimes seems to me that
many of the men I know to-day are only feeble reflections of
my father and his friends. It sometimes seems to me that my
father's generation did all there was to do, and left nothing to
the rest of us. Thus we have been left in a curious position.
Most of us have obeyed the older generation so implicitly that
now they are gone there is nothing left but to continue in the
pattern they have laid down for us. Or is it that we have not
the originality to change that pattern? Or is it that we have
not the wish? It may be, like the Chinese, that we are finally
ending in a definite and static state of ancestor worship, that
the achievements of the past are beyond our present capacities.
My father was that past.

This last paragraph in George Apley's memorial, as the result of maturer consideration, was never read in public, nor did
it appear in print. It remains in the original manuscript, with
pencil marks crossed through it, and is only quoted here because it shows Apley in one of his more erratic moods. In
allowing himself to embark on such totally inaccurate lines of
speculation, George Apley was indulging in a tendency which
some of his more intimate friends found both annoying and
alarming, although those who knew him best always understood that he was merely voicing an unconsidered whim.

It has always been the author's belief that in this clash with his father George Apley gained somewhat in stature; that he had afterwards an assurance which had been lacking before. The results he faced were even more serious than those indicated here, and the weight of them caused his mother to take to her bed. His own wife, obeying the dictates of her conscience, saw fit to side with Thomas Apley. A species of dissension thus arose which could not but have had unhappy consequences. But this was dissipated by an important piece of news. In the spring of 1898, when the Spanish War crisis was at its height, George Apley's sister Amelia announced her engagement to Newcomb Simmings. It need not be added that this was an important and interesting match. The Simmings Mills, situated on the Merrimack above Apley Falls, still indicate how welcome a union of these interests was to both the Simmings and the Apleys. There was at this time a very definite belief among well-informed persons that the Spanish fleet might make a sudden attack upon the Atlantic Coast, and the fortifications of Boston were ill-prepared to face such a danger. Although Thomas Apley had been in bad health for several years, he acted with his usual promptness. Collecting his silver and securities he commissioned George Apley to convey them for safekeeping to a bank in Worcester, and it was during George Apley's absence on this errand that Thomas Apley wrote him the following letter.

Dear George: —

A capital thing has happened since you have been in Worcester and you must come back at once. It is nothing less than that Newcomb Simmings has offered his hand in marriage to Amelia. No one could have been more astonished and delighted than I when Newcomb apprised me of his intentions.

As you must know he is very comfortably off indeed, so comfortably off that none of us need worry greatly about Amelia's future. The young man, of whom I am beginning to grow very fond now that I come to know him, has, it is true, not much presence nor many of the Simmings brains, but these lacks are more than made up for in other respects. It appears that he has admired Amelia from afar for many years, and that he finally gained the courage to speak only when he saw her here alone in danger. I admire him very greatly, as I know you will, particularly as I have feared for some time that your sister would not marry. I have blamed her more than once for passing many suitable opportunities, but I do so no longer. . . .

Letter from Elizabeth Apley.

Dearest George: —

You have heard the news from your dear father. Amelia is leaving the nest. I have been afraid she would not and this has made me unhappy for long, especially as poor dear Jane is still under doctors' care. Amelia is such a headstrong girl that sometimes I have been a little bit bewildered by her, but I know that she and dear Newcomb will get along splendidly. The wedding reception, of course, will be at Hillcrest and I think it might be well to bring the silver back with you, without telling your dear father, who is still greatly upset by rumours. He has not been at all well lately and cannot sleep. . . .

Letter from Catharine Apley.

Dearest George: —

I wish you would let me know definitely when you are coming back, as you have put off coming for two days already. Well, Amelia has caught Newcomb. It took her a long time —

but now she really has him. I wish your family were not quite as openly pleased as they are. You might think Newcomb was a crown prince. I could have married Newcomb myself, as you know, but we won't mention that. Johnnie and Nellie are doing splendidly and send you love and kisses. . . .

Letter from George Apley to Amelia Apley.

Dear Amelia: —

I was rejoiced to get your letter and with it its budget of good news. It seems a strange thing, doesn't it, to think what has happened to us both? It does not seem more than the year before last that you and I were pulling each other's hair in the pantry at Hillcrest, and now here you are getting married. Please do not say I am patronizing you.

I must say there is one thing, Amelia, which distresses me somewhat in your letter, or rather two things. One, that you seem convinced that Father is already dead, though he seemed very much alive the last time I saw him a week ago, and second that you seem convinced that Catharine and I will reach out and take something which is rightfully yours.

Surely there are enough heirlooms to satisfy you and Jane and me, without our having to squabble over them. In fact, Hillcrest and Beacon Street are so full of family silver, furniture, papers and draperies that there is not room for anything which is not family. None of our ancestors seems to have thrown away anything.

I do not know, as you seem to think I do, anything about the provisions of Father's will but I should suppose that the furniture and everything in the house will be left intact during Mother's lifetime. And now I suggest that we do not discuss this any further, for such speculations can seldom amount to anything. . . .

Although one cannot dispute the correctness of George Apley's attitude, it has been the amiable weakness of many persons to speculate upon the possibility of inheritance, a propensity which has frequently been encouraged by the very persons who have the power of giving or taking. The writer can recall several instances where dissension has risen to such an extent that it became public property some ten or fifteen years before there was a possibility that the will might be probated. One such dispute, which many who read this will remember, arose over nothing more important than a badly worn square of carpet upon which General Lafayette inadvertently spilled a glass of Madeira during his visit to Boston in the twenties. But differences concerning the Apley estate were little heard of outside the family circle; indeed all knowledge of them to-day rests only indirectly in the Apley correspondence. If a certain lack of sympathy between George Apley and his sister Amelia was apparent after Thomas Apley's death, it may safely be ascribed, as they both said themselves, to temperamental rather than material difficulties. There existed — and the writer hastens to lay his evidence with that of others — a mutual sense between those two of the responsibilities of a brother-and-sister relationship, and it was foreign to the character of either of them to forget these responsibilities. Thus during George Apley's entire lifetime, his sister Amelia supplied him with unflagging advice and suggestions. Her answer to George Apley is characteristic of this spirit.

Indeed, I wish to grasp at nothing [she wrote], but I think you should remember this: You may be the male heir, but I am the eldest child. As such, it is my duty to see that the house is kept in order. I do not think I am wrong in believing that I am vastly more interested in the family than you are.

For the last two years I have spent every morning arranging
the documents and papers of Moses Apley and many of the
earlier Apley letters. If there should be an examination I am
confident that I should win over you with high honours, and
that now the time has come when these sacrifices of mine should
have some recognition. I shall be glad to give up the silver tea
set, but I shall feel it very unkind of you if it is not understood
between us that I shall have the Apley papers to take to our
new house on Louisburg Square. You may have access to them,
of course, at any time you may desire. I also should like it understood that I take the portrait of John Apley, done by Copley. Newcomb is furnishing our house with some things taken
from the Simmings' country place in Winchester, but they are
all very hideous. This is hard on one who has been brought up
surrounded by important and beautiful objects.

I, for one, do not choose to have my personality as completely dominated as yours has been. The Simmings are not going to ride rough-shod over me as the Bosworths have over you.
I shall hope to have the self-respect not to allow myself to be
dominated by Newcomb as you have been by Catharine. As
you know, Mother and I have been much concerned about this
for some time, but our advice to you seems to have done no
good.

It has always been the characteristic of the Apleys and other
New England families to speak frankly within the family
circle, while preserving at the same time a graceful façade
toward the outer world. This momentary glimpse behind the
façade simply reveals the temporary impatience of a high-
minded, kind-hearted, but somewhat impetuous woman. It is
safe to rely on the understanding of those who read these
pages, without touching in greater detail upon this problem
as it affected George Apley's life, particularly as there is no

answer extant to these observations of his elder sister. The answer, however, must have been fully satisfactory, as George Apley served as best man to Newcomb Simmings at the wedding, although the acquaintance of these two had only been casual until this date.

It is pleasant to recall that this acquaintance ripened rapidly into friendship, as it soon became apparent to both Apley and Simmings that they had many interests and problems in common. Only a month after this wedding, which took place on the second of June, George Apley wrote: —

Dear Newcomb: —

Your invitation to go to your camp in Quebec, even though it is the black-fly season, appeals to me strongly and I am grateful to you, old man, for thinking of me in this connection. It does seem, as you suggest, high time that we loosed ourselves for a little while from the apron strings which bind us, but this cannot be at present. I am on the Board of the Summer Outing for the Berkley Club, and I am in charge of decorating the new playroom in the Boston Waifs' North End Sanctuary, and I have also promised Winty Vassal to sail his sloop with him in the forthcoming races. Besides all this, Catharine is very reluctant to have me leave home at present, as I seem to be the only person who can make Johnny do his multiplication tables. If these reasons were not enough, I find myself faced with the necessity of helping Harry Ripley with the new investments for the Winter estate, which has just reached the office in ten large japanned boxes.

My last and most cogent reason for not accepting your invitation I reserve until now. Father has been failing very markedly during the summer. Shortly after your wedding he had a spell of vertigo which we did not take seriously at the time. Now Dr. Grafton is afraid that it was a slight stroke. He has grown more restless and irritable than usual, and is somewhat of a trial to Mother, although she is perfectly splendid. In the last week he has ordered two of the elm trees at Hillcrest chopped down and has had the shrubbery by the stone wall near the main road moved ten feet back. These, and other similar indications, make me feel that his mind is not altogether reliable. I believe that he got overtired at the wedding, although he seemed very pleased at giving Amelia away.

Well, Newcomb, thanks again for asking me and better luck next time. . . .

CHAPTER XIV

———•———

ADDED BURDENS

*The Impact of Becoming the Head of a
Distinguished Family and Some
Immediate Consequences*

O N A sultry evening in mid-July Thomas Apley took his
customary two glasses of claret during dinner. His wife,
who sat opposite him, and other members of the household
waiting on the table, observed nothing unusual in his manner.
He discussed with considerable animation the international
situation, and made it known that he was unalterably opposed
to further extension of United States territory. He also discussed turning the old carriage horses, Tony and Jack, out to
pasture, since this handsome pair of bays had been in Apley
harness for over fifteen years and were beginning to show their
age. (As is well known, it was Thomas Apley's policy and
that of his son after him never to sell a horse from the Hillcrest stables.) He next asked with deep interest about the
health of the second gardener, Patrick Burke, whose hand had
become badly infected from a nail in the asparagus bed, and
he then alluded briefly to labor difficulties at the Apley Mills.
His conversation, in short, was that of an active man interested
in life.

Yet I should have known even then [Elizabeth Apley wrote to her old school friend Cynthia Fellowes] that something was very, very wrong with the sweetest husband in the world, for he suddenly turned to me and said: "Elizabeth, I have been thinking of something. I wonder if it would have been better if George had married that little Irish girl." Then, for the first time, I knew that Thomas Apley's mind and his judgment, upon which I had leaned for a lifetime, was not what it had been once. "Thomas," I said, "the hot weather has made you very tired; you had better not attempt to go to the office to-morrow." He replied that he should go to the office as he had done always, and then said that he would go to the library to read. A few moments later, as I was discussing with Norah, our dear waitress, the arrangements for next morning's breakfast, I was startled by a heavy fall. Thomas had been reaching for one of his favourite Waverley novels. . . .

He was seized in this act by a fatal apoplectic stroke, never regained consciousness, and died an hour after George and his sister Amelia reached his bedside.

"And so passed," George Apley wrote in his memorial, "one of the great men of his generation, and one of the greatest men whom I have ever known."

It would be a slur upon George Apley's integrity to doubt the absolute sincerity of his statement, that shows the strength of Thomas Apley's influence upon his son, and upon his entire family. The sure hand of Thomas Apley had guided wife and son and daughters benignly and accurately. The shock of losing such an influence was correspondingly great. It was only when he was removed from their midst forever that they realized the full force of his personality and how this personality had wound itself into every detail of their lives, and how Thomas assumed chivalrously many unnecessary burdens. Although he had spoken often of investments, he had been characteristically reticent regarding the details of his own financial affairs, and thus the provisions of his will came as a distinct surprise even to his widow.

I had always known [George Apley wrote some years later to his son], that we were comfortably off, but until the death of your grandfather, whom I am glad you were old enough to remember, I never dreamed how comfortably off. What he did for me, and indirectly for you, was to free us from the belittling task of money making, but not from the responsibility which springs from this freedom. It is a grave responsibility toward the community and toward others. You will feel it some day as I have. I hope you will be fitter than I to meet it.

It was true that Thomas Apley's will removed from his descendants the necessity for commercial livelihood, and it was evident that Thomas Apley's great preoccupation in the years before his death was the building and the conserving of an estate. He had arranged for the principal to remain intact until the death of his youngest grandchild. In an affectionate letter to his son he expressed a disbelief in George Apley's ability to handle personally interests of such proportions, thus explaining, but not apologizing for, the deed in trust.

When George Apley was confronted by the actual figures of the estate he could not but agree with his father's judgment. The bequests in Thomas Apley's will hint eloquently at the size of the remainder: To Harvard University, one million dollars to be known as "The Apley Fund," the income of which to be used to defray the tuition of deserving Protestant students from the vicinity of Milton; two hundred thousand dollars for the schools at Apley Falls; one million dollars to the city of Boston. In addition to this, there were liberal bequests to libraries, historical societies, and to other organizations of which Thomas Apley was a member. His office employees and the employees at Beacon Street and Hillcrest were also given legacies depending on their length of service, and George Apley was requested to provide for them in any future emergency. His solicitude went beyond the realms of human beings down to the dogs and horses on the Hillcrest estate. The grounds and gardens at Hillcrest were also endowed by a fund to cover taxes and upkeep. The remainder of his property, consisting of his holdings in the Apley Mills, and in a diversified list of securities, was placed in trust under William Apley and the firm of Ledyard and Hollins. The income was divided into four parts to be paid equally to the widow and the children. Even with this division the amount was an intense surprise to everyone concerned. In addition, George Apley was appointed the guardian of his sister, Jane, whose condition at the time demanded guardianship.

Until my father's death [George Apley wrote in another letter to his son], your mother and I were living on an income of ten thousand dollars a year, and this seemed adequate for all our needs. It was a great shock to me, as indeed it was to your mother, suddenly to find this income increased to such a great extent. Its size has caused us no little embarrassment for I have inherited, as I hope you have, a distaste for lavish expenditure. It has always seemed to me that great establishments are senseless and egotistical and do not help one's name in a community. It is better to think of one's self as a steward who owes the community a definite debt; and such I have always tried to be, as my father was before me.

My father once made a remark which I shall now repeat to you because it illustrates this attitude. One evening not very long before his death, when I was seated with him on the Hillcrest piazza watching the gold of the setting sun on the leaves of our great elms, I happened to make some casual remark about the servants, when my father stopped me by beating impatiently on the floor with his walking stick. "I do not like the word 'servants,' " he said, "when it is employed to differentiate a certain class of persons from ourselves. In a sense we all are servants, placed here on earth to serve. Some of us, by the will and the omniscience of the Divinity, have been given a greater task than others; I count myself, somewhat to my sorrow, as a member of that group. It is a very grave thought to me to think that I may soon have to render an account of my stewardship to my Maker. I have held control of some large industries in this country and through them I have controlled the lives of many people. This is a solemn thought and some day it will be a solemn thought for you. There are certain definite obligations for one in my position and one in yours — and one of them is to try to make your life worth while with the advantages God has given you. When one is the steward of a large fortune one should not dissipate it by useless spending. That is why I have always lived on a small fraction of my income, have reinvested another fraction against possible contingencies, and have given the rest to charity." This sentiment of my father's, I am afraid, is a little archaic to-day, but I am glad to see that it is still followed by many. There would be less trouble if everyone with property followed it.

I should like to give you one specific example of what I mean. As you know, for a number of years I have been making a collection of Chinese bronzes. I have tried to inform myself fully about these things, and I have spent much time with many wily Oriental dealers. I have not done this because I particularly like these bronzes. As a matter of fact, I think many of my best ones are overdecorated and look inappropriate in the Hillcrest library. I have made this collection out of duty rather than out of predilection, from the conviction that everyone in a certain position owes it to the community to collect something. In this way industries are stimulated and scholars are given definite occupations. In the end the public will be the gainer. I had perceived that our Art Museum was short of Chinese bronzes and I started my collection at your Uncle William's suggestion. They will, of course, be left by my will to the Museum, just as your Uncle William proposes to leave his own very extensive collection of Chinese ceramics. No one in our position should consider himself alone, but first he should consider his duty to the community.

It would be difficult to find a more accurate expression of the sentiment which has actuated so many individuals in our group. It may be true that George Apley did not live up entirely to these ideals — as, indeed, who has? — but in a measure they were before him always. They explain much of his own simplicity in life, in which to the last he took a definite, if perhaps an over meticulous, pride. It was always his ideal, for example, that anyone less fortunately situated than himself should feel at ease in his house and should not feel self-conscious because it was encumbered with the externals of luxury so prevalent in estates about New York, and so ridiculously manifested in Chicago and other points in the Middle West. It was always his endeavor, not invariably successful, to have matters of the intellect placed before material consideration. Thus in later years one very often found about the Apley table some person of interest to Boston — a professor, for example, who had distinguished himself by some discovery in literature or science, some itinerant writer whose work had sufficient merit to deserve intelligent attention, or perhaps some visiting Englishman or a Frenchman.

It is difficult to visualize either the extent or the significance of the changes to which George Apley was obliged to adjust himself as the result of his father's death. He had been busy before in the domestic pursuits resulting from matrimony; but now, almost overnight, he found himself the head of the Apley family, on whom many members he hardly knew existed drew for advice and often for more tangible support. He found himself in the position of receiving requests from charities and from educational institutions, and also demands of a more sinister sort from numerous charlatans and adventurers — which leads us to the revealing of a very painful situation. It may be useful, however, as illustrating the problems which beset George Apley and as showing also how unscrupulous and mercenary individuals may cast gratuitous and baseless slander upon an honest and respected name. A week after his father's will was probated, George Apley, still harassed by myriads of arrangements, received the following communication from New York, written by a lawyer named Presser, of whom no one had previously heard.

My dear sir: —
A client of mine, whose name I shall be glad to divulge to you in a private conversation, has asked me to do what I can for her. Some years ago she met your late father, Thomas Apley, on one of the many occasions when he was in New York on business. The acquaintance ripened into something more than friendship and the result is a son, now a boy of twelve years of age. My client states categorically that your late father moved her from a position as a stenographer in a Wall

Street firm and has furnished her for a number of years with
support. In addition to this, he had always assured my client
that he would make an adequate provision for her and her
child's future at the time of his death. I am communicating
with you to find what provision has been made, assuring you
that you may rely on my discretion. It is neither my client's
desire nor mine that this matter should be made public unless
absolutely necessary. I am placing myself at your disposal and
suggest that I visit Boston or, better, that you come to New
York. I am sorry that the matter is urgent but my client is in
immediate need of money.

The shock which this news caused George Apley is sufficiently
obvious not to demand specific description. It is the same as
any dutiful son must feel when, cognizant of the rectitude of a
parent, he finds that rectitude left open to slander and himself
the only one to refute it. George Apley had no precedent or
experience to guide him and had only to rely on his own
sound sense. The present writer has always felt it a great
honor that George Apley called for him in this great hour of
need, arranging a meeting in the Apley house on Beacon Street.
The house was closed during the summer months except for
the sitting-room and bedroom of Thomas Apley, which was
customarily kept open and dusted for the late owner's visits
to town. Thus, with the exception of the sitting-room, the house
had an air of mourning. George Apley, pale and nervous, but
with his lips closed imperturbably, paced the length of the
room and back.

"It is a lie!" he said, "a damnable, scurrilous lie!" And
then he added, "I have been through Father's checkbooks and
letters, and there is no mention in them whatsoever of any
such woman." It was only necessary to point out to him the

absurdity of such a liaison to relieve him of much of his distress. It was not a doubt of his late father's own blamelessness which assailed him as much as a fear of the natural cynicism of irresponsible individuals who might hear the news.

"You know as well as I do," he said, "that such things have happened. Every now and then one does hear gossip of illegitimacy. I must go down to New York. I must go down to New York."

As was always the case with Apley, the idea of action pleased him. We went down to New York that night — taking, I well remember, the Fall River boat. Once we were established in the comfortable dining saloon, with a very fair bottle of claret between us, George Apley partly dismissed the problem from his mind. He was once again the companion whom his friends had known in college days, thoughtful and almost gay.

"Will," he said, "this is something of a lark, to be getting out of Boston. I sometimes feel that all the rest of the world is like a foreign country."

We discussed this remark for a while as we finished the bottle of wine. We discussed the affairs of many of our friends, but all the while he was preoccupied, and finally he said: "Mother must never hear a breath of this. The family must never hear."

This generous feeling was the mainspring of all his actions in New York. After a confidential conversation with his father's New York attorneys, who were as deeply shocked at the news as the son, the man Presser was called for an interview. It soon became plain that neither Presser nor the woman he represented could offer more than the flimsiest line of evidence that such an alleged liaison had ever existed. It was only

Apley's dread and intense dislike of the slightest whisper against the family name which caused him to be generous upon the advice of New York counsel. The matter was finally compounded upon the payment of a lump sum, although George Apley held out against this until the end, on the ground that the payment was an admission of truth. The best evidence that the entire charge was absolutely groundless is that from that day to this nothing has been heard of the matter.

No sooner was this situation arranged than another arose of a different though of an equally painful nature. It concerned his intense love, Hillcrest, where he wished to move with his wife and family after his father's death, sharing the housekeeping with his mother. His wife and the Bosworths, however, were so distressed at the idea of leaving Mulberry Beach that this could not be arranged and for many years George and Catharine Apley contented themselves with frequent visits to Hillcrest.

It is not that I do not like Mulberry Beach [George Apley once wrote by way of explanation]. My one objection to it is that it is a long distance from Milton, being on diametrically the opposite side of Boston. My children must have their roots in the soil of Milton. It seems to me that the time is fast arriving when this rushing about, this uncertainty of the life which I have led so long must come to an end. My children must be brought up in a steady, congenial atmosphere, and Milton is the place.

This desire to establish himself in a firmly entrenched environment grew on him as time continued. His numerous activities filled him always with an increasing desire for peace, yet this desire seldom took shape in a wish to escape but rather in an anxiety for simplification. His life was too full; there were too many things to do. In September the attacks of indigestion, with which he had become stricken in the months following his marriage, and which had become chronic, grew more acute; and finally, on the advice of doctors, he took a much needed rest — in a sense one of his first vacations. Leaving his wife and family he went with two congenial friends, of whom the writer was one, on a camping trip to the woods of northern Maine. The success of this experiment caused him to repeat it for many years with the same congenial companions, going always to the same place, and this leads us to another phase of George Apley's life and to the founding of an institution very dear to many in Boston; the Pequod Island Camp. The story of this camp begins with this pioneering journey.

———•———

CHAPTER XV

PEQUOD ISLAND DAYS

*The Establishment of a
Beloved and Challenging Institution*

PEQUOD ISLAND CAMP and the life on that remote jewel of an island nestled in the clear blue waters of one of Maine's wilderness lakes has been described by the present writer in his memorial, "Pequod Island Days," which was distributed privately a few years back to those fortunate enough to know the spot. At the risk of injecting his own personality, a few selections from this work by the present writer are quoted, as they are so deeply concerned with Apley.

Well I remember the first day that anyone saw Pequod Island and thought of it as something more than a stopping place on a wilderness journey. It was in the latter part of a September afternoon, in the cool before sunset, that the canoes of three tired campers and their guides first broke the stillness of the waters of Pequod Lake after Half Mile Carry. In the party was our host, George Apley, Winthrop Vassal, and myself. Our guide was Norman Rowe, as fine a man as ever handled a canoe in white water, and one who, although he did not know it then, was for many years to be the guide, philosopher, and friend of every pilgrim to Pequod Island. There is little need to describe him here, for we all know him, a typical Yankee product of the woods, endowed with the quiet patience and the tolerance that is born of open spaces. We all know that drawling, singsong speech which George Apley was able so perfectly to imitate. We all know the dry, tolerant humor with which he regarded us "sports," as he called us. We have often seen him in later years at storytelling time around the campfire, with his perennial quid of tobacco tucked inside his cheek, exchanging pleasantries with his employer and dear friend; and the rapport between this son of Boston and this rough-handed, clear-eyed product of forest and stream was in many ways as amazing as it was beautiful — but perhaps it was not amazing after all. The son of Boston and the son of Maine were both sons of New England, who shared a common philosophy. It has sometimes amused me to speculate how Norman Rowe might have developed had he been brought up in Apley's own environment. At any rate, his exterior never for a moment concealed the sterling traits of a gentleman, for he had many of the same qualities which President Emeritus Eliot perceived in his rough fisher friend farther up the Maine coast, and of which he wrote so eloquently.

We were weary indeed as the canoes neared the golden bow of beach that fringed the wooded slopes of Pequod Island, but it was a carefree, happy weariness. As we went for a dip in the lake while the guides busied themselves expertly with putting up tents, cutting soft beds of balsam boughs and preparing trout, coffee, and flapjacks for supper, we were alone in a wilderness of woods and water, alone save for the mournful call of the loons and the splash of an occasional fish. Once seated about the campfire, according to his invariable habit of good fellowship Apley directed the guides to sit among us instead of modestly withdrawing into a corner by themselves. He had the faculty, inherited perhaps from his seafaring an-

cestors, of putting this type of person entirely at his ease, so
much so that one had the illusion that Apley was one of them.
He drew Norman Rowe into fanciful accounts of the habits
of moose and beaver; and as Norman Rowe's imagination became stimulated through his own narration, George Apley's
eye had that sly twinkle which those who knew him in the
woods so well remember. When Norman had finished his
story of a tame beaver at a lumber camp, who rang the dinner
bell whenever he was hungry, George Apley said: "I believe
you, Norman, we all believe you," and Norman shared in the
hearty laugh at his expense. Then George Apley placed a hand
in a friendly way on Norman's shoulder. "Norman," he said,
"you are too good a man to lose; I am going to buy this island
and I am going to put you on it."

That was the beginning of Pequod Island Camp.

Starting spontaneously, Pequod Island has never lost its
spontaneity, and one loves to think that the aura of good fellowship which enfolded it that evening and the carefree gayety
of that moment have never left it. Pequod Island has always
been a place where one may drink deeply and gayly of un-
spoiled nature, and where one may commune with the forest
about it. The great central cabin which now overlooks the
beach, christened facetiously by George Apley the "Forum
Romanum," with its enormous fieldstone fireplace and rawhide-
seated chairs, was George Apley's own idea, as indeed was
the arrangement of the outer cabins, each given the name for
some building of classical Rome. These even included the
dormitory of unmarried women, facetiously but racily called
"The Hall of the Vestal Virgins." Thus, the whole island
became in time an idealization of its owner's hospitality. It is
true that each guest paid a nominal fee for his or her board
and lodging, but this plan was only hit upon to free each visitor
from a certain sense of obligation to the host. Simple though

the life was at Pequod Island, the actual running expenses were vastly greater than any sums collected, and this difference was made up cheerfully by "Romulus" Apley, our host, a name which was facetiously given him by the present writer.

Everyone arriving at Pequod Island dock recalls the sign made in letters of rustic cedar twigs which so typifies the welcoming spirit of the place: ALL YE WHO STEP UPON THIS PIER, LEAVE THE WORLD BEHIND. In a sense this admonition has always been sedulously followed. The dross of the world we have known has always been left in the broad-beamed passenger launch, and only what is fine in the world, with an occasional unpleasant exception, has come to Pequod Island. Now and then, to be sure, an individual has stepped ashore who did not fit in, who could not share that carefree spirit, but he has never been asked again. It was George Apley's idea also that there should be no drinking and no smoking. As the sign over the fireplace in the Forum Romanum gayly said: "Wood smoke is enough." Incidentally, it was amazing how quickly everyone who arrived there was cured of his craving for tobacco.

It was first George Apley's idea that Pequod Island should be a haven for men, since he was under the illusion that its facilities were of too rough and ready a nature to appeal to the fairer sex. He was soon cheerfully to admit his error. After two years the fame of Pequod Island became so widely known in Boston that it could no longer serve exclusively as a retreat for the "mere male." On the third summer, perhaps out of sheer curiosity, Catharine Apley and Amelia Simmings asked to be included in the party; and they may have come to scoff, but they remained to pray. Much to Apley's surprise Pequod Island appealed to them also, and to them we owe much of the routine and tradition which still exist there to-day. The accurate social sense of Amelia and Catharine Apley has been largely responsible for the selection of divergent but congenial personalities, so that there has always been good talk and stimulating thought on Pequod Island. It was Catharine Apley's idea, so successfully carried out, that no one of the fair sex should give a thought to dress. The rules for costume which she rigidly laid down demanded a flannel shirtwaist, a khaki skirt, black cotton stockings, and black sneakers. After wading in the brook, or climbing to the top of Eagle Mountain across the lake, this costume might be changed but it was never varied. Thus it has often caused no small amusement among new guests to observe in the dining-hall that the village girls from the near-by town, employed as waitresses at the camp in summer, are universally more expensively dressed than those upon whom they wait. It was due to Amelia Simmings that the routine schedule of camp activities, which the rising generation considers as firm as the laws of the Medes and the Persians, was first adopted. Since Amelia Simmings first arrived at Pequod Island the rising bell has sounded at six-thirty, and it was she who thought of a derisive song to greet the tardy arrivals at table, the first lines of which must ring in the memory of every Pequod Islander.

Late, late, we all have ate,
And now a cold egg is your fate.

Amelia Simmings also arranged the institution of the After Breakfast Forum, to discuss, after a short prayer, the activities of the day. It was first her idea for George Apley to act as chairman of Parliamentary Meeting, but later Mrs. Simmings herself took over this office. Each day a variety of morning and afternoon projects were laid informally before the assembled company, old and young, so that there was something to meet each taste. The fishers, for example, might go to Sturgeon Cove, the berrypickers might betake themselves to the top of Eagle Mountain, the workers — for at Pequod Island there was always work to do — might be assigned to dam building, wood chopping, boat painting, or trail cutting. The "idlers" were customarily taken in hand by Professor Speyer, to sit quietly on the rustic benches beneath the trees of Indian Point, there to read some selections from good books. The youngsters — for here John and Eleanor Apley and many of their friends and contemporaries spent a large portion of their summers — might join any of these parties if they were not backward in their lessons. In the evening by the hospitable lamplight of the Forum the secretary of each group rendered its report for the day to the tune of friendly and whimsical mirth, and so Pequod Island would retire to well earned and dreamless repose.

To one who reads these pages, but who has never been on Pequod Island, this program may seem simple, but in truth it was not. The personalities that took part, and who contributed so much besides to our charades and pageants, were what leavened an otherwise dull loaf. It is needless to say that many famous figures appeared on Pequod Island and that eventually an invitation there was like an accolade. Poetry, philosophy, music, art and diplomacy, all have passed beneath the giant pines which guard the Forum's door. There has always been something provocative in the gay spirit of Pequod Island, but the feature one remembers best was the character of the host who ruled over it.

In all those years, particularly after the organization beneath the capable hand of Amelia Simmings and Catharine Apley, the spirit of George Apley was felt more than his presence — a genial, kindly, but retiring spirit. As time went on his love for the woods and solitude became more and more pronounced and he organized a group within the group at Pequod Island, known as the "camping crowd." The camping crowd was always directly under control of Norman Rowe, and frequently with its canoes and tents left the island for days, and sometimes weeks, for little known parts and for untouched beaches and streams. On one matter George Apley was always firm. Neither Catharine nor Amelia could interfere with the camping crowd. This was made up always of men, generally of his clubmates, and later his son John Apley and his college friends were admitted to the group.

You know [he wrote his friend, Dr. Sewell, by then a famous abdominal surgeon] how much I love Pequod Island. I fully realize that a part of its charm is that it makes other people happy, and I leave much of that to Catharine and Amelia. The Robin Hood festival which my dear mother arranged herself this year was particularly delightful, and so are the talks and the singing in the evening, but now and then I have a feeling which I am brave enough to express only to you and a few others. I had thought on first coming to Pequod Island that we might get away for a while from certain things, that we might have a moment's breathing space, a respite from what we know so well and love so much. I suppose that this was rather too much to hope for. It sometimes seems to me that Boston has come to Pequod Island. I suppose we cannot escape from it entirely, nor do we really wish to, but I know what you and I like: the dripping water from a canoe paddle, the scent of balsam, the sweet smell of pond lilies and mud, the weariness of a long carry. These things are still on tap at Pequod Island. Norman and I have the canoes ready, and you can either go with me or talk with Professor Speyer. Personally, my summer is under canvas, with a few days in camp in which to recuperate, and then off again. Yet, even in those trips we move in circles, we move in circles and come back. I wish to goodness my life was not always a circle. I wish I were not always resting beneath the umbrella of my own personality. You must bear with me when I say this, because you know me better than most, you know it is a mood and I'll soon get over it. The mood is on me to-night only because I have listened to several hours of intelligent conversation and I am not a very brilliant person. Sometimes here on Pequod Island and back again on Beacon Street, I have the most curious delusion that our world may be a little narrow. I cannot avoid the impression that something has gone out of it (what, I do not know), and that our little world moves in an orbit of its own, again one of those confounded circles, or possibly an ellipse. Do you suppose that it moves without any relation to anything else? That it is broken off from some greater planet like the moon? We talk of life, we talk of art, but do we actually know anything about either? Have any of us really lived? Sometimes I am not entirely sure; sometimes I am afraid that we are all amazing people, placed in an ancestral mould. There is no spring, there is no force. Of course you know better than this, you who plunge every day in the operating room of the Massachusetts General, into life itself. Come up here and tell me I am wrong.

Mr. Wong writes me from New York that he has a dozen new bronzes from the Han Dynasty. He will send them to Boston and I must look at them. I wish to heaven I had not started collecting them; it seems as hard to tell what is a real bronze as it is to tell who is a real person. Come up soon and explain this to me.

A letter written some years later to his son is in a somewhat different vein.

Dear John: —

I am sorry that you consider it advisable not to be with us here at Pequod Island for your usual month this summer, but instead to visit your college friends at Bar Harbor. There is an atmosphere of money at Bar Harbor which I, personally, have never liked, and I hope that you are not going there solely for that reason. It seems to me that you and the other young people whom I know are not as contented as I used to be at your age. I suppose it is because the world is moving faster. I was aware myself of this change when your mother and I gave up our carriage and began using an automobile.

What really worries me, however, about your not going to Pequod Island is that I am afraid you are neglecting a certain duty which you owe to others. Our little community at Pequod Island requires the coöperation of everyone to keep it together, and this coöperation, as I well know, not infrequently entails a certain sacrifice of personal inclination. Nevertheless, it is my obligation and yours, as my son, to make our guests here happy. You must be lenient with certain eccentricities. Believe me, I can understand how you feel about many of the requirements of your Aunt Amelia, because I agree with you that some of them are ridiculous. Frankly, I have sometimes wished that I were not invariably aroused at half-past six. I have often wished that I could spend the day doing exactly as I pleased; but I know now that such a wish is a luxury and a weakness. As time goes on it will become more and more evident to you that you are a part of a society whose dictates you must obey within certain prescribed limits and in every walk of life we must give way to the common will. Yes, there are certain things one does and others one does not do. One of the things which you and I must not do is to neglect our duties at Pequod Island.

I am afraid you will learn before you are much older that this general principle will run through much of your life. Take our downtown lunch club for instance — it comes into my mind as just such another group which has its customs and its manners. You will find, when you become a member as you doubtless will when you take up business in Boston, that you will not be cordially received at certain of the tables where the same people have customarily eaten for the last thirty years. Furthermore, you will discover if you go downstairs to smoke in the room reserved for the purpose that you should not linger there long over your cigar whether you have anything to do for the next hour or not. This, of course, is a trivial example and I simply give it as an illustration to show that you and I cannot and should not change established customs.

I want to tell you one thing more, John, and some day you will know how right I am. There are certain duties one cannot escape. I do not know just why. I consider this quite often without arriving at any just rationalization. It is, I think, because you and I have been born into a certain environment with very definite inherited instincts. We cannot escape that environment, John, because it is a part of you and me. You can leave Pequod Island for Bar Harbor but Pequod Island will nevertheless remain a part of you. You can go to the uttermost ends of the earth but, in a sense, you will still be in Boston; and this is not true alone with you and me; it has been the same with others. For many years after the discovery of the Sandwich Islands all Americans touching there were known to the natives as Bostonians. Believe me, this was not entirely an accident; in my opinion these individuals stood out in the childlike minds of the Polynesians as more distinct than other American nationals. They had brought something of Boston with them, just as you and I will bring it with us, always.

This is an inescapable fact but one, I believe, that we should be rather proud of than otherwise. It is something to be an integrated part of such a distinct group. It is somehow reassuring; at any rate you can go to Bar Harbor, John, but you cannot get away from Pequod Island. . . .

It is interesting to observe that John Apley himself appended a note to this letter which reads: "By God, you can't."

———— •◦• ————

CHAPTER XVI

PORTRAIT OF A GENTLEMAN

Civic Duties
And the Rising Tide of Change

AS ONE looks back upon the first decade of this century from the perspective of the present, one grows increasingly aware that it was a time of subtle change; subtle, because the material aspects of life as we have known it underwent no great marked exterior alteration. That change was rather a gathering of forces from within, the end of which we know not yet. George Apley himself was able to perceive the working of these forces during some of the most fruitful and interesting years of his life, for this decade was indeed important to him. It was in many ways the crowning decade of his career, since it found him in the full force of early manhood and left him in the prime of middle life. It was in this decade, in the year 1905 to be exact, that our great genius, John Sargent, painted George Apley's portrait, now the property of his son. Sargent's uncanny ability to evaluate a character through indefinable gradation of feature is very finely manifested in this work. It shows George Apley in a simple brown business suit, with the high starched collar of the period, standing with one hand leaning upon a bare table, the other half-thrust into the side pocket of his coat. It is a simple, austere picture of a slender man with a somewhat long brown mustache, but in some way George Apley has brought his world with him to the canvas so that one recalls almost immediately the line written to his son: "You cannot get away from it." The sharp nose and particularly the set of the mouth and jaw indicate their owner's definite reaction to his world. The hands are long and fine. In the attenuation of the features one is aware of distinctive breeding. It might be termed, as many another canvas by older great masters, "The Portrait of a Gentleman." There is a marked and gratifying similarity shared by Sargent's "Apley" and Titian's "Gentleman with a Glove" and Velasquez's and Rembrandt's gentlemen. There is the same leanness, the same courteous, reserved assurance — but here the resemblance ends. George Apley is not an Italian or a Spaniard; he is entirely his own type and completely true to type.

This was the Apley of State Street, of Mulberry Beach and Milton, who walked across the Common to his office of a winter morning in long, half-careless strides, a true son of Boston — the present writer likes to think — imbued with the love of his land and caste. This was the Apley who realized, like so many of his contemporaries, that his caste in a sense was threatened. The realization came to him when he encountered at first hand certain vicious phases in the city government. This occurred when he was given the place his name demanded on a committee selected by the Mayor of Boston to advise regarding certain plantings and improvements on the Commonwealth Avenue Mall. Though this was a matter of no very large importance, it was not his way to shirk a civic duty and he attended the meetings of this committee assiduously. The make-up of this committee, rather than its actions, amazed him most; and this example, coming at firsthand, drove him ever afterwards to take a more active interest in city affairs and threw him eventually with many who were trying to shed some light on the shadowy ways of our municipal politics. Thus, as early as 1902, we find him writing to Mr. Henry Salter, whose letters to the *Transcript* at the time were already causing no little discussion.

My dear Mr. Salter: —

I have heard you speak more than once of the incredible laxness, to use a mild expression, which has been appearing without our fully recognizing it, in our city affairs. I am afraid I have been guilty of not paying much attention to this, since I have been engaged in many other activities, until I found myself upon the advisory committee for the planting of the Commonwealth Avenue Mall. Then, for the first time I realized that Boston has indeed become a melting pot. As I listened to the discussions of this committee I was amazed to find myself in the company of a number of ill-bred men, mostly Irish, who seemed to take no real interest in improving the city. Such ideas as they had were illiterate and without any merit. What seemed to concern them most was that the work should go to one of two contractors for whom they appeared to have a deep personal friendship, although I could readily see that the bids these contractors had made for the proposed work were vastly higher than the bids of others. The matter of economy did not seem to concern my fellow committee members in the least. Their argument ran something like this: "Martin Casey will do a good job. He always does the work." What surprised me more was that no one paid much attention to anything I said. They appeared rather to resent some suggestions which I made and one of them actually said to me: "It's your name we want, we're used to this sort of business; sure, you wouldn't understand it, Mr. Apley." If this is indicative of the way our entire city is run, and I begin to be afraid that it is, surely something is very wrong. Those of us who should sway the taste and perhaps the conscience in municipal affairs have been careless of our trust. I, for one, hope that you will call on me to aid in any of the good works which you may be doing.

In all the amusing and erroneous criticisms directed against our city no one has been able to say that there has not always been a spirit of abnegation and self-sacrifice among our better element. The Puritanical idea of uplift ever lingers in the blood of the descendants of the first colonists of Massachusetts Bay. It may be true that occasionally they are shortsighted and oblivious to certain faults in their surroundings which may be obvious to others, but when their attention is directed toward these faults, they leave no stone unturned in an effort at rectification. In a sense the letter of George Apley indicates a marked awakening of conscience in the better element of Boston — or "consciousness" might be a fitter word.

It is clear to-day that this better element was already beginning to perceive that it had neglected certain phases of the life around it. Preoccupied with their own activities, and possibly judging the probity of others by their own, many persons did not observe the inevitable results of the rapid growth of our city until they became suddenly aware, perhaps more so in this decade than at any other time, that much of Boston had grown away from them. It was becoming increasingly evident that a species of organized corruption which had reared its ugly head in other American municipalities was only too apparent in Boston also. Imperceptibly, but at last surely, it was dawning on thoughtful observers of the public trend that the esprit and the spiritual pattern which had always distinguished the metropolis of New England was no longer sensitive to the influence of our better element.

If it had not been for external urging, it may have been that Apley would have allowed the matter to rest with this single unsavory committee experience. As he said in later years, he was never greatly interested in politics or sociology, nor had he, as he admitted himself, the pliability of mind or the tolerance to deal with demagogues; but the pressure of public conscience, and also the pressure of individuals including members of his own family, gradually aroused his sense of duty. Those who know the indefatigability and fearlessness of Henry Salter in his efforts at various branches of reform can readily appreciate the enthusiasm with which he welcomed an offer of assistance given by one of Apley's caliber.

I have never seen [George Apley wrote some time afterwards, in a paper entitled "Adventures in Reform"] a more dynamic man than Henry Salter. He had the leanness of face and the fixity of purpose which make up the ideal leader of a cause. His very eccentricities of dress and manner served only to accentuate his earnestness. He is the type of man who has made us what we are, and I am proud to have been associated in some of his activities.

Even a casual perusal of Salter's letters to George Apley give a definite idea of the effect they must have had on one of Apley's disposition, for they are calculated to open up new and startling vistas.

Do you remember Henry Salter? [We find Apley writing thus to his classmate, Walker.] I recall how we used to joke about him at Harvard, the pale bookworm with glasses. Believe me, he is quite a different sort of fellow now.

We are beginning to realize here that the better element has let things slide and that now there are incredible social abuses. Organized vice is rampant hardly a stone's throw from our very doors. I never knew it before, but bribery seems to be a common practice and many officials are growing rich on the taxpayers' money. More than this, there is an entire letdown in the general moral tone. The displays at some of the Music Halls are really too shocking to be mentioned, although I consider myself tolerably broad-minded.

It has always seemed to me until lately that these matters were beyond my province. In some way the better element must be organized and must make its influence felt. I do not know exactly how, because suddenly we seem to be very much in the minority.

More significant, perhaps, in his correspondence at this time is a hastily penned note from his sister, Amelia Simmings.

Dear George: —
Newcomb has just told me the news that you and he have been asked to serve on the organizing committee of a new organization which is to be called the Save Boston Association. Newcomb has overcome his usual reluctance to put himself forward in anything and, of course, will serve. You must do so also. Your name will be of great importance and we must be represented since everyone else will be. I have just come back from the Morning Reading Club where Henry Salter gave a talk. We must and we shall clean up Boston. If we do not, this will become an Irish city run by the Roman Catholic Church. For your own self-respect and for ours I am sure you will join Newcomb on this committee. . . .

If Apley was slow to act it was more because of natural caution than through lack of courage.

It seems to me [he wrote to his sister in an answering note] that all this business is rather sudden, that we may all of us be growing a trifle hysterical. I should like to consider more carefully what the "Save Boston Association" means and exactly what it is trying to do. We seem to forget that all these abuses have been going on for quite a long while without causing any of us any real discomfort. You know how quickly you jump at things, Amelia.

You will be glad to know, however, that Catharine is in hearty accord with you. I have never known her so deeply interested and we have been discussing this during the entire evening. I still do not feel that I am the man for the place.

His realization of the importance of the Save Boston Association to the ultimate public welfare finally overcame his disbelief in his own fitness and his name appears upon the list of early organizers. Once embarked on such a cause, Apley was not the sort to turn back. For many years he was indefatigable in raising money and in appealing personally to his friends to join the growing roster of members.

The work accomplished by Henry Salter and the Save Boston Association is too well known to need mention here, except in so far as its activities affected Apley himself. The political significance of the Save Boston Association, the effect which it had in stimulating the public conscience to many abuses, its fearless revelation of many irregularities, resulting even in the confusion of many public officials, all form a part of Boston history. Better yet, this association furnished the impetus for the inception of many other civic groups such as the "Teachers' Investigation Association" which has done so much to eradicate many deficiencies in our public teaching, and the "Guardian Association," and, in later years, the "Parents'

Association," which has brought startlingly to our attention many of the moral lapses of our own children.

It was a source of deep pain to Apley that this new interest of his met with doubt and opposition in certain quarters, even from members of his own family who saw affairs with a perspective with which George Apley could not agree. A letter from his Uncle William distressed him.

Dear George: —

From what you told me the other night when you came to me seeking a contribution for the Save Boston Association — take an old man's advice. You are biting off a good deal more than you can chew. I am pretty familiar with the type of person you are trying to attack because I have had a good deal to do with him. You do not understand him; he is too much for you and, mark my words, sooner or later he will get you into trouble. He doesn't care a button for anything you think. . . .

There is also extant a letter from his cousin, John Apley, expressing a somewhat different point of view: —

Dear George: —

You won't mind my giving you a piece of advice, will you, as we have always been friends? The other afternoon at the Club in Cambridge they were talking about you, saying that you were getting to be a reformer and that your ideas were almost radical. They tell me that you are in this new organization which seems to be designed to mind other people's business and that you are joining all the other Catos and censoring a lot of things that you really don't know anything about. You're too good a fellow, George, to get mixed up in anything like this. Besides, you know it's unsound; it isn't going to help you with the people you like and who like you. Make your horse jump

over the mud, don't try to gallop him through it and don't you
mind what Catharine says either. . . .

There is no doubt that Apley was subjected to much similar
advice. In the light of what we know, it might have been better
had he followed it, but in many ways it is to his credit that he
did not.

"I neither like nor enjoy what I am doing," he wrote to his
Uncle William. "You may be right in what you say, as you
nearly always are, but I feel this to be my duty. I am sorry I
must go ahead."

It is only on looking back over the events of a life which is
finished that individual episodes take their proper place, and
so it is with George Apley's emergence into public affairs. Only
when his entire life was completed could one fully understand
the difficulties which he was storing up for himself when he
took the position that he did, because he considered it his duty.

At this period in his life, however, his interest in these affairs
was more passive than it was later. His life at the time was vivid
with other concerns, several of which one may mention. The
most important is made self-explanatory by a copy of a letter
which he sent to the Committee on Admissions of the Province
Club, and marks the beginning of a collision which the present
writer knows that Apley would gladly have avoided.

My dear Sirs: —
I noticed to-day on the bulletin board that the name of
Marcus Ransome has been proposed by Mr. Storrel Moore and
Mr. Franklin Fields for resident membership in the Province
Club. I wish to express myself as unalterably opposed to his
admission.
I do not object to Ransome personally and I have sat with

him about the directors' tables of several small companies in which we are both associated. Although he has only been in Boston for ten years, he has good manners and is superficially a gentleman. He may not possess the same background and antecedents which characterize most members of the Province Club but I do not believe that his appearance here would be objectionable. I wish to make it clear that it is not because of Ransome personally that I move to oppose him.

Rather, I move to oppose the motive which actuates Messrs. Moore and Fields in putting this man up for membership. They are not doing so because of family connections, nor because of disinterested friendship, but rather because of business reasons. It is, perhaps, too well known for me to mention it that Mr. Ransome has been instrumental in bringing a very large amount of New York business to the banking house of Moore and Fields. This I do not think is reason enough to admit Mr. Ransome to the Province Club, a club which exists for social and not for business purposes. I, for one, shall feel that the Club has lost much of what is good in it if the Committee acts favorably on Mr. Ransome. I am sending a copy of this letter to Mr. Moore and another to Mr. Fields. . . .

It may readily be understood that the importance of the two above-mentioned gentlemen in Boston business was so great that this act of Apley's assumes the proportions of one of considerable moral courage. He was standing against his own kind for what he felt was a principle, and in the end he may be largely thanked that the Province Club to-day maintains its old standards and still remains known as the best club in Boston, broad-minded, yet conservative. This letter, however, aroused a species of dissension which has not been forgotten, for it struck a spark from the well-known high temper of Mr. Moore, which divided Boston into factions. Many persons who had never heard of Ransome before, including friends of George Apley, eagerly espoused his cause. The answering letter from Mr. Moore is still among the late George Apley's papers: —

My dear Apley: —
If you interested yourself in business more than in a variety of social pursuits you would know enough to mind your own business. What is the matter with Ransome that you should write this ridiculous and puerile letter to the Province Club? I ask you to reconsider it at once. . . .

The copy of Apley's letter which he preserved is equally curt.

My letter to the admission committee explains itself. I do not care to reconsider it.

When one recalls the ensuing excitement it is not surprising to find floods of protest still extant. There were letters of expostulation and letters of pleading from many who realized the embarrassments which Apley's stand would cause. There is even a letter from Hugh Tilton, Secretary of the Province Club. "I appreciate your objection," he writes, "but I wonder if you consider its implications." It is clear enough that Apley considered them.

If Mr. Ransome is elected, [he wrote in a second letter to the Committee] I myself shall be obliged to resign from the Province Club. You may consider this letter as my resignation, taking effect immediately upon Mr. Ransome's admission.

This statement of George Apley's, which was couched rather more in the form of a suggestion than an actual threat, reduced the situation *ad absurdum,* since Ransome could no longer be considered as a serious possibility. It is safe to believe that this stand of Apley's had repercussions which lasted until the day of his death and that he underwent much pain in doing what he always considered a disinterested service. What grieved him most was the impression gained by many that he was a "snob," for he had always prided himself upon maintaining democratic tolerance and anyone who has seen Apley at a single reunion of his college class can be quite sure that this is true.

On George Apley's fifteenth reunion and outing which was held at about this time at the Breaker House, near Pachogue Neck, Apley made an especial point of addressing every one of his classmates present, some of them less than mere acquaintances. More than this, he was careful to ask considerately and with real interest, how each was faring in the world; and he went so far as to call several by their first names for the first time in their acquaintanceship. This scrupulousness of Apley was commented upon freely by many of his intimates who had expected him to join the small group of Club members. There is no doubt that Apley would have preferred to do so, but he persisted strictly in this other course. Instead of being a snob, it would be more just to say that throughout his life George Apley was persistently democratic.

Greatly to his astonishment he was also taxed in many quarters with being personally hostile to Mr. Ransome himself — who, it appears, held a certain position in the downtown district and in West Newton, where he resided. This was the accusation which Apley denied most heatedly. Instead of disliking Ransome, he always asserted with perfect truth that he had a warm personal liking for the man and a general admiration for his business acumen. There are not many who know that George Apley had recourse to definite action to confirm these words. In the very heat of this dispute he went to considerable trouble to give Ransome some buying orders for securities that would ordinarily have fallen to another firm, and he could only express astonishment and bewilderment when Ransome refused to execute these orders. Nevertheless, his quiet interest in Ransome did not cease, and the present writer is one of the few who know that when Ransome was seriously embarrassed in the autumn of 1929 George Apley, though the two had not seen each other for many years, immediately came to his aid.

Enough has already been said of this episode to illustrate George Apley's point of view. It made him many friends, but also many enemies who to the end refused to understand his attitude. Many of these individuals also used the Province Club dispute as an actual precedent for doubting George Apley's integrity when he found himself faced with the final unmerited *débâcle* that did so much to shorten the latter end of his life and to sadden his latter days.

------·------

CHAPTER XVII

PARENTHOOD AND BIRD LORE

*Paternal and Other Responsibilities in the
Vicinity of Boston and Milton*

IN THE midst of these cares and demands which beset
any active life George Apley also found himself making
the welcome adjustments to the pressure of a growing family
for which the modest house in Gloucester Street, where he
and Catharine Apley still resided during the winter months,
was growing somewhat small. His children were now in
middle childhood; John Apley a thin, pale, and interesting
boy approaching twelve, and Eleanor Apley a golden-headed
girl of ten who had inherited much of the Apley looks and
charm. At this age, as George Apley once said himself, facetiously, he became obliged to regard these two as individuals
and not as playthings in the nursery. It had been Catharine
Apley's belief, inherited from her mother, that early childhood care and discipline were best administered by the woman
of the family; but now the younger Apleys had developed
sufficiently to break these ties and gave evidence of a deep
interest in their father's company which was returned with affection and solicitude. Thus, one finds the father considering
each year more deeply the problems of education; so, like other

parents, he found himself confronted by the many implications of this absorbing topic, which he faced with the earnestness characteristic of the best tradition.

His letters to his friend Walker at this period gave a very real insight into the life of the comfortable and well-regulated home.

I wish you might see Johnny [he writes]. I think he might amuse you because he seems in many ways like a reflection of me, when you and I attended Hobson's School, Micky, so many centuries ago. I have the curious sensation, common perhaps to all parents, of living over again a half-forgotten phase of my life in Johnny. I try to grope back into the past to make myself better understand his ideas and aspirations. Not very successfully, I am afraid. Catharine says I do not understand him at all, and possibly she is right. At her own request I have left the management of the children with Catharine until now, and I suppose they have been brought up much as Catharine and I were in our childhood. But now, quite suddenly, Johnny has become a person and so has Eleanor. I do not understand girls but I love her and I think she knows I do — at least I hope so.

Johnny is another matter. We have long talks together and I now make it a point each afternoon to return early from the office. I want very much for him to be happier than I have been, though heaven knows I have every reason to be happy enough. It is quite uncanny how much he understands of the characters in the household, particularly of his mother and me. Sometimes of an evening I read to him from the Waverley novels, of which my father was so fond. His great interest is football, which, of course, makes me very pleased, and I have told him about you and the football team at Harvard. We have also been out to Cambridge to see some games, but here I come to another point.

Something seems to be very wrong with Harvard athletics. For some reason the teams do not seem to have the fighting spirit which they had when we were young. The players seem soft, and I am sorry to say almost effeminate. I wish that you could come back before the Yale game and give them a talk. It seems utterly impossible any longer to beat Yale, and there is not much pleasure in attending a spectacle which is an inevitable defeat. I am glad to say that some of us at the Club are very much concerned about this and an informal graduates' committee is being formed, of which I am a member, to investigate the defects in our coaching system. I was told only last Tuesday at the Club lunch that one of our troubles is that certain players are not encouraged on account of social distinctions, that many fellows from South Boston and the suburbs who might make very good material indeed are frowned on by their teammates, who do not care to play with the type which we used to know as "mucker." This is all very well, if their team can beat Yale, but if it cannot I, for one, think these "muckers" should be encouraged, as long as they are Harvard men. The more of them the better, I say, if they can hold the Yale rush line.

I believe the time is coming when Johnny should go to one of these boarding schools. Of course they were not popular nor very well known in our day but now the consensus of opinion seems to be that they fit a boy for life better than the home. This may be right. At any rate, it gets them away from women into a healthy atmosphere of men where they can develop their minds and harden their bodies. This is why, if I can induce Catharine to part with him, I want to send Johnny to Groton. Even though I am a Unitarian and a pewholder at King's Chapel, my greatest wish is that he should be hard and strong. Eleanor is already entering Miss Rose's School. It is sensible and turns out a very good type of girl and the more I see of life the more sure I am that every individual should learn to conform to type.

This letter may be enough to indicate the trend of George Apley's thoughts along the line of education. It is evident that his ideas were eminently conservative but in the main thoroughly wholesome. He was quick to see the advantages of the Arnold and Rugby idea which has since chimed in so perfectly with Boston life. The product of this method, while the English importation was fresh and new and not softened by many of the radical and puerile innovations of the present, has, on the whole, been excellent. John Apley's contemporaries have been proof enough of this. They have nearly all upheld the best traditions of their class, having faced courageously the problems of a World War and the many social difficulties which have followed it. If the same cannot be said in as great a measure of still younger men, whose attitude toward sport and sex is sometimes shoddy, the present writer believes that this result is due to defections from the old system. It is true that some did not conform to the rigidity of that mould, including in a measure John Apley himself, but this was the fault of the individual, rather than of the system. George Apley's letters to his son during his years at school indicate his concern with this defect.

Dear Johnny: —
Of course Groton is not as comfortable as home but I did not send you there to be comfortable. I sent you there to grow used to a hard, clean life. A great many of us cannot do every-

thing we want. I want, for instance, to go abroad with your mother, you, and Eleanor, next summer; but I cannot because of business reasons and because of your grandmother's weak heart. I should like to go down to Carolina now with your great-uncle Horatio for the quail shooting, but I cannot because I am needed here. The thing that you must learn to do as quickly as possible is to learn how to get on with the other boys and to play football. . . .

Dear Johnny: —

I am very sorry you are unhappy and sometime soon I am coming up to see you, but you must remember that no one can be happy all the time. I believe that a large part of life consists of learning how to be unhappy without worrying too much about it. . . .

Dear Johnny: —

I cannot understand why your marks are so low. Both your mother and I are worried about this. We both know that you are not stupid and surely you are not lazy. Much of your life is going to be spent with very intelligent people and you also must learn to be intelligent. . . .

All of this is a parent's state of mind rather than George Apley's actual feelings toward his son. Beyond a concern for his son's success there was a deep affection and sometimes a genuine sympathy. As Eleanor Apley once said, a few years later, in the author's hearing: "Dad doesn't mean half what he says; half the time he's trying to be somebody else."

During the compilation of this volume John Apley himself has given his own impressions of this time, which may be extracted from his correspondence with the author: —

I don't blame Father very much for being disgusted with my record at school, for I can realize now that I was quite intolerable to most of my schoolmates and my masters. I should never have gone there because I did not fit in. Sometimes even then I think Father understood this in our talks at home or when we went walking in the country or sailing at Mulberry Beach or fishing at Pequod Island. At these times I think he understood me, particularly because I have a shrewd suspicion now that Father, much as he tried, had a good deal of difficulty himself in adjusting to his environment. He was always trying and making a pretty good job of it, but even then I could see that he was worried by a great many things. I don't believe he ever liked half of what he did, but simply everlastingly carried on, like the British Army. Of course, it doesn't alter the fact that I went through a good deal of hell at school. It helped me to see for one thing that Boston is a sort of Groton. Lord knows there are peculiar enough eccentric types but even these conform to a definite pattern of eccentricity.

It is amazing how much more a boy realizes than anyone thinks he does. I could understand, even when he was sharp with me, that Father had a great many worries, not the sort that would worry most people but genuine, none the less. In the first place, Mother didn't make things any too easy for him. She never really understood him, any more than he understood her. Then there were the details in his life, which he was working at conscientiously. He was getting himself involved in an infernal round of detail. Grandmother's health was failing and this worried him a great deal. There were all sorts of administrative affairs that had to do with dozens of small businesses at the office. Then there was his Club life, and his interest in undergraduate activities.

All these matters were assuming for him a peculiar and completely overestimated importance, so characteristically Bostonian. He was always doing a hundred things, not one of them amounting to much, and it was like him never to let anything go when he might have dropped the whole lot of them without any trouble. I never blamed him when he was hard on me because he was hard on himself — too hard.

This passage is only quoted to illustrate a point of view from one who was never wholly appreciative of George Apley's very genuine contribution to society and to his time. Yet, it is interesting that the son's letter, by some quirk of inheritance, is a repetition of the father's occasional doubts. I still can hear Apley saying, as he sometimes did, though he always smiled when he said it, "I seem to be getting nowhere." He said it, even when he knew very well that he was doing quite the opposite.

Thus, this picture which John Apley paints is, in many respects, overcolored and overexaggerated. There were many lighter moments in his life, nor was it without friendship and sympathy. A natural craving for exercise, which never entirely left him, set him to adopt the bicycle as a means of locomotion. In the early nineteen-hundreds it became his habit to arise each Saturday morning at four o'clock in the spring and autumn and to bicycle to the Caleb Goodrich's woods in Milton, where he gratified his love of nature and solitude by taking a bird walk and by jotting down in a notebook the number and species he encountered. These books have been subsequently left by bequest to the State ornithologist and their accuracy has awakened no little interest. It is to Catharine Apley's credit that she always understood completely his purpose in taking these weekly journeys, as he did not take them alone. For many years, in-

deed up to the last year of his life, he shared this interest in
bird lore with his old playmate and lifetime friend, Mrs. Clara
Goodrich.

It is truly astonishing [we find him writing] how much
Clara knows about birds and how little Caleb Goodrich knows.
In this respect Caleb and Catharine are very much the same.
Clara's feeling for nature is almost the same as mine. Caleb,
who occasionally accompanied us on these walks, has now given
it up and Clara and I wander farther afield with our spy glasses
and notebooks, particularly around the pools and marshes.

There can be no doubt that these walks were a great fulfillment to Apley, for we find him writing again: —

I always feel better after searching for birds with Clara.
The world seems to revolve more easily. I return home in a
better mood and all the cares of the office are no longer cares.

Again we find him writing: —

This morning, since we were spending the night at Hillcrest,
I took John and Eleanor on a bird walk with Clara Goodrich.
I was disappointed that they did not enjoy it as much as I did,
and Clara and I have both decided that they are too noisy to
come again.

At the author's suggestion Mrs. Goodrich herself has contributed to this reminiscence.

I like to think [she writes] that some of my dear lifelong
friend's happiest hours were spent in our forest and swamp-
land of a sunny early morning. If it is so, this alone is sufficient
reason for my husband's having maintained untouched this bit
of wilderness. Even to-day, as I walk alone, the kindly, quiet

spirit of George Apley seems to walk beside me. I can hear him saying in his quiet, gentle way, "I spied him first, Clara, the Carolina wren." I can see him still walking with the loose-limbed stride of a woodsman, his eyes alert, his notebook in his hands. The lines of perplexity were gone from his forehead then.

Following these Saturday walks, it was their invariable custom to join Mr. Caleb Goodrich at a hearty breakfast of baked beans, brown bread, and fishballs, a type of menu which was never altered from one year's end to the other.

Nothing could better refute the criticism of narrow-mindedness sometimes leveled against our society than the almost universal recognition of the platonic qualities of this relationship by all who knew George Apley and Mrs. Goodrich. This may be because they had the benefit of precedent of many other friendships between members of the opposite sex, and such freedom of social intercourse has fortunately been allowed to flourish here almost free from the blight of gossip or of suspicion. Caleb Goodrich and Catharine Apley were quick to recognize that this was simply one of the many instances of friendly devotion which they observed around them. Instead of trying to hinder this congeniality, they both accepted and tacitly encouraged it.

Curiously enough, the only protest which was ever heard came from a somewhat peculiar source, namely from the now ageing Nathaniel Pettingill who still made his daily call upon Elizabeth Apley each afternoon at a quarter after four.

Your dear mother [he wrote], who depends so on your devotion and whose every thought is an idealization of you, is naturally far too loyal to express any doubt as to your behaviour, nor, indeed do I, dear George, who have often felt myself in my poor way a second father to you. But I have known your mother so well and for so long that I sometimes feel I can read her thoughts, as we sit before the table in Beacon Street before turning to our Emerson. I believe she is worried, not because she has not the most absolute trust in her son, as I have also in you, but because she understands that appearances are important. It may be that I shall offend you but I do so in a good cause and as one who has been a devoted adherent to your family. Could you not arrange to see a little less of Clara Goodrich, or at any rate to visit her in the company of others? There is a connotation to these long bicycle rides and to these ramblings in the woods which may be misunderstood. Please consider this for your dear mother's sake, as she is far from well.

George Apley's reply is not extant, but at the time he was honestly indignant to the point of agitation. This indignation was shared by his own mother.

I have just heard that Nathaniel has sent you a very ill-considered letter [she writes]. I cannot understand why he is so peculiar, Georgie dear. He should know as well as I that there is nothing more beautiful than a pure friendship between a good man and a good woman. I have grown to love dear Clara, who has spoken of you so often, and I must say she gives you much that dear Catharine does not, and that is why Catharine is generous enough to love her too. I have spoken quite sharply to Nathaniel about this. You must give his letter no thought. No one will, no one can, share in his opinion.

There is something sadly pathetic in these lines of a loving mother to her son, nearly the last she ever wrote him. Elizabeth Apley must have seen, with that prescience of one who nears the end of a long journey, that George Apley would need the support and encouragement of another when she herself was taken from him, and much of that support in later years did come from Clara Goodrich.

------◆------

CHAPTER XVIII

SOLITUDE

The Severing of a
Last Tie and a Father's Growing Cares

ELIZABETH APLEY had persisted for many years in the custom of the Hillcrest Thanksgiving dinners. In November of the year 1908, ignoring protests of her physician, of her son, and of her daughter Amelia, the family festival was held as usual, correct in every detail. It was marked by the appearance of Jane Apley with an attendant, the first time in many years that George Apley's sister had attended such a large and public occasion. The pleasure of Elizabeth Apley may be readily realized. Indeed it was, in many ways, as she said herself, one of her happiest days. She is quoted as saying: "My fledgelings are with me again." Yet she may have had the premonition that it was the last time that they would be.

After the dinner the large front parlor was cleared, and Elizabeth Apley sat with her grandson John and her granddaughter Eleanor, watching a series of charades which had been arranged at her request by her son. With his customary ability to throw aside all appearance of care on such occasions, George Apley had given himself to the spirit of play. When the charades were over, his mother called to him, saying that she was

tired and would lie down, asking at the same time that Mr.
Pettingill come up to read to her. She was explicit that no one
must be disturbed, that the gayety must go on.

"Thus," George Apley wrote, "her thought of others persisted to the end."

An hour later, after most of the guests had gone, Mr. Pettingill descended the broad staircase into the front hall. There
was no need for him to speak. The strain of Thanksgiving had
been too much for Elizabeth Apley's heart. She had died as
her old friend read to her that afternoon, but the news was not
communicated to those outside the immediate family until
that evening.

Although George Apley had long realized the inevitability
of this blow, its suddenness took him unaware. Beneath the
calmness which he maintained was a shock of bereavement beyond his calculation. During all the adjustment in the weeks
that followed his reactions were slow.

I cannot express myself [he wrote in a letter to his aunt].
I still cannot believe that this support has been removed from
me forever. I cannot believe that there will never again be
someone who is convinced that everything I do is right. I cannot believe that the parlour in Beacon Street will be dark at
five o'clock and that her Sewing Circle will no longer meet
there on the first Tuesday of the month. I have never felt so
horribly, so completely alone. It is a very frightening feeling.
I can compare it only to my sensations when, as a little boy,
Mother would blow out the light and close the door and leave
me in the dark.

Under the circumstances it was not strange that he should
depend for a long time upon the consolation of memory. He

gave ten acres of woodland to the town of Milton, to be known as the "Elizabeth Apley Park." Her room in Beacon Street and her room in Milton he ordered locked, and he held the keys himself. He was assiduous in keeping every piece of furniture in the parlor at Hillcrest exactly as she had arranged it. He might have proceeded further along this line of action if he had not been prevented by the kindly good sense of Catharine Apley. When George Apley and his family moved to Hillcrest the next spring, Catharine Apley took complete charge, not only of the household indoors but of much of the grounds and gardens.

The unostentatious perfection of her arrangements must be recognized by everyone who has ever visited Hillcrest. The atmosphere of cheerful reality which her presence imparted to the whole estate could not but in the end be contagious and could not but serve finally to dispel much of George Apley's sadness. Indeed, those who knew him began to notice that he deferred increasingly to the executive ability of his wife. It was Catharine Apley who directed his mind to a subject which did much to interest him in the months following his mother's death.

In dusting and rearranging books on the high shelves of the long dark oak library at Hillcrest Catharine Apley came upon a volume which had been purchased from the George Washington library, probably by Moses Apley himself. George Apley, although he had prided himself in being familiar with the contents of the library, had somehow neglected this important item, which bore the indubitable signature of Washington upon the title page. His interest in it served to hold his attention even in this hour of his bereavement, and we find him writing to the librarian of Congress: —

On turning over the pages of a copy of a volume which formerly belonged to George Washington and which is now in my possession, I have discovered a single human hair in the centre of the book and my wife has encouraged me to write you about it. It is not the hair of either my grandfather or father, and no one else, as far as I know, has ever opened these pages. I wonder if it could be Washington's and I send it to you in the envelope enclosed herewith, in the hope that you may solve this mystery.

Many persons outside the Apley family must still remember the interest caused by this episode, which the Congressional Library also shared, although it was proved later that the hair came from another and unknown head.

"I feel as though everything for me had stopped," he wrote at about this time. But this was far from being the case. His conscientiousness for details was attracting a wider and more merited attention. Now that he was a partner in the law firm, whose name was changed to Ripley and Apley, his services were in growing demand as a trustee for estates, particularly of small properties held by charity. His services were also sought on various directors' boards. To list only a few of these latter gives some insight into the scope of his activity. Exclusive of a directorship in the Apley Mills which was his by right of birth, he was a director in the North End Cold Storage Warehouse Company, founded and controlled by his father, a director of the Water Carriers' Savings Bank when his uncle William Apley was president, a director of the North End, the South End, the Fenway, and the Basin Real Estate Trusts, a director in the Apley Heirs' Trust, of which his cousin John Apley was president, a director of the Apley Falls Gas Company, a director of the Apley Falls Water Works, a director of the Maine Pulp Land Trust, containing properties acquired by Thomas Apley, a director in the firm of Apley Brothers, and a director of the Apley Safe Deposit Vaults. Although it may be true that Apley had never assumed a leading position in any of these companies, his presence on the directorates was of considerable importance, as it did much to encourage others. It was his invariable habit to save the ten-dollar gold piece, customarily presented to the directors at these meetings, for distribution to the servants at Christmastime, for it pleased him to serve these various companies without actual pay.

If Apley had said that everything had stopped, it was only because he was being carried evenly on the stream of life, experiencing that same motionless sensation which a canoeist feels upon a quiet stream, although the landscape is gliding by on either side. Now and then some feature of this landscape would surprise him.

To-day John beat me a set of tennis [we find him writing to Catharine Apley from the Brent estate on Pachogue Neck]: John, who only yesterday was mewling and puking in his nurse's arms. It still only seems yesterday, Catharine. I declare I have no sense of the passing of the time. You and I are getting to be middle-aged people, although you do not look it and I do not think I do, either. Yet only to-day, at one of those clambakes on the rocks, Hugh Brent told me that I was getting set in my ways. I rather resented this. It seems to me that I have been broad-minded about a great many things always, too broad-minded. It seems to me that I have always been hospitable to new ideas, and that you and I have led a very free life. I told John as much, after we had finished that set of tennis, but he is still fresh from his visit to the Birchards on Long Island. He is still talking of dances and chauffeurs; he says the New York girls are prettier than the Boston girls and he wishes that we could be more like the Birchards. I told him that a fifth-former in Groton really did not know much about points of view, and I tried to explain to him that our relations of Pachogue Neck were some of the most liberal people in the world, that they are the products of the most liberal cultivation. Youth seems to be revolting these days but I am sure that this is not our fault. John is probably only feeling his oats. He says he has not got enough clothes, so I am sending him to McCulloch Barker's to buy two new suits. I am letting him select them himself and hope you do not mind.

Again a short time afterwards we find him writing to his friend, Walker: —

Can you believe it, my little girl is going to the Friday evenings? I saw her leave for the first time to-night with Hannah, Mother's old maid. What struck me most was her amazing beauty, inherited entirely from the Apleys. That beauty of hers distressed me a little. She was in a blue dress of a light, robin's-egg blue which Catharine had designed for her herself from one of her own old party dresses. She wore long gloves and patent leather slippers. As she stood in front of the fireplace for me to look at her, I had the impression of girls I used to know at dancing school at about the time when we used to hide downstairs in the cloakroom. Her hair added to this illusion. Catharine is not going to allow her to put it up until she comes out. Yet, as she stood there, I could see that she was more than a little girl; I could see that my little Eleanor is growing up. She is growing up and in some way I have never really known her. When she asked me whether I thought anyone would dance with her I could feel a lump rise in my throat. She was setting off with Hannah to face the world and she was afraid of it. I do not blame her much. Sometimes the world is a strange and brutal place. Life, they say, is what you put into it. For myself, I have tried to put in a great deal, and yet what is the result? I do not know my own daughter and I am afraid even that I shall never know her.

I should like to be friends with my children. It has always been my ideal to be a good companion to them and to have them treat me as one of themselves. But I wonder if this is ever possible. Enmeshed in the duties and perplexities of my own life, I cannot seem to adjust this life to theirs. They do not seem to be much interested in what I am doing. I had hoped that we might all take up gardening together at Hillcrest as my mother had taught Amelia and poor Jane and me, but somehow these children of mine do not seem interested in the flowers. I had hoped that we might play the same games together that we had played when we were children, that Catharine and John and Eleanor and I might be our own community, reading together and talking together in front of the fire of an evening. I can now understand the futility of this readily enough. The world seems constantly to be stepping in, or if it does not, neither Eleanor nor John seem to appreciate the value of these moments of relaxation. The great thing that John and I seem to have in common is a love of dogs, but as Catharine will allow no dog in the house, this does not take me very far. As for Eleanor, she has never been alone with me very much and now the world is stepping in to take her from me.

There is no doubt that this letter was penned in one of George Apley's more melancholy moods. Fortunately, these moods were not with him for long, as an early letter from Eleanor Apley herself attests.

Dear Father: —

I wish you were down here at Pachogue Neck. You always

have such a good time down here. You are different from the way you are at home because I don't suppose it is your house and you are different from the way you are at Pequod Island, too. Do you remember when we went out digging clams and how you slipped in the mud? I wonder if you could give me some money to get a new dress, just because I ask you. I should like to buy it myself, without Mother seeing me buy it. It would be a sort of a secret, wouldn't it?

Toward the end of this decade we find George Apley again in New York City. And again through no choice of his own, but because of the vicissitudes of his friend, Walker. These were caused by Walker's having contracted an alliance with a young woman named Mapes, who had appeared some years before in the extravaganza, "The Wizard of Oz." Although many of Walker's friends considered that this action of Walker no longer made them responsible, Apley remained loyal. We may add here, parenthetically, that this was only one example of a hundred individual kindnesses.

My father once gave me a very good piece of advice [he says in one of his letters to his son] and that is never to lend money to a friend. Friendship cannot be gauged in terms of money and should not be, yet you will probably find yourself, as I have, often beset by requests for loans from people who are hard pressed. You will sometimes be surprised from what quarters these appeals will come and most of them are the result of improvidence, gambling, and bad management. I have never been very successful, however, in reading these people a moral lecture. It has been my custom always to give the money outright and then as quickly as possible to forget about the whole transaction. I believe it is the kindest thing to do and I believe it is a duty.

It is quite probable that his visit to Walker included some such errand, but his reactions to the great metropolis, aside from Walker, have an individual interest. They concern the reactions of a denizen of another world, viewing what we must now consider as the beginning of a change for the worse in America. Thus the unconscious criticisms which he makes are peculiarly trenchant.

Apley stayed at that convenient hotel, the Belmont, now so unfortunately demolished for no good reason, a hotel which has extended its hospitality to so many from Boston. To many a man obliged to come to New York on business the facilities of this hostelry and the company he has met there have been so congenial that he has never left it except for reasons of absolute necessity. This was particularly true later in the post-war decade when the nervous excitement of New York City, the roar of its traffic, and the casualness of its manners assumed a rising crescendo. Nevertheless, it was necessary for many in these later years to visit New York in order to attend the theater, since producers who had once eagerly sought the commendation of a Boston public had turned a cold shoulder, due to the influx of an uneducated element in the audiences. When confronted with the problem of seeing a play and nothing else, the Belmont offered a happy solution. Close to the teeming Broadway district and closer still by good fortune to the Boston train, it was only necessary to take a few minutes' ride in a taxicab to reach the playhouse and, upon returning, there was always an acquaintance with whom to exchange ideas regarding the frequently unpleasant and oftentimes shocking dramatic spectacle.

I have never been as astonished at anything [George Apley writes to his wife] as I have been at New York. The Billy

Bradshaws and the Jack Jessups and I were speaking of it at breakfast this morning. They are taking the noon train back, but I cannot. Although we are Americans, we all seem like strangers in a foreign city. I do not like to think that it is setting the style for the future. If it is, I believe that the world is going mad, that we are reaching the end of an era. I can understand perfectly why you do not ever want to see it, for it is quite beyond our own philosophy. There are very few horses left on the streets; their place is taken by taxicabs and private automobiles with shining brasswork that pant beside the curbs. There is a pandemonium of motor horns and policemen. Broadway is full of strange electric signs that move in nervous patterns. My senses are stunned by gilded ostentation and shallowness. I wonder if the time will ever come when we shall hear only motor horns instead of the rattle of wheels and the slap-slap of horses' hoofs on Beacon Street. Old and young, everyone seems to be possessed with a sudden craze for dancing. At many restaurants where I have been with Walker and his wife, the floor is reserved for dancing and the diners dance between the courses of the meal.

Walker, genial as always, was much surprised at my *naïveté*. I do not object to dancing, as you know, and I flatter myself that I am considered a rather tolerable waltzer, but the steps here are surprising and frequently suggestive. I am sure I am as broad-minded as most people, but I could not suppress a start of astonishment; and I wonder what you would have said to behold men and women with their arms about each other, locked in a close embrace, walking and hopping to this "ragtime" which I once heard Eleanor playing upon the piano. The names of these dances reveal their nature: the Turkey Trot, the Bunny Hug, and the Grizzly Bear. What astonished me more was to see people whom we both know indulging in them freely. After watching for some time, Walker's wife asked me to follow their example. She said that she could teach me quite easily, as the steps were not much more than walking backwards and forwards in time to the very obvious beat of the music.

As a matter of fact, she proved a very able instructress and I actually enjoyed myself very much. I think people are quite wrong in their criticism of Walker. The Mapes girl is very charming and amazingly gay and beautiful. Natural, spontaneous, and yet quite different from anyone I have ever seen, she is really a very kind, simple person. She comes from Schenectady, New York.

I think I shall be very glad to get home and away from this restlessness and uncertainty. I wonder if this represents a phase of life that John and Eleanor must live. I can understand much better now certain snatches I have heard of their conversation and I think we must both be broad-minded and very tolerant. It may be a time of change and we must conform to it; we must try to combine what is good in the new with the good in the old.

There is no doubt that this visit to New York made a profound impression upon Apley. A short time after his return he gave a small, congenial dinner. After the meal was over the parlor floor was cleared, a professional appeared to play the piano, and Apley, and others versed in them, exhibited some of these new steps. Many of the company finally joined, and, later still, many took lessons, as it was found to be on the whole a healthy form of exercise, but Apley was already aware of the rumblings of a changing world.

I am quite convinced [he wrote] that we are approaching the end of an era. I don't know quite what will happen to us, but I have faith in our common sense, just as I have faith in our inheritance.

———•———

CHAPTER XIX

HARVARD AGAIN, AND ENGLAND

Old Haunts of Youth
Viewed through Maturer Eyes; and
More Cares of Parenthood

IN THE autumn of 1910 John Apley, after spending a large part of the summer at Dixon's tutoring school in Cambridge, successfully passed his entrance examinations for Harvard and entered the Freshman class, thus affording the father a new and vicarious interest. Cambridge, like the world at large, was changing. Though many of the landmarks still remained, the Cambridge which John Apley faced was more of a city than a town. There were available for the students many luxurious accommodations. The vicinity of Mt. Auburn Street was called facetiously in the press the "Gold Coast," and it was not difficult to understand the connotation, when one considers the huge new student dormitories which had been built up in that neighborhood — Dunster, Claverly, Randolph, and Westmorly Halls. In addition to these a subway, connecting Cambridge and Boston, was nearing completion and eventually Boston would be twelve minutes, instead of an hour's distance, from Cambridge. These changes deeply bothered Apley, and he could not view them all as improvements for the better. In his opinion matters were moving too fast, far too fast.

> The other day [he writes] I took my customary walk across the Common. The Common, due to unceasing vigilance, has undergone no great alteration. The façades of the buildings on upper Beacon Street and the State House dome are much the same, but what of Tremont Street and what of Boylston? The shops and theatres there are startling. Boston is growing to be a very large and restive place, yet, in a way, I am proud of its growth.

Letter to John Apley.

Dear John: —

I suppose a father always writes advice to his son upon the important moment of his entering college and I am no exception. A large part of your future life will be influenced by what you do this next year. The habits and ties you form will be with you always. At least, they have been with me, and I want you to do the right thing. There is a great deal of talk about democracy. I thought there was something in it once but now I am not so sure. You cannot be too careful to select friends who have the same bringing-up as your own, and I want your friends to be my friends. You must bring them around to Beacon Street as much as possible on Saturdays and Sundays. Besides helping yourself, this will also be a great help to Eleanor and I am sure we can all enjoy ourselves a great deal.

Sometimes it seems to me that you are reticent in talking to your parents. You are making a great mistake, John, for I really think that I could be a good deal of help to you. I am still quite well-known around the Club, you know, and your first object must be to "make" the Club. I believe that everything else, even including your studies, should be secondary to this. You may call this a piece of worldly counsel but it is worth while. I don't know what I should have done in life without the Club. When I leave Boston it is my shield. When I am in Boston it is one of my great diversions. The best people are always in it, the sort that you will understand and like. I once tried to understand a number of other people, but I am not so sure now that it was not a waste of time. Your own sort are the best friends and you will do well not to forget it.

I hope very much that you will do nothing to give you the reputation of being peculiar. I know well that it is hard always to be conventional, for one rather struggles against convention at your age. On the whole you will find that this struggle is a mistake and really a great waste of time. Do not try to be different from what you are because in the end you will find that you cannot be different. Learn to accept what you are as soon as possible, not arrogantly but philosophically. You represent something which is potentially very important. In a sense you are setting an example to other people. You will not believe it now, but you will later. I can see already how futile it is to give advice and yet I shall persist. It is only because I want you to be happier than I have been. It is only because I see so clearly that a great part of my uneasiness in previous years has been entirely wasted effort. I have been chafing in a way at an environment, and only lately it has been coming over me that it is the only environment in which I could possibly have survived. I am proud of it, I am thankful that I am in it. Some day you will be, John. I suppose now that you find yourself laughing at certain mannerisms and certain dictates of convention. You will not do so in time. You will find they are all very important, not only to yourself, but to other people.

It occurs to me that I am being more intimate and frank than I have been with you ever before but I am doing so for your own good. I am going to be so frank as to talk to you

about women. You will, of course, be honourable with all
women, because you are my son. You will treat them all, even
women of pleasure, if you see them, with invariable consideration and respect. I am not anxious about this. I go back only to
a certain phase which I went through when I was about your
age. It sometimes seemed to me that the type of girl with whom
I was brought up was somewhat dull, largely because I had
known her and her kind always. This is a very great mistake.
In the end she is the sort with whom you will get on best. Your
own mother is a perfect example of this. You know how much I
depend on her. I depend on her more and more each year.

If I had married someone from New York, or someone from
the Middle West, as some of my acquaintances have, there
would have been an inevitable clash between standards and environments. Believe me, marriage is difficult enough without
this added complication. It is well for you to keep this in the
back of your mind, though I don't suppose you will. The other
day my friend Vassal and I were talking and we both agreed
that after all Boston girls are the best.

This leaves me to make a confession to you because you are
my son. It is a matter of which I have seldom spoken but of
which I think a great deal and it has had more to do with my
life than I readily care to contemplate. I was once in love with
a girl whom I met on Central Square, and I will allow nothing
to be said against her. I owe it largely to my father, who saw
the folly of this infatuation, that I was not involved in quite
a different life from the one I have led. I have been bitter about
it for many years. I have sometimes wondered, as we all wonder about such things, whether it would not have been better
if I had married Mary Monahan. I suppose this may amuse
you; but it would not, if you had seen her. I am aware now
that it would have been a very great mistake. I mention it to
show you that I may not be such an old "fogey" as you think,

and also to show you that life is dangerous at your age. I have opened this page for you for a moment because I want you to realize that I have some authority to speak as I do in the beginning of this letter. For better or worse, we are what we are. Don't try to be different, John. . . .

Thus, at the end of this decade, we find Apley finally reconciled to that important precept, "Know Thyself." He had developed in stature both as to assurance and as to resignation. Catharine Apley herself appears to have felt this, when she traveled with George Apley and the Thomas Wilkinsons for a bicycle tour through England. She writes: —

Dear Mother: —
George has been perfectly sweet all the time and such a distinguished person. Of course, we visited Sir Thomas and Lady Hadley to see the portrait which George is thinking of buying for the museum. Everyone was really delighted with George and he seemed entirely at home in English country life, more at home I think than he really is in America. He no longer wants to wander away by himself in that lonely, moody way of his that you have noticed. Instead, at times, he has been the very life of the party. I think after this when he returns to Boston he is going to be a good deal more conscious of his position there and will do much more to take his place. He seems to realize that the things I have wanted of him for so long are really the important things. I think I have done very well with George and I am very proud of him. . . .

A letter from George Apley is couched in slightly different terms: —

I find it just as well to do what Catharine wants. It saves such a great deal of trouble. Thus I have let her buy the tickets and arrange everything. We have visited a great many Norman churches and a great many people to whom she has letters and, curiously enough, our old life seems to go with us everywhere. It is singular how many people there are from Boston. It reminds me of the last trip I took abroad, a long while ago, but this time I have found it pleasant. We all know each other so well and we all get on so well together.

I suppose this is because I am getting old. As I look back upon my life, nothing much seems to have happened to me. Perhaps this is just as well but I still wish that something might happen. I should somehow like to know what I am made of. I wonder if I ever shall.

He did not know, when he wrote this letter, how close he was approaching to this realization of self and what demands circumstance would make upon him. He did not know until the summer of 1914, which marked the outbreak of the European War. It was not until the time when he took his place among the few who were to arouse our national conscience that Apley was to find a true scope for his character. In a way his entire life was a preparation for this, as we shall see in dealing with this subject.

———— • ————

CHAPTER XX

WAR DAYS

*Dealing with the Difficulties
Of Living in a Reluctant and Neutral Nation*

THE ATTITUDE of Boston toward the questions involved in the World War was essentially George Ap-
ley's attitude. It would be difficult for this to be otherwise since
the conscience of those like Apley was the basis of the Boston
reaction. Those who say that New England has become decadent would do well to remember the lessons of the war. The
same inherent sense of justice and of differentiation between
right and wrong which brought Boston to the forefront in the
American Revolution and in the Civil War were to work
again with an equal force.

"To any rightly thinking person," George Apley wrote in
a letter to the *Boston Evening Transcript* in the early part of
1915, "there can be no compromise between wrong and right.
Germany is wrong and the Allies are right. The devastations of
Belgium and the atrocities of the invading horde of barbarians
are an outrage to civilized mankind."

This point of view he held in common with all but a few
radicals and eccentrics. From nearly the beginning of hostilities

George Apley began to devote the full force of his interest to the Allied cause. As the conflict spread and its vital issues became more pronounced, until it was patent that democracy and all human freedom were in the balance, Apley became more and more bewildered at the indifference of the rest of the country to this truth. He laid it, as many others did, to the vacillating tactics and to the intentional blindness of a Democratic administration. He watched with growing impatience our temporizing with Germany, which must forever be a blot upon this country. He felt it was his duty to express himself freely upon this subject and he was careful to do so on every occasion that offered itself.

Again, as in many other phases of his life, his letters to his friend Walker are of particular value here. He speaks for himself in them, with a spirit of conviction and sacrifice which even his enemies, and he made many in these years, could not but reluctantly admire. For nearly the first time in his life he was confronted with a real cause in which he could act from definite conviction. For the first time in his life he was at his best, a man of militance and fire.

I cannot understand George [we find Catharine Apley writing]. The war seems to have utterly upset him. He can talk of nothing else, nothing else seems to interest him. At the Caldwells' the other evening we met a Mr. Nixon who had studied at Heidelberg and who had some pro-German leanings. George was so upset by this that I was afraid he would grow violent, particularly when Mr. Nixon said that the German army was better equipped and disciplined than the French. The library at Beacon Street is one great mass of maps stuck with pins to indicate the opposing lines. I do hope for all our sakes that the war will be over in a little while.

Yet Catharine Apley herself was being carried forward on the tide of sentiment. She shared, with many others around her, a deep affection for France and for the cool courage and the debonair spirit of the *Poilu*. Thus we find her writing again in the spring of 1916: —

George brought the dearest French officer to dinner, who is over here on a mission to buy munitions. He was so beautiful in his new horizon-blue uniform and hardly older than John. His manners were absolutely perfect and I am so proud of the way Eleanor speaks French with him. Eleanor, of course, wants to be a nurse in France but this is completely absurd.

The present author, who served with Apley on many war committees, noticed a very great change in him, a new assurance, a new decisiveness, and a demand for action which is reflected in his letters to his old school and college friends.

Some of us [he writes] are trying very hard here to prepare public opinion for the inevitable. It is quite clear, from the information we are able to gather through several informal committees of which I am a member, that this country is riddled with German spies and the brains of the system are actually located beneath the very shadow of the Capitol Dome in Washington. There are a number of rumours here that we are endeavouring to run down of undercover activity. There are too many Germans in Boston and all of them should be watched, now that they have placed themselves beyond the pale of civilization by their policy of frightfulness. I believe it is absolutely true, as it is rumoured, that concrete emplacements are being built on the hills around here for heavy guns and that there are a number of wirelesses along the coast which signal to submarines. There is nothing to do now, of course, but to wait. In the meanwhile, I for one am very sorry that any tacit approval is given Germany by employing not only a German, but an ardent German sympathizer, as a director of our Symphony Orchestra. It may be true that the man is an artist, if any German can be an artist, which I very much doubt, but any sympathy with him is only a compromise with injustice. Besides this, the man is probably a spy besides being a musician. It is shocking to me also that there is a certain amount of tolerance in Harvard University. Thank Heaven, most of the students there take the right position, but John tells me that certain members of the teaching staff actually speak favourably of Germany in lectures. Obviously, a stand for neutrality is absurd in the face of overt hostility. It must be clear to everyone that Germany is endeavoring to embroil us in a war with Mexico, and yet nothing is done about it by the sentimentalists in Washington. Thank Heaven that there are a few voices crying aloud in the wilderness and I hope that my own is among them.

As one reads these letters in the light of the present, their contents may seem unreal, since much has happened in the way of disillusion. Weary tolerance has crept over many, which was not present at the time when George Apley wrote. His sentiments may have been right or wrong, but this in no way alters the strength of his deep conviction. Like his ancestors, Apley was standing squarely for the right. When the *Lusitania* was sunk on the seventh of May, 1915, he breathed a sigh of relief, for it was his opinion that his country would at last stand for the right. The amazingly supine attitude of the nation at large pained him, as did the temporizing tone of President Wilson's notes, which left an actual loophole for discussion; and his activities in the various protest meetings against the sinking of the *Lusitania* are very well remembered.

He writes to Walker at about this time: —

There is another ugly phase of the situation here. It has to
do with our racial situation here in Boston. Since the sinking
of the *Lusitania*, much of the Irish element, due to the fanatical
ideas of certain Irish Independence agitators, I suspect is tacitly
in sympathy with Germany. I heard yesterday that many persons are going about saying that Germany did very well to
sink the *Lusitania*, that she was an armed vessel carrying munitions. This seems incredible, but I have reason to believe that
it is absolutely true. In the event of war I dread that the Germans may stir up something close to strife in Boston. The hold
of the Catholic Church here is particularly sinister. In the last
few years a number of religious institutions have been buying
tracts of land for schools and orphan asylums. It is very noticeable that each one of these sites is selected on a piece of rising
ground, commanding a view of the country for miles about. It
is not reassuring to feel that these sites have been chosen with
suspicious military accuracy. An enormous amount of concrete
is being used in these constructions and it is even said that gun
emplacements are being made. It is certainly high time that
there should be some sort of preparedness. I wish there was
something active that I might do, but instead I have been born
at the wrong time. I have already volunteered for the American Ambulance, only to find that there is a need for younger
men. I had not realized that I was old. I do not feel particularly
old. All I can do is to contribute as largely as my means will
allow and I have offered John the opportunity to join this
ambulance service when he has finished his first year at Law
School. I am somewhat hurt that he does not take the idea as
seriously as I do. He has, however, agreed to attend the citizens'
camp at Plattsburg and this, at least, is something. I am anxious
to go myself but I am very busy with committee work.

A large number of committees are forming here, as I suppose they are everywhere else. A great many of us are trying to do what little we can in this crisis and in a sense I truly believe it is revitalizing Boston, that it is imbuing this city with some part of an old spirit, that it is refurbishing ideals. I am aware of a new vitality and a new pride everywhere around me. This is taking a tangible shape in the vast new Technology buildings on the other side of the river. It has a spiritual manifestation in the raising of our enormous new City Club, where every citizen is welcome as a member at a purely nominal cost and where our civic affairs and problems are open to discussion. I have attended several formal luncheons in this fine new building and I must confess that I have found the company there deeply interesting and refreshing. It is made up of individuals of a sort whom I have not an opportunity of meeting every day, but many of them are most congenial. We are in a great brotherhood there for the betterment of Boston. We all realize that we have a stake in this community. There are politicians and newspapermen, some of them very brilliant after one penetrates their rough exterior, lawyers and small businessmen. It helps me very much to form this contact with new minds and I hope that they benefit from me. Yes, it is highly stimulating, this rubbing of elbows intellectually.

And so it is with the war committees, a new burden which we are assuming besides our local charities. Besides several committees which have been formed to stimulate and to encourage positive action on the part of the administration, there are committees collecting funds and supplies of food and clothing for various groups of war sufferers, notably the Belgians, Serbs, and Poles. I regret that there is also a committee raising a fund for milk for German babies, but its efforts have made no great headway. Most of these groups are remarkably democratic; indeed many of their most active workers are persons of whom I have never heard before. This has raised a suspicion that certain persons are using this means to have themselves recognized by a section of society that has been more or less closed to them, but I do not believe this. At any rate, it is no time for social distinctions. I am very glad to see both Catharine and Eleanor, while they are making bandages for the Red Cross, rubbing elbows and laughing with women from the Newtons. It is all a part of this new spirit of camaraderie.

I have spoken to you before of this new spirit [he writes again]. It makes me very proud of the place I live in. Its genuineness is attested by a species of religious revival. We have just received one of the most remarkable men of the day here, of whom I had never heard, but perhaps you may have. The man's name is Billy Sunday, a revivalist with genuine oratorical gifts. He has erected a huge tabernacle on Huntington Avenue — a tent the size of a circus tent. His language is the sort that appeals to everyone. I was induced to go by my son, John, who said I would be interested. I was more than interested, so much so that after hearing him once I brought Catharine and Eleanor the next evening. The expressions of this man may be crude, but their very crudity is convincing enough to sway a multitude to tears and laughter. Although I admit I cannot agree intellectually with his Biblical interpretations, I am in deep sympathy with what he is trying to do. I met him at the end of one of the revivalist meetings and I shall never forget the interview. Sunday was seated in a space partitioned off behind the stage from which he had delivered his strange address. A dressing-gown was thrown over his shoulders. He was perspiring freely from his exertion. Sitting there he looked more like an athlete than a preacher. As a matter of fact, I believe that he is a professional baseball player. For the first few moments I found it hard to be natural with him. He seized my hand in a vise-like grip and asked me if I thought he was driving the Devil out of Boston. After a few moments he seemed quite as interested in me as I was in him. A middle-aged woman was sitting beside him, whom he introduced as "Ma." I was glad at the end of the interview to write him out a check for $5,000, provided he did not mention my name as a contributor. Yes, I am learning a great deal these days about all sorts of people. The more I learn, the more I see how much good there is in everyone. Sunday is coming down next week to give a ten-minute talk to the men at the Apley Sailors' Home.

It was about this time, as Apley was treading this broader stage, that he was obliged to make a stand of a very different nature, for he found himself confronted with a difficulty that concerned his own flesh and blood, his friend and second cousin John Apley. So much has already been said about this matter that it may seem like resurrecting useless gossip to air it in these pages. We include it only in that it illustrates the soundness of Apley's judgment.

One is safe in saying that Apley's cousin, John Apley, was of a different type, highly likeable and sought-after in society, but hotblooded and irresponsible. His marriage at the end of his senior year at Harvard, to Georgina Murch of Brookline, had left him comfortably off. The young couple had moved to the North Shore, where Apley's stables and his hunters are too well known to require much mention. The family passion, which amused and somewhat exasperated George Apley, was almost entirely confined to this peculiar sport.

I have just been to luncheon at my cousin's house [George Apley writes at about this time], an informal lunch with Catha-

rine and myself and Mr. and Mrs. Tom Brecking. The luncheon was quite informal and it was more like dining in a stable
than a house. Georgina had on a riding habit and John had on
riding breeches; so did the Breckings. Betty Brecking wore
breeches without a skirt. The plates had horses' heads upon
them and in the centre of the table was a silver horse, presented
to John by some hunt club. Nearly every room was decorated
with hunting prints and the hall was hung with riding crops
and even bridles. After lunch we three men retired for a while
to John's study to drink some very good brandy and there I
noticed that the inkwell on his desk was made out of a horse's
hoof. John talked to me for a while about the stock market
and I became quite alarmed at his ideas. Tom Brecking seemed
to me to be rather ill at ease. Once the brandy was finished, we
joined the ladies and went outside to a field where a number
of very fine horses were being led in a line by grooms. Then
Betty Brecking and John signified their intention of riding
some of these horses over a series of jumps, which they did
while the rest of us watched. It seemed to me that neither
Georgina nor Brecking appreciated the exhibition.

This quotation may be enough to foreshadow the ensuing
situation, although the writer very well knows that it burst
upon George Apley like a clap of thunder. Thus, the following letters from his cousin John Apley, which he kept in his
files, require no comment.

Dear George: —
I think you ought to know, among the first, that I am leaving
Georgina. We have never understood each other. I may add
that Betty Brecking is leaving her husband. I suppose this is
going to make a complicated situation but I think you may
understand it, George, better than most. . . .

Dear George: —

Your answer is incredible. When I consider you and Clara Goodrich, I don't see why you are in any very great position to read me a lecture about family. I know that this is the first time such a thing has happened to the Apleys — and what of it? . . .

Dear George: —

I have thought over our talk of yesterday, as you have suggested that I should, and I am still somewhat shocked by it. Betty and Georgina and Tom and I have all listened to you carefully and I must say I never knew you would have quite the character to lay your cards on the table the way you did. I must say you have us very nearly where you want us. I know that I have been financially obligated to you for a long while and now you have tied my hands. I even admit that you have done so out of your own perverted sense of justice. I admit that you believe in keeping the family together at the risk of ruining lives. Well, you've done it and due to you we are going to go along as though nothing whatsoever had happened. Believe me, my relationship with Betty will be as beautiful as yours but there's one thing that I hope. I hope to heaven some day I may be able to give you a little sound advice and meanwhile I should like very much to think that I shall never have to speak to you again. Don't worry. I shall, of course. . . .

Those who were close to Apley at the time know best the pain that was caused him by this complex affair. In spite of his satisfaction in knowing that the stand he had taken was just, it was hard to pay the cost of losing the affection of a relative and a lifelong friend. In doing so, however, he gained the respect of many others, among them his uncle, William Apley, who was failing in health.

In putting the screws on him [the old gentleman says in one of his last letters] you did, of course, the only thing possible. I would not have known you were capable of it, but now I know you are your father's son.

George Apley scarcely alluded to the matter to his own son, as he naturally considered the less said about such a scandal the better. His one allusion was indirect. It is contained in a letter written his son during a vacation in the latter's second year at the Harvard Law School, which he was spending with friends in New York.

I have just been confronted with a very difficult family crisis, one that has played heavily upon my emotions. Much as I hope it will not, it will probably come to your ears some day. If it should I hope you will remember that your father acted for the best, according to his lights. You are reaching a time when you will find out what my own father pointed out to me at a very trying time in my own career: that family is more important than the individual, that a family must be solid before the world, no matter what the faults may be of a single member, that a family has a heritage to hand down which must be protected. I can give you a number of interesting examples of this in the lives of people whom you have known always, but you probably know of these yourself. Several individuals in my own generation have been sent to the South and West, where they are probably making new lives for themselves, but here their names are no longer mentioned. A girl I knew at dancing school became involved with a public-hack driver. I do not believe you would ever know her name, because the matter has been kept as silent as the tomb. There is another man, a friend of mine once, who abstracted family silver from the safe-deposit vault and pawned it in order to pay a gambling debt. I do not know where he is to-day. These examples may seem harsh to you and perhaps somewhat ridiculous. They did to me, when I was young, but believe me they will not as you live longer. These matters are not actuated by pride because they are beyond pride. There are some things which one does not speak about and you will learn to follow this same reticence. I am glad to tell you before I leave this subject that there are very few skeletons in our family closet.

I am sorry that you are not here with your mother and sister and me during your vacation. This gadabout habit you have assumed of wandering away from Boston will not pay you in the end. Above all, I cannot imagine what you see in New York. You are not really fitted to cope with the place, and surely you can't like it. You face a foreign philosophy down there, but I suppose one is venturesome when one is young.

Your mother and Eleanor are both well. Eleanor is the centre of a great deal of society but the young men who come to the house do not seem to me particularly worth while and I am sorry that many of them are your friends. Though their manners are interesting enough, very few of them seem to have any definite prospects; and I can find out very little of most of their backgrounds as they nearly all are students from out of town. Eleanor takes the same lofty attitude about this as you do, that such things do not matter. I am not speaking entirely of money, because I hope that you and Eleanor will both be comfortably off. I am speaking of something that money can't buy — congeniality of habits and manners.

This reticence of which George Apley speaks, regarding family matters, did not confine itself to scandals. It was his rule also never to speak of his generosity toward many distant and impoverished branches of the Apley family. Only after his death did it become apparent how many of his relatives had him to thank for saving them through crisis and illness, for educating the younger generation, and, more than anything else, for saving many who became involved in the disastrous crash of 1929. It would be safe to assume that the estate which George Apley left at his death would have been even larger except for his family loyalty, especially as he suffered like so many others from trusting too much to local institutions. It was fortunate for his issue that a large part of his fortune was in trust when the firm of Apley Brothers became involved at that time through the unforeseen machinations of one of its partners; otherwise Apley would have stepped into the breach with all his resources simply because of the family name, for at that time there was no Apley in the firm.

CHAPTER XXI

―――――・―――――

THE WAR STRIKES HOME

*A Son in Texas
And Other Family Difficulties*

IN THESE years Apley had little time for more than casual writing and almost none for quiet meditation. He was deeply involved in the Preparedness Parade and the Allied Bazaar, and finally the actuality of war came home to him with the troubles on the Mexican Border. The present writer recalls a certain evening very well when Apley telephoned him in deep agitation. "Come to see me," he said. "John is going to the Border. John is going to war."

He was sitting in his library at Beacon Street and his son, John Apley, was with him. George Apley had taken the occasion to open a bottle of Madeira, for the news which had been conveyed to him that very evening that his son had joined the National Guard came as a distinct shock.

I never knew how much Father cared about me [John Apley wrote some time later] until the night I told him I was going down to the Border as a private of artillery, and he called me up to the library to speak to me alone. Incidentally,

we thought at the time that there was going to be real fighting
and that we would go in with Pershing's column.

"Of course," Father said, "it is the only thing for you to do,"
— and he paused and blew his nose, — "particularly considering that everyone else is going. I am glad that you are going
with a distinctly Boston battery, but this upsets a great many
of my plans." I knew what he meant by that, although of
course we did not allude to it. He meant that a permanence
which he had always been striving for was threatened. That
whole world of his was being threatened. He was thinking of
the portraits and the silver, but he was thinking of me, too.
He said, "John, when are you going into camp?" And I told
him the next day, and then he cleared his throat.

"John," he said, "perhaps I shouldn't keep you here. There
may be some girl that you would like to see to-night." I told
him there wasn't and he cleared his throat again. I could see
that he was very much embarrassed.

"I think it might be nice," he said, "if you went to call on
Evelyn Newcomb, don't you?"

"You mean you want me to get married and leave an heir?"
I said.

This was almost the only time I ever saw him blush and he
said, "Certainly not, but if you should wish to get married,
John, I should not blame you in the least," and I told him that
I would think it over. He changed the subject and began speaking of my immediate plans, but later, when he opened the
bottle of Madeira, he came back to it again.

"John," he said, "as man to man, is there anyone you care
about?" Then I told him that I had met a girl in New York
last spring.

"Good God," he said. "New York?" And then he took another glass. "I don't think anything I've done will amount to
anything."

I could understand him then. He was counting on me in a way. I had never known him quite as well as I did that night. I remember a single other remark he made. "I wish to heaven," he said, "that there had been a war when I was young. I wonder . . . Things might have been quite different." And then he shook hands with me and said, "I want you to be happy, John."

That was all, but as I say, I knew him better than I ever had before. He seemed to step out of the frame of his Sargent portrait. I don't suppose I ever realized till then that Father was a frustrated man, but then I could see that he had been trying all his life to get through the meshes of a net, a net which he could never break, and in a sense it was a net of his own contriving.

The imminence of war which was largely averted by the time that John Apley and his companions were leaving Framingham for the Border was succeeded for George Apley by a crisis of a somewhat different nature, occasioned by the death and burial of Mrs. Henry Apley, a somewhat distant family connection. Her sons, entirely within their right, buried their mother in the Apley lot of the Mt. Auburn Cemetery — that gracious, well-endowed, and beautifully attended piece of ground where so many have found their final resting place and where others hope to, including the present writer. It was Apley's invariable custom to attend every funeral of the family, but on this occasion, being much pressed for time, he was not among those present at the grave, nor did he attend to the grave's location, although he was one of the trustees of the Apley lot. Instead, he entrusted these details to his second cousin, Roger Apley, greatly to his subsequent regret. His letters, however, are self-explanatory: —

Dear Roger: —

Yesterday, happening to be motoring with Catharine toward Concord, we stopped at Mt. Auburn Cemetery as is our habit whenever we pass by it. I was particularly anxious to see how the young arbor vitae which we decided, after so much debate, to plant on the southern border, were surviving the early summer heat. I was pleased to see that they were doing very well indeed and, in fact, was about to leave when I noticed that Cousin Hattie had been placed in that part of the lot which I had always understood, and which I believe everyone in the family has understood, was reserved for my particular branch. I refer to the part of ground around the oak tree which my father had ordered planted. This was a favourite place of his and has a peculiarly sentimental significance to me and to my children. As you know, these matters grow more important with the growing years. I cannot conceive what prompted you to allow Cousin Hattie to occupy this spot. Not only do I think she should not be there, but also her pink granite headstone with the recumbent figure on top of it, which I suppose represents an angel, makes a garish contrast to our own plain, white marble stones.

I admit that the Henry Apleys are connections of the family, though so distant that they might almost not be considered as such. I might also call to your attention that the Henry Apleys, due to their straitened circumstances, did not and have never contributed to the purchase and maintenance fund of our ground. Except for Thanksgiving dinner, I do not recall ever having seen Cousin Hattie except twice when she had difficulty in meeting her grandson's tuition bills. Under these circumstances it seems to me somewhat pushing and presumptuous, although I like neither of the words, of the Henry Apleys to preëmpt the place they did without at least consulting me. I may tell you confidentially that I was very much disturbed by the reaction of Adam, our chauffeur, who came with us, carrying some potted geraniums, slips from some which my mother had planted. It was clear to both Catharine and me that Adam was very much shocked, from his manner, if not from any words.

It is no use to embroider any further upon this, but I cannot forget that I left these arrangements to you, as a member of the trustees' committee. I feel very sure you did not realize how your decision would have affected me, and how it would affect my Uncle William who is planning to rest near that spot, I am afraid in the very near future. Uncle William, as you know, has a series of violent dislikes and among them was Cousin Hattie. I hesitate to tell him that she is there, and yet I am afraid I must do so because he has asked me to go with him next week to Mt. Auburn so that he may pick out the exact spot he desires. I dread the repercussions of his discovery so much that I think it is up to you to make representations to the Henry Apley branch and to arrange that Cousin Hattie be exhumed and placed near the arbor vitae trees on the other slope. This section of the lot is not occupied at present. Will you please let me know what you can do about this. . . .

Dear Roger: —

I am very much gratified that you realize the seriousness of this situation. I agree with you it requires delicacy in handling, but I do not agree with you that it is too late to do anything about it. When the subway was built under Boston Common a great many bodies were exhumed from the old graveyard there and again buried. I note that you feel that you cannot see the Henry Apleys yourself, therefore you had better refer them to me. I shall write to Henry Apley to-day as you suggest. . . .

Dear Henry: —

Through a piece of mismanagement which I cannot believe is any fault of yours, your mother's remains have been placed in a spot in our family ground which I have always felt was tacitly at the disposal of our branch. I am afraid I must come to the point at once and ask that your mother be removed near the arbor vitae hedges on the opposite slope. I hope very much that you will agree with me when you consider the various implications involved, and believe me, I realize that my request may be trying to you in this period of your grief. I cannot avoid the feeling also that this accident has occurred because of my own pre-occupation in other matters, therefore I want you to realize that I, of course, shall defray all expenses. Please let me know at once about this as the matter is important. . . .

Dear Henry: —

I can ascribe much of your letter to the natural agitation which you must feel at such a time, but I see no reason for your final decision. The plot is family property until it is fully occupied. My one objection was regarding location. I do not feel that I have the slightest right in suggesting that your mother's remains be removed from the Apley plot, and I beg you to remember that I never did suggest it.

If, however, you feel that this removal is the most satisfactory solution of this difficulty and will relieve your own feelings, I shall not urge you not to do it. I repeat again that I stand ready to defray all expenses.

Such a contretemps, it will be recognized, bears no great novelty; rather it is a difficulty which has been faced by so many that nearly any reader may feel a sympathy for Apley's point of view and may comprehend as well the importance of such a negotiation. The consequence obviously foreshadowed a rift within the family and explains the reason for many breaches which are yet unhealed. At the time Apley was considerably surprised and not a little hurt by the unsympathetic, if not actually hostile, reactions of his own blood relations. He became aware for the first time that in spite of his most generous efforts certain of his own kin harbored for him a tacit resentment that bordered dangerously on dislike. It may only be added that he faced it with his usual composure in the belief that he had conscientiously done what was right.

Even his own uncle, Horatio Brent, who was suffering severely at the time from gout and from heart complications, saw fit in spite of his devotion to George Apley to remonstrate with his nephew's point of view. His letter, which is quoted here, is additionally useful in showing the impression that George Apley was making upon a certain segment of his own group. If this impression is neither a true nor a welcome one to those who admired him most, it serves merely as another proof that no man of definite character can help but create opposition.

Dear George: —

Here I am at Pachogue Neck. I am sitting on the old piazza where you have been so often, with my foot swathed in bandages. Your aunt, who sends you her love, will not allow me to take stimulants and is arranging to have an elevator installed to pull me upstairs to bed. Old Bess, my pointer bitch, who you remember took first prize in the Dedham Field Trial six years back, is sitting here beside me creaky in her joints and I am afraid the vet will have to put her out of the way by autumn. Frankly, I wish we had vets instead of doctors, because I believe I should be put out of the way too quite as much as Bess.

It seems funny to see the whole world look as young as ever, to smell the salt air and to see the water sparkling on the bay, and to be so old myself. Frankly, George, it is damnably unpleasant. I think of all the good times we had together. I think of when your aunt and I took you to Paris with Henrietta to get you over that abortive romance. You can laugh at it now, I guess. I think of lots of things, because there is nothing else to do, and I hope you won't mind your uncle writing a few words to you because he is fond of you.

Of course I have heard about the Mt. Auburn Cemetery row. Everybody at Pachogue Neck has been talking about it for the past two weeks. I don't mind where Hattie is buried. I don't mind much where anyone is buried except that I do not like the idea of throwing around ashes, but I wonder if you see yourself the way other people see you. I don't like people outside of the family to be laughing at you, George. I don't like to have them say that you are exhibiting a sense of your own pompousness and your own importance, because I know that you are not. I know what the trouble is with you: it is the *galère* in which we have all had to live. We have all been told from the nursery that we are important and that we must do the right thing. Believe me you don't feel important when you have the gout. I want to tell you something that it won't hurt to remember. I know that I have forgotten it often enough myself, but here it is. Most people in the world don't know who the Apleys are and they don't give a damn. I don't intend this as rudeness but as a sort of comfort. I know it has been a comfort to me sometimes when talking with your aunt. Just remember that most people don't give a damn. When you remember it, you won't feel the necessity of taking the Apleys so seriously. I hope you know the way I mean it. . . .

Although George Apley undoubtedly sympathized with this point of view, at the same time it bothered him; and his letters to his son John, who was stationed at the Border, showed that he was as keenly aware as ever of his own responsibilities. They show, besides, a growing solicitude for his children's welfare, and more than that a fear that his children might be hostile. In fact Apley was reaching that stage which every parent must face who observes that universal phenomenon, the perennial revolt of youth from the ways of its parents.

Dear John: —

I am glad to hear that everything is comfortable for you in Texas. Your letter sounds most interesting, although I cannot understand a large part of it. Of course this matter of preparedness is vitally important. It will be a perpetual blot always on the history of this country that we have not drawn the sword long ago to defend our national honour in the face of German frightfulness. Here at home we are doing what we can to help the Allies and at least we have not the torpid lack of interest of the hyphenated Americans and of the pacifists in the Middle West. The Boston Defense Committee, of which I am a member, is organizing a series of meetings. We are doing everything we can to arouse the public and to make them understand that heroic England and chivalrous France are standing shoulder to shoulder to save our own shamefully slothful country from the Hun. There are certain very well-informed people at the Lunch Club who believe that the Washington Administration is actually pro-German. I hope that you understand my point of view in spite of the levity with which you sometimes treat these matters. You must, since you are in your country's service.

There is also a belief here that the city is riddled with German spies who are doing their best to foist their propaganda on the public. They have certainly succeeded in reaching a large section of our South Boston Irish population which shows a definite hostility to England and an unbelievable sympathy in the revolutionary tendencies of Ireland. It is said also, and I have reasons for believing it, that the Irish Catholic Church here is actually pro-German. I am sure when you return you will not joke about these matters as you have in the past. . . .

Dear John: —

Your reply to my letter shows that you simply do not understand how scrious things are with us here in Boston. I hope you are not turning into a pacifist (believe me, I only say this jestingly because it is unthinkable), but such an attitude on your part is not even amusing, on the contrary, very dangerous. You must not forget that your name is up for the Province Club and such things as you have said in your last letter, if said in public, would really hurt you greatly.

One very agreeable thing has happened here recently. A British major, wounded and on leave, has been here giving a series of lectures to various discussion groups. He has given us a very real impression of what is going on in the battlefields of France. Besides this, he is really a capital fellow. His name is Fitzhugh Darcy, and he is staying with us at Hillcrest. With his help I have mounted an additional large map of the Western Front in the library with pins to show the various positions in Somme offensive. As soon as the *Transcript* arrives, he and Eleanor arrange these pins each evening. I may tell you frankly that Eleanor seems much interested in him and your mother and I are both delighted. . . .

Dear John: —

I cannot understand the tone of your last letter. I should think you might leave Major Darcy's background to my own good judgment. I certainly feel that I am able to tell a gentleman when I see one. When you caution me that he may be an adventurer, your caution seems to me gratuitous, to say the least. Everyone here is charmed with his manners. He is a public school man who has finished at Sandhurst and he knows everyone whom I know in England, which I believe you will agree is sufficient. He also has two medals for bravery, besides which his manners are utterly delightful. There is every reason why Eleanor should be interested in him. You would be too if you could hear him tell modestly after dinner how his regiment "carried on" in the Marne offensive. Your mother is charmed with him also. He says quite truthfully that Hillcrest is like a bit of home and quite different from establishments which he has visited on Long Island. I shall write to the Embassy in Washington about him as you suggest, though such a precaution is really needless.

One very shocking thing has happened since you have been away. The two great elms on the driveway circle are turning yellow. At the first sign of this, I telephoned the Arboretum and now a dozen men are investigating their roots. Major Darcy and Eleanor are out there with them as I write. They are going for a picnic on the top of Blue Hill. We have been very busy raising subscriptions for the French and British Loans. . . .

Dear John: —

Although I am quite sure that a communication I received from Washington to-day is utterly false, the question which it has raised has been resolved by the departure of Major Darcy. He has left after incurring debts up to five thousand dollars which I am gladly offering to underwrite. In spite of this your mother and I still feel that he is essentially a gentleman and not an adventurer. If he has been careless in financial matters, we both believe, as do many others who are in a better position than you to know, that his forgetfulness is caused by the frightful strain under which he has laboured. I am sure that he will be back with us before long.

I do not understand why Eleanor feels the way you do, but then there is a great deal about you both which I do not understand. Your friend, Royall, has stopped in to see her on his way to some small summer resort in New Hampshire. I have asked you before and I wish after this that you would be more careful about the friends you invite to the house. You must learn to realize that what may seem like a casual piece of hospitality to you may be a serious matter to Eleanor and to all of us. I have nothing against Royall personally, but the fact remains that no one has ever heard of him. Not only was he not in the Club at Harvard, but I cannot find that he was in any other club. His interest in Eleanor, which is somewhat marked, — sufficiently so to cause your mother to speak to me about it last evening, — can only be on account of her money, though such a thing means so little to me that I dislike to mention it. I believe nevertheless that he is not our sort of person. . . .

Dear John: —

Your reply about young Royall disturbs me very much. It almost makes me believe that you have been bitten by the doctrine of Socialism. You must think of this very carefully. Legislation is becoming rapidly more and more Socialistic. There has actually been a bill here before the Legislature for the State support of the elderly. This, of course, is a matter for private charity and not for Government interference. I was amazed last night to hear Eleanor speak warmly and favorably of such a measure, and I am afraid that her views come from you. I cannot see why you do not understand that such a philosophy is utterly subversive and spoils individual initiative.

The elm trees in the driveway circle are being artificially fed and look better. You will be interested to know that we have purchased a new Packard. I called on your Uncle William yesterday, who is very poorly; he asked after you particularly, and surprised me by saying that he liked you. His mind has been wandering a good deal of late. I think it would be well if you wrote him a letter. . . .

Dear John: —

Matters have been very difficult here during the last week. I want to bring them to your attention seriously, as the time is approaching when you must eventually take your position here as the son of the house. I have noticed that you have shirked this responsibility, but undoubtedly your military training in Texas will change you.

The matter concerns the lower rose garden. As you know it contains a number of Damask roses which your grandfather transplanted from your great-grandfather's garden in Salem. It is true that the bushes are growing old, and that the blooms are not particularly attractive. Nevertheless the idea of having them removed seems to me unthinkable, yet this is exactly what your mother proposes to do. I came upon her myself this afternoon and saw her tying ribbons around five of them. You know that I admire your mother more than any other woman, but nevertheless she has a very determined character. Although your Aunt Amelia has been to see her this afternoon about the bushes, she is still determined to have them removed. It has not been my custom to cross your mother when her mind is made up, but this is a time when I must do so. I am sorry to say that Eleanor takes her side. When you get this letter, will you please send a telegram saying that you do not wish the bushes to be removed. If there is no telegraph office near your artillery camp, I am sure that your captain or your colonel will allow you to go in town for the purpose if you tell him that the matter is important. It is important. . . .

CHAPTER XXII

WILLIAM APLEY

*The Natural Concern
Of a Nephew for an Uncle and for
The Honor of the Family*

IT WAS toward the end of this disturbed summer that an event occurred in the Apley family which was to tax the patience of George Apley, and indeed that of all his nearer relations, almost to the uttermost. The event to which we allude is sufficiently well known to all who read these pages, as indeed it is to a great many more besides.

During this period of intense activity, so soon to reach a climax by our nation's tardy entrance into the war, George Apley did not permit his preoccupations to interfere with the very nearly filial duty of calling each afternoon upon his Uncle William Apley, who because of failing health had been obliged to remain, since he refused to go to a hospital, in his Boston house. He had been there during the past year under the care of a Miss Prentiss, a trained nurse from the Massachusetts General Hospital. In spite of his illness, he still held firm to the management of the Apley Mills to an extent that obliged William Pritchard, the office manager of Apley Brothers and later president of the Apley Mills themselves, to call each day at the house.

Pritchard, who was at Harvard some years after the present writer and who is well known still as one of the most active contributors to Harvard athletic funds, has left an interesting account of these visits, in a memorial read at William Apley's death before the Apley Library Foundation at Apley Falls.

I believe [he writes] that the hold of this great man, who must be recognized as one of the true founders of New England, was loosened after the incredible difficulties of the Lawrence strike in 1912. Although then he was well over eighty it is through his efforts alone that Apley Falls did not feel the blight of unionism. It is due to his initiative that this paralyzing strike was stopped at the very boundary of the Apley Mills Township, and that the workers' union did not throw its lot in with the national organization.

When certain radical agitators appeared in town to disturb the Apley workers, always adequately paid and decently cared for in blocks of brick houses built at the time of the Civil War, it was William Apley who took a step which his younger associates frankly hesitated to envisage. It was William Apley who arranged for the arrest and expulsion from the Apley Falls Municipality not only of these agitators but of a certain subversive group within the Mills, whose names had been placed before him. By this decisive act, high-handed perhaps, yet fully justified in the interest of social justice, William Apley kept the relationship between owners and workers in the Apley Mills that of one large and happy family as it had been in the past, and may it remain so in the future.

Nevertheless those who admire him most have always thought that the moral force necessary to rise to this emergency had weakened "Uncle Will," as his younger associates were beginning to call that grand old gentleman. In those last days of 1916 his thoughts seemed to be more on the comfort of his employees than upon the increasing orders which were beginning to come to us from abroad.

Although not definitely connected with the management of the Apley Mills, George Apley always maintained the keenest interest in them as a family institution, and during his daily calls on William Apley frequently discussed the situation on the Merrimack.

Uncle William [we find him writing somewhat facetiously to his friend Walker] is as keen and bright as ever these days. He has the same impatience with me as he used to have when I was sent to learn the business at Apley Falls. Just this afternoon he said to me: —

"George, you don't know what you are talking about. Your father did right not to put you into the business."

Perhaps in a sense the old gentleman is right. He almost always is. At any rate he is still an imposing sight seated swathed in his armchair, looking like one of the Apley portraits, with Miss Prentiss, his nurse, standing behind him to arrange his shawls. Even in his enfeebled condition I feel the same respect for him that I have always felt. It is hard to escape the ties of youth. Yes, Uncle William's mind is very keen. Only yesterday he made another remark:—

"The Mills are going to make money out of this war," he said. "No matter what happens, keep the hands contented."

It is very reassuring to have someone in the house as competent, sympathetic, and sensible as Miss Prentiss. There had been trouble with other nurses, but at last Miss Prentiss seems to fill the bill.

The following letter from George Apley to his son, still on the Texas border, is self-explanatory and requires no further comment: —

Dear John: —

My telegram which was sent you last night has already apprised you of the blow which has fallen upon us. It is a bitter blow and not a little shocking in that it reflects in a sense upon the family name. I had feared for some time that your Great-Uncle William's mind was wandering, and now there can be no doubt of it. Without a word of warning to me or to any other member of the family, your great-uncle has married Miss Prentiss, his trained nurse. Of course the gesture is unbecoming enough to excite ridicule, and your mother and I and all of us are deeply upset, since it cannot help but remind many people of the vagaries of other old gentlemen. That this should have befallen your great uncle, a man of very real importance, is a sad thing. What I worry about most is that he will be remembered ludicrously on account of it. I think I am honest in saying that I do not feel concerned about the financial interest involved, but rather on account of your Great-Uncle William.

Yesterday, your mother and I spent the entire day in calling on the family and on friends to say that we were completely delighted and that we had known of this for a long while. This afternoon we have given a tea at Hillcrest for your new Aunt Emeline, which is Miss Prentiss's first name. I need not tell you that the family must stay together. If you have not done so already, I want you to send your Aunt Emeline at once a telegram of congratulation, also you must write to your friends saying that you have known of this for a long time and that you, like everyone else in the family, are pleased by this expected bit of news. It might be well for you to add, as I have, that your Uncle William considered this gesture as the most suitable way by which he could express his gratitude for Miss Prentiss's care. I do not think it would be a bad idea for you to send a telegram to your Uncle William. As I say, the family must stand together. . . .

It would have probably done no good had some friend attempted to explain to George Apley that he was unduly sensitive about this matter, for at such a time the cares of family preclude all breadth of vision. Nevertheless any man of the world must realize that such crises are of not infrequent occurrence. It has been recognized by many that there is a certain phase in the life of the aged when the warmth of the heart seems to increase in direct proportion with the years. This is a time of life when a solicitous family does well to watch affectionately over the vagaries of its unattached relatives, particularly of those who are comfortably off. Although this need is generally recognized in New England, one can recall a number of relapses and sudden surprises in the experience of one's own sphere of acquaintance. Such embarrassments, which are a part of life, have on the whole caused but little harm. Several former teachers, housekeepers, companions, and nurses have become in this way a recognized part of our society, and one is now pleased to acknowledge Emeline Prentiss Apley in that category. It may be added that all who have known her have come to admire her, and that to-day the Friday Afternoon Sewing Circle meets monthly at her home.

If Apley was not able at the time to envisage the broader aspects of the situation, he and the rest of his family carried off the affair with instinctive dignity. There was never a breath of criticism heard outside of the family circle. Nevertheless developments of the next few days could not but afford him considerable relief.

Letter to John Apley.

Dear John: —

I need not tell you that I am greatly pleased both with your attitude and with the interest you have displayed in regard to your Great-Uncle William. Of course it is exactly what I would have expected from a son of mine. I can even under stand your remark about your military interests and the deserts of Texas making the affair seem more remote to you than it might otherwise. Still you have understood its importance and have acted promptly.

I now can bring you what I am sure you will agree with me is a piece of very good news and a reward, I think, for meeting this crisis bravely and squarely. Yesterday, I had a conversation with your Uncle William and your Aunt Emeline. Your great-uncle, as I should have known, still has the interest of the family at heart, and frankly after my talk with him I feel guilty that I should ever have suspected otherwise. In many respects, indeed in nearly all, your great-uncle's mind is as clear as ever. It is his intention, now placed in legal form, that his property shall remain in the family. In fact he proposes simply that a comfortable allowance be made to your Aunt Emeline out of a portion of his estate during her lifetime, the remainder will go to you and Eleanor in trust. I have objected to this decision, believing that the remainder should go to me for my lifetime, the income to be distributed by me to you and Eleanor as I might see fit. You understand, of course, that I have no need for this money, but I feel that my experience and knowledge of life renders me a fitter steward for this responsibility than either of you two children. Frankly, I feel that you and Eleanor are both displaying certain tendencies which I believe you may regret in later years and which I should prefer to be able to control. However, your Uncle William's views are different and so the matter must rest.

On the whole I am very much relieved. I have been particularly pleased with the sensible and reasonable attitude of your Aunt Emeline. I can even sympathize with some of your great-uncle's feeling toward her. She is anxious to be helpful in every way; she is fully cognizant of the great good fortune which has befallen her, and recognizes the responsibilities of her new position as a member of the family. I am taking her on Saturday for a bird walk with Clara Goodrich.

There is one thing now which I think you must realize and to which you must give great thought. It is, in the event of your Great-Uncle William's death, which I am afraid cannot be many months off, that you will be very comfortably situated indeed in your own right. I cannot estimate exactly how comfortably. Your Aunt Amelia is writing to you about this also and though her advice may seem to you and me somewhat snobbish and strait-laced, basically it is sound. It is time, John, that you recognize more than you have in the past the importance of your new position. You can never forget now, whether you like it or not, that you bear the family name. It may not mean much to you now but it will. You will be beset with many difficulties. You will be harassed by a number of requests for contributions. You must learn to spend your money wisely and I need not say that your father will be ready with advice. Half of your income should be re-invested annually. The remaining half should be divided between living expenses and charity. I shall give you a list of suitable charities. The main thing is not to have too much money to spend. This I have found always bewildering and a sure pathway to extravagance and foolishness. You have only to look about you here among the unhappy members of the horsey and sporting set to see what happens when there is too much loose money in the bank. I have two immediate suggestions to make: one is that you start a collection of something, let us say of tapestries; the other is that you buy one of the large islands near to Pequod Camp. These two methods will use up profitably and pleasantly a great deal of loose money in a way which no one can criticize. I have found it very important to avoid criticism, and it does not look well to be extravagant. I beg of you to be careful about this and to remember always what we owe to the community.

If John Apley did not follow this advice, the results surely require no comment or criticism in these pages. Aside from sensible views on worldly matters, this letter exhibits a growing concern on George Apley's part about the development of his children. In the correspondence now in the author's hands, there is ample evidence of this concern, which cast somewhat of a shadow on his sunset years. Another one of his letters to his son, one of many filled with sound advice which John Apley has considerately turned over to the author, speaks of this new phase: —

Dear John: —
I hope that you will be coming back from the Border soon. I still cannot understand why the authorities were so inconsiderate as not to permit you to leave for your great-uncle's funeral. Our dear old friend, Colonel Stanhope, whom I have always regarded as one of the most important figures in Boston, feels as I do. He was kind enough to write to the Adjutant-General in Washington and later to the Secretary of War explaining why you should be granted a leave. There seems to have been some misunderstanding, but now it is too late to have it cleared up. I do wish though that you would write to

Major Stanhope on some paper, better than the Y. M. C. A. stationery which you use in corresponding with me, thanking him for his trouble and signing yourself "Affectionately," which I think will be quite right under the circumstances as Major Stanhope is one of the executors for your great-uncle's estate.

I hope very much that you will return soon as you are needed here much more than in Texas, especially as there seems no prospect of our being involved with the Mexicans. From many things I hear, there is danger of your falling in with a fast set. Although I rely on your good sense, there are reports here of heavy gambling and drinking and worse in El Paso. You must not let yourself be led to any lengths which you may regret by trying to be a "good fellow." I hope that I am as broad-minded as others, and you have always seen a decanter of wine on my table.

I am not as concerned with wine as I am with women, but surely your attitude on this subject is the same as mine. Perhaps I should have spoken to you before about some of the dangers, although I believe that silence is enough. There is only one thing for you to remember: that someday you will meet the girl that you will wish to marry. You will feel sorry if you cannot tell her truthfully about your past. I know that I felt so with your own mother. When you get home we must have a long quiet talk about this. In the meanwhile I need not tell you to remember that you are a gentleman and one that has the responsibility of setting an example to others. You have in my opinion been away too long from Boston, much longer than I ever have even on my trips to Europe. I do not think that this is a good thing, but I like to feel that you are with a Boston battery and that in the evenings you gather in your tents and talk about home and about the Club. That reminds me that your name will soon be passed on for the

Province Club. Some of your friends at my suggestion are also doing what they can for you at the Berkley Club. I think you might get a little more forward here if you were to write something, say a paper on the social conditions in El Paso. I should be very pleased to have you read it as my guest at some meeting at Beacon Street next winter, and if you have trouble with your facts, there is a very useful man in the History Department at Harvard who would be glad to help you to assemble them. He helped me on the occasion last week when I read an address on preparedness on the Boston Common. Although of course the ideas were my own, I did not have time to get the facts about the Ancient and Honourable Artillery myself.

I have been very busy here, rising at six in the morning, to prepare for my committee work before going to the office. There has been a great deal of trouble with the drains beneath the tennis court. Last week a skunk was caught beneath the piazza. I will leave it to you to imagine the condition of the front parlour. The sixteenth-century Apley blanket chest had to be opened and the handloom work had to be aired for a week. It was just as well that the chest was opened, as there were mice in it. I was obliged to spend an hour yesterday complaining to the company which is supposed to keep the house rid of mice.

———◆———

CHAPTER XXIII

A PARENT'S VIGIL

Intimate Aspects
In the Challenge of a Changing World

DEAR JOHN: —
One of the first things I want you to do when you get back, which we hear will be soon, is to have a serious long talk with your sister Eleanor, who I feel may listen to your advice. Your mother is writing to you about this also, but, as you know, she has not our breadth of view.

I need not tell you to keep this matter entirely to yourself as any further talk might do Eleanor everlasting harm. Last week Eleanor left Hillcrest in the motor for the North Station to take the five o'clock train to visit her aunt in Nahant. She did not arrive there until eleven in the evening, and then not from the railroad station. When she did, it was by motor, accompanied by a man named Searing who she says is a friend of yours. According to her aunt, who is quite broad-minded about such matters, young Searing was actually unsteady when he helped Eleanor from the car and there was an appreciable odour of liquor on Eleanor's breath. It appears that these two went without chaperonage to a certain roadhouse on the Newburyport Turnpike, of which Eleanor says you have sometimes spoken. I have found after inquiry in certain

quarters that this place is frequented by stenographers and
worse. Under the circumstances I have been obliged to send
for Searing here at the office and I have also spoken to his
parents. I will do him the justice to say that he was contrite
about the whole affair; and I believe, within limits, acted like
a gentleman. He understands by now that any mention of
this will militate seriously against your sister and has agreed
to keep silent. It relieves me that they both assure me that
they saw no one who might know them. Of course Searing
cannot be received again at the house. Even Eleanor understands this.

What worries me most is her attitude about the entire affair.
She appears resentful toward me for the steps I have taken to
the point that we have barely exchanged a word for two days.
I cannot understand how a child of mine, my own little girl
who has had every advantage, could have done such a thing
as this and afterwards have expressed no regrets. You and
Eleanor both have everything. Your mother and I have striven
to confront you with an example of a happy marriage. You
have a congenial home and congenial friends. Eleanor can
have the parlour for callers whenever she wishes, except when
the Wednesday Night Club meets.

When you get back, I think we must have some parties for
Eleanor and perhaps even a dance at Beacon Street. I shall not
write further. Family matters besides my other activities are
placing a very great burden on me. Sometimes I do not understand what is happening to either you or Eleanor. You know
that I not only am your father, but wish to be your friend and
companion. I hope that when you come back we can all do some
things together if I can only find the time. . . .

The above letter was shown to Eleanor Apley recently by
the present writer, who felt a natural reluctance in including it

even among such intimate pages as this memoir. That Eleanor
Apley did not share his opinion is the reason for its inclusion,
and her reply may surely be considered as characteristic of that
generation, the reply of "a daughter of change" so strange to
Apley's eyes.

Why not use it if you want [she writes]? The only reason
why I should hesitate is because it dates me. You know I had
nearly forgotten how completely changed things are. Poor
Father — he lived to see the era when girls went out un-
chaperoned even after dark. I remember the whole occasion
now — a curiously Boston occasion, and one that I do not believe could have happened anywhere else. Phil Searing was
really a darling, although he now lives rather unattractively
on Marlborough Street. We both of us wanted to see what
sin was like, so we planned to go to that roadhouse. It was not
inspiring. New Englanders hitting the high places are generally not a gay party. There were booths, a dance floor, paper
streamers, a piano, a lot of painted hussies, and traveling sales-
men, but it was sin incarnate to Phil and me. We stayed there
for two hours. I had one gin fizz, and Phil may have had
more. Back in the car he asked if it would be all right to kiss
me even if we were not engaged, and he did once, though we
both felt rather guilty about it. It is rather pathetic, isn't it, in
the light of the present methods of selection? I am glad that
I had sense enough to realize that it did not amount to much
when it was all over. I had already been out three years, but I
do not believe that any girl in my Sewing Circle had ever gone
to such a place or had gambled so recklessly with her reputation. I should not have dared if I had not been rather unattrac-
tive and had not always been getting stuck at dances. It was a
sort of a revolt, you see. John and I had a good deal to revolt
from, but I had more than John. Mother generally designed

my dresses herself — but then you know the Apleys. The only thing that made me feel badly was how keenly poor Father felt. In his eyes I was the "girl gone wrong." Nothing I ever did after that shocked him very much, because he always understood that I had bad blood in me, inherited from the Bosworths. But I don't mean to make fun of him really. Father was always sweet to me. He was always trying to set me on a pedestal, probably because he could not set Mother there, but it was his tradition with all women — a rather horrible tradition. He was always trying to be friendly, but then he had so much on his mind. How could he be friendly at Pequod Island and at Sunday luncheons with roast beef and Yorkshire pudding and white ice cream? How could he be friendly when we had charades and parlor games? I remember him looking at me sometimes, wistfully, puzzled. You know he was really a splendid man.

I remember what John said to me when he got back from the Border. That was really a great occasion when the Battery marched down Beacon Street and all the horses went slipping on the asphalt. John came into the parlor looking thin and brown. The parlor was just as it had been when Grandmama had arranged it — all those curious knickknacks on the mantelpiece and the fire screen of pressed ferns that Grandmama had made.

"Hi, El," John had said, and he looked around to be sure that we were alone — "so you didn't marry the British hero?"

"No," I said, "but he tried to."

"I have been hearing about you," he said. And he looked around the room again. It made me feel a little strange, because he did not seem to belong there.

"I had forgotten how the old place looked," he said. "El, we have to get out of this before it gets us too."

I knew exactly what he meant. You would too if you had been John or me — but then it doesn't matter, does it?

This quotation, like so many others included in this volume needs but little comment. One of the strangest phenomena of the last two decades was the illogical desire of many of the younger generation to escape physically from Boston. We have witnessed daughters with an excellent position of their own, situated in circumstances which required no such exertion, living in small New York flats and working in department stores, in the position, even, of saleswomen, and even obeying aspirations to appear publicly upon the stage. Sons of families too well known to be mentioned have left Boston and an acceptable background for trips on tramp steamers, expeditions to the South Pole or banana plantations, and even for work as radio announcers in New York. What is the more unaccountable, these young people have left Boston under no compulsion and for no definite reason, unless to fulfill a relentless desire for change which was, on the whole, properly controlled in this writer's generation. We have seen that George Apley, himself, was once beset by this restiveness and that a definite sense of responsibility enabled him to overcome any such desire. That this same weakness should have been manifested in his children, although perhaps an axiom of inheritance, was none the less a cross for him to bear.

Much of a parent's life in the course of all events is devoted to making a place for the children. If the children do not desire this place, something is obviously lacking in fulfillment. It was, however, Apley's great good fortune that his life was full enough and rich enough for him to face this disappointment in a measure philosophically. As for any normal duty which his children may have owed him, it remains for them, in this writer's opinion, to decide in their own consciences whether they have fulfilled this obligation of the Decalogue. It would be interesting, whatever their motives and justifications, to speculate whether their lives have been any happier or fuller than the lives of their parents.

In conclusion we cannot refrain from adding that it is a tribute to the broad-mindedness of George Apley that he could sympathize with his own daughter's desire for change, when she elected at the time of her marriage some years later to join her husband in another section of the country — instead of inducing him, as Apley himself suggested, to take up a lucrative and interesting literary position in the Boston offices of the Apley Mills.

In some ways, my dear, I can understand your point of view [we find him writing on this occasion]. If it is not the same as mine, at least let me try to understand it, and let me tell you a secret: I once felt as you do myself.

His reaction to his son's marriage when this event occurred was different for different reasons, but this matter, since it must be dealt with at all, will be reserved for brief mention in subsequent pages. It will be sufficient here to say that John Apley married a divorcée.

The activities of George Apley when his country finally entered the World War are sufficiently well known and so much in common with the experiences of others who shared in that soul-purifying event as to need no great mention of them at length. The task of the present biographer has been to set the frame for the man, to set the stage on which he played his part, and to indicate certain forces and motivations which led to what was the final crisis in his career, a crisis which left him misunderstood by some of his best friends. It was a crisis as serious to his reputation as the stand which certain persons took, in more recent years out of conscience, in the well-known Sacco-Vanzetti Case. (It may be said here, parenthetically, that in this issue Apley's position was eminently the right one — that the two men were radicals who had been found guilty under the laws of Massachusetts, whose case was delayed solely through the efforts of fellow radicals and of emotionally unbalanced sentimentalists who had interested themselves in their defense. These two men, in Apley's opinion, had been allowed further an unusual privilege of having their case examined by three unprejudiced and eminent citizens whose probity was as well-known to Apley as to the entire Commonwealth. It seemed to Apley that justice should take its course, unimpeded by the parades, placards and denouncements of certain elements whose increasing purpose has patently been to undermine society as determined by our Constitution.)

This parenthesis, however, brings us far afield. It is simply an example, one of many, that exhibits the basic soundness of the man in a period of crisis. Now, in this epoch of war, Boston was calling for men with the steadfast courage of their convictions; and it is natural to find Apley taking his place as leader, a leadership bringing the inevitable increase in stature which marked Apley for subsequent events. His home throughout the War was a haven for boys, regardless of their rank or previous background, who were about to embark for their service overseas. His entertainment of the various military missions needs no mention in these pages. His heavy subscription to the Liberty Loan Campaign was a matter of duty rather than pride,

as was his own cheerful acceptance of the hardship of the sugar-
less days and the meatless days, which we so well remember.
With the exception of his butler, a man in late middle age who
was suffering from a complicated form of indigestion, Apley
has pointed out that no one ate bacon in his house during the
entire period of conflict. Apley was also one of the first to take
the lead in planting lawn gardens, ordering his entire expanse
of lawn at Hillcrest, as an example to others, to be plowed up
for corn and potatoes, although there were many other fields
available; and this lawn, always a source of pride to his father
and himself, although reseeded the day of the Armistice, has
never recovered its former texture. In fact, standing on the
piazza at Hillcrest to-day, one can still see the ghosts of fur-
rows on that lawn — memories of what Apley himself called
afterwards "the brave days."

The efforts of Apley, in another farseeing group, to prevent
espionage and sabotage are a contribution of his which will not
be forgotten. It was this same group which was to stand guard
against radical activities during the first turbulent years of the
Russian Revolution. It is true, as Apley was the first to admit,
that such small efforts were only a part of every citizen's duty
— small sacrifices to be made cheerfully and without stint.

CHAPTER XXIV

A SON AT THE FRONT

Experiences of John Apley
As Seen Through a Father's Eyes

WE FIND Apley's wife writing to her father, a year after her mother's death: —

George is drilling with the Home Defense Corps to-night. He looks very handsome in his belt. I am very proud of George, and proud of Eleanor who is in the Home Motor Corps, but we are prouder still of John at the Front. There has been no letter from him for two weeks, which makes us sure that his Division has moved to the Front, exactly where George and I both want him. No one can say that our family are slackers. I hope that you are feeling much better. I shall call after the Red Cross Meeting to-morrow, I hope in time to see the doctor. George sends you his love.

A single letter of Apley's may be enough to paint that vanished scene, together with one taken at random from his letters to his son. The first is written to his friend Walker.

Dear Mike: —

It is hell to be old in these days and to be able to do so little. I should be glad to be where John is and so would you. In some sense it would allow me to vindicate myself. This has been denied us and instead we find ourselves with the women and children indulging in the trivalities of meatless days and gasolene-less Sundays. The spirit of everyone here is very high as indeed it should be with our sons at the Front. The horrible news of the Germans' break-through toward Paris makes us all pray that we have not joined our allies too late and that we may still be true to the spirit of Lafayette. In the meanwhile there is nothing to do but to wait for news.

Yet no matter what happens, I shall be able to hold my head high, I think, because John is with the Second Division at the Front. He may have taken the matter lightly. He said he was going because everyone was going, which of course was only a gay way of hiding his real convictions. At any rate he went among the first as cheerfully as he might have gone to breakfast and certainly will be in the forefront of the battle. Again, I say, I wish you and I were with him. We often used to speak about going to war, at the Club. There are not many men of my age to-day who can be as proud as I, because John is at the Front.

In a way, I think, I am making as great a sacrifice as he, for I cannot envisage life without him. Everything I have done would amount to nothing then. As for him, if he dies on the Field of Honour, I say to you frankly, for such is my state of mind, that he may be saving himself a good deal of trouble, a good deal of disillusion, a good deal of difficulty with personalities. He will have died in the full vigour of his strength, and that is something. Yet, of course, he must come back. I cannot comfort myself with any other thought. I have tried to think what it is like out there, but none of us can know. . . .

Dear John: —

Your letter from the Base Hospital has reached us and has allayed all the fears that have haunted us since you were reported wounded in action. If the leg wound is coming on as you say, the scar will be a badge of honour for you always and one which I am personally sorry I do not bear. I know without your telling me that you received that piece of shrapnel doing your duty and leading your men as you should. In doing so, you have brought honour to the family. There are not many families in Boston who have a wounded son.

I wish that your Uncle William and that your Uncle Horatio Brent and that your two grandfathers were alive to hear of it. There was a service for you at church last Wednesday afternoon. When we received your letter, I read it to the in-servants and the out-servants at Hillcrest assembled on the lawn, because they have known you always and are all fond of you. They join their congratulations with mine. I have cabled the Embassy to see if there is anything you need and of course they have been in touch with you.

Everything here is going capitally. We are only waiting for our boy to come back. When you do, we shall get out of this and try to have other plans. You would not know the place now; the lawn is full of potatoes, and the Common is full of soldiers. A toast was offered to you at the Monday lunch of the Province Club. God bless you, dear John, and come home soon. . . .

It was Apley's belief to the day of his death, a belief shared by many others including this writer, that the Allied Forces, when the tide turned so gloriously in the early autumn of 1918, failed to make the most of their opportunities. And those opportunities were great, with the German Army battered to its knees and with the scions of a Prussian autocracy hastening for shelter to the arms of neutral nations. The way was clear to Berlin and the way was clear also for a decisive defeat which would have eliminated the German nation as a world menace for many years to come. Subsequent events prove only too eloquently the justice of Apley's belief. That this opportunity was not grasped, in his opinion was due almost entirely to the weak and temporizing policy of the Administration at Washington with the pronouncement of its "Fourteen Points" and of "Peace without Victory." It was due to Apley's vigor that several petitions were circulated in an effort to stem this wave of sentimentality.

"Now is not the time to stop," we find him writing in one of his numerous letters to the *Boston Evening Transcript*, letters of such cogency and force that they were frequently reprinted next morning in the *Boston Herald;* and incidentally, these letters were also made available in pamphlet form. He continues: —

Now that we have so tardily grasped the sword, we cannot, we must not, let it fall supinely from our hands for reasons of mercy to a foe which has shown no mercy. We must strengthen our consciousness of justice with a memory of the women and children who have perished at the hands of a rapacious militaristic nation. The Mad Dog of Europe must be chained. After this is done, there will be ample time for pity. We must not forget our debt to the steadfastness of England and the chivalry of France that have stood for years, protecting us from something worse than death while we have waxed fat on profits. What will it profit America if she loses her soul? Can we face the memories of our dead, who have given their lives in a war to end war upon the shell-pocked fields of Château-Thierry, St. Mihiel and in the shrapnel-swept thickets of the Argonne? If we do not now lift the burden from the weary shoulders of our brave Allies, if we do not, how can we look our boys in the face when they come back from Over There?

What explanation can we give our sons, who have shed their blood in France, or to our boys training here in camp who have struggled through a winter of influenza and who are now straining to join their more fortunate comrades in the front lines? What shall we say to them if we do not let them go?

The eloquence of this and other letters could not help but bring Apley before the public eye. These letters quite rightly earned the commendation of Senator Henry Cabot Lodge, under whose banner Apley fought in the next year against that instrument, the League of Nations. It is not generally known that in the autumn of 1918 after President Wilson made his demagogic plea for a Democratic congress, that many of Apley's friends and well-wishers suggested that he run as a Republican for the national body. He refused only on the grounds that he would be more useful at home, where he better understood the situation. There was need then, indeed, for right-thinking men at home.

Even in the crisis of conflict there were certain subversive elements in Boston, which after the example set by Washington were becoming vocal. Apley like many others saw this danger. His well-known letter to the Board of Governors of the Province Club indicates the stand which he took in public and in private.

Gentlemen: —
While seated upon the brick terrace yesterday after luncheon, I was amazed to hear certain members of the Province Club, whose names I shall gladly furnish should I be called before your Board, advocating a Peace without Victory. In my humble opinion every member of the Province Club should not forget that this nation is in a state of War, and that our Divi-

sions are moving forward against a demoralized enemy. At such a time any talk of peace is patently pro-German, and we who admire the unanimity of the Province Club should surely not tolerate it. It is my suggestion that these members be called before your Board and suitably admonished.

There is no answer to this letter extant in Apley's files.

When the terms of the Armistice were finally announced, these seemed to Apley, in a measure, a vindication of his efforts, although perhaps a partial vindication. It had been his hope, shared by so many others, that there might be peace after the war was over instead of the trying times that followed. It was his hope that time might be allowed him for family affairs, which badly needed his attention, but instead he was enmeshed in an increasing complication of public and semi-public activities. His name and his presence rightly enough were in demand by various civic organizations, for dinners and committees of welcome. His efforts in finding work for the boys who were returning home need no mention here, and his increased contributions to various social agencies are something for which he would desire to take no credit, since those sacrifices were shared by nearly everyone in New England.

For the first time since the hoards of insect pests have invaded us [he writes to his friend Walker] the elms at Hillcrest will not have their dormant oil spray. The money will go where it is needed more — to the Fourth Liberty Loan. I am arranging so that everyone who works for me will contribute and we are also seeing that every worker at Apley Mills will be assisted in continuing his contributions. This is a time for giving without stint, and no time for saving income to be added to principal. Everyone must be encouraged in small forms of thrift for giving.

Yet in spite of the financial and physical strain under which he was laboring, there is a spirit of elation in Apley's letters at this period born naturally from a sense of vindication.

It really seems [he writes to Walker] as though the people who are fitted by education and tradition are taking the lead again in civic affairs; even the professional politicians seem to be turning to them for advice. This is a very hopeful sign. At this time, when we are facing great changes, we must be sure that all of them are for the better. We must combat the spirit of restiveness here in Boston.

Those changes to the world which we once knew, the last of which are not yet in sight — those changes, which began so subtly in the first decade of the century, were moving faster, and Apley's insight perceived them. In fact the following letter to his son, John, is in a sense prophetic: —

Dear John: —
    I hope by now that you will be out of the Convalescent Hospital at Aix. Now that the War is over, I cannot see what delays you, especially since I have ascertained that arrangements can be made through Washington for your return at any time that your health permits; and from your letters, both your mother and I gather that your health is very good. Now that you are able to walk with a cane, surely you can stand an ocean voyage. You speak of getting some sort of job at the Peace Conference; surely you have done enough for your country. I have every sympathy with your desire for a period of relaxation, but every opportunity for a good time can be afforded to you here where your family and friends long to see you. I have agreed with you that you should see something of France "besides corpses and roofless buildings," as you so trenchantly put it. For me

France has always been my mistress, but she is ample enough for us both to share the same love. We must have long talks about her when you come home.

I am glad that the young nurses at Aix are so agreeable. We never can thank them enough for what they have done for us, but I only hope that they are not *too* agreeable. There are times, if a man is in a weakened condition, when his loneliness and his natural sense of gratitude overcome saner dictates. We have already had one example in the family, but I know that I need not say any more to a son of mine. Your relations with these girls, of course, are all in a spirit of comradeship and friendship. Your mother and I are both anxious to have Miss Jelke, who has been giving you leg exercises, at Hillcrest for some weekend. When you get back here, there are plenty of hearts in Boston for you to break. Evelyn Newcomb was asking for you only yesterday. She is one of the girls from the Vincent Club who has been serving doughnuts and coffee at the Boston Common Canteen and working in the evenings at the Radio Boys' Social Hour. She looks very pretty in her uniform.

There is a rather amusing thing about one of the girls whom you must remember, because I have seen you dancing with her for long periods at the Somerset — Dot Wills. In the last two years she has grown quite surprisingly attractive, perhaps because of the new styles in dress which seem to have certain advantages. During the War, she was on the Committee which made mobilization plans to move the virgins inland in case of an enemy invasion. The idea amused me at the time, as I know it will you, especially as I am told at the Berkley Club that you have a Rabelaisian sense of humor. There have been many amusing things about the War which you and I must talk about over cigars.

There have been many serious things also, and seriously you are needed at home.

I think you will be as surprised as I am at certain changes when you get back. Firstly, there is a strange lack of reticence in the younger generation which extends to your contemporaries. In spite of the imminence of Prohibition, which is a deplorable blow to the rights of the individual, there seems to be a wave of drinking, and it is even said that young girls whom we both know have been seen to take too much. One cocktail before dinner on a gay occasion is well enough; I do not like to see your sister Eleanor taking two, although I must say she seems to show no effects. Worse than this, certain people who should be setting an example are letting things slide very badly.

I am much afraid that the War has not helped morals between the sexes. I could tell you a good deal that would surprise you, but I have never been a gossip. Worse than this, there is a wave of discontent among the working classes, although they have never been so exorbitantly paid. Instead of saving their money, they are attending motion-picture theatres and their women are buying silk stockings and even fur coats. The craze for purchasing automobiles which they cannot afford to run is driving many into debt, and several families in Apley Falls are doing without wholesome nourishment in order to own a car. There is no doubt that Russian agents are at work in the building trades and even on our railroads. Everywhere strikes are breaking out. I am afraid that we are going to have serious times. . . .

This concern with the Red Menace was to occupy much of Apley's attention during the next years, and he was not alone in seeing the threat. Subsequently he was active in endeavoring to curb the utterances of certain visionaries in Harvard University whose names are too familiar to require specific mention. At this time, however, we find much of his attention devoted to the affairs of his son, who had returned from France during the summer of 1919 and who resumed his work at the Harvard Law School that same autumn. Like so many events in this life which have been anticipated with the greatest zest, there is frequently a sense of disappointment in the final actuality. It is regrettable that such disappointment should have appeared in Apley's relationship with his son, although this is shown only in the letters to his old friend, Walker.

———•———

CHAPTER XXV

BROKEN BARRIERS

The Problem of a Son
Who Has Been Too Long away from Boston

APLEY writes: —

I cannot understand why it is that the War seems to have drawn John and me apart. I have tried again and again to gather some of the firsthand impressions which he may have had in battle. I have tried to induce him at one of the men's dinners which I gave for him on his return home, where only my oldest friends and of course his also were present, to speak about events in France. In spite of my encouragement he has exhibited a reticence which surprises me. I cannot get at him, for he appears to suffer from a species of shell-shock when subjects of which he should be proud are mentioned. On the other hand, he seems pleased enough to speak of certain re-unions in Paris which seem to have been held nearly always at a friend's house in the Rue du Bray, though, even about the happenings there, he is sometimes reticent. All in all I can gather from him only something of the lighter side of war which seemed to consist principally of dinners with young women in the Red Cross. Nevertheless, he seems to have learnt a great deal of French, and I wonder how he managed it. He is surprisingly proficient, considering that he did not serve with the French Army. You know that I am not a prude. If ever young men had a right to sow their wild oats within limits, our boys in France had, and yet John always seems to feel that I will criticize him. Thus I cannot really find what he has done at or behind the Front. Only the other evening I asked him what it all had taught him. His only answer was that it had taught him that he was lucky to be alive, and this does not seem to be very much. Both his mother and I have wanted to show our boy to our friends and we have urged him to wear his uniform with his wound stripe as is quite permissible under regulations. He has never been willing to do this. It sometimes seems as though he were ashamed of the uniform.

What worries me most are his criticisms about the places and the people among whom he must take up his life's position. He is polite enough, but now and then he lets drop a word. Nothing that I am doing appears to interest him, not even the building of the high wall by the front drive at Hillcrest. He has gone with me to the Lunch Club and has been several times to the Province Club, but I cannot say that he seems to enter into the spirit of either place.

When it was suggested that he sing in the Hallowe'en Chorus at the Berkley Club, an occasion where every good Berkleyite always does his part, he actually refused. I can attribute this only to the deep emotional upset which John must have experienced, since in many ways the War has seared his soul. No games or gayety seem to interest him, but his mother and I are making every effort to distract his attention by a series of dinners and by week-end parties where he can meet some really nice girls. Though he is always polite, I cannot see that he takes any real interest in any of them. Yet surely he must understand that it is time to settle down. He is often going to New York where I hope he looks you up, although I am afraid he does not. I have heard that he has been to luncheon there once with the editors of a magazine called the *New Republic,* but I have hesitated to speak to him about this. His whole attitude reminds me of the way he was during his early years at Groton. You know that he did not fit in there and he has never evinced a desire to return there for a week end. Nevertheless he got through Groton and I am sure that he will get through this phase as well.

This lack of interest of his son's was changed momentarily by an event which shook not only Boston, but the entire nation. There is no occasion here to outline the circumstances leading to the Police Strike out of which emerged the national figure of Calvin Coolidge. Its effect, however, on both the Apleys, father and son, is of considerable importance. In those few days of mob rule and disruption Apley, himself, patrolled the streets and John Apley, at the head of some War Veterans, cleared a portion of Commonwealth Avenue of a mob.

There can be no doubts any longer about John [Apley writes]. He has made a place for himself in Boston and that is one of the best things which has come out of this horrible situation, that and a knowledge that we have a strong man in the State House whose very name has a ring of reassurance. I am proud that I have such a son, although he only did his part with the sons of our other friends. He went into the thing as cheerfully as he might have gone to breakfast and I have been told that his suggestions were very valuable. Without any desire to boast, I know that John has the makings of a leader in him. He seems to me more and more like his great-grandfather.

On Apley himself the dangers inherent in this situation made a deep impression, for here once again he met at first hand the supineness, the corruption, and the inefficiencies of the local City Government. In a sense this occasion marks the beginning of the fight he waged — a losing battle — to stamp out this inefficiency; but before turning to this phase of Apley's life it is necessary to deal briefly with two disappointments which were as bitter as they were undeserved.

In June of 1921, John Apley on a visit to New York accepted employment in a downtown law firm and categorically refused to take the place that had been reserved for him in the Boston firm of Apley and Reid. It need not be stated that this decision of the son was a disappointment to the father, and it was obviously more than that. It brought to George Apley a realization of many of the fears that he had envisaged at the prospect of John Apley's death in France; and the circumstance, it is needless to say, would not be mentioned in these pages except for the son's own explicit request; and so George Apley's letter to him is published here only at John Apley's suggestion.

Dear John: —

I have not answered your letter for two days because I have been ill in bed, one of the first times that I have been ill in many years. Your letter came just as I was dressing in preparation to read a paper on "War Days Past and Present" before my dinner club. I got through my paper well enough, but something at the dinner so disagreed with me that I have been under doctor's care ever since. I am up and about now, but your letter has taken something out of life — I do not know just what. I do know that it has robbed me of what I had hoped for most in life, the companionship of a son, and this was something that was very dear to me, how dear, I am afraid I have never shown you. Now that you have gone to New York, I know that I shall never have it. I might beg you to alter your decision, but I will not, for I suppose that you have given the matter very careful attention. You have surely seen what there was here for you. It would have been, I think, a fuller and a happier life where your traditions lie than it will ever be elsewhere. I cannot think that what your mother and I have tried to do for you has gone for nothing. I cannot think that you do not love this place as I love it. It is impossible for me to believe that you can fit anywhere else. I am so sure of it that I have a hope that in a year or two you will reconsider. If you do not, who will look after Hillcrest when I am gone? I am older than you and the older I grow the more convinced I am that there must be some sort of continuity in this changing world, something to which one must hold fast. It is something too precious to be dropped lightly. It is something which we have here.

I know you have laughed at many people and at many customs, as I have in my time, but I hope that you have laughed kindly as I have. At any rate, when the jest is over, continuity remains. You will find, as I have, a solace in background and tradition. It will always be waiting for you here.

It may be the fault of the times that our great figures have left us. I remember many of them in my own youth and boyhood, such as Dr. Holmes and Mr. Whittier. The memories of others were still fresh, of our historians, of Emerson, of Thoreau, of Margaret Fuller. I have heard Dr. Hale preach; I have heard the sermons of Phillips Brooks. Their words here are not entirely stilled, and I have hoped, I know wrongly now, that you would hear an echo of them. I am sorry that you have not heard. Instead you say that Boston has become a backwater in which the greatest activity is the conserving of wealth and the raking of literary ash heaps. I can understand in some sense what you mean. You are young as I was once. You wish to be in the tide of change. I wished it also once, but the time will come when you will long for continuity and peace. I shall do my best to see that you will get it, or at any rate that your children will get it.

In the meanwhile I am glad that I have other interests. These seem vital and worth while to me, if they do not to you. I wish to make the place where I am living better, I wish to try in my poor way to carry out what others have planned. If you have left me, I must do this alone and wish you God speed, but I hope you will come back.

Your mother is writing you also. I am afraid it will be an angry letter, as she is very deeply shocked. I think the least that you can do is to promise her that you will come up to Pequod Island for a month each summer, no matter what happens. For the rest you must remember that your mother has a very strong will and is so little used to having her wishes disregarded that she may say many things that she does not actually mean. The same will be true with your Aunt Amelia, who has always had a great liking for you. What the rest of the family will think, I do not like to conjecture. I can only promise to do my best for you here and to try to take your part. I am already saying, which I hope is true, that your position in New York is a very important one, which will lead you eventually to Washington and possibly into international law. If this is so, many people will understand more readily why you are leaving us.

Would it not be possible for you to take some place in the diplomatic service? Such a step as that would be completely understood. . . .

After this decision of John Apley's, an incomprehensible one to many of his family and to his friends, George Apley did not cease his correspondence with his son as might quite reasonably have been expected, for Apley's instinctive flair for tolerance and for good sportsmanship was such as not to permit any such narrow attitude of resentment to cross his mind. Once a week for many years, except for such time as John Apley was in Boston, George Apley wrote his son a letter. As one runs to-day through this rich store of manuscript, which brings up a thousand vivid memories of events and personalities, one cannot escape a certain wistfulness on the part of the writer and even an understanding of his son's motives not shared by others. Here one finds him painting a picture of home, in colors calculated to rouse a desire in his son to return to it. Here again, with that subtle contradiction which to many was a lovable part of Apley's character, the father deliberately seems to lay stress on amusing eccentricities of his environment. But through all of this correspondence is a thread of longing — of a father's natural and never-to-be-attained desire to share in his son's alien interest.

I wish you could be here with me to-night [he writes on one occasion]. Your mother and I have just returned from hearing that fine young Englishman, Philip Gibbs, speak out his mind in Symphony Hall to everyone here in Boston who really matters. Your mother has gone to bed, I think emotionally exhausted, and it is one of the first times that I have ever known her to be tired. Have you heard that slim, pale young man speak? He seemed hardly more than a boy on the platform, although so impeccably and correctly dressed, and yet like all of his generation, a man. Truly nothing in the world is quite so fine as an English gentleman; there is a politeness, an air and an *esprit* which cannot but make us all a little bit ashamed. Believe me, he made us all very much ashamed to-night, for he spoke without mincing words of what we owe to England, to England which has borne the real brunt of saving civilization for posterity. He spoke modestly, in a repressed voice, as a good sportsman who has "carried on" through thick and thin, of the burden which is borne by our former Mother Country and of the indissoluble ties which bind every branch of the Anglo-Saxon race. I was especially asked to meet him afterwards for a quiet little supper with half a dozen others, but frankly I was too ashamed to meet him. I was too ashamed after he had shown us so politely but clearly the crass commercial policy of our nation toward England. I am ashamed to think that we are demanding in full a payment of a war debt by England, as though money mattered compared to the British lives which have been spent in our defense. Yes, I am thoroughly and bitterly humiliated; I feel that we are taking advantage of England's weakness to build up our navy beyond her strength when England's very life depends on ruling the seas. I am having at my own expense a number of copies of his address printed in pamphlet form, and I shall send you several hundred for distribution among your friends, who must feel, as I am sure you do, the inherent justice of England's cause.

I repeat, I wish you were here to-night, as I sit looking across the Charles River Basin, so that we might talk of the lecture over one of S. S. Pierce's new brand of cigars, and perhaps have a touch of the old Madeira. There are still a few bottles in the cellar waiting for you, John, though I am afraid the increasing motor traffic on Beacon Street has shaken them a bit. There is a fine breeze whipping down the river which makes the windows rattle and I can see the lights of the Massachusetts Avenue Bridge and the lights of Technology twinkling through the black. It is rather beautiful, even in spite of the hideous interpolation of two electric signs which the Basin Protective Society, of which I am chairman, is striving to have taken down. It all makes me feel very snug here inside the library when I turn and look at the tooled bindings of your grandfather's Dickens, Thackeray, and of my own beloved mystic radical Thoreau. You must remember to have lanolin put on those bindings once a month after I am gone. As I say, it makes me very comfortable now that I sit here alone, with your mother safe in bed. I do not know where Eleanor is tonight, but I shall when she comes in, for I always sit up for her. After all there is nothing like a good cigar and good books, and we have both of these in Boston.

Dear John: —

We have been having a great deal of difficulty here this week. Young Balch from Balch, Balch, and Steffins, whose grandfather made so many additions to Hillcrest, has been here making plans. There can be no longer any dodging of the fact that the roof of the conservatory is too small for your mother's rubber tree. You know that she sets a great store by it, as indeed I begin to, since it has been with us so long. When your mother brought it to the house when we were married, I felt toward it somewhat as Napoleon must have reacted toward Josephine's little dog when the latter bit him. As you know the tree was given to your mother when she was six years old and ever since then she has tended it herself. Once it was possible to jest about this tree, but now it is not. It is a family tree. Professor Sargent at the Arboretum tells me that it is certainly the oldest rubber tree in New England. Your mother will not think of cutting the branches back. The conservatory is being enlarged.

Your great-great-grandfather's silver can has gone on its annual visit to Park Street for overhauling. Old Seldon, there, has again taken up the question of removing the dent. I still prefer to have it remain. You may do what you like when you get it.

Of a morning the same people start out for State Street. I do not need a watch, when I see Mr. Bolles appear on his stoop with his umbrella. One of the elms near the Civil War Monument on the Common has lost a limb — a limb, not a leg. I am not such a prude as you think, John. . . .

———•———

CHAPTER XXVI

NEW IMPACTS

*Conservative Comments upon
Unfamiliar Environments and Ideas*

DEAR JOHN: —
Sometime before long, if I can ever get my affairs straightened out here so that I can once have a few days' breathing spell, I wish to come down to see you in New York. Now that I come to think of it it has been a good many years since I have had the time to travel so far. I shall not think of troubling you in your flat (I dislike the more modern name "apartment") but I shall ask you to get me a quiet room and bath at the Belmont, where no doubt the management remembers me. When I come I want you to take me to some of the new plays, and please don't feel that I shall be shocked by them. Your father can stand a good deal, John, and he has heard most of the simple Anglo-Saxon monosyllables. Nevertheless I should like to hear for myself whether the one-syllable word for prostitute is spoken out loud in one of these productions. I have been told that this is so, but an old man must be convinced to believe it. I also want to see that very strong play called "What Price Glory"; I should also like to see the musical comedy in which young Chickering appears as a chorus man. His father will appreciate it if I go.

My work in many ways has kept me out of touch with many changes of which I hear. Fortunately I do not think they are very apparent among us, although I hear some of the younger men speak of them now and then at teatime at the Berkley Club. Is it true in New York and in other cities farther south such as Philadelphia and Baltimore that young debutantes practise promiscuously what is known as "petting" or "necking"? Eleanor is evasive on the subject. I should like to know what "necking" and "petting" mean. I have also heard it said that boys and girls sit alone in automobiles and drink from pocket flasks. As a matter of fact one young couple was expelled from the Mulberry Club last summer for doing that very thing. These practices surely cannot be prevalent among people whom you and I know.

I should also like to have you take me to one of these "speak-easies" where liquor is dispensed against the law, as I take a very deep interest in these. Anything that can be done, even at the expense of possible arrest and disgrace which may demonstrate a citizen's disapproval of a law which flouts the rights of the individual, is something in which your father will gladly coöperate. In short I want to see the town and even paint it red a little. We can certainly have a good dinner together at the Century Club. . . .

Dear John: —

There is no doubt that Eleanor had a very good time on her visit with you in New York. Your mother and I have both commented on her cheerfulness since she has returned, in spite of her seeming rather pale and tired. There is only one thing which actually disturbs me about her visit. I know you will understand me and not take it amiss when I tell you of it, since it means that you have been away so long that you have forgotten that New York girls, whose parents doubtless have their own good reasons for permitting them, can do certain things and still escape the censure which a girl in Eleanor's position cannot. Last night while Hopkins Balch and your cousin Nate Hancock were here at a little dinner which your mother gave for Eleanor, Eleanor dropped the remark quite casually that you had taken her to dine at one of these "speak-easies." Afterwards in the library over the cigars, I asked both of the boys not to mention it, and I think I may rely on their sense of chivalry, as they are both gentlemen. Your mother did the same with the girls in the parlour, who also promised, though I fear there may be trouble there, for women will talk. Nevertheless I do not feel that any very lasting harm has been done. In trying honestly to give Eleanor a "good time," you have simply forgotten how such an escapade may strike us old "fogies" up here. I know that I need not say any more about it.

My back is quite stiff from curling this afternoon at the Country Club. I did not wish to curl to-day, but being the Chairman of the Curling Committee of course I had to show myself. The cellar here was flooded last week, inexplicably so. Young Balch has been very thoughtful about it and has been down in the cellar every evening measuring the water with Eleanor's help. Their last advice is that it will not reach the furnace.

I am pleased to hear that you are going about so much, as is quite right for one of your age and your position. I do not know why you should speak apologetically about lunching with the literary set at the Algonquin Hotel, since nothing which you have told me for months has pleased me more. I only wish that your dear grandmother were alive to hear of it. She always had a soft spot in her heart for the scriveners; and now that Boston has passed the torch of creative literature to New York, it is only natural that one of our family should be a member of the group. I hope your contact with these minds will encourage you to write something yourself. You know very well that even a pamphlet of a few pages written by you would give all of your family and your old friends here the greatest pleasure. What good talks you must have around the Algonquin Table! It is kind of you to tell me that your new friends are all anxious to meet me and wish me to go with you to the Algonquin when I visit you in New York, but for the life of me I cannot see why you think I would not enjoy it. I want you to send me by the next mail a parcel of their books, some of which I understand are banned by our Save Boston Committee. You must get over this absurd idea that I am a prude. You have certainly heard me tell stories at the Club at the last dinner in February which show that I am not, and even the undergraduates enjoyed them. As a matter of fact I think you and I were both perhaps a bit on our beam ends that night, but then that is what a Club dinner is for, isn't it? And they only come once a year, and your mother was visiting your aunt at Pachogue Neck. . . .

Dear John: —

I am still a little bewildered by my trip to New York, but not so bewildered that I cannot thank you for it. To me it was an amazing experience, amazing.

You need not be afraid that I told much about it to your mother. It was very thoughtful of you to give me the catalogues of the chief picture exhibitions. I read them coming home on the train. I still cannot imagine why you bought me that seat in the parlour car. It had never occurred to me that you ever travelled that way and certainly I never have, and I still consider it a useless waste of money, although of course there are a few thousand shares of Pullman stock in the family portfolio. At the end of the trip I was able to make your mother feel that we had spent a great deal of time in the galleries and had seen the worth-while things.

For the rest, frankly, my impressions are chaotic, and no doubt the world has moved beyond me. I know now that it is a mad world, but I hold to the belief that New York is not an American city. We have our Irish and you your Jews, and both of them are crosses to bear. Out of habit I am afraid that I prefer South Boston. I shall tell you in more detail in another letter how much I enjoyed it because I did, even the grass skirt dance at that Negro night club. How intelligent the coloured people are, and how physical! Yet now that it is over and I have been to count the crocuses on the lawn at Hillcrest and to walk with Mrs. Goodrich through the Blue Hill woods where our first summer visitors are returning from the South, I know that New York is not meant for me. It was never meant for me, and I am happy where I am. There is no more beautiful approach to the city than our Fenway; no city can boast of a Museum like dear Mrs. Jack Gardner's, and after all our Symphony Orchestra can show New York "plenty" as you would doubtless put it. . . .

Dear John: —

I think I spoke to you the last time I saw you about Hopkins Balch and about the very obvious attentions he has been paying to Eleanor. I also asked you to say nothing to Eleanor about it nor to anyone else, as you know how important it is to allow nothing to disturb such a thing in its initial stages. For our own parts, your mother and I have made every effort to be as casual and natural as possible in spite of our deep interest and in spite of our natural desire to know how each detail of this little affair has been progressing.

I need not tell you about Hopkins Balch because you know him as well as I know his father. Our families have always been congenial and think the same way about nearly all important matters. When that damnable effort was made by the Park Commissioner to have a children's merry-go-round installed near the Public Garden Pond, Hopkins was a great help to me, and I have been distinctly in favour of him ever since. He may not be as comfortably off as Eleanor, but there are times, and this is an excellent example, when it is not necessary to be worldly. Hopkins really has a great artistic flair. The time may very well come when he will be a second Richardson. When you are here next, I want you to see for yourself the group of buildings which he has made for the Play Day Pre-School in Cambridge. To my mind they are a very pretty little group.

I do not want you to feel, simply because I like Hopkins' buildings, that I am wholly in favour of these novel methods of education, which have cropped up hereabouts, together with all the other new ideas which we are endeavouring to assimilate. Nevertheless, I am not narrow-minded about them and they furnish an interesting topic for casual dinner-table conversation. I personally believe that there must be some very real thought behind them because Mrs. Goodrich is deeply interested in this whole new modern movement. She has pointed out the remarkable results it has had on some of the offspring of your early married contemporaries.

I have heard you comment on the behaviour of Tom and Anstis Oswell's little daughter, Lucretia, Mrs. Goodrich's grandniece. The child, as you will remember, has never eaten her cereal and has been seized with regular fits of hysterics at bedtime. For a long while it seemed as though the unfortunate mental weakness of the Oswell branch was cropping out again even unto the seventh generation. However, now that Lucretia has been under the care of Miss Fox at the Play Day School, her entire attitude has changed. She has developed what is called by modern educators "group consciousness." Mrs. Good-rich, herself, took me to see Lucretia take a leading part in the Thanksgiving pageant in which both the parents and the pupils of the Play Day School coöperate. Lucretia's father, after con-siderable urging, consented to be Miles Standish and Lucre-tia was one of the Indians who gave the Pilgrims turkeys. The Project Class of the school had made the turkeys themselves out of floor mops and feather dusters. Lucretia is also being taught responsibility by having the sole care of a mother guinea pig with six young ones. Miss Fox says that nothing should be done for several years, except indirectly, about teaching Lu-cretia to read and to write. The surprising thing about all this is that Lucretia now eats her cereal regularly and her screaming fits have diminished to one a week.

I know that you will laugh at all this, John, and I am in-clined to laugh at it myself, but one must have a tolerant point of view in these days; one must try to see the constructive good in everything. I wonder if it would not have been the making of my poor sister, Jane, who now must have three nurses, if she had gone to such a school. I wonder if there is not something in all this modern trend. I try to think that there is, even though I instinctively shy away from most of it. . . .

Dear John: —

At a small dinner last night, which your mother and I gave for Eleanor, your sister suddenly began discussing psychology. To my amazement, she seems to have been spending a great deal of time in the Athenaeum lately reading the works of a certain doctor named Sigmund Freud. Have you ever heard of this man? I believe I recall overhearing some of your friends mention his name in New York. I am writing by this same mail to the Trustees of the Athenaeum asking that all works by Freud be put into the Locked Room. They are certainly too strong for public consumption and certainly not the books which an Athenaeum Proprietor wishes to have exposed for an unmarried girl's perusal.

The effect which this man Freud has had upon Eleanor has upset your mother very greatly. Neither of us had ever heard sex mentioned before across a dinner table. I could see that Hopkins Balch, who was present, was distressed by Eleanor's speaking of certain things about which even men in a library are customarily reticent, and I could feel, with a certain amount of justice, that his distress was a direct reflection upon me. Eleanor told us that the entire mainspring of civilization is the desire of mankind to reproduce. She says that sex underlies all art and all philosophy. She then said that a frank understanding of sex would change a great many individuals in Boston, whose names she mentioned. Before the subject could be changed, she added that there is a distinct sexual antagonism between men and women here, which is why both sexes enjoy withdrawing into segregated groups. She then said that a great many women who have been married for years — mentioning their names — have what she calls the Outraged Virgin Complex.

Now you have more influence with Eleanor than we have, John. I wish when you get this letter you would ask her down to New York, or better come up here and speak to her sensibly. This letter is, of course, completely confidential as man to man and it might be just as well if you would burn it.

This disposition to throw all reticence to the wind, to speak frankly of things which had better not be mentioned, may be all right in a way. Certainly it seems hard these days to find a good clean novel, so hard that I have given up reading any but the works of Conrad and Archibald Marshall. At any rate this sort of thing is distinctly not good for women. Yesterday, I found that your mother had actually taken this Freud book out of the Athenaeum. She was embarrassed when I found her reading it in the small music-room, and gave as her reason that she wished to know what Eleanor was doing. I am now reading the book myself for the same reason.

You know and I know that all this idea of sex is largely "bosh." I can frankly say that sex has not played a dominant part in my own life, and I trust that it has not in yours. No right-thinking man permits his mind to dwell upon such things, and the same must be true of women. And now this is enough of this unsavoury subject.

On Sunday we had our usual game of indoor baseball on the lawn at Hillcrest and afterwards picnicked on the piazza. On Saturday I went for my usual bird walk with Clara Goodrich. We saw six thrushes, a Wilson snipe, and a Baltimore oriole. I am not entirely sure about the snipe. . . .

Dear John: —

I wish there weren't quite so many new ideas. Where do they come from? You seem to play with them and toss them aside, but I cannot. I try to think what is in back of them and speculation often disturbs my sleep. Why is everyone trying to break away from what we all know is sane and good? There is only one right way to live; there is only one right way to write and to paint. Yet all you youngsters seem to be searching for another way to do everything. What worries me most is that you seem to be searching for an easier way and a pleasanter way. Nothing which is worth while is easy, nor in my experience is the actual doing of it particularly pleasant. The pleasure arises from completion and from the knowledge that one has done the right thing and has stood by one's convictions. Don't forget, John, that the only real satisfaction of life must be derived from this.

I do not want to be an "old fogey." I try to keep my mind

open to everything. This afternoon your sister invited Hopkins and me to an exhibition of modern painting in Newbury Street in which she seems to be deeply interested. Of course, I have heard of Cubism before the War and have laughed as heartily as anyone at the Nude Descending the Staircase, but now to see supposedly intelligent people gaping at a wall full of paint slobbered willy-nilly over canvas makes me feel that the world is going mad. Eleanor, who appears to have read about it, endeavoured to explain something of the theory, but the Monets at the Art Museum are radical enough for me. I want to know what I am looking at. Surely so does everyone else in his proper senses. I am glad to say that Hopkins agrees with me. He is very kind to Eleanor, though, and I believe tries his level best to share in her interests. . . .

Dear John: —

There is no use beating about the bush; Eleanor has refused Hopkins Balch. He proposed to her last evening after asking my permission. I have tried to think that her refusal was the result of the suddenness of his proposal and soon would be changed to womanly surrender, but after a talk with her in the library this evening I am forced to conclude that her refusal is categorical. I cannot understand this; neither can your mother. In our day a girl was brought up to understand that her first duty was to find a suitable husband and to establish a home of her own. Surely Eleanor must realize this. I do not like to think that she is the sort of girl to lead Hopkins on. Yet surely she must have given him some sort of encouragement. He is by far the most suitable man that has ever come into the house, and I cannot escape the conviction that she could love him if she tried, especially when these two have so much in common in background and in tradition. Instead of making an effort to see the good in Hopkins, she has allowed herself to be swayed entirely by his mental and physical defects. It is true that Hopkins has the Balch nose and wears glasses, but what of it? What worries me most is that this cavalier treatment of Hopkins may be very serious for Eleanor, since it will inevitably give her the reputation of being a flirt. I am afraid that young fellows with serious intentions will begin to avoid her.

I must tell you frankly that I had built up my hopes on this more than I should have. I should like to see my children happy and settled. I was married and settled when I was your age. Both of you must see that the time has come for you to settle down. Why don't you settle down? I wish you would, if only to please your mother who seems to be under the impression, why I cannot fancy, that this is all my fault. When your friends in New York mention this matter of Eleanor and Hopkins, as they doubtless will, you must adopt my attitude. It will be best to tell them that Eleanor and Hopkins have been childhood friends and that there has never been anything between them but the comradeship natural to boys and girls who have played together and who will play together always. . . .

As has been said, out of the rich store of material available, these letters have been chosen almost at random. Yet even this casual selection is sufficient to illustrate the eagerness in Apley to assimilate new ideas and the inevitable difficulty which he experienced in the assimilation. It was a difficulty shared by many of his contemporaries, who, appalled, have watched the rising tide of alien theories which still threatens to engulf us and which has done so much to undermine moral fabric and inherent sound sense. Thanks to men of Apley's stamp, who have been able to keep before them through all this stress a realization of abstract right and wrong and a practical philos-

ophy, little real harm has yet been done. The foundations
which have been assailed still stand.

To quote the words of one of the ablest fiction delineators of
Boston since the mantle of interpretation descended on him
from the shoulders of William Dean Howells — "Everything
is certain to swing back." This quotation is taken from a novel
dealing with our locale published in 1931, when, as this novelist
has said, the cocksure new generation "was beginning to perceive that its vaunted philosophy of utter naturalness at the cost
of all formulae was Dead Sea fruit." We may quote further the
words of a main character, in themselves both hopeful and
prophetic: —

Everything is certain to swing back. . . . But I am wondering, though, who'll comfort the others who went the pace and
showed such scorn for the rest of us. The unleashed, cocksure
spirits, youths and maidens, who glorified filth in the name of
liberty and crammed it down our throats. For only think,
they're already in the shadow and their public has turned to
detective stories and the private lives of bandits. Boston is a
pretty stable place to live in, dear old boy.

It is a relief and in a very definite way a vindication to the
present writer to see a new generation rising which is turning
from the war-jaded individuals of John Apley's time. It is a
satisfaction to see that we are at a turning of the ways, where
the path bends back toward the security of the formulae for
which George Apley and the rest of us have stood. We are
learning, from the example which George Apley gave by living, if not from his precepts, that he did not live in vain. It is
because of him that there is a kindliness, a keen concern for the

good of others, an uncompromising honesty still extant here in Boston. In a decade where the pledged word has been lightly broken even by the elected leaders of our nation, there are still men in these environs whose word is good. There are still men here who can stand and fall by their convictions, honestly formed, no matter what these convictions may be, or where they may ultimately lead, as long as they are convictions.

I am very much afraid [George Apley wrote toward the end of his life] that John and Eleanor are sailing upon uncharted seas while I am safe in harbour.

CHAPTER XXVII

THE TURBULENT TWENTIES

*A Defense of Position and
Marital Implications*

IF THE reader has gathered from these letters that George
Apley's life had grown more leisurely, that he was indulging in criticisms unconfirmed by action, this is a mistake
— for Apley was primarily a man of action. Throughout these
turbulent years of the twenties, Apley identified himself more
and more with Henry Salter and the Save Boston Society. He
did so instinctively, as one might who felt that his traditions
were endangered, as indeed they were. He did so, however,
with reservations.

There is much in Salter's methods that I do not like [he
writes]. I do not quite go his lengths in endeavouring to raise
the moral tone of the community. I believe that there are
limits in tastes and behaviour beyond which one should not im-
pose his will. I believe that straightforward education is better
than censorship and I am not by nature a "snooper" who strives
to uncover concealed vice. It may be a weakness of mine, but
I cannot find myself aroused until vice is actually endangering
the whole community. At such a time I shall yield to no man
my place in the forefront of the battle. I think that Salter is

wasting many of his great talents in seeking to prosecute sellers of obscene postcards and to stir up an indifferent police about performances given in such places as the Old Howard Athenaeum. At Salter's instigation, I have been several times to that beautiful old theatre, really a landmark of the old days, and have observed the performance. While much of it is undoubtedly censurable, I cannot believe that it does any great harm to the type of person who sees it and within limits I think we should adhere to the doctrine "live and let live." Nevertheless, I greatly admire Salter's undeviating courage and his devotion to the public good. My check for a larger amount than usual goes again to the Save Boston Society.

When it comes to uncovering the manifest corruption which exists in the municipal affairs, I am behind Salter heart and soul. I am ashamed at the cowardice manifested by so many persons who should know better and who are high enough up in business to be leaders of the community. These people who should strike for the right are seldom there at the proper time. Should the hour of need arise I hope that I shall not be found among the shirkers.

This quotation should be an ample answer to those who have criticized through ignorance Apley's membership on the Save Boston Committee. It need only be added that on several occasions he followed his own dictates and even collided with Salter. Thus when the radical editor of a nationally known periodical was arrested on Boston Common for selling his magazine containing a doubtful article Apley objected to the futility of the whole performance. Although the article was distasteful to him personally, he felt that it dealt truthfully and artistically with a social evil that needs a certain wholesome recognition. It was only due to the persuasion of his wife and of his sister, Amelia Newcomb, that he did not offer financial help to this editor in the ensuing legal battle. With this prelude it is necessary to turn to the episode, so well known and so frequently misunderstood, when Apley appeared in the center of the stage to take up the cudgels against a lawyer and a faithless civil servant.

This [one of his friends has written] was the one great mistake of Apley's life. He should have let well enough alone. He was warned to let well enough alone. George was no match for an unscrupulous Irish politician. He might as well have tried to enter the ring with Jack Dempsey. Nevertheless, he chose to do it.

It is to Apley's credit that he chose seldom to speak about this affair when it was over, deeply as it must have moved him, but resorted rather to a dignified silence. Thus it is difficult at this time to find what interested Apley first in a notorious matter which never reached a final conclusion. Now that the entire episode has quieted down it is fortunately well on the way toward being forgotten, like so many other scandalous pieces of civic maladministration. Even at the time the stir subsided quickly, since fortunately an aroused public was faced with monstrous and alleged blackmail in a far higher public office; but this scandal, the resultant legal battles, and the characters involved are a part of our somewhat turgid city history. Compared to this excitement the drama in which Apley played a leading part is modest, in that it seems to have concerned only a certain element of the police force backed by a lawyer who appears to have had only the limited support of certain unscrupulous political interests.

It is, incidentally, vastly to the credit of the Boston press that nothing of this appeared at the time in print either in the *Boston Evening Transcript* or the *Boston Herald*. Only in two lesser journals were there a few "squibs" on the subject. These did little or no harm, since they could have been read by few of Apley's friends outside of the garage and the kitchen or were generally not given serious attention. It may be added here that our better-known public prints have more than once done yeoman's service in protecting the name and reputation of our better element. It is only in later years that some have succumbed to the disease of sensationalism to such an extent that this writer is told on good authority, by persons who should know, that it is more and more difficult to convince certain journalists that there are facts which either should be suppressed or should, if necessity absolutely demands it, be placed in a small "squib" on one of the rear pages.

But we are getting far afield. This phase of Boston journalism is only mentioned as proof of the utter needlessness, in this writer's opinion, for bringing up this side of Apley's life at the present time. As one of Apley's oldest friends and admirers, he consents to do so now only for three reasons. First, this little volume, because of its limited circulation, will only appear before the sympathetic eyes of Apley's own immediate family. Second, Apley's son, out of some eccentric wish to deal honestly with his father's memory by exaggerating certain phases, has demanded its inclusion in spite of all objections. The third reason is a more subtle one. It has to do with an element of drama which, try as one may to avoid it, creeps mysteriously into the life of every human being. Apley himself, with that rightness of perception which has ever characterized him, was able to see this element and to observe its gentle irony.

I wish, Will [he wrote, not long before his death, confidentially to the present writer], that I had your great powers of expression, powers which have borne such fruit and which are so universally recognized. I wish that I had your trenchant, pungent pen, your painstaking concentration, and with it your ability to probe deep beneath the veneer of character. If I had it I should spend the time, now that the doctor does not allow me to walk up and down stairs more than once a day, in writing a bit of my own life, proving that the past, which one has well-nigh forgotten, may return again in an odd moment — a bit of the past that was rather beautiful came to help me once in the sordidness of the present. I shall always revere that memory. I think you understand to what I allude. It seems so much more beautiful to me than the crass realism of present fiction. She had grown a trifle stout. Age had touched her, as it has touched us all, but still she was very beautiful.

The above quotation is ample evidence of Apley's idealism. He shared, in common with many State Street bankers, as has been evidenced by certain transactions in the present financial chaos, the belief that all men in every walk of life must be actuated by the high principles taught our class. Granted that this belief has caused much hardship in recent years to many widows and orphans, whose slender investments have been swept away on account of it, it none the less has merit. Thus, when Apley was confronted, because of the investigations of his friend Salter in behalf of the Save Boston Committee, with certain patent irregularities in the Police Department, he was deeply shocked.

That such a thing should come to pass here beneath our very noses [we find him writing] is to me incredible. I had thought after the Police Strike that the fine young fellows who had been taken into the service — young men who for the most part had served their country bravely overseas — would be beyond taint and corruption. This thing smells as much to heaven as the muckrakings of the radical Sinclair Lewis who is doing so much to discredit America. Something must be done.

To individuals of a different stamp, grown cynical by exposure to such matters, among whose number unfortunately must be included the younger members of Apley's own family, the peccadilloes of the Boston police would not have appeared so important. In spite of the shafts which have been launched at us by the envious from other sections of the country, the Boston police are no more corrupt than the police in other large centers — witness the scandals in New York and Chicago. In such large enforcement organizations there must of necessity be certain unscrupulous members.

Apley's own son took this point of view, and a letter of his from his father's files deals plainly with the case in a language which this writer will not claim for his own.

Dear Father: —
Your letter makes me worried about you. I have always thought that Salter would get you into trouble sometime because he is one of these people who can never mind his own business. This penchant for reforming the world is one of our very worst puritanical traits. Now I am really afraid that he is getting you into deep water. There is plenty of vice everywhere. It exists and you and I can't do anything about it. I note what you say about the two detectives on the Vice Squad. It is an old game, that of getting a woman to lure some man with money into a room in some disreputable hotel, and then having detectives break in and make an arrest. When Noah got out of the Ark there was probably an attorney outside in

the hall ready to compose matters by the payment of what you term blackmail. I wish you could realize that there is nothing new in it and nothing startling. Your letter which you ask me to burn does not give me a single indignant quiver.

In my opinion any old dodo, whether he is in the Social Register or not, who gets himself caught upstairs in a hotel room where he does not belong, ought to be made to pay for it. It's his funeral. It isn't yours.

Have you ever thought why Salter wants to push you into this thing? I'll tell you why — because he hasn't got the guts himself. I hate to speak so strongly but I feel it. You say that other private attorneys have not the courage or the public spirit to take up the case. In my humble opinion they are showing very good sense. You are not a criminal lawyer and you never have been. Your work in Apley and Reid has been almost entirely trust work. If you get mixed up with shyster lawyers you'll get hurt. It is all right when it comes to protesting against electric signs on the Common and about changes on the Esplanade, but let it go at that.

At any rate, don't do anything until I have seen you. Since you have cautioned me not to speak to Mother about it, I won't. But I feel so strongly about this that I am coming up to Boston next weekend. There are some plans of my own which I wish to speak about at any rate. . . .

This letter requires but little comment. It represents a practical and compromising point of view which was foreign to Apley's nature when he was thoroughly aroused. Why this situation should have aroused him does not perhaps admit of any easy explanation unless one casts back over the threads of his life. There may have been in his actions something of personal vindication but more than that it reveals the inherent contradiction of his character. On the one hand, we have found him struggling for security; on the other, we have found him struggling against it. Something of this personal tumult which may never wholly be resolved is reflected in an intimate letter to his friend, Walker, written at the time. It was written when Apley was recovering from a bad bout with the grippe and the ensuing physical weakness may have caused him to give way to a definite weakness of character.

For several days, while lying still in bed, listening to Catharine read me "The Decline and Fall of the Roman Empire," I have had a good deal of time to think about myself and not so pleasantly either, Mike. Here I am getting to be an old man. I seem to have done nothing except develop a few convictions. I have been busy, and even now detail work and the household bills are creeping up on me; but I have really done nothing. I have sat and have watched the things which I have cared for most in life being threatened on every side. I fully realize that I have never struck an honest blow for them. It is time for someone to strike a blow, and now I have an opportunity. I will tell you about it later.

Just this morning, however, just when I was recovered enough to be able to crawl down to the library and to take down a Waverley, which seems to stick in my mind better than Gibbon, I received a piece of news which demanded nearly all my attention. John has written me that he has been secretly married for two months to a Mrs. McCullogh of Bay Heights, Long Island. He has spoken of her sometimes, but I never conceived, believing that John was basically sound, that such an eventuality would be possible. From all I have been able to gather, Mrs. McCullogh comes of a reasonably good New York family, but this is not the point. The point is that Mrs. McCullogh was in Reno, Nevada, six months ago, where she obtained a divorce from her husband, on the grounds of cruel and abusive treatment. Although I cannot and will not believe for a moment that John, in any way whatsoever, had anything to do with this divorce, at the same time the matter presents an aspect which makes me glad at last that John's activities are centred about New York instead of here. I had hoped that he might be back with us again but now this will be impossible, at least for several years. Of course his mother, who is more upset than I am, has been out already telling our friends and the family that she is pleased with the news and glad that at last John is settling down. She is adding, as I hope that you will add, that our new daughter-in-law is a very fine person and that John is fortunate in every way. His aunt and his cousins have been so splendid about it that I am very proud of the family. John is coming to see me to-morrow. His wife is staying in New York.

Frankly, I had hoped better things of John but now that he has in quite a real sense left us, I feel more than ever a sense of responsibility toward the family. It is time that some one of us took a definite and a strong position. Due to the kindness of Henry Salter, the opportunity is ready for my hand. When I am able to leave the house I am going to gather together material which will result in the conviction of a lawyer here named O'Reilly and two plain-clothes detectives for blackmail.

This letter, written at a dark moment, similar to several which we have found crowding on his life through no fault of his own, mirrors only one of these rare gloomy moods. In many ways he was to be pleasantly surprised at many aspects of this seemingly impossible union. Indeed a few years later Apley's fondness for his new daughter-in-law, which was considered by some to verge on almost unjust partiality, was mentioned by both his wife and daughter, but always in a cheerful spirit; in fact, everyone who has met Louise Hogarth Apley has succumbed to her charm and it is gratifying to many, now that John Apley's duty and position have made his thoughts turn more and more to the city of his birth, that his gracious and talented wife is now the new hostess of Hillcrest. Even after his first conversation with his son, George Apley's worst fears were allayed.

Dear John: —

I cannot for the life of me see why you did not tell me in the first place that Louise, whom I am growing more and more anxious daily to set eyes upon, was one of the Hogarths of Connecticut. This, of course, makes a very great difference, foolish, perhaps, in your eyes, but not in mine. It has always been a most important thing with me to place a person. Many of us are accused unjustly of being snobbish. This is not the case. The so-called snobbishness is generally due to one's inability to place the subject of it in the accepted social scale. Louise's being a Hogarth places her perfectly. I am sure that the man McCullogh must have been a very bad hat.

There is one thing which pleases me even more than this. That is your news that Louise is very comfortably off in her own right. While the actual financial element fortunately makes very little difference, as we all seem to be a little more comfortably off no matter what happens, the appearance of everything is much better. There can be no possibility of talk of Louise's marrying you for your money, and an even division of property on each side makes on the whole for a happy marriage, according to my observation.

Your mother is redecorating your old room and putting twin beds in it, as seems to be the new fashion. She wishes me to write Louise, as I certainly shall, and as she is doing also, asking you both to come up next week. I may add that you owe it to the family yourself. They have stood by you like nailers through this thing. Even your Cousin Henry Apley has written me a letter of congratulation, which I do not think is ironical. This was on the whole broad-minded of him, considering his pique about moving Cousin Harriet. I am glad that I have been to the cemetery to see where she has finally been placed.

Besides all this, I think it is a very important thing for you to show your face at both the Province and the Berkley Club. That Tennis and Squash Club of yours, where there is so much drinking, does not really matter. I need not say that I shall be glad to take the time to appear with you at both the Province and the Berkley Clubs and even think it might be well to arrange a small dinner for you at both. This, if ever, is a time when the head must be held high, and you may not realize, as I do, what a store casual people place on such gestures.

There is one thing, though, on which my mind is set and upon which you are hardly in a position to judge. You have had your fling, John, and I shall have mine. Before I have finished, this man O'Reilly will face the jury of the criminal court, let the chips fall where they may. Again I caution you not to mention this to your mother. Things are going very well in this direction. I believe I very nearly induced one of the victims of this petty blackmail ring to prepare himself to testify. O'Reilly himself is disturbed and has been around to see me. He is red-faced and noisy, with the makings of a demagogue. He wishes, of course, for me to "lay off," as he puts it, but I shall do nothing of the sort. I feel ten years younger since I have taken up the cudgels in this matter. . . .

Always happy in activity, it may very well be that the next few months were some of the happiest in Apley's life. He was finding himself and was playing a part in the world which he had not known, always a stimulating matter. His personality was making itself felt there, as it had in the life where his lot had placed him. In many ways, under suitable circumstances, his sympathy and his sense of humor were very keen. An adept, from long experience, in collating facts, his work in this self-imposed task was in a measure congenial. The letters which he wrote to his friend Walker, now as ever his favorite confidant, betray an elation which is perhaps not entirely healthy. He speaks of standing on his own feet at last. He even speaks almost jeeringly of certain institutions and of certain friends who did not share this liberation of the spirit.

In many ways [he writes] I wish that I had embraced criminal law, for there is certainly nothing humdrum about this business, and one is face to face with life. Salter is a brick about everything. He has detailed two investigators under my orders. These fellows dig up all sorts of matters and bring the most amazing types into the office. Reid, who has grown to be pretty much of an "old fogey" now that he is growing older, has obliged me to take another office across the hall as he says that my new clients, as he calls them, disturb our old clients who come in to discuss their investments. Be this as it may, my new clients are most amusing. I can tell you some good stories about them, Mike, when next we meet.

Do you remember the old days when we had the snowball battles on the Common — the North End against the West End? This experience reminds me very much of those days. I see the same sort of fellows and a lot of them are capital people. I am glad now that I have always made it a point of going once every two weeks to chat with the men in the Apley Sailors' Home. My experience there helps me a great deal here. It leads to the definite conviction that there is a lot of good in everyone.

This O'Reilly cannot be very popular as many persons in

every walk of life are anxious to have him punished. I have looked up his record. He went to the Boston Latin School which proves that I was right in always thinking that this school has been losing its grip since my father's time. What is not a little exasperating is the very great difficulty in getting any *bona fide* evidence in such a case, since no one wishes to appear, for private reasons. One generally seems to have to talk to friends of friends. Only this afternoon, however, matters seemed to be clearing up. A man has come to me, introduced by one of Salter's agents, who has a friend living at a hotel in the south part of the city, the name of which I have never heard before and which would certainly mean nothing to you. His friend has been one of those who has been victimized by O'Reilly and requests a personal interview. These poor fellows are all shy. He is afraid to come to the office, but his friend is arranging things so that I can go to the hotel and see him to-morrow afternoon.

It is great to be doing something, Mike. For the first time in a long while I feel that life amounts to something.

CHAPTER XXVIII

—————•—————

CRISIS

*The Facing of an Event
Which Had Far Better Not Have Been Included
In This Work*

IT IS this writer's experience that at some time or other the best of us is inclined to "take the bit in his teeth." Such can be the only explanation for Apley's lack of judgment, that and his confiding belief that other men acted according to his own lights. Always a man of caution and acumen in conducting the affairs of others, to the extent that he came through the depression with the reputation of being one of the best trustees in Boston, Apley in this instance was neglectful of his own interests. It will be remembered that Apley was one of the few who sensed the impending difficulties in the orgy of the 1929 market, but this man was not the Apley who embarked upon an errand about which many of his friends had cautioned him, including the present writer. At five o'clock, on a February afternoon, Apley left his office in State Street, a man without a blemish. At seven o'clock that evening George Apley was under arrest in a Precinct Police Station house under charges of having been discovered in a hotel bedroom with a woman of doubtful reputation. This unbelievable change in affairs, as is well enough known now, was engineered by the man O'Reilly, who must have long been waiting the opportunity to tar with his own brush a man of public spirit and beyond reasonable reproach. Although no one living can doubt the folly of this accusation, the very absurdity has cast its own shadow, for, while granting its absurdity, many who knew him best ever afterwards took a light view of George Apley's ability, going even so far as to indulge in mistakenly humorous comments, and this for Apley was a very real burden. There is no doubt that through this unforeseen accident Apley lost a certain position as a man of affairs. Thus it must largely be ascribed to these circumstances more than to any desire for ease on his part that Apley's name did not appear as often of later years on committees where he had been formerly one of the most useful and indefatigable guiding spirits. Only toward the end of Apley's life did certain persons realize their error.

It was a time when Apley was at last to know his true friends and their loyalty he never forgot. His first action on being freed on bail was to offer his resignation to the Province and the Berkley Clubs, in two identical letters: —

Gentlemen: —

Through no fault of mine, I find myself accused of a crime the commission of which I trust I will be considered incapable. As I have every fear that my name will appear in this connection in the public prints, I offer my resignation to this Club. I do so as much out of consideration to myself as to others. I cannot appear in any company any member of which may harbour a doubt regarding my reputation. . . .

It is needless to add that Apley's resignation was not accepted, nor was it accepted from any other organization where it was tendered. As many friends told him, this high-minded gesture was not necessary, and in the perspective of years it is very clear that altogether too much was made of the matter. It can remain now only as a tribute to Apley's integrity that he took the affair so seriously. Any man as high-minded as he might have found himself in a similar predicament.

The more responsible members of our community were deeply aroused, even many who knew Apley's name without having had the honor of his acquaintance. There was a general feeling of indignation that our legal system, with its myriad delays and innumerable loopholes of escape for the criminal, could be such as to impugn the motives of a man of Apley's stamp to the length of threatening him with an appearance before the bar of justice. To many it seemed a strange irony that there should be any necessity for Apley's word being balanced against the words of two presumably faithless public servants. An informal and secret committee was formed at once of men of affairs with political and other connections, to take full charge of Apley's interests, and the important sections of the press hastened to coöperate. Almost overnight representations were made in political quarters where they would do the most good, including, it has been said, the Governor of the Commonwealth. It was unfortunate at the time that Salter, who would have been of great help, was in Florida investigating prison camps.

Although in the best informed quarters the spirit against the man O'Reilly ran high, it seems peculiar in the light of the present that there should have been a cleavage along certain national and religious lines. The fact remains, however, that those political demagogues, who are always with us, showed unmistakable and dangerous signs of using this incident to fan

the fictitious flame of class antagonism. In twenty-four hours
those familiar with the beat of the popular pulse reluctantly
reached the conclusion that a very real crisis was arising out
of the ill-considered talk among politicians who were "making hay." There were actually murmurs, undoubtedly fostered
by the man O'Reilly, of privilege and of persecution of the
poor.

Fortunately, perhaps, there was but one simple thought in
the mind of everyone who heard of this, which stood out
above any desire to comment. It concerned the natural question
of how Apley had ever fallen into this predicament. This question has been answered frankly by Apley himself, whose
dignified attitude through all this trying time could not have
been improved upon. It is answered by him in a frank memorial
written at the time for benefit of friends and family, and read
afterwards at several dinner clubs: —

There are times when one must be frank. I have always
been willing to admit my faults and I should be a very "bad
sport" now if I did not plead guilty to the faults of carelessness and stupidity. The man who gave his name as Morrissey,
and whom I have never seen nor heard of since, much as I
should like to meet him, accompanied me to the hotel in
question, where, I may add, he seemed well known to the employees, although these subsequently have consistently denied
all knowledge of him. He led me, with the tacit consent of
those employees, up one flight of stairs and along a corridor
where there were sounds of phonograph music and worse, to
a door midway down this corridor, which he opened without
knocking, and invited me inside. I was dull enough to accept
his invitation. Saying that he would be back in a moment, he
closed the door behind me, permitting me to find myself in

a shoddily furnished apartment and to discover that the man whom I was seeking was not there. Instead I found myself facing a woman whom I had never seen before, quite patently in *négligée*. Before I even had the opportunity to excuse my presence and to say that there must be some mistake there was a thundering knock on the door. Before I was allowed time to answer this summons the door was broken open. I had not realized that it was secured by a spring lock. Two men appeared, with police badges, who refused cynically, almost rudely, to accept my natural explanation. This is my honest version of an affair which may be believed or disbelieved by anyone who knows me.

I may add that five minutes later, before I left this place, Mr. O'Reilly appeared and presented in garbled language a proposal for settling the matter then and there. I did not find myself in a position to accept his proposal. I demanded at once to be taken to the nearest station house. I was pleased that my learned opponent, Mr. O'Reilly, seemed surprised and even somewhat disconcerted by this demand. I told him he did not know whom he was dealing with.

In the ensuing days Mr. O'Reilly was to realize very definitely the type of man with whom he was dealing. There is one doubt which no one who is acquainted with this affair can harbor against George Apley, that is any reflection upon his undisputed coolness, fortitude, and courage. From the outset, he expressed not only a willingness but a definite desire to appear in Court and to seek vindication. It was this desire which made the good offices of his friends both embarrassing and difficult, for there were certain very cogent reasons at the time why this matter should have been hushed up, and every representation was laid before him.

To the present writer's certain knowledge a conference was

arranged behind closed doors in a well-known law firm, where O'Reilly and Apley met face to face in an effort to compose their difficulties. By this time, however, it was too late. Certain slanderous insinuations had come to Apley's ears, emanating from the turbulent political element which has been our curse. According to everything this writer has been able to gather, the man O'Reilly was hotheaded and importunate. He also demanded a trial for what he had the ill grace to call his own personal vindication. Three days after Apley's apprehension the situation was increasingly ugly. It seemed as though Apley and many others were to be involved in a very unsavory quarrel.

The reason why Apley allowed the matter to drop even today is not very generally known. The explanation lies at the present writer's hand and it will now be given light. It is included in the following letter, and in a letter to his friend Walker. The letter which is now quoted was found with two others in a secret drawer of Apley's desk.

Dear Mr. Apley: —

I wonder if you still remember who I am? It has all been such a long while ago, but I still remember you and I have thought about you a great deal and I have always been glad that I knew you. I remember you as a fine gentleman. I know you are still. I know it has been a long while since our paths have crossed, but now the time has come when I really must see you for your own sake, because knowing you, I will not see you hurt. Can I call on you at your own house privately at five o'clock to-morrow afternoon?

I sign myself by the name which I still hope that you remember, —

MARY MONAHAN.

It is of interest to note that on the same date that the above letter was written Apley himself wrote as follows, to a friend of his in a public position of very great importance — so great that names will not be mentioned even in these intimate pages: —

I am grateful and I am honoured by your concern in me personally. I can also understand your worry over such a public airing of a controversy on the eve of an election.

If you will pardon my saying so, I do not think your concern on the last point does you credit. It is out of keeping with the high place which your family has always held in state and national councils. We have compromised too long with principle here and elsewhere. I do not propose to make any such compromise.

Any mental anguish which a complete airing of this matter may cause me or my family is something which I shall gladly endure for the sake of principle. I am ready and anxious to have my day in Court. I am anxious to take my place among the few who do not compromise for personal or for material reasons.

If Apley's point of view, so categorically expressed above, underwent a change after the interview foreshadowed by the letter of the former Miss Monahan, his reasons are deeply personal and private. It was only when an unforeseen aspect of the situation was presented to him that Apley consented to change his position. This change was not due to an alteration of principle but due to a human element involved which appealed to Apley's sense of chivalry. It is fortunate that something of his reaction is still extant in a communication to his friend Walker, now in this writer's hands.

I have been very deeply moved this afternoon [he writes] and I am still a little bewildered at myself. In a most unforeseen way the long arm of the past has reached out through the haze of memories and has touched me on the shoulder. This afternoon a figure of my past came back like a ghost, but a living ghost. It was a strange experience in the agony which I have suffered of late and strange for the humdrum world in which we live. I wonder if you remember something which happened in college, of which I made you a confidant. If you do, I need only say that she came back in my hour of need and sat with me alone in my library on Beacon Street, for two hours, a sort of a ghost of an Annabelle Lee. We had our own kingdom by the sea once and a little of that kingdom came back too. At any rate, a very strange thing occurred. She was much more real to me and the time we spent is a much more real space of time than anything in the dull years which have elapsed. In those two hours I could believe that I was alive again after a period of partial paralysis and I know she felt as I did. Her voice called something back. She had come to help me in my hour of need. I was glad to be able to help her instead, but I could not have done otherwise.

One must be loyal to one's people and I know now that she has been one of my own people always. When she told me that the man O'Reilly was her husband's cousin this was enough. I cannot and I shall not raise my hand against anything which belongs to her. Though I do not agree with her point of view I can sympathize with it, because it is based on family. She has a position quite apart from ours but none the less important. She is connected by family with many of our officials. I believe after this talk that something may be arranged.

When I told Catharine about this, when she tapped on the library door at the end of an hour and a half, Catharine's pleasure in itself was a reward. Those two, although I could not have believed it, were sisters under the skin, little as I have ever liked the expression and little as I approve of Kipling's jingles. I shall never forget the light in Catharine's eyes when she took her hand with most unusual impulsiveness and said: "I am so glad that you are looking after George. He needs it sometimes, doesn't he?" I did not try to disabuse her of her error. Catharine would never understand that I was looking after memory.

This letter, vague in itself, shows a human side of Apley which may have been neglected. It illustrates the depth of his nature and betrays a hint of that melancholy, as well as of that frustration prevalent in many of us, which he customarily hid beneath his common sense and cheerfulness. It shows that Apley was what this biographer has striven perhaps vainly to show — a man in every sense, a man of flesh and blood and a generous, tolerant man. The result of this single interview quickly became apparent.

I have spent this afternoon talking to O'Reilly [he writes again to Walker]. In many ways the man is a capital fellow. He knows a great deal about pugilism and sport, and seems surprised that I was once interested in boxing. He was more surprised at several things which his cousin had told him. We all met together pleasantly and informally in South Boston. I tell you this confidentially as no one else knows of it and no one must know, including Catharine. I am glad to be able to turn some work over to O'Reilly, which is quite different from the sort of thing he has been doing. In the course of the afternoon a number of his friends came to call, who also turned out to be very good fellows indeed. Now that we know each other, I think all difficulty is over. I have agreed to give — anonymously of course — a sum for the building and the upkeep of a municipal gymnasium in South Boston. It was a pleasure to be able to relieve O'Reilly of certain small financial difficulties. The two detectives who arrested me were also present at the meeting. They, too, turned out to be surprisingly human, with wives and children of their own. One of them served in John's army organization and was actually present when John received his wound. The world is a small place after all. Both these men, at my inducement, are gladly withdrawing from the police force to take positions as watchmen at the Apley Mills, where I think they will be very useful. Furthermore, O'Reilly in the most generous possible spirit has volunteered to write a letter, which will be made public, explaining that the whole matter centred around the mistaken number of the room and ending with a very handsome and manly apology. I think that everyone concerned in this affair is to be congratulated.

The actual details of these negotiations have never been made public, nor is there any need to speculate upon them at present except to say that whatever they may have been, they were a result of Apley's generosity. It is worth while noting here also that in after years Apley's attitude toward our South Boston element was marked by kindliness and understanding. Opportunities were often taken by various persons politically popular in that section to say a commendatory word for Apley. In fact, in certain diatribes against so-called "bluestocking" classes Apley's name was frequently specifically mentioned as an exception. The floral tributes which appeared at his funeral from many Hibernian organizations were proof enough of the esteem in which he was held.

There is no doubt that in the broader sense Apley was a man beloved by all. There are many who still remember in the last years of Apley's life, when he volunteered to take a place on the Hoover Flying Caravan, which penetrated even the most hostile and violent districts of South Boston, that when Apley arose to speak there against Bossism, much to the concern of many of his friends, he was greeted with a round of cheers which lasted for five minutes. In fact, the applause was so great at various periods of his speech that he had real difficulty in making himself understood. Indeed, after his reception, many of the politically wise were much surprised when this district turned out solidly for the present incumbent in the White House, and reëlected every one of the local individuals against whom Apley had so emphatically spoken. It may be added, however, that after this crisis in his life we find Apley standing more and more on the side lines, as an interested observer, taking less and less part in the more picturesque efforts of his contemporaries. His reasons are adequately expressed in an address which he delivered before a coffee party during one of the municipal political campaigns.

"I am glad to see so many young men here," he said, "because it shows that you young fellows at last are becoming aware that you and not my generation are responsible for making Boston a decent place to live in. I think it is high time that we oldsters turned over the business to you. I for one do not believe in standing in the way of younger men. This is my reason for refusing a place on this committee. Nevertheless, as in the past, I am ready at any time with my advice and I can promise you that what little I contribute financially will be as large as ever."

Thus we have reached a phase when Apley's public life, in a very considerable sense, may be considered as over. His thoughts were turning more and more, as an older man's must, toward home. But his observations on the increasing complexities of the world around him were quite as keen as ever and the inherent soundness of his conclusions was unaltered. Yet it must not be supposed that he shirked leadership in certain crises. When the proposal was made to have a motor speedway along the Esplanade, Apley was again in the forefront of the battle, nor was it due to Apley's indifference that a large electric sign, advertising a certain inexpensive variety of motor car still flaunts itself insolently over the Boston Common. He justly called this sign, to the end of his days, "Our Badge of Shame." Aside from the cares of family, his thoughts were ever on the purpose of making Boston a better place to live in.

"And indeed," said Apley, "it is a good place to live in, taken all in all. Probably the best place in this neurotic world, with the possible exception of London, although I am not even sure about this. At any rate, it is the only place I care to live in."

———•———

CHAPTER XXIX

RING IN THE NEW

A Grandfather's Salutation
To a New and, One Must Hope,
A Sounder Generation

IN THE AUTUMN of 1928 a new pleasure and a very great joy came into Apley's life. It need hardly be said here that this concerned the birth of a son to his own son and daughter-in-law, John and Louise Apley.

Dear John: —

I still cannot understand why you have insisted on the newfangled idea of having my grandson — because I know he will be a boy, since something must work out right sometime — brought into the world in the delivery room of a hospital. Your mother and I had both hoped that dear Louise might be induced to come to Hillcrest to be cared for by Doctor Hadley, who brought you into the world. Certainly she would have been as well cared for and I think that I might have been of some help to you in this trying time. I could explain to you by word of mouth, instead of by letter, that women on such occasions are apt to be a little bit difficult. You must be very careful of Louise.

I am sending down your porringer, as well as the little mug, which belonged to the first John Apley. I need not say that of course he will bear that name, unless you wish to name him Thomas, after your own grandfather.

Of course, the christening will be held at Hillcrest and my own dear mother's lifelong friend Mr. Pettingill will perform the ceremony, if his health will permit him. The big parlour is being newly decorated for this purpose by your mother. I am seeing that your own little room by the back stairs is made into a nursery. The new nursery is being redecorated, and I have been up to the attic myself to get out some of my own old toys. You may tell Louise that they will all be disinfected, although I am not sure that this is necessary. I am also having that sharp curve in the driveway straightened. It was well enough for carriages but not so for motors. This means that one of the large rhododendron bushes must be removed. The tree surgeons have been working on it this afternoon with a derrick and they will place it on the second terrace. I have been in communication with Groton School already and shall see that his name is entered at the first possible moment.

I wish I were not so busy here, because I should like to be in New York myself. Your mother, of course, is coming down, so is your Aunt Amelia, and I have cabled Eleanor to cut her visit to Paris short and to return at once. Is there anything else you think I ought to do? I am setting a small fund aside for him to-morrow in Liberty and Municipal bonds. Your little pony which is still in the stable seems stiff in the legs, being now twenty-eight years old. I am inquiring about another one, but the cart and the saddle both seem very good. Of course, he will be christened in the dress which your great-grandmother embroidered for your grandfather and which I wore and which you wore. . . .

Dear John: —

I need not tell you how deeply moved I was when I received your telegram. At last it seems as though my life were really worth while. My thoughts have been with you all day long, for I know you have been through a great ordeal. No ordeal that I have experienced, and I have passed through several lately, is greater than parenthood. I am glad Louise is doing well and I am sending my dear daughter-in-law your grandmother's pearl chaplet which has not seen the light for a long while. You may tell her that steps are already being taken to replace those pearls which have lost their lustre in the safe-deposit vault. A wire and a confirming letter have already gone to Groton School. I have been busy all day receiving congratulations. You will not understand until you grow older that this child is in a very real sense my own.

There is one thing which worries me very deeply. Now that they take newborn babies and place them upon shelves in a warm room, with all the other children, no matter whose, that may be born in the hospital, I think that there is a very reasonable chance for error. You must take every precaution about this and you must have him removed from that place at the first possible moment. I do not like the idea of my grandson being placed in a vault with a lot of casual screaming brats and with the ever-present danger not only of disease but of being placed in the wrong bassinet. Please let me know that I need not worry about this and let me know at the earliest moment when you can arrive at Hillcrest. I am already working over a list of invitations and of course we must know the date. . . .

It is pleasing to note here that the wishes of George Apley were scrupulously followed by his son. John Apley, Jr., was christened at Hillcrest January 15, 1929, the house being especially opened for the occasion. Except that through some oversight no arrangements had been made for the distaff side of the family until the Hogarths arrived quite unexpectedly, the occasion moved with very little friction.

Dear John: —

I did not sleep well last night. As one grows older sleep does
not come as easily. I put on my dressing-gown and went into
your mother's sewing parlour at the front of the house to read,
but I could not keep my mind on the pages of my book although it was my Emerson, who I believe is one of the greatest men ever produced by this nation, certainly by Harvard.
I could not keep my mind on the book because my thoughts
were like a book in themselves. I had taken two cups of
coffee last night after dinner in order to fortify myself against
Professor Speyer's paper, "Certain Dangerous Modern Tendencies," which he read before the Eight O'Clock Club. Being
Secretary of this organization I was obliged to keep alert
enough to make an abstract of the speaker's remarks. I have
never liked the practice of borrowing the speaker's paper later,
which is indulged in by some secretaries I might mention. Of
late years this necessity for concentration is apt to give me a
bad night afterward.

My mind was like the pages of a book. It fluttered here and
there as pages do when the wind blows them, out under the
pines at Pequod Island. The house was very quiet. Outside
the fronts of Beacon Street, the brick walks and the asphalt
shone emptily beneath those new glaring street lights that il-
luminate our front rooms and disturb our slumber. For one of
the first times I can remember it seemed to me that Beacon
Street was a trifle sad in its emptiness. It was as though something had left it. It was like that street in Ecclesiastes "when
the sound of the grinding is low." I began thinking about you
and about the newest and most welcome member of our family.
I hoped that you were not bringing our new boy into as changing a world as the one into which I introduced you. I had never
thought before that this devastating effect of almost uncalcu-
lable change is what has made you different from what I might

have expected, but I believe that this is the reason that you are sometimes somewhat of an enigma to me. You are a part of this new Frankenstein-like world which will always be a little bit beyond my powers of comprehension.

Have you ever stopped to think how great this material revolution has been? You have probably not done so any more than I, because we accept the obvious so easily. When I was a boy I went to bed by candlelight. The old candlesticks are still on the shelf by the cellar stairs, and later there were jokes about country bumpkins blowing out the gas. I washed out of a pitcher and a basin. Later there was a single zinc tub for the entire family. I remember how it surprised me even five years ago when a salesman demonstrated to me that it was quite possible to arrange modern plumbing facilities in a place like Pequod Island. The human voice can now reach around the world. It is a simple afternoon's diversion to drive eighty or ninety miles. Our two heroes, Byrd and Lindbergh, — by far the most hopeful, indeed to my mind the only hopeful, human products arising from this chaotic change, — have spanned the Atlantic Ocean. (We are all not a little gratified incidentally that Richard Byrd is among us here in Boston. I proposed him myself for the Berkley Club.) There is no use reciting any more of the obvious. I have given reason enough why you should all be changed. This material change has made you all materialists, and yet it has rendered your grasp on reality uncertain. It has made you rely on the material gratification of the senses. It has made you worship Mammon and in this new material world everything comes too easily. Heat comes too easily and cold. Money comes too easily. Don't forget that it will go as easily too. Romance comes too easily, and success. We have all grown soft from this ease. Position changes too easily. Values shift elusively. When everything is totalled up we have evolved a fine variety of flushing toilets but not a very good world, if you will excuse the coarseness of the simile.

I hope for our new boy's sake that this change is very nearly over. I hope, when he grows up, that those who are comfortably off will begin to realize again their duty to the community. I hope, when he grows up, that he may be able to recognize a lady by her manner and by her dress. I hope that he will see what so many of you have forgotten, that there must be certain standards, that there must be certain formulae in art and thought and manners. There must be a class which sets a tone, not for its own pleasure, but because of the responsibility which it owes to others. In a sense it may be what the demagogues call a privileged class, but it must know how to pay for its privilege.

Such a class must always have its eccentricities, but it should also have its ideals. I think that I am safe in saying that we have such a class here, which is what raises us above mediocrity. We have contrived to maintain something of the spirit in spite of all this change. In my opinion it is the best heritage which we can pass to another generation. I hope that I may not live to see the time when this is swept away. I hope that you may understand this now that you have a son.

Yesterday I bowled at the Province Club and my back is very lame. I have also been reading a book which has made me very sad. It is by a new author named Hemingway entitled "The Sun also Rises." I am not a prude but I do not like it. This Hemingway is obviously not a gentleman nor are his characters gentlemen or ladies, yet I am broad-minded enough to admit that the man has a certain startling and crude power, although I feel that he resorts to artistically unfair sensational and mechanical tricks.

When this book came up before our Beacon Street Circulating Library Committee I stood out against all the others except Mrs. Sill, who always likes to be contradictory, for having it included on our recommended list. I did so because the book, gross, sexual, and unmoral though it be, points a very definite moral. It is that this wretched promiscuity so widely practised does not and cannot pay. It shows the unhappiness of those who practise it. Yet surely Mr. Hemingway must exaggerate somewhat. From what I am able to observe of the new members of the Club in Cambridge these young fellows are of as fine a type as ever, though I do believe they drink more than is good for them. . . .

Dear John: —

In my opinion one of the most damnable examples of the materialism which we face is the new School of Business Administration at Harvard. Though widely different, it is as great a threat to idealism as Prohibition itself. I have, of course, not been to see it and when I motor by it I look the other way; but I hear that there is a tablet upon one of the buildings which greatly amuses me. If I am not mistaken it speaks of business as the "newest of the arts and the oldest of the professions." If this is so, it is wrong on both counts. Certainly there is one profession which is older.

By the by, I have a new bootlegger. He is really a capital fellow. He gets his supplies, a few bottles at a time, from Pullman car porters coming from Montreal. I am buying from him liberally, purely out of principle as of course I stocked the cellar full enough to last my lifetime before that damnable amendment came into force. Also, of course, there is your grandfather's cellar at Hillcrest over which I am placing a special watchman. The papers last week report three deaths by wood alcohol poisoning and there have been two murders in bootleggers' feuds in the North End. All this is capital and I hope teaches everyone a lesson. . . .

Dear John: —

It is always a pleasure to write you because I know that I

can speak to you freely — a thing which is not always possible hereabouts. Eleanor brought a strange man home to dinner last night, since this seems to be a day of casual acquaintances. She was evasive as to where she met him but he appears to be a graduate student of Harvard. His peculiarity of speech and manner indicate that he comes from a very long distance, probably the Middle West, a place I have not seen, nor do I wish to see it.

What amused both your mother and me was his total misconception of our position. As you know, we have always tried to live simply and I dislike doing rooms over, so that the house may be a trifle musty, which may be why our guest laboured under the delusion that we were not comfortably off. This must have been his delusion because he spoke in a radical manner, favouring the cutting down of large inheritances. I did not care to disabuse him. In fact, in the library over cigars I agreed with him.

I think it would be a very good thing if a large number of the colossal fortunes now being accumulated by the uneducated were eventually handed over to the Government. This, of course, does not apply to people who are used to the responsibilities which go with inherited wealth. This is a small class but one of the greatest importance. Upon our shoulders rests the future of all educational and philanthropic institutions. It is the very basis of the world as we know it, but once our class loses its sense of responsibility it is lost. The employees in the Apley Mills are well-fed and well-clothed and they always must be. We must also do what little we can to relieve the sufferings of those less fortunate than ourselves—less fortunate, perhaps, but it must be remembered also that these persons have a freedom of action which is denied us. You must be very careful about this when I am gone. One of the most important things these days is to live unostentatiously. Thus nothing has pleased me so much as the belief of Eleanor's new friend that we are not comfortably off. . . .

Dear John:—

I have incurred a great deal of difficulty in taking a stand which may surprise you. I heard a number of the younger members of the Club speaking of an allegedly obscene book called "Lady Chatterley's Lover" by one of these new writers named Lawrence, not to be confused with the British hero who has done so much for Arabia. I laid hands upon this book expecting to be greatly shocked, as I have been by nearly every bit of literature which has come my way of late. At first I was stunned but now, in my opinion, this book is a work of art. Even your mother and I have quarrelled violently on the subject—a thing which has not happened in years. I made a great mistake in allowing your mother to read it. It is now in the safe with the silver so that Eleanor cannot lay her hands on it. Things go on here much as usual; I am glad that this is so. Boston is a pretty good place to live in. . . .

One attitude of strangers in our midst, which has always been a source of amazement to this writer and to others, is an impression which they bring away of a narrow-minded dourness among those who set our social and intellectual tone. In this they are very wrong. We have for years harbored minorities. When one penetrates beneath the meticulous exterior, one finds here a mellow broad-mindedness and a cheerful optimism for the future, not manifest elsewhere. Age was making Apley mellow; age was gradually giving him a confidence unknown to him in earlier manhood.

A great many things have been going on here [we find him writing to his friend Walker]. A great many "crackpots" have

advanced a great many absurd ideas, but these do not disturb
me as they used to. I notice that every time good sound common sense triumphs in the end. There is a substratum of common sense upon which we can all count. We all know in our
heart of hearts that we are a good deal more comfortably off
than we would be anywhere else. The stock market reflects
this feeling, but it is a great deal too high. I am now well out
of it and back into tax-exempt Governments and Municipals.
I really believe that my total Income Tax this year will not
exceed seventy-five dollars, which I think under the circumstances is doing rather well.

This mellowness of Apley, not unlike the sunset which casts
a glow which gives an infinite softness to the bricks of Beacon
Hill, is manifest in his attitude toward the whimsies of the
younger generation. So much has been written about this phase
of postwar madness, now fortunately waning, that unpleasant
details need not be mentioned. Apley, whose sense of pro-
priety was strong, was also among the first to sound a note of
hope. We quote from another letter to Walker, which displays
that same breadth of vision that allowed him to see the good in
so many things, as in "Lady Chatterley's Lover."

Dorothy and Johnny Stillwell asked me to their daughter,
Jane's, coming-out party at the Somerset. I attended frankly
to lend the Stillwells my support as I have always admired
the sensible way this nice little couple has behaved. It was
the first time that I have attended such a party since the War.
I was prepared for surprises, but not for what I saw. It seems
to me that this "cutting-in" system has turned a formal function into a grotesque rout. The very music to which the young
people danced was calculated to arouse rather than to suppress
desire. I for one am not averse to seeing romance bud upon

the ballroom floor, and the Somerset can be thanked for many of our more successful marriages. Indeed, I believe, that is what the Somerset is for. Yet there can be no real romance with such music, especially when the orchestra leader bursts into song rich in expressions from the stable and the gutter. There no longer seems to be any discipline in the stag line. Indeed, almost the entire floor is covered with indolent young men, many of doubtful antecedents, some of whom are smoking and some frankly intoxicated.

A few years ago, this whole unsavoury sight would have made me feel that the world was over, but we oldsters are not as easily shocked as we used to be. I know now, after talking with certain young fellows at the Club who are quite frank about it, that most of this exterior is largely "bosh." You have only to look at the faces of these youngsters to know that they are as moral as we were and that their ideals are quite as high as ours. If there is a certain lack of reticence in their dealings with young girls, who certainly look very sweet and athletic in the new dresses, this frankness is probably all for the best. As Kipling so aptly puts it, "a kiss or two is nothing to you." Perhaps it meant a good deal more to us, Mike, than was absolutely necessary. I am sure that the relationships of these young people are all founded, as ours were, on a spirit of companionship. Considering their family tradition it would be absurd to think of anything else.

It even occurs to me to-night, although this is simply a whim of the moment and probably not quite sound, that you and I may have missed something in our day, Mike. In a great many ways I envy these children their freedom and their companionship with its many possibilities for the outlet of natural high spirits. I am sure, for them as they did for us, that most things will turn out right in the end, and perhaps they will all be better wives and husbands for it. At any rate it all seems a little beyond me now. It is time for younger people to bother about these things. It is time for us to sit by the side of the road and to watch the parade go by.

At any rate there is one thing I am certain of. This business will not last, this extravagance of thought and money is abnormal; it is bound to be, with General Electric selling where it is to-day.

CHAPTER XXX

———•———

LAST PILGRIMAGE

Rome Through the Eyes of an Euthusiast,
Although in Failing Health

IN THE AUTUMN of 1929 we find a pleasant interlude
in Apley's life, for at this time he took a much needed
rest from his great activities and we see him embarking from
Boston upon a trip to Europe and particularly for an extended
visit to Rome, a city of his dreams which he had never visited.
There were two reasons for this decision. The first largely
concerned the important post which was given that year to a
distant cousin, Horatio Apley, in the United States Embassy at
Rome. Although George Apley had only met Horatio Apley
once, at a football game many years before, this lack of acquaintance did not dim his interest in this relative's unexpected
success. He speaks affectionately of Horatio Apley in a letter to
his son.

Dear John: —
  You have doubtless heard the news about your Cousin
Horatio and the Embassy. This is one of the reasons why we
are all going to Rome for some months. I think we owe it to
Horatio as well as to others to show him that the family is
squarely behind him in his spectacular success. Not since your
Cousin Applegate married Sir George, the baronet, has such

a really worth-while tribute been paid the family. We must do our part, even though I have never approved of Horatio from what I have heard of him.

Besides this, it will give Eleanor an opportunity to see something of the gay cosmopolitan world where it is pleasant to know a place is always reserved for us. I have sent Horatio a cable telling him that we are coming and asking that we be included in some of the more exclusive social functions for the coming months. I have explained to him that I should prefer not to meet His Holiness. As for that remarkable man, Mussolini, who seems to have had the courage to stamp out radicalism, that is quite another matter. Of course, Horatio will be glad to attend to all of this. We do not wish to stay at his house, but in some near-by hotel.

Between you and me, I greatly hope that all this may turn Eleanor's mind in another direction. I have asked you before what you think of this man William Budd, and you were noncommittal. I for one am not. How my daughter, my own little girl, should be able to abide such a man is more than I can imagine. Though I may not have always shown it, Eleanor has always seemed to me one of the most delicate, sweet, and sensitive flowers in our family. That this blossom which has cheered me so often should be plucked by the fingers of a penniless journalist, none of whose work is even familiar to me, fills me with a very honest indignation. When Budd called to see me last week, I was frankly too ill to receive him. He is obviously an adventurer, utterly unfamiliar with the world which he is trying to enter. He is obviously marrying Eleanor for her money and position. I cannot for the life of me see why Eleanor should be delighted, nor can I see, speaking to you frankly, why you have not taken a more definite stand. Surely you must dislike this man, Budd, as intensely as I do, because Eleanor is, after all, your sister. . . .

This allusion will be almost sufficient for what was to Apley, and is still to nearly all the family, a sad example of infatuation.

It was thus that Apley was absent from America at the time of the stock market crash which has caused such deserved and undeserved misfortune, the end of which is not yet. His absence from home, however, did not remove his thoughts from home. He recognized that we were facing another real crisis.

Dear John: —

I am just back from a very interesting walk with Clara Goodrich on the Palatine Hill where there are so many interesting foundations of imperial palaces. Your mother and Eleanor and the Chickerings elected to go to an Embassy tea party as did Mr. Goodrich, so that Clara and I had the palaces quite to ourselves, except for a very loquacious guide who charged me ten lire more than was correct — I still do not know quite how. On my return, I found that the worst has happened; the market has collapsed. I am sending you a list of certain friends who I believe may be seriously involved through their own carelessness. Tell them I am standing ready to help them, but I wish nothing to be said about it. Good always comes out of these panics and this one should show our working people how necessary it is to save in good times instead of buying worthless odds and ends and becoming softened by a new mode of living. They must get back to basic principles; we all must.

Rome is really a delightful place, particularly when one brings one's own group with one. Having a group does away with a great deal of what I consider the danger of travel. The danger is that travel always gets one a little bit out of touch with home; the sight of new faces and the reception of new ideas is sometimes a little bit unsettling to the best of us, and makes for the restlessness which you felt when you returned from the War. I am too old to be restless now. To-day Rome only teaches me the beauties of the place I live in.

It seems to me that Mrs. Gardner has brought back to us all that is really best of Rome and Italy and has considerately left the rest behind. A visit to her Fenway Palace really suffices to show one everything. The head of Aphrodite in our Museum is superior to anything I have seen in the Vatican. I also think that we have by far the better half of the so-called Ludovici Throne. I wish the Coliseum was situated in a more open space as is our Harvard Stadium, so that one could view its proportions at a single glance. I have been, of course, to see the grave of Keats, but that burying ground does not seem to me as interesting as our own Granary burying ground which one can see so comfortably from the upper windows of our own Athenaeum. I know that you will laugh at me for all this, but I really mean it, in a way. Of course Rome is the Eternal City; its yellow bricks, its masses of old construction, its old tombs in the Campagna give a great sense of antiquity. Rome has been loved by everyone. That is why we have brought so much of it home. I suppose I am getting old. I suppose this is why so much of it makes me homesick. I see in it the ruins of so many hopes greater than any of mine. Personally, I long to get back, but I think that the change is doing Eleanor a great deal of good. Although Horatio is very busy, he is doing what he can for us, a luncheon and two teas where we have met nearly everyone who is worth while. Yet I still feel a little out of touch with things. Will you please, if you can spare the time, go up to Boston and see if the roof at Hillcrest, near the angle by the Terrace, is still leaking. I have been having great difficulty with the carpenter about this. I should also like to know what is being done about the family of squirrels which has invaded the attic. I do not want them killed, but I do want them put out of the attic. This worries me very

much. Eleanor sends her love. As far as I know she has not
written to Budd for the last three days. Your mother and I
both think that she is getting over it, and that is reason enough
for the sacrifice we make in being here. I picked up a flea yesterday, I think in one of the small churches. That is one thing
which we have not got at home. . . .

Dear John: —

I have just been to the Villa at Frascati. As I looked at the
numerous fountains, I could not for the life of me remember
whether or not the plumbing has been turned off at Hillcrest.
Will you please wire about this? Also the cypresses reminded
me that the evergreen hedge in the family lot has not been cut
back at the cemetery. Will you please see about this, too? I cannot go away without neglecting a great deal. Eleanor has met a
young man in the Guarda Nobile, and I do hope he will take
her mind off Budd. He seems to be making the effort. I have
bought several pictures for little John. Will you please get
him the very best rocking horse that you can find for his
Christmas present? I am counting the days when I can get
home; so is Clara Goodrich. Your mother keeps wishing to
remain. Believe me, I am only here on account of Eleanor.
If Rome is beautiful, the food is not good. Will you please
see that the locks are secure on the wine cellar at Beacon
Street? . . .

Dear John: —

I have been very ill for the last three weeks, one of the
first times that I have been ill in my life. It started with a cold
I contracted from looking too long at the sunset. It developed
into influenza. I still am very weak. The only good that has
come out of all this trip is what it may do for Eleanor. She
and your mother have been with me constantly. The thing
which worries me, as your mother may have written, but you

must not believe too much of it, is something one of the doctors has said about my heart. Please do not say anything about this to anyone. My heart has always been all right, and after all I am not so old. At any rate these Italian doctors have not improved since the days of Benvenuto Cellini, and they are all unsanitary. I shall not be in the least worried until I get an overhauling at home, and I don't want you to be. Clara Goodrich has been reading me the "Marble Faun." I do think Hawthorne has hit off the spirit of this place excellently. Again I caution you not to tell anyone about my heart because it is all bosh. . . .

Thus we have the first intimation ever conveyed that Apley's health was failing. That he faced this failing in health with the gallantry of his kind is natural, and part of his tradition. Though he treated the matter lightly this opinion was not shared by his wife or daughter, and doubtless he himself secretly knew that there was reason to fear. This may account for his activities in the last years of his life and for his anxiety to set his mind and his house in order. Ever after this illness, one receives the very definite impression that Apley is taking leave of something, that he is balancing accounts with himself, that he is living more and more in a world of memory. He was more and more the spectator watching the world pass by. Even the marriage of his daughter Eleanor with William Budd, a New York journalist from Lancaster, Pennsylvania, did not disturb him as it might have in former years. Apley's only comment was that he had done his best.

I have done my best [he writes to his friend Walker]. And that is all anyone can do. It is now time for someone else to try. The doctors, who seem to me to be painfully ignorant men, are keeping me very still at Hillcrest this summer, but

I have insisted on my Saturday bird walk with Clara Goodrich, and Catharine and the doctors can't stop that. As for Eleanor I am glad to say that I have never in any way tried to influence my children. She must lead her own life. I have led mine. The wedding, of course, was an important one, and I think at last my new son-in-law understands what he is getting into. He seemed quite shaken when I gave Eleanor away. At the reception, he appeared to do his best to pull himself together, but his manner was distrait. He and Eleanor are now somewhere on the West Coast. Of course, I am telling everyone that I am greatly pleased with Budd, and we shall let it go at that. This seems to me the definite end of a chapter. I am glad that my little grandson is here with me, now able to walk. I seem to have more in common with him than I have with most people. He has the Apley eyes and the same yellow hair. His nurse, both his grandmother and I feel, neglects him shamefully, but he seems to survive it.

My real reason for this letter is to ask you to come up to see me. I have not seen you for a long while, Mike. I really think you have been away from Boston long enough so that there would be no great flutter of gossip if you came back here on a little visit. I should see that only our own crowd met you, and we could have some good talks about the old days. I really do not think it would do any harm if you came up now on the grounds of seeing an old friend who is not well, although this talk of my not being well is largely bosh.

There are many reasons against the inclusion of the following letter, as it was written quite obviously at this time when Apley's health was failing. When one remembers the gallantry with which he faced as an active man the impairment of his physical faculties, for medical examination had proved only too clearly the existence of serious constitutional organic defects, the publication of this letter may seem unsportsmanlike; yet despite the depression of mood which it illustrates it contains an inherent soundness and is besides such an exposition of his philosophy that it cannot but be included.

Dear John: —

I have a good deal of time on my hands these days, more than I ever remember having. Except for two hours in the morning managing correspondence with Miss Fearing from the office I seem to spend most of my time on the porch watching John, Jr., playing in the sand pile we have built for him. I have been impressed to-day that he seems to do the same thing over and over again. He has definite limitations of activity and thought, but then that is true with most of us. We all do the same things over and over again.

I have been amusing myself to-day by reading Emerson's essay on Self-Reliance. There is a brave ring to the words. There is a courage about them which I like to think that Emerson and the rest of us, in a lesser measure, have drawn from the rocky soil and from this harsh climate. I like to think we are all self-reliant in a way, but sometimes Emerson leads one's thoughts along disturbing channels. Emerson disturbed me this afternoon.

He made me do something which I have never really done. He made me examine my life objectively, and I cannot say that I liked it very much; however, I could see myself as perhaps you and some others see me. It seems to me that, although I have tried, I have achieved surprisingly little compared with my own father and his father, for instance. I repeat that this negative result has not been for want of trying. The difficulty seems to have been that something has always stepped in the way to prevent me. I have always been faced from childhood by the obligation of convention, and all of these conventions have been made by others, formed from the fabric of the past. In some way these have stepped in between me and life. I had to realize that they were designed to do just that. They were designed to promote stability and inheritance. Perhaps they have gone a little bit too far.

When I stopped to think of it, I had the unpleasant conviction that everything I have done has amounted almost to nothing. I tried to think of the things which I have cared about most. In all conscience they have been simple things. They have been the relaxation after physical weariness — the feel of wind on the face, the feel of cold water on the body. I may say parenthetically that the doctors will no longer permit me to take my daily cold tub. Now and then something has come to me in unexpected moments when I have been near the woods or water at sundown. I have felt at such odd times a peace and happiness amounting to a belief that I was in tune with a sort of infinity. It has been like moments I have had with you and Eleanor when you were growing up. I have known the joys of companionship now and then, and I have known the deep satisfaction of friendship. I have known the satisfaction of accomplishing something on which I have centred all my energies and hopes. I have known the feeling of warm earth. I have heard the sleigh bells sound in winter. All this has been very good. Yet somehow I seem to have enjoyed very little of these pleasures, for I have never seemed to have had the time to enjoy them. More than this, I will tell you frankly I have sometimes deliberately tried not to enjoy them. I have turned away from them because I have believed that most of these were pleasures of the senses rather than of the intellect. I have been taught since boyhood not to give way to sensuality. I think this afternoon, now that it is almost too late, that this viewpoint may be a little wrong. There has been too much talk in my life. There has been too little action.

These thoughts were still in my mind when I came in here to the library to write this letter, and now that I am here, I feel very much better. The family portraits are all around me. There is my grandfather painted on one of his visits to Paris. There is my own father when he was a young man. There are the Chippendale chairs and the tall clock and the gate-legged table. All these objects are very consoling this afternoon. I can realize now that these are the things which make people like you and me behave, the exacting tyrants from which we cannot escape, but there is something beneficial in their rule. Memory and tradition are the tyrants of our environment. You cannot be very radical or very wrong when you see Moses Apley's face. He made me think of some other things on the favorable ledger of my life. I have always told the truth. I have never shirked standing by my convictions. I have tried to realize that my position demanded and still demands the giving of help to others. I have tried in my poor way to behave toward all men in a manner which might not disgrace that position. Now I can feel a humble sense of pride that I have done so.

I have not had a very good time in doing it. There is a great deal of talk in these days about happiness. An English woman named Mrs. Bertrand Russell, whose life in many ways has not been the same as mine, has written a strange book entitled "The Right To Be Happy" which has disturbed even your mother's admirable sense of balance. It seems to me to-day in all this unhappy country there is a loud, lonely cry for happiness. Perhaps it would be better if people realized that happiness comes only by indirection, that it can never exist by any conscious effort of the will. I think this is a mistake that you and Eleanor and all the rest of you are making. When the hour comes for you to balance your accounts I wonder if you will have had any better time than I. I doubt it.

At any rate, I feel that I have been the means of continuing something which is worth more than happiness. I have stood for many things which I hope will not vanish from the earth. I am only one of many here who have done so. The world I have lived in may be in a certain sense restricted but it has been a good world and a just world. Much of it may have been built on a sense of security which is now disappearing but it has also been built on certain elements of the spirit which will always be secure: on honour and on courage and on truth.

I have been engaged during the past two weeks in going over the details of my will. I am very anxious that certain small possessions go to the right people and that you and Eleanor will not quarrel over my wishes. I have sent the bronzes to the Art Museum yesterday, where they will be exhibited on the Apley side of the large wing. I, for one, am very glad to have them out of the house. The silver is being carefully listed and so is the furniture. I want you to take particular care to look after Norman Rowe at Pequod Island. There is also a fund being set aside for the servants. Do you want your great-grandmother's locket with your great-grandfather's hair inside it? If you don't I shall give it to the Historical Society. I am very much puzzled about what to do with certain family letters. I do not think there is anything in them which will do much harm and I do not wish to burn them. They are in five tin boxes on the left-hand side of the attic stairs. As you know, most of the Apley letter books are on loan at the Essex Institute, where I imagine you will be willing to leave them. For the rest you must come up here to see me. Copies of my own letters, pamphlets, and papers I am having arranged in suitable boxes marked and documented. A great many people are coming to call on me every afternoon, all sorts of younger members of the family and many older friends. I had not realized that I was so popular. . . .

CHAPTER XXXI

———•———

A HOUSE IN ORDER

The Final Arrangements For a Pilgrim's Departure

DEAR JOHN:—
 This letter may seem a gloomy one to you but it is not to me. It is prompted by a conversation I had with my doctor, Minot Wingate. I am convinced that he is an alarmist, as in many ways I have never felt better in my life or more appreciative of everything which is going on around me. Yet it is necessary at a certain time to make certain arrangements. These requests and suggestions I am making to you are in no sense urgent but will stand for a number of years.

In the event of my death a good deal of pressure will be brought to bear on you to have an elaborate funeral. All the societies to which I belong and also the philanthropic organizations will in the nature of things send representatives, who will in all probability seek positions as honorary pallbearers. In this way the church aisle is apt to become very crowded and uncomfortable and this tendency seems to be growing, according to my observations of the funerals which I have attended recently. For myself I do not want anything of the sort. I simply want places reserved in the middle of the church for these representatives. The elaborate floral wreaths which they will present I want placed to one side as inconspicuously as is compatible with politeness. The order in which the family are to sit may be somewhat confusing to you. As you may not be as conversant with the various branches as I am, I am giving you a memorandum and a diagram. I am also giving a list of pallbearers and their order. You notice that I include Norman Rowe and our old coachman, if he is still alive, and also according to custom one representative to be chosen among the workers of the Apley Mills. This I think will give the necessary simplicity of tone. I need not tell you that these men must be treated with the same courtesy and respect which is accorded to the other pallbearers. After the funeral you will have special refreshments served to these three in the small servants' dining-room, either at Beacon Street or Hillcrest. My only reason for this is that I do not wish them to be embarrassed by the weight of the other company. I want you to spend at least fifteen minutes with them yourself and to take a personal interest in seeing that all their wants are satisfied. Also, you are to give each of them a twenty-dollar gold piece as coming directly from me, with my kindest regards.

I want you to be especially careful to see that the secretary and officers of my Harvard class are made comfortable and are treated cordially. There must be whisky and cigars for these and a few others in the library, including of course the executors. I want you to be particularly careful that any friends of mine who may attend the church and whose dress and appearance may cause them embarrassment are looked out for with every possible attention and are thanked by you or by some other representative of the family personally for their thoughtfulness in attending. You may add, in speaking to them, that this was my particular wish.

A word about the family will be enough. In my experience these occasions are apt to be the source of friction and ill feeling which may last over a period of years. There is apt to be a certain amount of jealousy displayed by those who wish to show themselves as having stood high in the regard of the deceased. Your mother and my sister Amelia will help you in estimating exactly the degree of attention which you must show to everyone. The Douglas Apleys will be apt as always to be somewhat officious and pushing. It may be as well to put them in one of the pews farther back. I shall hope that your Aunt Jane, if she is alive, may be able to attend but you must leave this decision to the doctors of the institution. In other words, I want everything to go as smoothly as though I were here myself to oversee it.

The arrangements about the stone have been already made. I do not want any verse or inscription added. These few words with the memoranda I am giving you will cover the whole matter, except for a few afterthoughts I may have from time to time that will relieve you of considerable responsibility. There is one task which I am leaving up to you and which I want you to oversee personally in such a way that no gossip may be connected with it. I have put together a few odd articles, including some books which I owned in college. These I want you to bring yourself to a Mrs. Monahan O'Reilly, whose address you will find in my address book. I want you to see her personally and to tell her that it was my wish that she should have these things and my wish also, which you will agree to fulfill, that she shall come to you for your assistance in any time that she may be in any difficulty. I shall not say anything more about this matter but shall rely on your tact and your good judgment.

If I do not get around to it myself I wish you to remember that the joists in the cellar beneath the old laundry at Hillcrest are in very bad condition. They all have dry-rotted and should be replaced. If you attend to this I want you to get a new carpenter. The one I have has taken advantage of me of late in his bills. You must learn to watch this sort of person very carefully. I do not need to recommend to your care the four dogs on the place and the horses, because you have always been very fond of animals. Jacob the groom has been drinking heavily lately. You must wink at this as much as you possibly can. Jacob in many ways has been a fine fellow and has taught you to ride, himself. Somehow horses and liquor have a way of going together. Perhaps it is not for either of us to reason why.

Things have been very gay and cheerful around here during the last few weeks. I have never had so many callers. A special dinner is being given for me at the Province Club and two old salts from the Apley Sailors' Home who remember your grandfather have come up especially to see me. Your great-uncle's gardener from Pachogue Neck has come up also and Norman Rowe has come down from Maine. Cousins of yours come in every day to see me. I think they are fine young people. Their ideas may be slightly different from mine but on the whole the family traits are about the same, and I am very proud to be related to them.

Preparations are on foot already for the customary Thanksgiving party which will be a large one this year as I wish every possible member of the family to be included. I shall want, if it can be arranged, you and Louise to come up a week in advance. Your ideas are needed for the pencil and paper games and I am composing a small family pageant. You, of course, are to take the part of the first John Apley. I have found some of his old clothes in the attic, which I hope will fit you. It is high time for you to enter into the spirit of this occasion rather more assiduously than you have in the past.

During the last week I have been working on several plans to rid the attic of those gray squirrels. I think now the only thing to do is to keep watch near the limb of the elm tree and to shoot them as they enter by that hole under the gutter. If the hole is stopped up they simply gnaw another. I should rather have you shoot them than one of the hired men. I really think it would look better. . . .

My dear boy:—

I cannot tell you how deeply your last letter, with its budget of good news, has moved me. You must give me credit for always knowing that you had the "right stuff" in you. If the War put some odd notions in your head, you cannot be blamed for that. In many ways it made me a little bit eccentric myself. I have always known in the back of my mind that eventually you would settle down and that you would find that New York, though it may be agreeable in a way, is not the right place to raise children. Your acquaintances there may be more sprightly and amusing but they are not the same as old friends here. What makes me happier than anything else is the knowledge that you have come to this decision without my urging. I have told you more than once that there are certain things you cannot get away from and now you know it. You have had your fling and now you are coming back, as one of our flesh and blood inevitably must, to take up your responsibilities. I cannot be thankful enough that I have lived to see the time when all this "bosh" and nonsense is over with.

You will understand, of course, that your long absence from Boston will be a considerable loss to you always. You and Louise will find difficulties and annoyances in taking up the position which was always waiting for you here. As you say that Louise is really the person who is obliging you to take this step, perhaps she will understand these difficulties better than you. Your mother is already writing to her and is taking steps to have her made a member of the Sewing Circle suitable to her age. By the time she arrives she will also find herself a member of the Thursday Afternoon Debating Club, which has given your mother and your Aunt Amelia such pleasure always. If she comes up a month from now she will have the opportunity of discussing "Is True Happiness Derived from Work Rather Than from Play?" The ladies all like these questions very much. Perhaps you and I can think of something more amusing, in the library, over a good cigar. The doctors still allow me one cigar a day. I shall take two on the day you come. Be sure to bring up some of the latest stories with you.

It goes without saying that you will face many problems on your return among us. I am planning to resign from several boards, nominating you in my place. You will of necessity be the next president of the Apley Sailors' Home but a membership on the Lending Library is a different matter. I do not think you had better attempt this until your views on literature are a little bit more sound.

Here, by the way, is something which I wish to advance to you confidentially. I have heard from very good authority that there may be a vacancy in the Harvard Corporation. Certain of us are looking for a younger man and one of the right sort. There is altogether too much sentiment here lately for getting outsiders and so-called "new blood" into Harvard. The traditions of the place must not be spoiled. There is actually some talk about a new president, about whom no one seems to have heard. Needless to say, this is only one of the wild rumours which circulate at such a time. Harvard will be Harvard, just as Harvard was old Harvard when Yale was but a pup. Seriously, I think you might be fitted to take your place on the corporation. It is true you have never been a scholar but now that you are actually going to live in Boston this does not really make much difference. I shall have some of the right people meet you and we shall see what can be done.

There will be a good deal of hard work ahead for you at both the Province and the Berkley Clubs. Though you have been a member of both for some years you have not really identified yourself with either. This will take a long time because there are certain cliques in each with which one must cope very carefully. I do think, however, given the requisite amount of patience, you may be able to do rather well. There is one thing you must remember. Although you must show yourself at both these places as often as possible, even at the expense of other social obligations, you must try on the whole to be silent and observing. Do not above anything else, until you have been in Boston for at least five years, become involved in discussions with any of the regular members. This sort of thing creates a very bad general impression. The Berkley Club, which is founded on a more informal spirit, you must never treat too lightly. Although you must unbend there as much as possible be sure to unbend in a friendly way. You will doubtless be called upon, on one of the regular evenings, to tell some sort of story or perhaps to sing a song. Be sure that you pick out a very good story indeed because you will be largely identified by this first venture and you will frequently be called upon to repeat the same story. I have noticed that you are interested in certain social questions. Be sure to deal with these very lightly, if at all—better not at all. You must understand that the Berkley Club and the Province Club are both havens of refuge where no one wishes to be emotionally disturbed.

But I am getting very far afield. I am speaking very prosily, out of sheer joy at having you come back. We can talk about all these matters together much more sensibly than I can ever put them down on paper. My mind and my heart are both too full for writing. I repeat I always knew that you had the right stuff in you and now we will have a chance to get to know each other. What I want particularly is to have a great many small men's dinners. There is so much to say. There is so much to talk about. God bless you. . . .

George Apley died in his own house on Beacon Street on the thirteenth of December, 1933, two weeks after John Apley returned to Boston.

ABOUT THE AUTHOR

John P. Marquand (1893-1960) was awarded the Pulitzer Prize in 1938 for his novel *The Late George Apley.* Among his other widely admired and bestselling novels are *Wickford Point* (1939), *H. M. Pulham, Esquire* (1941), *So Little Time* (1943), *Point of No Return* (1949), and *Women and Thomas Harrow* (1958). He was also the author of the highly successful series of Mr. Moto detective novels.

Also by John P. Marquand
Wickford Point

"A notable and original novel, shrewd in characterization, richly quotable, and individual as all get out.... Some of the scenes are written in Mr. Marquand's best vein of ironic comedy."
—Stephen Vincent Benét, *Saturday Review*

"Despite all the intelligent purpose of the novel, *Wickford Point* is written with an easy informality and a sparkle that make it fascinating reading.... Mr. Marquand has created as varied and entertaining a gallery of character portraits as any novel has contained in a long while.... Whether he is being sentimental, or brusque, or satirical, or yielding a little to pathos, Mr. Marquand bubbles with entertainment. I think there is not a single dull page in his novel — and that is extraordinary for a Pulitzer Prize winner."
—William Soskin, *New York Herald Tribune*

"The impression I first received from reading *Wickford Point*, as I see now, was one of overemphasis on the humor, the almost continuous entertainment provided by the novel, the satire on a family run to seed. But in retrospect these features, although in no wise dimmed, are no longer exclusive. John Marquand's deep reading of character overshadows them.... The true worth of *Wickford Point* lies below its satiric surface. It is a novel of importance because its underlying emphasis is upon the springs of human behavior."
—Percy Hutchison, *New York Times Book Review*

"This reviewer can remember no American novel since *The Great Gatsby* which he has read with so much delight as *Wickford Point*."
—Graham Green, *Spectator*

BACK BAY BOOKS
Available wherever paperbacks are sold

GREAT FICTION IN PAPERBACK

The Ice Storm
A novel by Rick Moody

"A bitter and loving and damning tribute to the American family. . . . This is a good book, packed with keen observation and sympathy for human failure."
> — Adam Begley, *Chicago Tribune*

"A gripping roller-coaster ride through the dark side of the American Dream. . . . Moody possesses a near-encyclopedic knowledge of his suburban turf." — Dani Shapiro, *People*

Martin Sloane
A novel by Michael Redhill

"Reading *Martin Sloane* made me feel melancholic, hopeful, amused, energized, enlightened, unnerved, touched, and finally grateful that occasionally a writer comes along who gets real life just right." — Bliss Broyard, *New York Times*

"A superb novel. . . . *Martin Sloane* makes you realize just how thin and fleeting most of what passes for good fiction is."
> — Noah Richler, *National Post*

BACK BAY BOOKS
Available wherever books are sold

Made in the USA
Columbia, SC
30 November 2020